THE
LAST
FLAME

ROSEBOURNE KINGDOM: BOOK ONE

BROOKE ANDERSON

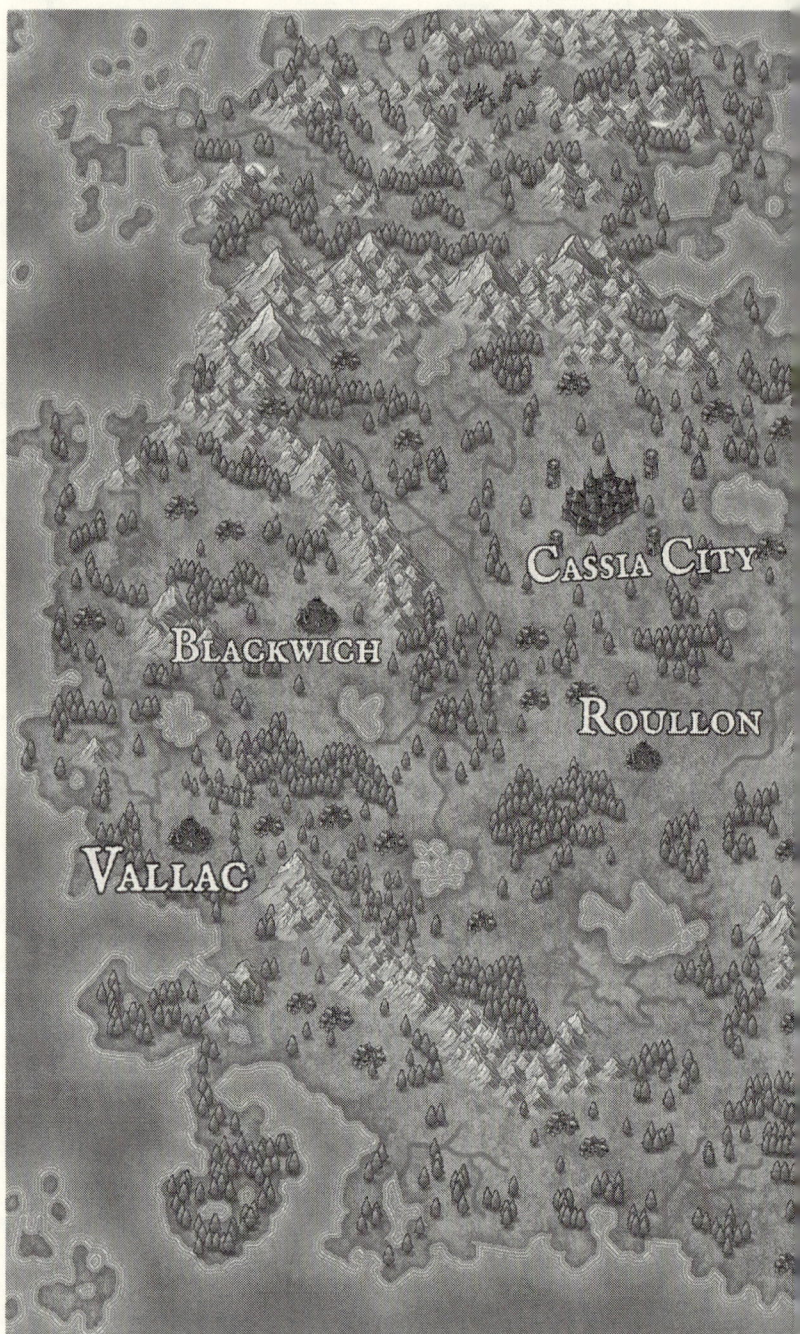

ROSEBOURNE KINGDOM

TANIN

AUBERTEAUX

NAERON

To my sister, Skylee, who has yet to read this, but I am duty-bound to mention due to an agreement made by my young self. Jokes aside, I appreciate your support and being the guinea pig for the other disastrous version of this novel. I promise, this one is far better.

And to all the beautiful, big, bad bitches who wanted nothing more than to see a fantasy heroine who didn't struggle with her "extra weight" but thrived with it.

Chapter 1

Myla Yules should have turned around. She should have followed her instincts. However, one thought of her best friend, Wrynn, quashed that idea spectacularly. He wanted her here—nearly begged her—and she couldn't let him down again. She knew he only wanted what was best for her and was looking out for her best interests. As he had told her, what sort of aspiring general didn't take the time to bond with fellow knights? Nonexistent ones.

"After you become general, then you can ignore us lower ranks," Wrynn had teased her while trying to convince her to go to the tavern with him and the rest of the recruits.

She'd argued that a general wasn't an elected position, but he'd quickly pointed out the most crucial thing considered when appointing a general: the camaraderie between fellow troops.

"No one will vouch for you, let alone fight for you if they don't like you."

Myla knew Wrynn had good points, so she pushed open the tavern doors rather than turning around and returning to the training yard.

Garith's Tavern was crowded, and almost every table and booth was occupied. The wood floor was darker in places where ale and food had stained it. To the right, a small crowd danced before a man playing the fiddle on a platform only two inches from the ground. People were laughing and yelling over each other to hear their companions. She could feel her eyebrows pull together as she failed to hide her disgust. Perhaps it made her a little stuck-up for not wanting to spend her evenings in a place reeking of body odor and bad decisions. She preferred a quieter space, which was one of the many reasons she spent her nights off doing some extra training while the other recruits bonded over shared ale.

Myla likely wouldn't have any friends had she not met Wrynn a few years ago. As soon as she'd turned eighteen, she'd begged her father to let her join the knights. He'd refused, and being the general gave him the right to refuse anyone he deemed unfit. Myla, refusing to be deterred, had taken to practicing alone. She'd met Wrynn one night after sneaking into the training arena in the middle of the night. He'd just become a recruit and was putting in extra training hours at the time. Rather than turn her in, he offered to train her. Two years later, Myla, masked in dark coloring and a scarf that only exposed her eyes, easily completed the physical evaluation. She revealed her identity only after her father and the other two high-ranked officers dubbed her fit for duty. Unable to rescind his offer, she joined the recruits, and he'd been pushing her to her limit ever since. She knew he wanted her to quit, but the pressure only made her work harder.

Myla walked up to the bar and pushed herself between two men. The older and plumper man was already passed out on his stool, bald head gleaming with sweat and drool dripping from his open lips. The other was flirting with a woman half his age whose breasts were nearly spilling from her dress. From what she could tell, the woman didn't seem uncomfortable or seeking an exit, so she turned her attention away from the pair. It wouldn't do well to cause a fight and get kicked out before she even ordered a drink. But, she was willing to keep her options open if the need arose.

She waved her hand to get the barkeep's attention before ordering two ales for her and Wrynn. She slipped the barkeep a few copper pieces. The barkeep grunted in response and dropped the coins into his apron. Myla turned around and leaned her back against the bar. Her eyes scanned across the crowd, trying to find the familiar mop of black hair. Before she could even scan half the room, someone entered her line of sight. She sighed deeply through her nose as she met the familiar dark brown eyes of someone she had hoped to avoid.

"Assar," Myla said, crossing her arms over her chest.

Desmond Assar was a fellow recruit and resident asshole. She could admit he was a decent fighter, but he carried himself like the best in the class even when she'd held that record for eight months now. Myla knew that was why he chose to pick fights with her nearly every day. He was an aggravating, petty man with mountainous insecurities she didn't want to deal with tonight.

Desmond smirked at her. "Yules, surprised to see you here mingling with us peasants."

Myla rolled her eyes. "I don't know where you got the idea that I think I'm above everyone—"

"Maybe because your father's the general and gives you special treatment. It's the only reason to explain how you passed the physical evaluation."

3

Myla really did not want to deal with his nonsense now, or ever, for that matter. He was among the few who didn't think she had proven her skills enough. "Or maybe I passed because I worked and trained my ass off for two years before the evaluation."

Desmond's eyes scanned Myla from head to toe. His gaze lingered on her wide hips and large breasts that refused to slim down despite her consistent training before huffing out a laugh. "Right, sure."

The barkeep behind her set down one of her ales, and she picked it up, taking a long sip. Myla straightened and pushed her shoulders back. Even at her full height, she was still a few inches shorter than Desmond. He was broader than her, too, his body coiled with muscle. She might not be able to bulk up like the other men in training, but she knew her strength and had proven it to him on multiple occasions.

"And here I thought we settled this on the sparring mat yesterday when I sliced your chest open before you were even able to swing your blade." Myla tapped Desmond's chest, right between his two pectoral muscles. "Do you need a refresher so soon? I'd be happy to knock you on your ass again if it'll get you to shut up."

Desmond sneered, and out of the corner of her eye, she could see Maxith and Canon walking closer to them. Those two were never far behind Desmond—always ready to back him up in any case. If they wanted to fight with him, that was fine by her. Myla relished the challenge.

Desmond put his hand up, effectively calling off his attack dogs. His sneer turned into a smirk as he stepped closer. "I let you cut me so I would be sent to the medical ward. A beautiful woman works there—long dark hair, hazel eyes, and the body of a goddess. Rikia's her name. At least, I think it is. I was too busy admiring her ample bosom—"

"Stay the fuck away from my sister," Myla growled. Rage boiled in the pit of her stomach along with something

4

else. Something she needed to keep at bay lest it expose her in a tavern full of soon-to-be knights who would kill her if they found out what she was.

Desmond grinned. "That's right. I always forget she's your sister since she looks nothing like you. Obviously, she got all the good looks in the family and left you with nothing."

Myla tightened her hold on the jug of ale—willing herself to calm down. She didn't care that Desmond thought her sister was more beautiful than she was. Myla thought that herself. But if he tried to lay a hand on her—

"I'm going back there tomorrow so she can check out the wound. Then I can show my appreciation by bending her over and—"

The ale burst out of her jug, splattering them both. Desmond stumbled back, spewing out expletives. He wiped his face with his sleeve, but ale continued to drip onto his forehead from his short, brown hair.

He blinked at her, face screwing up in fury. "You're dead—"

Heart thundering in her chest, Myla dropped the jug and punched Desmond in the face before he could say another word. He fell back onto Maxith and Canon, who barely kept him from toppling to the floor. Myla didn't give him time to recover before she sprinted out the door.

Chapter 2

The dark sky lit up as lightning slashed across it—
thunder rumbling not far behind. Rain poured onto the dirt
road. The mud squelched under Myla's knee-length boots as
she ran out of the tavern. She ducked her head, pulling her
hood so it nearly fell over her eyes. She curled her shoulders
in, wrapping her arms around herself to combat the biting
wind as she disappeared into the shrinking crowd. She
twisted around a carriage so fast her hood came off,
exposing her long, dark waves. Not bothering to pull it back
up, she darted farther down the streets toward the alleyway
between her favorite bakery and the medical ward where
her sister worked. She rested her back against the stone wall
and peered around the corner.

Desmond stood before Garith's Tavern, scanning the
crowd around him. His green cloak fluttered around him,
allowing the rain to soak through his loose-fitted, white
shirt. He was snapping at his friends standing under the

safety of the tavern's awning. Though she couldn't hear them, she could guess what Desmond had ordered them to do, especially when they stood at attention before splitting up to search the crowd.

Myla looked away and placed her hand over her beating heart, willing herself to calm down. He didn't know—he couldn't. If anyone else thought something unnatural was happening, she wouldn't have been able to leave. There was no guarantee that a hunter was in the tavern tonight, but it was likely, given how many her father knew were around. They blended in with the denizens around Cassia City—the better to catch magic wielders unaware. Not that there were many of them left in the city or kingdom. Not since the War on Magic two hundred years ago. The foundation of Rosebourne Kingdom was created on the bones of dragons that were slaughtered to eradicate magic so that all citizens could be equal. The practice had continued, and as far as Myla knew, only a few were left. She'd never met another who could wield magic, let alone seen a dragon. For her to have been born with magic meant there was at least one dragon out there—far from this kingdom, no doubt. If anyone knew she had magic, they'd use her to find the dragon before killing them both.

At least she could tell that Desmond hadn't put the pieces together, not that it surprised Myla. He'd never been the sharpest sword in the armory. He wouldn't be the one to turn her in. She just hoped that no one around them had noticed anything unusual either. It probably looked like Myla had thrown a drink in Desmond's face. She hoped.

Myla peeked back around the corner and immediately regretted it. Desmond's eyes locked with hers, and his lip curled into a snarl. Myla swore and looked away before bolting down the alleyway. She didn't dare look behind to see if Desmond was following. The storm and her splattering footsteps made it impossible for her to hear him either. She kept running past the market that made up the town center and into the neighboring street, where towering apartments were placed. Trash littered the ground, and more than a few people were passed out in ditches, sheltering under blankets.

Myla turned so fast between two apartment buildings that she slammed into the wall. Pain flared in her shoulder, but she quickly pushed off the wall and kept running. A fence was at the end of the alley, but Myla knew two panels were just loose enough for someone to slip through. She pushed through them, ensuring they fell back into place before running between the two manors on the other side. On this side of the neighborhood, the dirt road turned to cobblestones. There were cobblestone sections around the town center, but they only lined the stores and taverns, leaving the middle of the road packed with dirt.

She passed row after row of houses, and with each turn, the rows of houses grew in size and improved in look. The lawns became greener, and the bricks less worn. Turning down her street, she headed toward her home—a three-story house with shining bricks painted a startlingly white. The roof and grand double doors were painted black along with the windowpanes overlooking the lush, green yard. Nestled in front of the porch were flowers of various shades of purple, blue, and red.

Myla stopped in front of the gate to her home and finally looked behind her. Desmond was nowhere in sight, nor anyone else for that matter. The neighborhood was quiet save for the rain. Myla rested her hands on her knees and tried to catch her breath. Her breath steadily returned to her, but her heart rate wouldn't slow. That was close—too close. She couldn't be sure that no one had seen her. There was no telling if she'd caught the attention of a hunter—a hunter waiting for her to make another mistake. The magic in her body thrummed at the thought as she tried to wrangle her panic. Her magic had always felt like two sides of a coin. One side was entirely her own that fed off her emotions—brimming with unrealized potential and growing every day she practiced. The other side was like a presence in her mind hidden behind a door reinforced with brick layers. She assumed the presence was her dragon. She'd read in a history book that a mental bond between wielder and dragon allowed them to communicate, but it hadn't gone into detail about it. The history books tended to focus on the negative aspects of magic wielders. All her knowledge was from her own experiences and a few mentions in history books.

The sound of approaching footsteps caused the hair on the back of her neck to stand on end. Slowly, she reached for the dagger sheathed to her thigh. She pulled it free, the blade gleaming in the moonlight. She held it close and loosened her body to prepare for a fight. The footsteps grew louder, and when she was sure they were close enough to stab, she spun around. She launched herself at the man, pushing the blade against the chest of—

"Wrynn!" Myla let the blade drop between them and sighed in relief. "Sorry, I thought you were someone else."

"Clearly." Wrynn smiled, but it quickly washed away as worry etched his face. "I saw what happened. Well, part of what happened. Are you okay? I tried to catch you but lost you in the storm before figuring you'd probably head home."

"I'm fine," Myla replied, sheathing her dagger. "Desmond was just being an ass, so I threw my drink in his face and punched him."

Wrynn's cinnamon-colored, narrow eyes were alight with amusement as he raised a dark eyebrow. "Sounds like him and you. What exactly did he say?"

Myla leaned back against the gate and wiped the sweat from her brow. "Disgusting things about my sister and what he wants to do to her."

9

Wrynn grimaced. "Shit. Sounds like he deserved what came to him."

"Of course. Would I punch someone for no reason?" Myla asked sweetly.

Wrynn snorted. "Not for no reason, but definitely for less of a reason." His hood was thrown back, leaving his wavy dark hair to lie limply on his forehead. He always loved the rain and never cared if he got soaked through. Myla was surprised he even bothered with the cloak, as it did nothing to prevent his dark shirt from clinging to his lean, muscular frame.

"Did Desmond say anything after I left?" Myla asked, her voice surprisingly even despite her spiked nerves.

Wrynn shrugged. "I only heard pieces. Just your name followed by a bunch of swearing."

Myla nodded and let out a small breath. She'd figured as much but was lightened to hear it from Wrynn. She just hoped others at the tavern were as oblivious.

"Okay, that's fine. I'm used to his threats by now."

Wrynn searched her face, frowning slightly. "Are you sure you're all right, Sea Storm? You seem rattled."

Myla smiled and took his hand in hers—his skin a few shades darker than her own. "I'm good. Just annoyed at myself for letting him get to me."

"Nothing wrong with being protective of your siblings. Had he said that about my sister, I would have done the same thing."

Myla nodded. "I'll just have to kick his ass twice as hard tomorrow during training to make up for it."

Wrynn snorted. "That's the spirit."

Chapter 3

Sleep eluded Myla most of the night. Her dreams were burdened with vengeful mobs and daggers in her back. So, she was more than a little disoriented walking into the training arena the following day. She struggled through each drill—her muscles protesting even the most basic workout. Of course, her father noticed immediately and pushed her harder. She refused to give him the satisfaction of seeing her fail and quit—not after last night. No, if anything, she had even more to prove. She wouldn't allow herself to make another mistake.

They ended the day as usual, with sparing matches. Myla had hoped to be paired with Desmond to take him down a peg, but the general paired her with Wrynn. As someone close to completing his recruit training, Wrynn was a worthy competitor—to most people. Since Wrynn had been the one to teach her for years, she was familiar with his shortcomings as he was with hers. It made for a rather stale fight, and they often chose other partners when given the chance so they could improve their skills.

Myla raised her sword, and Wrynn mirrored her. He was smiling, but she could tell he was worried about her. He knew better than to show it on his face, but she knew well enough to know when he was hiding his true feelings. General rang the bell, and Myla rushed forward. Her sword clashed with his with a responding shriek. That and the clang of steel meeting steel echoing around them made for a discordant orchestra.

She slashed as Wrynn struggled to meet each blow. He shuffled back, his leather boots scuffing against the floor and kicking up dirt as he tried to stand his ground. Frustration bloomed in her chest when she realized he was holding back. She narrowed her eyes at him, pulling her blade back so she could kick him in the stomach. He bent, coughing in surprise.

"Don't you fucking dare hold back," Myla growled.

He straightened with a grimace. "Myla–"

"No excuses." She pointed her sword at him. "We're going again, and if I sense you're still holding back, I'll cut off your ridiculous little ponytail."

Wrynn suppressed a smile, brushing his fingers over the ponytail on top of his head that kept the hair out of his eyes. "You wouldn't."

Myla couldn't help but smile in kind. "Try me."

He lifted his blade in response—her only warning before he rushed toward her. Myla deflected the blow, twisting around him. He quickly turned to face her and struck again. He didn't hold back, striking repeatedly as she tried not to falter. Her muscles were tight and fought against her with every swing of her sword. Her frustration grew as she fought to be on the offense. Knowing it would make her sloppy, she tried to rein in her emotions. Her father had drilled that into her for nearly a year now, but topped with her exhaustion, she didn't stand a chance. Her grip on her sword slipped, and the second it took to regain the blade cost her.

Pain lashed through her arm as Wrynn cut a deep line in her bicep. Myla swore, dropping her sword to grip the wound. Blood seeped through her fingers—hot and sticky—staining her white shirt. Wrynn's eyes widened as he dropped his sword, too.

"Shit, Myla, I didn't mean—"

"It's just a scratch," Myla replied through clenched teeth.

"It's not, you're going to need stitches—"

"What happened here?"

Wrynn jumped as Myla's father appeared behind him, green eyes fixed on Myla's wound.

"I'm fine, General—"

"Take her to the medical ward, *now*," he barked at Wrynn.

"I can just wrap it up, and it'll be fine," Myla argued.

Her father ignored her, turning his attention to Wrynn. "Now, recruit."

Wrynn gave a curt nod. "Yes, sir."

He darted to Myla's side and grabbed the elbow of her uninjured arm. Myla sighed but allowed Wrynn to lead her out of the training arena. She knew better than anyone when letting an argument with her father drop was best. She'd inherited his stubbornness, after all.

"It's nothing—"

"No arguing," Wrynn interrupted.

He tore off a piece of his shirt and wrapped it around her wound as a makeshift bandage. To her

13

annoyance, blood immediately soaked the fabric. She'd probably need stitches, which would not help her case.

"Now tell me what's wrong," Wrynn said, retaking her elbow to lead her down the street.

"I don't know what you mean," Myla replied defensively.

Wrynn rolled his eyes. "You've never missed a simple block like that in years. You're distracted, not just because of a bad night's rest."

Maybe it's because I possibly have a target on my back, Myla thought bitterly. *All because I couldn't keep my temper in check.*

"Maybe the pressure my dad's putting on me is finally reaching its breaking point," Myla said instead. It wasn't a lie. She'd been struggling for months to prove him wrong and show him she had what it took to be general one day. She understood why he didn't want her anywhere near the monarchy or troops in the royal army. It brought attention to her when she should be hiding away from the diligent sights of those who seek to kill magic. It was dangerous and reckless even to be a recruit, but it was all Myla had ever wanted. She didn't want her magic to define her or her purpose in life. She could be general and keep her magic a secret. She'd been hiding it for her entire life and would need to, even if she wasn't the general.

An unhelpful voice in the back of her head reminded her that she'd let her magic slip over a disgusting comment from a spineless asshole. If she couldn't even hold it together in that case, what if she slipped up on the battlefield? The adrenaline and fear would be running high, not to mention the likelihood of watching comrades die around her. Of course, her father had told her all this, but she'd brushed it off. She trusted in her strength—or had when arguing with her father. What if he'd been right this whole time? What did that make her?

14

Wrynn's face softened, and he gripped her hand. "I'm sorry, Myla. I didn't even think about that. I know it can't be easy, but he just wants you to be prepared. He knows what it's like to be a soldier and doesn't want you to go in blind."

"He wants me to quit," Myla corrected.

"Yes, but only because he doesn't want you in harm's way."

"I know. Dad doesn't see me as anything other than a child, and I'm sick of it." It was the closest thing to the truth Myla could give him. She hated keeping secrets from him because he'd become family over the years, but she wouldn't risk him. Enough people she loved were at risk as it was.

"Give it time," Wrynn assured. "He'll come around."

Chapter 4

"Hi, Rikia," Myla said with a wave.

Her sister stood behind the front counter to the medical ward, studying various charts before her. Her long, dark hair was pulled back into an elaborate updo that Myla could never dream of doing herself. A few strands had fallen away and clung to her forehead from sweat. Her slim form was clad in the medical uniform of a white blouse and black trousers under a long, white coat.

Rikia looked up with a smile before her hazel eyes took in the state of her arm. "What happened?"

"Just a sparring accident," Myla assured. "Would you mind taking a look?"

Rikia nodded. "Of course. Come on back."

Myla looked up at Wrynn. "You can head back to training—I'm in good hands here."

Wrynn dropped a kiss on Myla's head. "Meet at the tavern later?"

Myla grimaced. "I don't know—"

"Come on, Aryn and Eloria have been dying to spend more time with you."

She blinked in surprise. "They have?"

Wrynn smiled. "Of course, because they got good instincts."

Myla snorted. "That or you've been talking me up and raising their expectations way too high."

"Semantics. I'll see you tonight!" Wrynn was out the door before she could argue further.

Myla sighed and turned back to her sister, who gave her an amused look. Rikia was a few years younger than Myla and was her opposite in almost every aspect. She was beautiful, skinny, and longed to be married. Someone was looking at her or pining for her attention everywhere she went. Despite only being seventeen years old, she had been proposed to at least three times (that Myla was aware of). Rikia could be stubborn at times but hated conflict—she only tended to argue with Myla. Myla wouldn't ever admit this out loud, but she had always been a little jealous of Rikia's beauty. She did not wish to get the attention Rikia always got, knowing how fast it could turn into a hostile situation if Rikia didn't respond properly. A small part of her, though, couldn't help but look at her sister—seeing how different they looked—and wonder where it went wrong with Myla.

"Don't give me that look," Myla told her sister as she followed her to the back, where dozens of cots were laid out. Most of the beds were empty, save for a few people sleeping. This medical ward mostly catered to recruits and soldiers since it was more of an emergency trauma center. Though, in the corner, Myla could make out the local butcher, Direk, with his hand bandaged up. For someone so adept with knives, it surprised Myla how often Rikia said he found himself here.

"I think Wrynn's right. You work too hard and deserve a break," Rikia responded, gesturing for Myla to sit on one of the empty cots.

"This wound is proof the opposite is true," she said, taking a seat.

"Or your body's finally giving into exhaustion. When's the last time you've gone out instead of training alone?"

"Yesterday," Myla countered.

Rikia rolled her eyes, unwrapping the makeshift bandage on her arm. "Before that."

Truthfully, Myla had no idea. Before she became a recruit, most likely. There were nights she'd spend time with Wrynn or her family, but that was always after she'd trained alone for at least a few hours. She hadn't bothered to put in any effort to spend time with other recruits. It was partly because she feared the others had similar ideas about her that Desmond did. She wanted to show them that she became a recruit through her own merit and not due to her last name. Perhaps it was more than just a part of the reason. She wouldn't be disappointed if she never put herself out there. Not to mention, she feared getting close to others and accidentally exposing her magic. It hadn't happened, but there had been a lot of close calls. She'd learned the hard way that when she suppressed her magic and didn't use it at least a little once a week, it would burst out of her like an ill-timed firework.

"It's not that simple," Myla finally replied, wincing as her sister cleaned the wound.

Her sister's eyes softened in understanding. Of course, her entire family knew of her magic. It was impossible to hide it from them. It wasn't until she got older that she realized how momentous it was for them to keep her secret. If anyone found out that her family knew the entire time and did nothing, they'd be killed along with her. She owed everything to her family and knew deep down that she shouldn't be pushing her father like this. He never questioned her strength or determination—only worrying about her magic. In the wake of what happened yesterday, she should probably reevaluate her situation. But, in the meantime, maybe she should let loose for one evening.

"But maybe I'll relax tonight."

Her sister smiled at that and handed Myla a strip of leather to put between her teeth. "Good."

Myla put the piece of leather between her teeth as her sister got to work sewing up the wound. She bit down hard and flinched, barely able to contain herself from wrenching her arm out of her sister's grasp. Glancing away from the wound, Myla concentrated on breathing to distract from the pain. When Rikia finished, she rubbed soothing cream to help with the pain and healing before wrapping it up in gauze. Myla spat out the leather and placed it on the small table beside the cot.

"Thanks, Ri."

She nodded. "How'd this happen anyway?" Rikia asked, gesturing to her arm.

"Wrynn got in a good swipe before I could dodge."

She raised an eyebrow. "What's wrong?"

"I don't—"

Her sister leveled her with a look. "You don't miss, especially when you're fighting Wrynn. Did something happen?"

"I'm not without flaws, you know," Myla replied, frustrated. "I can have a bad day of training."

"Is that all this is?"

Myla glanced around the mostly empty room. A few healers and patients were around—too many for her to have this conversation.

"I'll tell you about it when I get home," Myla promised.

Rikia nodded, understanding immediately what the nature of Myla's problem was. "Okay."

She bid her sister farewell and headed back to the training arena. Training should be over by now, which hopefully meant everyone had cleared out. She needed to grab her things and didn't want to run into anyone after her embarrassing display. Everyone else would have been focused on their own sparring matches, but the fact that she had left injured didn't look good. Myla didn't have the energy today to deal with criticism.

Prickles of awareness skittered across the back of Myla's neck, and she stiffened. She was being watched. Myla crouched down and made a show of retying the laces on her boots before glancing around her. From what she could tell, no one was watching her. The streets were mostly bare, and those walking around didn't give her a second glance. Whoever was watching her was hiding themselves because that feeling did not lie. She'd honed that skill to better prepare herself for battle; now, it was a base instinct she had never ignored.

Ice water rushed down Myla's spine as she thought what this could mean. Had she caught the attention of the dragon hunters? Who else would possibly be following her around? Desmond? Was he looking to take revenge? Whatever the case, she wouldn't let her guard down for a moment. She'd find out who it was and ensure they never followed her again.

Chapter 5

By the time Myla returned to the training arena, they'd wrapped up for the day. Unfortunately, everyone was still there. She crept inside—sure to stay out of her father's line of sight—before hurrying to the corner where everyone stored their belongings. It was lined with cubbies and a few benches. Some of the recruits changed there, but Myla (like most of the other women) preferred walking home in their training gear to change in private. Today, since she'd come in early after giving up on sleeping, she'd changed here. If it had just been her clothes, she wouldn't have bothered returning, but she'd also left her sword there. It wasn't one of the training swords but the one her father had gifted her when she became a recruit. It had been crafted and balanced specifically for Myla and even had her initials engraved on the hilt. It was a gift she cherished more than anything.

She remembered distinctly what he'd told her when he gave it to her. "If I can't stop you from fighting, I'll be damned sure to arm you properly."

At that moment, Myla knew that it was the closest she'd get to approval from her father. No matter how stoic he presented himself, she could see the tiny spark of pride in his forest-green eyes. If she didn't have magic, he would have been over the moon for her to follow in his footsteps.

Keeping her head down, Myla eased between other recruits and toward her cubby. She quickly grabbed her things, but before she could make a run for it, Aryn stepped into her line of sight.

"Hey, nice job today," Aryn said.

Myla bristled—expecting cruel taunts about her incompetence—but to her surprise, Aryn gave her a genuine smile. Aryn was on the shorter side, with long blond hair braided down her back and big, beautiful, blue eyes. She was swift and agile, which made her deadly with a blade.

Myla smiled back, feeling her shoulders relax. "Thanks, you too. I only saw part of your match, but Eloria clearly didn't stand a chance."

"Just wait until hand-to-hand next week," Eloria said, coming up to stand next to Aryn. "I'll kick both of your asses."

Eloria grinned, her teeth startlingly white against her chestnut skin. Her dark hair was pulled back into two dense buns. She was about as tall as Myla, and her entire body was coiled with muscle. Due to that, she was on the slower side but could deal a lot more damage when given a shot.

"We'll see about that," Myla chuckled, feeling her spirit rise at the gentle ease of bantering with comrades.

Her eyes moved past Eloria and Aryn to see Desmond, Canon, and Maxith standing near one of the sparring mats. They were whispering about something, and

Desmond looked up in time to catch her eye. Myla held his stare—trying to discern what he was thinking—but his face remained neutral. She tried to remember if he'd been standing there when she'd come in. She couldn't remember, so it was possible he followed her—

"Myla?"

Myla snapped her gaze away from him to Aryn, who was looking at her expectantly. "Sorry, what?"

"Do you want to get drinks with us?" Eloria asked and nodded to Wrynn, who stood behind her talking to Kadyn. "With Wrynn, of course. I know Aryn would appreciate his company in particular."

Aryn blushed furiously and jabbed Eloria in the side with her elbow. "Dear gods, please shut up."

Myla smiled. "I'd love to, but I can't tonight. What about tomorrow?"

"No problem, tomorrow's good," Eloria replied.

"We're out there almost every night anyway," Aryn agreed.

"Good for the spirits, but bad for my head the next morning." Eloria chuckled.

She huffed out a laugh. "For sure. I'll see you tomorrow."

They bid her farewell as Myla walked away. She'd nearly made it to the door when her father stopped her.

"A word, Myla." It was more of a command than a request as he guided her outside without giving her time to respond.

"Yes, Father?"

"What's going on? You've been off all day."

"I'm just tired. Tomorrow will be better after a good night's rest."

Her father stared at her, quietly assessing her expression and words. "Why'd you come home early yesterday? You said you were going to get drinks with the other recruits, but Megra told me you were barely out an hour."

Damn, Myla had forgotten she'd run into the housekeeper after she got home yesterday. She should have known Megra would sell her out to her father. She couldn't tell him the truth of what happened. Even telling him she'd decided to leave because Desmond had been disrespectful to her sister would end badly. Her father would rip Desmond's head off if he found out. The last thing she wanted to do was prove Desmond right by crying to Daddy.

"I got in an argument with one of the recruits and didn't feel like sticking around."

Dad's eyebrows pulled together. "What kind of argument? Did it get physical?"

"It's nothing I couldn't handle."

"Myla, if the other recruits are—"

"It's fine. I told you to treat me like the other recruits. Would you care this much if I was anyone else?"

Her father sighed. "Fine. But you would tell me if it was anything serious, right?"

She forced herself to hold his gaze as she nodded. "Of course, Father."

****

When Myla got home, she found her sister waiting in her room. Rikia sat at her desk next to a steaming bag with an emblem Myla immediately recognized.

Her sister smiled and gestured to the bag. "Seemed like a glazed scone kind of conversation."

Myla grinned back. The scone tradition between them had started five years ago. It had been her sister's first

24

day at a new school. She'd been nervous, so she wore her favorite white dress with pale pink pansies to make her feel more confident. When Myla met up with Rikia after school, she'd been in tears—her favorite dress torn at the hem and covered in mud. Her sister wouldn't tell her what happened and locked herself in her room. So, Myla, not knowing what else to do, went to their favorite bakery and bought scones. It had been the only thing that got Rikia out of her room. They'd talked over the glazed sweets, and her sister told her she'd been picked on. The next day, Myla found that bully and ensured he would never pick on her little sister again. Thus began the tradition that had gotten them both through various challenging situations, from bad breakups to even worse days.

"Good call," Myla replied, grabbing a scone and plopping down on her bed. Then she launched into the story of what happened the other night. She debated leaving out what Desmond had said about her sister, but Myla wanted her to know in case he ever came skulking around the medical ward.

Rikia grimaced and placed her half-eaten scone back in the bag. "Why are men so disgusting?"

Myla shook her head. "Not all of them. But Desmond, along with his lackeys, don't have a decent bone in their bodies."

"And you're sure he didn't notice you wield?"

She nodded. "If he had, he would have shouted for all to hear."

"Well, that's something, at least," Rikia replied, still looking uneasy. "But that doesn't mean no one noticed something off."

Myla worried her lip between her teeth. "I know. And today, I think someone was following me after I left you."

"This is serious. Myla, if the hunters caught even a whiff—"

"I know," she cut her sister off. "But what's there to do?"

"Maybe Father will have some ideas." Rikia got to her feet. "I'll go get him—"

"No," Myla insisted, stepping between her sister and the door. "If we tell him, he will send me to live with our uncles across the kingdom."

"If it'll keep you safe—"

"Maybe, but that'll leave you all vulnerable. I'm not going to leave you to face my consequences."

"Either way, we're all going to be facing dire consequences. Which is why we need to tell Dad."

"What if I'm just being paranoid? If a hunter had seen me, why would they let me leave? Even a suspicion of magic would have gotten me arrested."

"Unless they know you're the general's daughter and needed to be sure before they brought you in."

Myla's stomach soured at the thought. Setting her scone on her desk, she slumped back onto her bed. "That's a valid point. So, I should just keep a low profile for a while and act as if nothing happened. If I start panicking and disrupting my schedule, that's a sure sign of guilt—if someone's following me."

"Myla," her sister whined, fear lacing her voice. "We can't just do nothing."

"Just give me a few days. If I still think someone's following me, I promise I'll talk to Dad."

Rikia tugged nervously on the strands of her hair. "I don't like this."

"Just a few days." Myla gave her sister the most encouraging smile she could muster. "I'm probably making this into a bigger deal than it is. It'll all work out."

Chapter 6

The entire night was plagued with nightmares. Myla thought she'd be able to sleep well given her lack of it the previous night. Of course, the universe had other plans. She woke up multiple times throughout the night, covered in sweat and her heart hammering in her chest. She didn't remember the specifics of the dreams, only glimpses of a shadowy monster and golden eyes. She wanted nothing more than to crawl back under the covers and stay in bed all day but couldn't. Her parents would get suspicious if she slept in too late, even on her day off. No, she needed to pretend everything was normal.

With a groan, Myla pulled herself out of bed and stumbled over to her wardrobe. She grabbed the first thing she could and threw it onto her bed. It happened to be the only shirt she owned with a high collar. It was a gift from her mother to wear to some event. Her mother disapproved of all of Myla's low tops and gifted the shirt to her in hopes that Myla would start wearing more of them. Myla hadn't appreciated it at the time, but she was too tired to care.

She got dressed quickly, tucking her shirt into a pair of black, cloth trousers. Over the shirt, she laced up her corset—blue with a cream-colored lace pattern. To finish the look, she tied on her favorite knee-high boots and pulled on a navy, knee-length overcoat. She went into the washroom and brushed out her unruly curls. Not bothering with her typical updo she did for training days, she let her natural waves fall down her back. Satisfied with the look, she walked downstairs and into the dining room.

Her family was already sitting at the table, enjoying breakfast. The table was laden with a spread of scrambled eggs, bacon, a pot of coffee, and chopped fruit. Her father sat at the head of the table wearing his dark green uniform blazer decorated with medals and badges to signify his rank. Her mother sat to his left in a floor-length, light pink dress with long sleeves and a pattern of golden flowers along her corset. Her long salt and pepper curls were twisted and pinned to the back of her head with small, golden flower clips. Rikia was on their father's other side. Her dress was light blue and sleeveless, with a pattern of silver leaves that decorated the corset and hem of her dress. Her straight dark hair was left down—long strands nearly falling to her waist. Myla slipped into the chair next to her sister.

"You slept in quite a bit," her father observed. "Out late last night?"

"No, just thought it would be nice to catch up on some sleep," Myla replied, filling her plate with a generous portion of food.

Her father only hummed in response, and Myla felt herself bristle. She could hear the disapproval in just that

28

noise, and she wanted to scream. Nothing she did was ever good enough. When she used her time off to train, it was too much training. And if she strayed away from her routine for a few extra hours of sleep, she was lazy.

Myla opened her mouth to retort when Rikia spoke. "Is that a new necklace, Mother? It's gorgeous."

Their mother smiled and touched the small, green stone that rested on her sternum. "Yes, it is. Your father gave it to me the other day."

While Rikia and her mother gushed over the stone, Myla turned to her father. "If you're worried about my training—don't be. Yesterday was rough, but I won't let myself get distracted again. I'll probably go to the arena to get some extra practice in this afternoon."

"You know that's not why I worry."

"And I can't have this conversation with you again," Myla responded with a scowl.

Her father sighed. "Fine. But remember, your year's almost up. If you can't pass my test, I'll dismiss you from the recruits."

When Myla had joined the recruits, she'd made a deal with her father. He promised her one year to hone her skills. In exchange, she needed to endure his test to ensure she would have no magical incidents on a battlefield. If she passed, he'd let her continue her training. Fail, and she'd be forced to quit.

Myla turned back to her food. "I understand, Father," she replied before shoving some food into her mouth.

Her father watched her for a moment longer before turning back to his own food. Myla was feeling an odd mixture of nausea and hunger. She gulped down the orange juice in front of her—trying to settle her stomach. She knew it would look odd if she didn't finish at least most of her food, so she ate as much as she could stomach before getting up from the table. After saying goodbye to her family, she walked out of the dining room. Throwing open the front door, she startled when she nearly ran into Wrynn.

"Oh!" Myla exclaimed, taking a step back. "Hey."

"Sorry," Wrynn said sheepishly and took a step back. "Do you want to walk around?"

"Sure," Myla said, stepping out and shutting the door behind her. "Let's go."

They started down the street, passing large estates as they went. Her family was well-off since her father was promoted to general almost twenty years ago. When her father was around her age, he was sent into battle against Adratus, the kingdom southeast of theirs. During the battle, the general died, and Myla's father took charge. He led the remaining troops into battle and beat the odds. Shortly after returning, he was promoted to general and was given a generous pay raise that allowed her mother to pursue her passion for learning. Myla's mother went to university and was now one of their most valued professors. She was a renowned scholar who specialized in languages, culture, and history.

"I'm sorry again for yesterday," Wrynn said, turning down the street that led farther into Rosebourne Kingdom's capital, Cassia City.

"It's fine," Myla assured, flexing her arm. "It only needed a few stitches, and it barely hurts."

"That's good." Wrynn smiled. "Maybe we should go back to training with the wooden swords."

Myla scoffed. "You got one lucky shot. It won't happen again. Besides, training with wooden swords is useless. It doesn't have the same feel as a blade."

"If I cut you again, your dad just might make us."

"Won't be necessary," she replied then quickly changed the subject. "Anyway, did you go out to Garith's last night?"

He nodded. "Just for an hour or so. Desmond and his goons showed up, and I didn't feel like hanging around."

"Did you spend some time with Aryn before you left?"

Wrynn gave her an inquisitive look. "Aryn? A little. Why?"

Myla shrugged. Obviously, Aryn hadn't gotten up the courage to admit her feelings, and Myla wasn't about to rat the girl out. "No reason. She and Eloria were the ones who invited me out, and I told them I'd see them tonight."

His face lit up. "Really?"

Myla nodded. "Yeah, and hopefully, Desmond will be decent enough to leave me be. If I punch him again, I might not be welcome back at Garith's for a while."

"Well, if he comes looking for a fight, I'll punch him so you won't get banned."

Myla snorted. "And that's why we're best friends," she responded, making Wrynn chuckle.

After that, they walked in silence for a while before heading into the heart of the city. They walked along the shops and booths, admiring the various wares, including ornate rugs, paintings, clothing, beautifully hand-crafted pottery decor, stunning jewelry, flower bouquets, and newly forged weapons.

Myla felt herself relax. She didn't realize how tense she had been the last few days until she felt the weight lift off her. Being around Wrynn always calmed her. He had become a constant for her in the few years they'd known each other, and she never realized how much she had come to rely on him until that moment.

31

They sat down on a bench near a bakery—the fresh smell of bread and sweet pastries wafting over them. Wrynn was looking out across the street, watching the baker pull out a loaf of bread from his display case to give to a woman with a child balanced on her hip. He didn't even notice the group of women giggling and staring at Wrynn as they passed. Wrynn had always been oblivious to attention like that for as long as she'd known him. Wherever they went, women and men would ogle him or blatantly flirt with him, but Wrynn never seemed to notice, or maybe he didn't care. Myla wondered sometimes if he even wanted any sort of romantic relationship.

"Do you ever wonder what you would be doing if you weren't a recruit?" He asked.

Myla blinked, taken aback by the question. "Uh, no, not really. This is the path I've always wanted to take."

Wrynn nodded.

She studied his expression, which had turned almost wistful. "Was there something you wanted to be more than a recruit?"

"I did—I thought about being a baker, but they weren't paying enough. The only job I could get with good wages without advanced education was a recruit." He smiled at Myla. "I wouldn't change anything, though."

Myla smiled back. "Good, because I'm not letting you quit on me. We're in this for the long haul, Einar."

Wrynn laughed. "In that case, maybe I should rethink things—"

She nudged his shoulder. "With a little over a year left, I don't see you quitting."

His smile faltered at that. "Yeah, I suppose I'm almost done."

"Which is good...right?"

He shrugged. "Yeah. I mean, I'll get a higher wage, but I have no idea where they'll station me. What if I'm sent to Naeron? Or Tanin? I would never have enough leave to visit you or my family."

"Just for a few years," Myla reasoned. "And you know I'll keep an eye on your family. Not that they need it. Your youngest sister is what...almost twelve? So, she'll be in school with Veric and Rayna. Barion just got a job working with a blacksmith. Not to mention, your mom's been putting in hours at the university and will be done with her degree before you leave. My mom's even talked about a position she'd be great for. Your family's going to be just fine while you're gone." She placed a reassuring hand on his shoulder. "And if it'll make you feel better, I'd be more than happy to write you as many times as you want with updates. Okay?"

Wrynn smiled. "Thanks, Sea Storm."

Chapter 7

The rest of the afternoon, Myla and Wrynn wandered the town. She'd planned on getting some extra practice in, but Wrynn had convinced her otherwise. Besides, she didn't want to reopen her wound. They bought some lunch at a cafe on the outskirts of the city, then hiked their favorite trail to waste the day away. It had been a while since Myla had relaxed like that, and it took her mind off the hunters for a few glorious hours. By the time the evening rolled around, she was feeling refreshed and ready to head to the tavern.

To Myla's immense relief, Desmond didn't show his face that night. She spent hours drinking and dancing with Aryn, Eloria, Wrynn, and Kadyn. It was the best night out she'd had in a long time. She pulled Eloria up to the front of the stage and danced as the fiddler played a jaunty tune. She laughed as she saw Aryn and Wrynn behind them—Aryn dancing awkwardly with her pale cheeks stained red from embarrassment or drink, Myla could only guess. Eloria followed her gaze and grinned.

"How precious!" Eloria called over the crowd.

Myla laughed. "You should show them how it's done." She nodded to a woman with tawny skin and a springy, ebony afro who had been staring at Eloria all night. Myla didn't recognize her, so she wasn't a recruit. Garith's may be dubbed as the 'recruits' tavern,' but that didn't mean others didn't wander in.

Eloria followed her gaze and smiled at the woman. "I think I will," Eloria said, walking over to her.

Myla grinned as Eloria sidled up next to the woman and started talking to her. From the way the other woman was giggling and smiling—Myla thought it must be going well. She turned to Wrynn and Aryn, but they had disappeared into the crowd. She spotted Kadyn dancing with another recruit, Pyke, Myla thought her name was. Pyke had her chest nearly flush against Kadyn's while they danced. They were smiling fondly at one another, and his hands were clasped firmly on Pyke's hips.

Myla pushed her way out of the crowd toward a table and slumped down in a seat. She'd only drank a few ales and was already starting to feel them wear off. Since the rest of her companions had paired off, Myla thought it was about time to head home. She tried to catch Wrynn's eye to tell him she was off, but he seemed to be having an intense conversation with Aryn. Deciding it best not to interrupt, Myla left the tavern and headed toward her house.

It was raining again, harder than it had a few nights before. The wind was howling, and thunder rumbled through her bones. It nearly drowned out the sounds around her.

35

Though, unlike others, the rain didn't hinder her senses. With her water magic coursing through her blood, the rain became almost like an extension of her. She may not hear others around her, but she could feel where the rain shifted to fall against a roof or a person's cloak. Which was how she knew someone was following her.

Myla couldn't go home, and she wasn't sure if she could face this person either. If it was a hunter like she suspected, she wouldn't stand a chance in a fight. They were trained to fight those with magic, and she couldn't confirm his suspicions. No, she needed a place to lie low that wouldn't put anyone else at risk.

Quickening her pace, she continued toward her house as if nothing were amiss. She prayed the person would go away, but they only matched her pace—keeping a safe distance away. Cursing herself for not grabbing her sword this morning, Myla took stock of the weapons she did have. One knife sheaved to her thigh, one in each boot, and two small ones sewn into her corset. Not much, but enough if it turned into a fight.

Myla passed her family manor and continued toward the river nearby. There was a path hidden behind the last house on her street. The dirt path led through the tall oak trees along the outskirts of the river, which eventually led to a waterfall. Only when she was obscured in the trees did she start running. She used her magic to hide her form in the storm, but the footprints in the mud would make her easy to track. She veered off the path onto the rocky shore, a place where she ironically always practiced her magic.

Running to the farthest tree on the bank, she wasted no time climbing it. She settled in the branches, hand resting over her hammering heart. She wrapped her cloak tighter around herself as the chill rain settled in her bones. The smell of damp earth and leaves wafted over her as she tried to slow her breathing. However, with panic running through her veins, it made the task impossible. She was forced to cover her mouth when, moments later, a man walked onto the shore. A golden curl peeked out from under his hood—a stark contrast to his all-black ensemble. His gloved hand rested on the hilt of his sword as he searched for her.

Myla didn't recognize the man, which only terrified her more. He had to be a hunter, which meant if she got out of this alive, she'd need to run—forced to leave her life behind all because she couldn't keep her temper in check. Unless she got rid of him, the thought of killing another human made her queasy, but the thought of losing her life here was unthinkable. Unseathing her dagger, she held it carefully between her fingers. Throwing knives had never been her strong suit, but with all the practice with Wrynn, she rarely missed.

She nocked it back, holding the blade against her ear. It would be a simple shot from here. One simple flick and her problems would be washed down the river. Staring, she tried to picture him as another training dummy. Unfortunately, she'd never been good at imagining things. Myla squeezed her eyes shut and moved her hand away from her mouth to grip the branch beneath her. One life for hers. It was bound to happen at some point. But, when she thought of that day, she was facing the person—blade to blade and eye to eye. There was no honor in being an assassin.

The blade lowered until it was clutched to her chest. She'd come up with a new plan. Once the hunter left, she'd talk to her father. He would know what to do.

Thunder rumbled overhead, and lightning streaked across the sky. A loud crack sounded as a nearby tree caught the blast. Smoking branches fell, and by the smell, they were burning nearby. Near enough that the tree Myla was nestled in could catch fire at any minute. She was so started that she nearly fell off her branch. Her boot slipped and crashed hard into the trunk. The rain wasn't loud enough to muffle the sound.

The hunter whipped his head up, the hood falling back to reveal his cruel face. "Gotcha."

Chapter 8

Myla stared at the man, dagger still clutched in her hand. He didn't appear to be much older than she was. He was all sharp edges—leaner than she expected a dragon hunter to be. A long scar gleamed on his neck as he stepped into the moonlight directly under her tree.

"Who are you?" Myla demanded. "What do you want?"

His brown eyes were alight with amusement as he replied, "I think you know, Myla Yules. Why else would you run?"

"Maybe because some psycho followed me home in the dark."

"I was there that night at Garith's Tavern," he continued as if she hadn't spoken. "You lost your temper and control of your magic. You were quick on your feet, I admit—pretending that you threw the drink in his face. But,

I've been at this awhile. Seen enough of your kind to know the signs. You're a dractactus."

The grip on her dagger tightened as she tried to keep her face neutral. "You're delusional."

He bared his teeth in a sinister smile. "That's exactly what my comrades said. 'The general's daughter, a wielder, not a chance.' I'll be the one laughing when I hand you over to their majesties to claim the water wielder bounty."

The last part of his sentence pinged around her mind, but Myla didn't have time to ponder it. She needed to find a way to convince him she was normal—preferably before the fire reached her tree. There were two options. One, fight him—though she didn't love her chances with that one. Or two, try and talk him down. Both options weren't ideal.

"Now." He unsheathed his sword and pointed up at her. "Are you going to make this easy on yourself? Or wait until the flames force you down?"

"You don't have any proof," Myla told him. "And who do you think the king and queen will believe? You—a nobody hunter—or my father—their general."

"Oh, I'll have proof." He grinned. "There are always ways of getting you lot to crack. For instance." He pulled a dagger from his boot and then turned to fling it into the darkness of the treeline behind him.

A cry rang through the air, and Myla's heart jumped into her throat. To her horror, Wrynn stumbled into view—pulling the dagger out of his shoulder.

"I find torturing a loved one speeds things along."

The hunter darted toward Wrynn, lifting his blade to strike. Wrynn rolled out of the way, grabbing his own sword. The time for talking was over. Myla lept from the tree and landed in a crouch she quickly rolled out of. Rocks dug uncomfortably into her skin, but it was the farthest thing

40

from her mind. She charged toward the hunter, cursing herself again for not having her sword. The hunter kicked Wrynn to the ground before rounding on Myla. His blade caught her dagger—flinging it from her grasp. Staggering back, she reached for another blade and threw it.

The dagger cut across his arm, but it did nothing to slow him down. The hunter swung his sword just as Wrynn came up behind him. Myla dodged the blow just in time to watch Wrynn cut a gash down the hunter's back. He turned with a snarl, shoving Wrynn back. Myla ran at him—throwing herself onto the hunter's back. With a tight grip around his neck, the hunter stumbled back, but he was quick to regain his balance. The hunter snarled and grabbed her hands. With a strong, fluid movement, he dislodged her grip and flung Myla into the icy river.

Her head struck a sharp rock, causing stars to dance in her vision. She surfaced with a gasp, struggling to find footing. Thankfully, the river wasn't deep, but the current was strong. Unable to help it, lest she got swept downstream, she used her magic to lift herself into a standing position. She turned to Wrynn, only to see the hunter slam the hilt of his sword into Wrynn's temple.

Myla cried out as her best friend crumpled to the ground. Anger roared in her veins, and the storm responded. Thunder boomed overhead, and the rain fell in heavier sheets. The hunter glanced up and smirked—knowing exactly what caused the shift.

"All the same," he said with a smirk. "Always too emotional to hide your monstrous nature."

It was reckless and extremely idiotic, but Myla allowed her emotions to take over. He already knew of her magic, so either way, one of them would not make it out of this alive. She refused to be the one dead.

Raising her arms, she flowed all of her anger into the storm and river churning beneath her. The wind and rain roared together—strong enough that the hunter staggered. Myla imagined the water reaching out like hands and dragging the hunter underwater. The river around her complied, reaching toward the hunter. He dodged, pulling something out of his pocket. The water reached for him again, but not before he threw something. It was a small ball that quickly expanded into a net that coiled around her. Crashing back into the water, Myla steered her concentration to parting the river around her. She grabbed her last dagger and sawed at the ropes. She was nearly free when the hunter appeared above her.

He knelt over her and grabbed her wrists, wrestling the dagger from her grip. She tried to slash at him, but he grabbed the net and pulled it tighter around her. The rope dug into her skin and forced her arms to her chest. She was forced to release the dagger before it could tear into her throat.

The hunter swiped the dagger with his free hand. "Gotcha," he said again with a wicked smile.

Myla barred her teeth right back. "Not on your life."

She'd been trained on how to get out of positions like this. With a good foothold and solid hip motion, it was easy. Though, being trapped under a net would make things trickier. Before she could try, he pointed the dagger toward the shore.

"Make another move against me, and this blade will find a home in your boyfriend's skull."

Myla froze at the words, glancing over at her friend, who was miraculously still breathing. Unfortunately, he didn't seem to be coming to any time soon. She wouldn't risk his life for hers. With a glare, she relaxed her body.

His grin widened. "Good girl."

The hunter got to his feet, and Myla followed suit— slowly. Only once they were back on the shore did she let up on her magic that kept the river parted. She didn't move as he collected his sword and sheathed her dagger in his boot. He pulled out a small length of rope from his cloak pocket and tied Myla's wrists together. He gave it a firm tug—hard enough that she had to fight not to flinch. Then, walking over to Wrynn, he slung him over one shoulder.

"So nice of your friend to save me the trouble of finding proof," the hunter said. "Now we're ready to meet their majesties."

Chapter 9

There were hundreds of tunnels hidden beneath the city. Some lead out of the city, and others lead straight onto the castle grounds. They'd been there as long as the city had—built in case of sieges or, later, dragon attacks. The stone walls were embedded with crystals that cast a dim glow, allowing people to pass through without a torch. Myla had been only eight years old when her father told her about them. There was an entrance to one near her house that she'd been told could be used in case of an emergency. For years, he drilled into her the directions she'd need to take in order to make it out of the city. Right, left, left, right, right, right. Her father had carved a giant X into the stone next to the exit she'd need to take to freedom. It wasn't until years later that she figured out the emergency was if anyone found out about her magic.

Taking the tunnels now, with Wrynn unconscious and Myla being pulled along like cattle, made her gut churn. She couldn't believe she'd let this happen. If only she'd talked to her father sooner or if only Wrynn hadn't followed her. She didn't know how much Wrynn had heard, but it was likely he knew of her magic. Not that it mattered at this point. She was as good as dead. She just prayed they'd spare Wrynn.

The smell of damp earth and mold plagued her nose as she tried to think of a way out of this situation. The hunter was stronger and faster than her, not to mention, he was holding her best friend hostage. There wasn't much she could do unless Wrynn woke up. She kept glancing at him. The trickle of blood on his temple had slowed, but he looked too pale. Even with a healer in the family, Myla knew nothing when it came to injuries. A head injury was obviously bad, but how could she tell if it was severe? What if he fell into a coma or worse?

The spiraling anxious thoughts were so consuming that Myla was jerked back after failing to notice the hunter's slowed steps. In front of them loomed a steep staircase with a trapdoor above. The hunter gestured for Myla to go first, and she did so begrudgingly. As soon as she pushed open the door, a sword appeared at her throat. Myla lifted her bound hands as the hunter called behind her.

"Only me, Oyvim, with a gift for their majesties."

The sword moved away, and Myla was able to climb into what looked to be a cell. Myla immediately recognized the man in front of her as the captain of the royal guard. She'd met him once or twice before. He was around her father's age with black hair streaked with grey shorn to his scalp. Taller than her father by a few inches, but he was nearly as broad. His skin was the color of mahogany, and his eyes were a shade of brown so dark it could be mistaken for black. His muscular frame was clad in full body armor made of shining silver, and a dark red cape was thrown over one shoulder to signify his rank.

Captain Oyvim's eyes widened a fraction as he recognized Myla as well. He glared at the hunter as he deposited Wrynn onto the ground. "What's the meaning of this?"

"She's a water wielder," the hunter explained with a smug smile. "Just what they were looking for."

"How do you know?" The captain demanded. "Do you know who she is?"

"Yes, yes, the general's daughter. I know it seems far-fetched. But who better to keep a wielder under their majesties' noses than their own general?"

"Do you have any proof?"

"I saw her do magic myself, and he—" The hunter gestured to Wrynn. "Is a friend of hers to use in case she doesn't cooperate."

The captain glanced between all of them skeptically. "You're sure?"

"Completely. And I'd be happy to show their majesties."

"That won't be necessary. I'll take them myself."

The hunter's grin faltered. "And have you taken all the glory? I don't think so. I want my reward."

"Which you'll get," he responded cooly. "If you cooperate."

"Not going to happen," he said, tugging on Myla's rope. She stumbled away from Oyvim and closer to the hunter.

Captain Oyvim signed in exasperation. Then, in a flash, he swung his sword. Myla flinched, sure the blow was for her, but the steel missed her entirely. A choked gasp escaped the hunter's lips, causing Myla to glance his way. She sucked in a breath to see the blade plunged deep into his gut. The captain pulled it away, and the hunter stumbled back. He released the rope and grasped at his bleeding middle. His lips parted as if to speak, but only blood fell from his lips. With one final step back, the hunter crumbled to the ground. Myla could only stare in horror as the light drained from his eyes before he became still.

"Should have taken my offer," Captain Oyvim tsked before sheathing his sword.

Just then, Wrynn stirred with a groan. She would have been relieved to see him sitting up if not for the dread-filled horror swirling in her chest. Wrynn glanced around, confused, eyes finding Myla's in the haze.

"What's—"

"Time to move," the captain cut Wrynn off. "On your feet, boy."

Wrynn, noticing the hunter for the first time, paled before quickly getting to his feet. He swayed slightly, and Myla reached out to steady him. Neither of them spoke as the captain ushered them from the cell-like room. Surprisingly, the room led into a grand hallway rather than the dungeon she'd imagined. She had never been inside the palace before but knew instantly that's where they were.

The walls were painted a light blue and were trimmed with gold. The floor was marble, and lined down the middle was one long red and gold rug. Chandeliers hung from the ceiling, but most of the light came from the full moon gleaming from the many windows that lined the right wall. Myla tried to keep track of where they were going, but all the halls looked the same. After a while, they stopped in front of a pair of large wooden doors—the golden handles gleaming. Two guards stood at the entrance, saluting to their captain. He must have nodded to them because a second later, they were pushing open the grand doors. Myla stiffened and took a step back. Captain Oyvim's large hand landed on her back and shoved her forward.

Wrynn looped his arm in hers, and unable to do anything else, they walked into the throne room.

Chapter 10

The room was large and mostly bare. The marble floor was white—so bright that she couldn't look directly at it. A long blue rug ran down the middle of the room, stopping at the base of two thrones elevated by three steps. The thrones were twice as big as their occupants and were made of a mixture of gold and metal and outlined in...Myla's eyes widened. The thrones were outlined in dragon scales of various colors.

Stone statues lined the walls of the room—depicting the ten Gods and Goddesses they worshiped in the Old Faith. Queen goddess Rornja was in the front, outlined in gold. Dakdarr, the god of war, wielding twin blades, came next. The Goddess of death, Thadea, was the only one kneeling— her face shrouded in a veil. Nuva, the goddess of Nature, had her arms outstretched with trees growing at her feet.

Voxdite, the god of the seas, was parting the ocean at his feet. The god of luck, Oros, was whom Myla sent a quick prayer to as she passed—her stomach bubbling with nerves. His hands were full of money, the coins dripping to his feet. Evella, the goddess of love, had her hands pressed to the foreheads of a couple kneeling at her feet—a soft smile curling her lips as she blessed them. The goddess of knowledge, Brerena, was the one that Myla recognized the most next to Dakdarr, as she was the goddess her mother prayed to often. Her shrewd eyes seemed to follow Myla as she passed—judging her for making such a ridiculous mistake that resulted in her being here. Dumis, the goddess of craft, held welding tools in her powerful hands, poised over a nearly completed sword. Last was Mestus, god of medicine, with his golden hands hovering over a mortal who lay dying at his feet.

Myla's heart was in her throat by the time they finally reached the foot of the steps after what seemed like hours. With her arm still tucked into Wrynn's, they bowed together.

"Captain, what's the meaning of this?" The king demanded. Despite his gruff tone, he looked relaxed on his throne. His golden crown lay on his short grey hair, matching the gold seams of his loose-fitted cloth trousers. He wore freshly shined, knee-length black boots and an elaborately designed blue and gold overcoat that was buttoned to his throat, which brightened his blue eyes. He had a sword strapped to his belt, but Myla knew it was mostly decorative. All the kings and queens before him had worn it around their waist. It was said that the sword was used by the king's ancestors in the War on Magic, and it was with that blade that the last dragon was slain. At least, that's what they wanted everyone in Rosebourne to believe. Myla's existence negated that fact, for it was a dragon that gifted Myla with power when she was born. They even explained away the continued existence of hunters as having the purpose of

49

finding the wielders. It was because of Myla's father that she knew the truth of things.

"She's the one you've been searching for, Your Majesty," the captain responded.

His eyes lit up, and he leaned forward. "Truly?"

Captain Oyvim nodded. "Brought in by a hunter, who has been dealt with."

King Otois nodded to Wrynn. "And him?"

"Proof, should you need it."

"Take him outside for now. We will speak with Miss Yules alone."

The captain bowed and escorted Wrynn away. He shot her a worried glance that Myla could do nothing to assuage. She tried to with a smile, but it only made his expression turn fearful. Forcing herself to look away from her friend, she turned to the king and queen.

Queen Deona furrowed her brow and looked at her husband. "Yules? As in, General Yules?"

"The same."

The queen looked over Myla with newfound interest. She was wearing a floor-length lilac-colored dress. The dress was sleeveless, cinched her waist, and flowed out at her hips in layers of thick fabric. Her neck was adorned with a thick diamond necklace, and her wrists were decorated with an assortment of silver bangles. The queen's dark brown eyes were lined with black, and her lips were painted a deep purple. Her long white-blonde hair was styled in an intricate updo with diamonds sparkling throughout the strands. Her crown was woven into her hair to give the illusion that the crown was a part of her.

The queen tilted her head at her and smirked slightly. "I always forget that our general has two daughters. Your younger sister looks just like your mother, Brie, and yet you..." she trailed off, her smirk widening. "Don't exactly fit. Makes me wonder if you belong at all."

Myla clenched her jaw. She had been told that her entire life. Her mother and sister were both thin and beautiful and often passed as sisters to those who did not know better. She had more features in common with her father, but it was subtle. The shape of their eyes were the same and the slope of their foreheads, but that's where the similarities ended. Her father was made of sharp edges and thick muscles, and Myla had a soft, round face. Though the year and a half of training had formed muscles along her arms and legs, she was still soft in the middle. It didn't matter to her because she knew she was her father's daughter through her personality. Both were strong-headed and determined—willing to do whatever they set their minds to and not willing to back down from a challenge. Myla didn't appreciate what the queen was insinuating about her birth.

"Your Majesty is quite astute," Myla replied, fighting to keep the sarcasm out of her voice. "I've been told I take after my father's mother, though she passed before I was born."

The queen only hummed in response.

"You come before us accused of being a dractactus with the ability to wield water," the king spoke. "However, given your father, I'm willing to give you the benefit of the doubt. Tell us what happened to bring you here."

This was it—her one chance to explain herself with no hunter to dispute her story. She only needed to make it convincing.

Myla took a steadying breath. "A few nights' ago, I went to the tavern with some of my fellow recruits. One in particular insulted my sister, and I threw a drink in his face and punched him. A hunter watched the entire encounter and was convinced I used magic on my drink. He started following me and decided to confront me tonight. He told me that he would have turned me in sooner, but none of his comrades believed the general's daughter could be a magic wielder. Hence, why he followed me for a few days until he got tired of it." Myla wrung her hands nervously, scratching at the ropes still clinging to her skin. "He attacked me without provocation and demanded I use my magic. He was so angry and kept going on about some reward he'd get with my surrender. Assuming the storm was somehow my doing, he only grew more determined. Wrynn tried to come to my aid, but the hunter bested us both and dragged us here."

"I see," the king mused, rubbing a hand across his bearded chin. "So, you claim that you do not possess any magic?"

"Do you truly believe the general would keep me a secret if I possessed magic?"

"It's unlikely," the king replied. "However, as a recruit of the knights, I am sure you are aware that we must do everything within our power to root out the dractactus."

Myla swallowed tightly. "Of course, Your Majesty."

"There is one surefire way to expose the magic in a dractactus," the queen said, leaning back on her throne. "Which is subjecting them to high levels of torture."

Her knees buckled as she struggled to stay standing.

"Magic seems to have a sort of defensive instinct. When the wielder is in danger, the magic will protect them, and this is the case for the wielder's loved ones as well. Since you are the general's daughter, and we did not want to risk turning him against us—we are not going to torture you. Your friend, on the other hand, is more expendable. If you can stand watching your friend beaten and no magic appears, then we will consider this matter settled. If not..." The king trailed off, his blue eyes scanning over Myla's face in a way that made her want to squirm. "Well, we'll cross that bridge if we get there."

The king gestured behind her, and Myla nearly jumped out of her skin when a royal guard placed a bucket of water behind her. She hadn't even noticed that he had come back into the room. At the king's command, he cut the ropes off her hands as well. The royal guard headed back toward the door to go get Wrynn, and Myla scrambled for a way to get them both out of this mess.

"I am more than willing to do whatever is necessary to prove myself, your majesties," Myla said, clasping her sweaty palms behind her back to hide their shaking. "But Wrynn isn't the right person for this. He is an acquaintance at best. He is one of the nicer ones out of the recruits, but I wouldn't call us friends." She heard the great doors behind her open and the sound of three sets of footsteps. "Perhaps there is a better way?"

"Even so," Queen Deona replied. "He is the closest that you have to a friend, so he will have to do."

Myla looked back and saw Wrynn standing between the two royal guards. He was rising from his bow, and his eyes locked with hers. His eyes widened slightly when he saw the blatant fear in her eyes before one guard punched him in the stomach.

Chapter 11

Myla was glad her back was to the king and queen because her face would have given away her lie about Wrynn. Wrynn slumped forward, taken aback by the blow. The other guard kicked him in the back, and he went sprawling to his knees before he could react.

Myla's body was tense—her hands clasped in front of her tightly. The guards started kicking Wrynn, who had curled into a ball, biting his lip to keep from crying out. One of the guards kicked Wrynn in the face with a sickening crack. Blood gushed out of Wrynn's nose as he called out. Myla fell to her knees, tears streaming down her face. She couldn't take it anymore. She sobbed at them to please stop—that Wrynn had nothing to do with this.

She wrapped her arms around herself, bowing her head as she felt the unmistakable pull of her magic in the pit of her stomach. The water in the bucket in front of her started to ripple. She tamped down on it, which felt like trying to cover a geyser with a wooden plank. Her body began to shake with exertion—the ripples in the water growing larger. She tried to divert her mind, but all she could hear was Wrynn's cries of pain and confusion. Then she heard a wet snap as the guard stomped on Wrynn's arm.

Wrynn screamed, and her magic exploded. The water burst from the bucket toward the guards—turning into icicles in the air. The icicles bombarded the guards, not hard enough to do permanent damage but enough to draw blood and cause the guards to stumble back. Myla crawled to Wrynn, who had stilled, having passed out from pain. There were cuts along his arms and chest—a bloody knife discarded next to his still form. She knelt in his blood and pulled his head into her lap. She pushed a lock of hair out of his eyes and rested her forehead against his. Her tears dripped onto his cheeks as she apologized over and over.

Others were speaking, but she wasn't listening—her ears were ringing with Wrynn's cries. She hugged him closer, covering her body with his. This was all her fault. How could she let this happen to him? She should have confessed when she had the chance. She was a fool to think that she could hide her magic forever.

Myla felt a prick in her neck, and she flinched, thrusting out her arm to hurl icicles at the assailant, but the water didn't respond. She could feel her magic in the pit of her stomach, but it was like clawing with broken fingernails for something at the bottom of a frozen lake. She turned to see one guard with a syringe in his hand. He took a step back—his eyes shone with fear, but when Myla didn't retaliate with magic, he took another step forward. The other guard started to pull Wrynn out of her arms, but she fought him. Eventually, the two guards were able to pull her away, kicking and screaming. They shackled her hands and forced her to her knees. With a boot to her back, she could only watch as one guard carried Wrynn out of the throne room.

She deflated, the fight leaving her as the grand doors shut. She let her head fall—hair curtaining her face. She didn't dare look at the king and queen—terrified of what would come next. Would they behead her right here and now? Would they at least let her say goodbye to her family first? Or let her apologize to Wrynn for everything?

"Leave us," the king commanded.

Myla lifted her head slightly at that.

"B-but, Your Majesty—" the guard spluttered, confused.

"Now," the king barked.

Myla felt the weight of his boot lift off her back and heard hurried footsteps. She straightened slightly and finally looked at the king and queen as the doors shut.

The queen was looking at the king with confusion. "What are you doing? Let's get her execution over with—"

"No," the king said firmly.

"What—"

"We're not going to kill her."

Myla barely kept her mouth from falling open.

The queen looked equally shocked. "Otois—"

"We are not going to hurt you," the king said, turning his attention to Myla. "We have need of you."

"What possible purpose could she have?" The queen challenged.

"She's going to bring our daughter home."

Myla had heard stories of the lost princess. Over ten years ago, the princess was being escorted to boarding school when bandits attacked their caravan, and the princess was taken. No one knew who had kidnapped the princess, and no ransom had been asked of her. There were even rumors that a dragon had taken her, but that had never been proven. Most believed she had died, but the king and queen never gave up looking for her. But why they thought Myla could be of any use—

"Otois, we can't just let another one of them slip away—"

Another one. Did that mean—

The king glared at his wife. "She didn't slip away. She was taken. And I will get her back."

"The chances that she's even alive—"

"She is," the king insisted. "I would know if she wasn't."

"Otois—"

"Enough," the king snapped. He didn't raise his voice, but there was finality in his tone that brooked no argument. "It has been decided."

The queen's lips thinned, but she didn't argue further.

"What we are about to tell you is confidential," King Otois said, the intensity of his gaze making Myla want to shrink in on herself. "You are not to breathe a word of this to anyone. If we find out that you leaked any information, you will be executed. Is that understood?"

Myla swallowed tightly and nodded.

"Good." The king leaned back on his throne. "You may have heard the story that the princess was kidnapped by bandits, but that's not completely true. Our daughter, Zaya, and her escorts were attacked by bandits, but she wasn't kidnapped by them. A dragon took her. A dragon that we believe gifted her with her flame magic."

Myla blanched. Their daughter had magic—she wasn't the only one left.

"We don't know where the dragon is keeping her, and we have scoured the kingdom, but those we have sent have never been heard from again. Someone or something is keeping our daughter away from us," the king continued. "We are forced to assume it is the beast that took her and won't let her go. If any of the knights got close to her, the dragon most likely killed them—seeing them as obvious threats. But you will be different."

"You don't truly believe the prophecy, do you?" The queen asked, askance. "There's a reason seers aren't used anymore."

"They may have fallen from grace, but I believe in their worth. They've been known to predict war outcomes and prevent coups. My seer will bring our daughter home."

"It's not even magic. If it was, they would have been run out with the rest of the dractactus."

"Their powers were gifted by the gods." The king snapped.

"Allegedly—"

"Enough." He snarled before glancing back at Myla. "On the day our daughter was taken, I was given a prophecy. *In the waves of destiny, a hope shall gleam. A water-kissed soul, a hero's dream. A princess wanders unseen, by ocean's embrace, shall the kingdom reclaim their future queen.* Ever since I've searched for one who could wield water. With your magic, you will be able to get close to the beast. Close enough to get rid of it for good and bring our daughter home. By whatever means necessary."

The queen cut a look at her husband. "You plan to send her alone? We might as well set her free!"

King Otois clenched his jaw. "If you'd allow me to finish." He shot a quick glare at his wife before turning his gaze to Myla. "You won't go alone. One of our appointed dragon hunters will accompany you. We won't tell him what you are, so this is your only warning. If he finds out, he will kill you."

Myla had so many questions, but she knew that the king and queen had no reason to answer them. Maybe if she went on this assignment, she'd learn more. Not that she had much of a choice. She could either die now or go on a deadly quest and most likely die later.

"If I do this," Myla said slowly, still trying to process everything she'd been told. "Then what will happen?"

"If you succeed, then you'll come back a hero. Anyone who knows about your magic will be taken care of, and I will knight you myself—if that is what you choose." The king leaned forward. "But if you fail and try to return empty-handed, we will have no choice but to execute you as our law states. That also goes if you succeed and carelessly allow someone else to learn of your magic."

"Then I would be honored to bring the princess home, your majesties."

Chapter 12

Myla was escorted out of the throne room and to the dungeon below the castle, where she would wait until the dragon hunter came to fetch her. With two guards on either side of her, holding each of her arms, Myla could only follow. The dungeon was located under the barracks, where sunlight could not penetrate. As soon as she walked down the long, winding staircase, the potent scent of mold and human waste hit her. Suppressing a gag, she focused ahead. The stone walls were damp, with sparse torches in the sconces along both sides. There was a guard stationed in front of the entrance to the dungeon, and he stood at attention as soon as he heard them walking down the hall.

Lifting her head slightly, her eyes widened when she recognized the tall, Black man with shorn salt and pepper curls.

"Myla?" Shiy asked, blinking and squinting as if his eyes were deceiving him.

She gave her father's oldest friend a wobbly smile. "Hi, Shiy."

Shiy cast his brown eyes from one guard to the next. "What is the meaning of this? Is the general aware that you're taking his daughter to the dungeons? And on what grounds?"

The guard on her left sneered—tightening his hold to the point that Myla almost flinched. "The general is not informed of every arrest made, and this was made personally by their majesties. The reason does not need to be conveyed to you."

The guard on her right pulled out a slip of paper and handed it over to Shiy. "Now, if you wouldn't mind letting us do our jobs so we can go about our day—it would be appreciated."

Shiy read the note, the color slowly draining from his face. When he looked back up at Myla, her gut knotted at the fear in his eyes.

"It's okay," Myla said. "It won't be long."

"This isn't—"

"Enough," the left guard snapped. "You have all you need. Now let us through."

Shiy clenched his jaw but did as they asked. Unlocking the entrance door, he revealed row after row of cells—most of them already occupied. She was led to the very last cell in that hallway, the torch nearby unlit. Through the shadows, she could make out hay covering the floor, and a small cot was set up in the far corner across from a rusty bucket. The guards shoved her in, and she barely kept herself from tumbling to her knees. The door shut behind her with a resounding clang and click of a lock. She turned in time to watch the guards retreat down the hall, leaving her alone.

****

The entire night she spent in her cell—tossing and turning on her feeble excuse of a cot. Myla had expected someone to come by during the night, but she was left alone. The entire dungeon was eerily quiet, save faint rustling from time to time that was either rat or human—she could not tell.

For the first hour, she paced around, thinking about Wrynn. She needed to know he was all right and being taken care of. He wasn't like her—at least, she didn't think so. Regardless, he didn't deserve to suffer because of what she was. She wanted to ask Shiy to check up on him, but he hadn't come by her cell like she had expected. It made her wonder if something in the note from their majesties had caused him to hesitate.

Eventually, she gave up on waiting and lied down. Even with exhaustion weighing heavy, she barely slept. With no sunlight, it was impossible to tell how much time had passed. It could have been eight hours or one when she gave up on sleeping.

Sitting up, Myla sighed and ran her hands down her face. She felt like such an idiot. Of course, a hunter had seen her. She should have gone to her father as soon as she figured out someone was following her. Tears filled her eyes, and she quickly blinked them away. She wouldn't break down—not now. She had been given a chance to prove herself. Even if all those before her had failed, Myla would make sure that she didn't. She was going to find the princess and bring her home, even if it was the last thing she did. As for the dragon hunter, she'd worry about that later.

The creaking sound of a door down the hall, followed by hurried footsteps, caused Myla to straighten. They echoed closer and closer until someone appeared.

Myla sprung to her feet as her father stopped in front of her cell. She rushed to the bars, nearly smacking her face on the cold metal.

"Dad!"

"Myla." Her father gripped her hands through the cell bars. "Shiy told me what happened. I'm sorry I wasn't here sooner. He couldn't leave his post until this morning."

"It's okay, I'm fine," Myla lied with a wobbly smile.

He squeezed her hands, his brow tight with sympathy. "I'm taking you home. Everything will be fine." He turned to the guard on his right before barking out, "Let my daughter out. *Now.*"

The guard was a tall, skinny man who looked to be only a few years older than Myla. He swallowed tightly—his Adam's apple bobbing. "I-I can't, sir," he stuttered, blue eyes darting between them. "I'm under strict orders—"

"I'm ordering you otherwise," Myla's father snapped.

The guard took a step back. "I'm s-sorry, sir. Their majesties were clear that she is only to be let out when her escort arrives."

Her father let go of her to turn and glare at the guard—a glare he reserved for those who really angered him. Myla had seen trained adults flee at the sight of it. This guard didn't, but she could see him trembling under the intense weight of it.

"I swear to all the gods, Tarson, if you don't let her go this instant, I will make sure that you get stuck doing night shifts in the town square for the rest of your career," her father growled, stepping toward the guard.

Tarson scurried back. "I—"

"If I didn't know any better, General, I'd say you weren't respecting the decree of our esteemed king and queen," another spoke from farther down the hall. "I'd hate for word of that to get around. I can think of at least ten people who would love an excuse to push you into early retirement."

The guard turned, and his whole body relaxed when he saw the other person who was still out of Myla's line of sight. "Thank Rornja, you're here," he said, praising the queen goddess.

Myla's father stiffened. "Raevyn Telius. I didn't know you decided to follow in your father's footsteps. I assume you're to be my daughter's escort on this...assignment."

Her father cut a glance at Myla and her stomach dropped when she saw the panic in his green eyes. He looked back down the hall, and she followed his gaze in time to see Raevyn stop in front of her cell.

Myla's eyes widened. Her escort was only a few years older than her, which was unexpected. So, too, was his blatant beauty. He appeared to be in his mid-twenties with a slight stubble lining his sharp jawline and three small hoop earrings in his right ear. He was tall with thick muscles barely contained under his dark red tunic. His dense, inky curls were cut short on the top and shaved on the sides. A few shades darker than his rich umber skin, his eyes gleamed nearly black in the gloom. Though Myla thought there were flecks of gold in there as well, but couldn't be sure. A scar ran the length of his face from just below his eye to his jawline. Myla couldn't help but wonder if he had any other scars hiding under his obscenely tight leather trousers.

Realizing she was staring, she snapped her eyes up to meet his, only to notice his gaze trail slowly over Myla. He started at her muddy boots, moving all the way up to her dark curls that Myla was sure were a mess from sleep. Her stomach fluttered, and her cheeks grew warm at the intense scrutiny, but she refused to squirm. To her surprise, her magic perked up at his gaze—churning in her gut like nervous energy. It was a warning, no doubt, that she needed to keep her guard up around him. As if she needed the reminder. When he finally looked away, he focused his attention back on her father.

"Yes, and lucky for your daughter, I'm the best at what I do. Even better than my father was."

Her father's expression suggested that he didn't consider anything about this lucky, and Myla was inclined to agree.

"I have no doubt," her father replied. "My daughter, on the other hand, is still training. She hasn't even finished her first year. I would not dream of questioning their majesties' rationale, but I wonder if someone else would be better suited for the task. Maybe someone with years of training under their belt."

Myla had to bite her tongue from arguing her worth as a fighter. Yes, she wasn't finished with her first year of training, but she was in the top five of her year. Knowing her father was trying to get her out of this situation, she refrained from arguing.

Raevyn looked back at Myla and raised an eyebrow. "What do you think? Are you as worthless as your father's insinuating?"

Myla clenched her jaw but refused to rise to the bait.

Raevyn smirked as if he knew exactly what she was thinking before looking back at her father. "Worthless or not, it's been ordered, so it shall be. It's their majesties' minds you need to change, not mine. For now, Tarson, let the girl out. We've got a long journey to prepare for."

Tarson scurried back over and unlocked the latch before doing the same to Myla's chains. Myla strolled out as if she was leaving her house and not a jail cell before turning her blue eyes on Raevyn. Since he had no power to change her fate, she might as well tell him exactly who he'd be traveling with for the foreseeable future.

65

"I'm a woman, not some sniveling little girl," Myla told him, raising her chin. With her shoulders pushed back, she tried to give the impression she was as tall as him even though the top of her head barely grazed his chin. "And as you'll soon find out, I'm anything but worthless."

He looked her up and down once more, his lips pulling up in the corners. "We shall see."

Chapter 13

Myla followed Raevyn out of the dungeons into the streets of Cassia City toward her house. Before she left, her father promised he would fix everything. She didn't believe that was possible but knew better than to tell him otherwise. Her only request was that he tell Wrynn that Myla would explain everything when she got back and that she was sorry. She knew it wasn't nearly enough and wasn't what Wrynn deserved, but she was helpless to do anything else. Raevyn couldn't know what she was, and she had a sinking feeling that he was going to be her shadow until she either died or brought the princess home. Myla prayed for the latter.

Her mother and sister must have heard the news because they were waiting when Myla strolled into the house with Raevyn close on her heels. Usually, during this time, her mother would be at the university at least until supper time, and her sister would be at the medical ward. Instead, they were sitting in the drawing room. They both sprung up and brought Myla into a hug without even giving Raevyn a second glance.

Unbidden, tears filled Myla's eyes as she hugged them back. "I'm okay," she told them, pulling back.

"What did they tell you?" Her mother demanded. "What's going on?"

Myla could feel Raevyn's eyes on her as she responded, "I'm going to bring the princess home. It is both my punishment and salvation."

"But why?" Rikia asked.

She needed to figure out a way to explain without revealing too much. If Raevyn was as good at fighting dragons as he'd said, she knew that he would be equally good at sniffing out those with magic.

"They are giving me a chance to atone for what I have done. Their majesties are quite generous. I won't be traveling alone, either." Gesturing back to Raevyn without taking her eyes off her family, Myla continued. "Raevyn, a dragon hunter, will be my companion for as long as it takes."

Her family finally looked back at Raevyn, both their expressions turning grave.

"I see," her mother said, taking hold of Myla's hands. "And this is set in stone?"

"Father will explain more once he's back from speaking with their majesties. In the meantime, I have to pack." Myla squeezed her mother's hands before letting go.

Unable to say anything more without giving away her secret, Myla walked up to her room. Silently, she started packing up her rucksack with clothes and other necessities. Raevyn didn't say anything as he sat on her window seat and watched her work. Myla didn't let herself think about his unnervingly beautiful eyes watching and assessing her as she tried to figure out what exactly she should pack and how much. She could be gone for years, but knew she couldn't

68

pack her entire wardrobe. Should she even bother packing any of her summer clothes?

"You're packing way too much shit," Raevyn commented as he propped his dirty shoes on the white cushion of her seat.

Myla scowled, hands fisting around the green tunic she'd pulled from her bag. "I don't know how long we'll be gone. I'd rather be prepared than not."

"You should only be packing what you can carry on your back. This isn't a vacation. There is no destination where we can drop off all of our things and be on our way. There'll be times when we need to make a quick getaway, but that won't happen if you try to pack everything you own. If there are things that we need later, we'll just buy them. This entire assignment was funded by their majesties, and I've been given enough gold for lodgings and other supplies to last at least a decade."

The thought of being gone for that long—of not being able to see her friends or family and being stuck in the company of the one person she'd never be truly safe with— made Myla's stomach sour. She had to succeed, or it wouldn't be the dragon that killed her.

"I know it's not a vacation," Myla growled as she emptied her rucksack once again. "Your company alone will be a constant reminder of that."

Raevyn snorted. "The feeling's mutual. You think I want to be slowed down by a novice? One I'm constantly trying to keep alive because, for some unknown reason, their majesties think is the key to finding their daughter once and for all? No, but we're stuck together, sunshine."

Myla blinked in surprise at the nickname and was annoyed when a wave of butterflies filled her stomach. Narrowing her eyes at him, she told him, "Don't call me that."

He grinned, exposing godsdamn dimples—as if he weren't attractive enough. "What? Sunshine? I think it fits you quite well. You're just full of warmth."

This fucking guy.

Rolling her eyes, Myla didn't deign to respond as she finished packing. She placed her packed rucksack next to the door and turned to Raevyn.

"I assume we're leaving today?"

He nodded.

"Then get out. I need to bathe and change before we leave."

Instead of getting up, Raevyn settled farther back into the cushions. "Not a chance, sunshine. I'm not about to get punished for allowing you to bolt before this assignment has even started."

"And I'm not about to *allow* you to see a free peepshow, pervert," Myla countered, crossing her arms.

Raevyn rolled his eyes. "You have a folding screen in the corner you can change behind, and I'm not stopping you from bathing. I checked when I came in here, and there aren't any windows in the washroom. Meaning the only two visible exit points are the window behind me and the door across from me. Both of which I plan to keep in my line of sight."

Myla sighed through her nose. "Is this how it's going to be the entire time? I'm never going to have any privacy?"

Raevyn didn't look the least bit sympathetic as he said, "Shouldn't have fucked up and gotten yourself arrested. What did you do, anyway? All I was told was this was a punishment for you, and the only reason you're not rotting in a cell is because you have a certain skill set that will help us find the princess."

"None of your business," she retorted.

Raevyn only nodded. "I thought you'd say as much. Now hurry up and get ready. I'd prefer to leave before the sun sets."

She clenched her fists and barely kept herself from punching his stupidly beautiful face.

****

As Myla bathed, she was able to take stock of her injuries. Luckily, her stitches hadn't been torn during her fight. She was covered in small cuts and bruises with a large bump on the back of her head. Other than that, she'd gotten out of her scuffle relatively well, thanks in no small part to Wrynn.

As Myla stared down at the water, fogging up from the filth scrubbed off her body, she thought of the hunter. She had no sympathy for the man who got her into this situation, but she couldn't stop seeing his face. The smug look turned surprised as the captain ran him through. It had been so sudden and brutal. And for what? To keep this prophecy a secret? Perhaps to keep their majesties from looking weak for trusting a seer. Whatever the case, it didn't make Myla feel any better about what her fate would be even if she were to miraculously save the princess.

This might be it. This might be the last time she was ever in here. The last time she sat down with her family for a meal while they chatted about their days or the last time she could walk down the hall to bug her sister when she herself felt bored. The finality of it all was overwhelming, and she had to push all of it from her mind before it crushed her.

Myla dressed in riding trousers, a long, white tunic, a black cloak, and knee-length boots. She braided her long, brown hair before strapping her weapons on—a dagger in each boot, another strapped to her right thigh, and her sword against her hip. Myla was lacing her boots on her bed—pointedly not looking at Raevyn—when her door banged open. With a jolt, she looked up, relaxing when she saw it was only her father. She smiled, but the smile quickly disappeared when she saw the desolate look on his face.

"I'm sorry," he said and pulled her into a tight hug.

Myla's eyes filled with tears as her walls crumbled—the weight of everything that transpired over the last twenty-four hours crashing into her. Burying her face in her father's shoulder, she tried to hide the abrupt sob that clawed from her throat. She had known he wouldn't succeed, but there had been a small kernel of hope she'd held onto that had kept her from breaking down completely. Now that it was gone, she couldn't hold it in anymore. She hated the fact that Raevyn was seeing her break down after she had told him she wasn't a sniveling girl, but she was helpless to stop.

"The king and queen told me everything," her father whispered as he rubbed soothing circles into her back. "Why didn't you tell me? I could have helped."

Myla swallowed tightly and pulled back so she could wipe the tears from her cheeks. "I thought I had handled it. The last thing I wanted was to cause you unnecessary stress. And I was afraid that you would make me pull out of training. Being a knight is all I want, and I know I'll be good at it even if you don't think so."

Her father lifted her chin so she had to look into his steely green eyes. "I never thought you weren't good enough. I've been hard on you because I didn't want you to end up like me. I didn't want you to have to experience the bloodshed of battle or be haunted by the lives you will be forced to take if you pledge yourself to the sword. I wanted you away from all that and living the life you dreamed for yourself."

"Being a knight *is* my dream, Dad. And after I succeed with this assignment, I will finally be one."

Her father smiled slightly, taking her hands in his and squeezing them. "If anyone can do it, you can."

Myla smiled. "Thank you."

He pulled her into another hug and whispered so low that Myla barely heard him. "Always keep your guard up. Follow your gut, and whatever you do, don't trust Raevyn. Stay alive by whatever means necessary. Promise me."

Myla nodded against his shoulder—knowing it was impossible to promise such a thing, but knowing he needed to hear it. "I promise."

Chapter 14

With her rucksack thrown over one shoulder, Myla followed her father down the stairs—Raevyn a shadow behind them. Her father explained to her that as far as anyone else was concerned, her assignment didn't come from the king and queen. She was not to tell anyone that they were involved if the nature of her assignment came to light. Her father had been instructed to tell anyone who asked that Myla was staying with family outside the capital for the foreseeable future. What the story would change into if Myla succeeded in bringing the princess home, she wasn't sure. And if the king and queen knew—her father hadn't been privy to that information.

Her mother and sister were waiting by the door with equally somber looks on their faces. Myla didn't like what their expressions meant—that they didn't think they would see her again. She tried to give them a reassuring smile, but her mother burst into tears, and Myla could do nothing to stop her eyes from filling with tears in reply. Wrapping her

74

mother into a hug, she rested her head on top of hers. Rikia joined the hug, wrapping her arms around Myla and her mother. Finally, her father gave in and hugged them all.

"I promise I'll be okay," Myla said, pulling back and blinking away the tears before they could fall. "I've got this."

"Of course you do," Her mother smiled softly.

"I want you to have this," her father handed her a small leather journal. "It's a journal of all the information I have about the possible whereabouts of the princess as well as all we know of her and the dragon. It's limited, but hopefully, it'll give you some idea of what you'll be dealing with."

"I got some elixirs from work for you as well," Rikia said. "I put them in one of the packs on your horse."

Heart full of love and gratitude tinged with an ache at the possibility of never seeing them again, Myla smiled. "Thank you. I love you all."

They smiled back and pulled her into one last hug before walking her outside. Myla had almost forgotten Raevyn was there since he had been so quiet. Sending him a quick glance, she was surprised to see he had a thoughtful expression on his face. Myla had the urge to ask what was on his mind, along with a litany of questions regarding dragons and magic. If the princess was a wielder, how many more were out there? And how had she remained hidden with her dragon for so long? There were countless dragon hunters around the kingdom unless that had been a lie, too. Maybe they weren't as good at eradicating dragons and magic wielders as their majesties would like the kingdom to believe. Since their daughter was a wielder, did that mean they were sympathetic to others? Was that part of the reason they chose not to kill her? If so, why keep up the ruse?

Those were only the beginning of what Myla wanted to ask Raevyn, but she had no reason to believe he'd be truthful with her. Tamping down her curiosity, she mounted her horse, Cass. A young boy stood next to the house gate holding the reins of a black horse. He wore the palace staff uniform of black trousers and a white tunic with the royal crest in the center. He had a large rucksack strapped to his back, and the poor boy looked like a small gust of wind away from toppling under its weight. Raevyn strolled over to him and pulled the bag off his back with ease before strapping it to his own. The boy sagged in relief and handed Raevyn the reins before scurrying down the street.

Raevyn swung up onto his horse and urged it down the street in a slight trot. Waving one last time to her family, stomach full of nerves, Myla followed him.

****

Myla usually didn't mind silence. Most of the time, she craved it, but it had been four hours, and Raevyn hadn't said a word. She had been given an impossible task and had no idea what to expect or even where to begin. Raevyn knew, at least to an extent, which was far more than her. The urge to ask him all the questions jostling through her mind was becoming increasingly hard to ignore. So, when they finally made camp for the night, Myla broke the silence.

"How has a woman with a dragon stayed hidden for so long?" She asked as she laid out her bedroll.

Raevyn was crouched in front of the fire he had just built. When he looked up at her, Myla saw that she had been right about his eyes. The firelight illuminated the gold flecks along his irises, and his long lashes cast shadows over his cheeks.

"If I knew, we wouldn't be here," he replied.

"How do we even know she's in the kingdom?"

"We don't."

"Would another kingdom harbor her?"

Raevyn got to his feet and grabbed his bedroll. "Perhaps."

"Have you searched? Or have other hunters?"

"That's need to know," Raevyn replied as he positioned his bedroll across from hers, near the horses. "And you do not."

Myla scowled. "Seems relevant to know where she isn't so we can find out where she is."

"Didn't your father give you a book with location information? Why don't you consult that rather than bothering me." Raevyn settled down cross-legged on his bedroll.

"If you insist on being this difficult, it's going to be a long journey." She snapped. "As you said, we're stuck together, and if we're going to succeed, then we have to work together."

He gave her a bored look. "To work together, I'd need to trust you. And I don't trust criminals."

Her lips pulled into a tight line as she fought the urge to argue. She wanted to tell him that she didn't trust dragon hunters but didn't want the questions that were sure to follow. To make matters worse, she actually agreed with him. They would need to trust each other to some extent to be able to work together.

"Then how about a mutual exchange of information?" Myla suggested, sitting on her own bedroll and leaning back on her hands. "To even the odds."

"Alright then." He leaned forward. "Why did their majesties really send you to find their daughter?"

Something told her that if she lied, Raevyn would know. That left half-truths in order to make her story convincing. It was a risk, but she trusted her instincts.

"It was prophesied by a seer."

It was clear he hadn't expected that answer. He raised an eyebrow. "The king consults a seer?"

"Apparently not publicly," Myla replied. "But, yes."

"If it was prophesied, then why arrest you? And why not send you earlier?"

"It wasn't clear to them that I was the one from the prophecy until I got arrested. Once they figured it out, they agreed to forgive my crime if I found their daughter."

He let out a breath of air that sounded almost like a laugh. "Well then, if it was *prophesied*, then we can't fail."

"I never said it was logical," Myla snapped, straightening. "I think the king's desperate enough to try anything at this point."

At that, he nodded. "That I can believe."

"If that's all your questions—"

"Just one last question, sunshine. Why were you arrested?"

Myla had been expecting this one but hadn't ironed out the details in her mind. To give her more time, she studied Raevyn's face as if sizing him up. The corners of his lips were curled up slightly as if by an invisible string. If she hadn't known better, she would have guessed he was amused. Thinking of how his stony face would look cracked with amusement made her chest warm for reasons she could not fathom.

"I killed a dragon hunter."

When surprise flickered across Raevyn's face for a second time, Myla concluded she liked surprising him. She enjoyed doing anything that made emotion appear in his expression—even if it was fleeting.

"I find that hard to believe," Raevyn replied, returning his neutral mask. "You haven't even finished your first year as a recruit."

"Because no one can learn how to defend themselves unless they're a recruit," she countered with a smug smile. "Do you really think my father wouldn't have taught me how to defend myself? How to kill a man before they could do the same to me?"

Myla shouldn't have been shocked when Raevyn didn't look repulsed. He'd no doubt killed many himself. Innocent people whose only crime was being born with magic. She should be the one repulsed, and yet, there was something about him. Something that felt like seeing an object or place that reminded you of a dream. She didn't understand it, nor did she trust it. What she did trust was her father, whose warning was ringing like alarm bells in her head.

"Why was a dragon hunter after you?" Raevyn asked, his voice low.

"The hunter came for my friend," Myla lied smoothly. "We'd wandered over to the stream near my home after a night at the tavern. I'd been up in a tree, talking with him when the hunter found us. Well, found my friend. He didn't notice me and accused my friend of being a wielder. The entire accusation was ludicrous, and instead of taking my friend to their majesties, the hunter attacked. It was clear he was only out for blood, so I defended my friend." The hunter's cold, expressionless face flashed in Myla's mind, and she grimaced. "I hadn't intended to kill him, but I couldn't let him hurt Wrynn." If only that were true. If only Myla hadn't been a coward and confessed to her sins earlier. "Some patrolling knights found us not long after, and we were brought before their majesties."

Raevyn studied her face in the same scrutinous way he had when they met. This time, Myla did not blush. She stared right back, waiting. She was careful not to let her expression change. She was no stranger to lying—often to spare the feelings of others. This, however, was far more

79

dangerous. Taking stock of the weapons on her person, she estimated it would take a few seconds to pull the dagger from the sheath on her thigh. Raevyn's sword was behind him, but she didn't doubt he had other weapons on his person. Not that he'd need them. Taller and broader than Myla, it wouldn't take him much effort to overpower her. She'd just need to be faster.

Finally, he said. "And Wrynn...was he a wielder?"

"No. They tested him, but he didn't show any signs of magic. He was set free, but that didn't erase my crime." She glanced down at her hands, tracing her fingers over the calluses along her palm. "*A princess wanders unseen, and by a knight disgraced, shall the kingdom reclaim their future queen.*"

The silence stretched on between them until Myla couldn't stand it. She glanced up through her lashes to find he hadn't looked away. There was no clear emotion on his face, but she thought she glimpsed a glimmer of understanding in his dark eyes. As if he could understand what it was like to have the burden of fate on one's back.

"Doesn't sound like complete nonsense," he replied with a genuine smile. It was small—barely creasing his cheeks—but it felt like so much more. It felt like potential.

"Does that mean I've earned questions of my own?"

"Tomorrow," he promised. "Now, sleep. We're leaving at dawn tomorrow."

The urge to argue was nearly overwhelming, but Myla let it go. She was exhausted after the day she had and knew she'd have countless nights like this to ask her questions. It seemed less daunting now than it had a few hours earlier, as if they were both reaching for common ground.

So, she lay on her side and pulled her blanket up to her chin. "Good night then, Telius."

"Good night, sunshine."

Chapter 15

Chirping birds overhead roused Myla the next morning. The rising sun trickled through the branches, casting light through the morning dew upon the grass. Sitting up with a stretch, she flinched as her muscles strained in protest. It had been almost a decade since she'd slept on the forest floor. When she was younger, she'd go camping with her father at least once a month. He'd taught her everything she needed to know to survive in the woods. It had been a lot for a twelve-year-old to shoulder, but he'd been preparing her for the worst-case scenario. Her father wouldn't ever say so, and she was too young to consider needing to run away from home to stay alive. All she knew was she didn't want to let her father down. She remembered waiting for her father to fall asleep and crying over the remains of the animal they'd killed for dinner. As well as the times her father had shouted at her when she'd picked the wrong berries or failed to catch a fish. They'd stopped going after only a year when her father got busier with work and

Myla with her school work. She wished she remembered more of the skills her father had taught her so she wouldn't need to rely on Raevyn.

Myla jolted when Raevyn dropped a leather pouch in front of her. Peering inside, she saw it was full of nuts and dried berries.

"Breakfast," Raevyn said, pocketing a similar bag in his cloak. "That you can enjoy on the road."

She glanced around. His gear had already been packed onto his horse. Raevyn, himself, had changed, and he'd washed his face. Tiny droplets gleamed in his stubble, and the collar of his shirt was damp. He'd changed his dark red tunic for a black one that matched the rest of his ensemble.

"How long have you been awake?" Myla asked, plopping a few berries into her mouth.

"Long enough," he replied. "Now, let's get moving."

She slipped the pouch into her pocket before folding her blanket. "What's the rush?"

"We have a lot of ground to cover."

"Starting where exactly? Do you even have a plan?"

"Do you?" He challenged. "You're the one with the *special skill.*"

Myla rolled her eyes and crouched next to her bed roll so she could roll it up. "You're the one who's traipsed around this kingdom for who knows how long. Where should we start?"

"Roullon, and from there, I'll let you lead."

Tucking her bedroll under her arm, she got to her feet with a smirk. "You don't seem the type to give up control."

His lips quirked. "Oh, I'm not giving up anything, sunshine. I'm merely letting fate take the reins."

A breathy laugh escaped her lips, and she shook her head. "Very funny. I knew telling you about the seer would be a mistake."

Myla walked over to Cass and started strapping up her gear.

"I only wish they'd found you sooner. Five years ago, it could have made for a great story. A teenager who aspires to be a knight finds out she's the hero they'd been waiting for. The story practically writes itself."

Mounting Cass, she gave Raevyn an unimpressed look. "Too bad you wouldn't have been able to read it. I expect they skip over reading and math in dragon hunter school."

Raevyn mounted his horse with ease, and she tried not to admire the way his muscles flexed even under his clothes.

"No cartography either, which is why we spend most of our time wandering around."

Myla snorted, pleasantly surprised to find he had a sense of humor under all his bravado. "It all makes sense now."

****

Since winter was still months away, the main road between Roullon and Cassia City was fairly crowded. Myla had wanted to ask her questions since she'd been deprived the night before but wouldn't with so many wandering ears. Nearly three hours passed before the road quieted, and they were alone.

"Alright, Telius. It's my turn to ask questions," Myla spoke, guiding Cass away from a fallen branch.

Raevyn glanced over at her from the corner of his eye. "I suppose that's fair."

"What do you know about the princess?"

84

"Her name is Zaya Griffin. She was allegedly kidnapped when she was eight—"

"Wait, allegedly? You don't think she was taken?"

"As part of my job, I had to learn everything I could about dragons and dractactus. And with that knowledge, I can say with almost certainty, that the princess is staying with the dragon willingly. A magical bond like that is stronger and unlike any bond we normal humans can comprehend. Not to mention, I know how the princess's home life was before she left, and suffice to say, I wouldn't have stuck around either."

"If they treated her so badly, why do they want her back? I know, she's the only heir, but couldn't they have tried to make other heirs or appoint one?"

"She may be a monster, but she's still their daughter. I know at least the king loves her."

Myla wanted to retort that he didn't know the princess. He only thought she was a monster because of her magic—magic she didn't ask for. And she has killed hundreds, the voice in the back of her head reminded her. Or her dragon had to protect her. Regardless, neither of them knew exactly who the princess was or what she was capable of.

"That's not love," Myla said instead. "If anything, I'd say it's guilt motivating him more than anything else."

"We don't need to understand the why to get this job done," Raevyn pointed out. "Anyway, she's been gone for thirteen years. She was supposedly a frail child with thin, white-blond hair and dull, brown eyes. Based on the height of both her parents, we estimate that she's on the taller side—a few inches taller than you, give or take. And she has a birthmark on the base of her neck that resembles flames. We believe that's her magic symbol."

"What's a magic symbol?"

"It's something a dractactus is born with that signifies their magic and bond with their dragon. It darkens the stronger the bond is between them. If my hunch is correct, the princess's mark should be as dark as a tattoo when before it had been light—almost like a scar."

A tremor of heat trailed along Myla's rib, and she barely kept herself from touching it. Three wavy lines were etched into the skin—itchy now with awareness. It had been there as long as she could remember. She had thought that it was just a birthmark, but maybe that was her magic symbol—three little waves, like the water she controlled.

"What happens to the mark once the dragon dies?"

"It fades, just like the magic in the dractactus would."

"So, if we kill her dragon, then will the princess still have magic?"

"Only a small fraction," Raevyn replied, arching his back in a stretch. "She'd be able to do parlor tricks like lighting candles without a match."

That meant that Myla's dragon was alive. Somewhere out there. The thought brought on a mixture of exhilaration and terror. She didn't know how powerful she was—she had always been too scared to test it—but she could do a lot more than parlor tricks. There was a deep well of magic inside her, and she wondered if she would ever figure out her limits. Would her magic get stronger if she found her dragon? Was it possible? They had stayed hidden for at least as long as Myla's been alive. Would they even want to meet her?

"Someone with white-blond hair would be fairly easy to spot. That's not a common hair color, especially not naturally."

Raevyn nodded. "Which is why we think she dyed her hair or shaved it."

"She wouldn't have shaved it because that would leave the magic symbol on her neck exposed."

"That's true. Then she probably always has her hair down."

"Is there anything else distinctive about her? Any visible scars?"

"None that I know of."

"Do you have any more insight from your other assignments? I assume this isn't your first time looking for the princess."

"You're asking far more questions of me than I did you," he groused.

Myla raised an expectant brow in response.

"It's complicated." He sighed, his fingers flexing around the reins.

"How is it complicated? You told my father you're the best at what you do," she accused. "Are you telling me that this is your first assignment?"

"I've been deployed many times, but the princess isn't our only target."

"What sort of assignments—"

"That's enough questions for today," Raevyn cut her off, gazing away from her.

It was clear that whatever his last assignment was—hadn't been pleasant. Not that dragon hunting could ever be considered such. Myla decided to let it go for now. If his previous journey hadn't involved the princess, she didn't need to know about it. But, the way his jaw was clenched, and his brows were pulled together unnerved her. She had the sudden urge to know what was wrong, which went beyond her insatiable curiosity.

Myla turned her gaze from him, focusing on the road ahead. She needed to stay focused and remember where they both stood. They may have reached an unsteady accord last night, but that didn't mean caring for what troubled the other. She had to keep a fair distance between them because they couldn't be more than enemies. He didn't know it yet, but if he were to find out what she was, he'd kill her without remorse or question. Myla had to strive to be just as ruthless.

Chapter 16

It was well past dark when they finally made camp for the night. Myla was exhausted and sore as she slid off Cass's back. She'd never been much of a rider, especially lately. It had thrilled her to learn as a child, but as she grew older, her hobbies turned elsewhere. She still made time to groom and care for Cass but usually left her exercise to the family stablehand.

Myla started the fire this time around, staying close to its warmth as the wind picked up. She positioned her bedroll close to the flames and settled down with her dinner of bread and cheese. Taking a bite of the sharp cheese, she glanced up at Raevyn. He was draping a cover over the low branches of a tree under which his gear sat. Looking up into the sky, Myla noted the dark clouds overhead. She'd always been good at sensing when a storm was near. The hairs on her arms stood on end, and the magic in her veins thrummed. She could feel it approaching, but it would be a drizzle at best—not enough to warrant shelter.

"Afraid of a little rain, hunter?" Myla asked sweetly.

"Ask me that again in the morning when you're drenched and near frostbitten." Raevyn bit back.

She smiled around a bite of bread. "Nice to know you care."

He only grunted in response, grabbing his pack and sitting down under his shelter. Turning her gaze back to the fire, Myla pulled off a piece of bread to eat with a bite of cheese. After all the questions she'd asked earlier, they'd rode the rest of the time in near silence. For some reason, she felt the need to extend an olive branch. She didn't let herself think past the obvious reason that it would be easier to work together if they were civil. Though she knew there was more to it than that.

"It's your turn now," Myla said, pulling her cloak tighter around herself. "Ask me whatever you like."

Casting her a sidelong glance, he replied, "I already know everything I need to know about you, sunshine."

She knew for a fact that wasn't true but didn't say as much. Nor did she give any mind to the twinge of pain she felt at his words. "The questions don't have to be about me. You can ask me whatever you like."

"So you can ask all of yours?"

"And who said hunters weren't smart?"

Raevyn leaned back on his hands, leaving his jerky forgotten next to him. "Alright, smartass, who was the hunter you killed?"

"He didn't exactly introduce himself before he tried to kill my friend."

"What did he look like?"

"Tall and lean with curly blond hair, brown eyes, and a scar down his neck."

Raevyn's eyes widened in recognition before he furrowed his brow. "That sounds like Ashyr. Though, he was never the bloodthirsty sort."

"Aren't you all?" Myla countered. "Can't exactly be a good hunter without it."

His eyes narrowed. "That's rich coming from the murdering recruit."

"I was protecting my friend." She snapped, fist tightening around her cloak. "What's your excuse?"

"It's my duty, just as yours will be if you ever become a knight. You will pledge yourself to kill at their majesties' demand—how is that any different from me?"

Rage boiled in Myla's stomach at his words and her lack. He was right. She could argue that those she would fight in battle weren't innocent, but weren't they? They'd be honor and duty-bound to do as their monarch decreed. Not many she'd fight would be doing so for the thrill of killing. Raevyn may be hunting wielders like animals, but she might one day do the same against a rival kingdom. The thought that they weren't all that different made Myla's stomach sour, and she was no longer hungry.

She shoved her food back into her pack and grabbed her blanket. "I think that's enough questions for one night."

Laying down on her side, she turned her back to Raevyn. She pulled the blanket up to her chin just as she felt the first drops of rain on her cheek. To her utter annoyance, the storm picked up. Rain pelted heavily against her face until she raised her blanket over it. The patter of droplets intensified and echoed loudly in her ears, causing a headache to spike. Just another thing Raevyn had been right about. She refused to give him the satisfaction of finding shelter. It would pass soon enough.

An hour passed, the rain refusing to let up. At this point, Myla was drenched and trying not to shiver. The fire

91

had been snuffed out, and her blanket was useless in keeping her warm. She turned onto her other side and peeked over at Raevyn. She'd been waiting for him to fall asleep so she could create a shelter of her own, but the bastard was still wide awake. Even through the gloom, she could make out his eyes watching her—no doubt waiting for her to cave. Well, he could just keep on waiting.

"Are you always this stubborn?" Raevyn asked over the booming thunder.

"I'm perfectly fine here," she responded through chattering teeth.

"The rain's not going to let up any time soon."

"Good. I like the rain." Turning her back to him once again, she held her freezing fingers against her chest.

She tried to focus her mind away from the cold, but her thoughts weren't comforting. They bounced around memories of the dead hunter, her tortured friend, and saying goodbye to her family—possibly for the last time. It sat heavy like stones, all the guilt and unknowns, not to mention Raevyn's words that they were the same. The only difference was Myla's dream was painted in brighter hues. Being a knight was honorable and well-respected while being a hunter was mysterious and terror-inducing. Well, it was terror-inducing for magic wielders like herself. They were two sides of the same coin commanded by a monarch.

****

Her first thought when she woke up was she couldn't see the trees or sky above her. She squinted and blinked before realizing she was staring at the canvas cover of Raevyn's shelter. Her blanket had been discarded as well, replaced with a dry one that smelled faintly of bergamot mixed with mahogany. She turned her head to see Raevyn sleeping mere inches from her, curled up to keep warm without his blanket. His eyelashes brushed gently against his cheekbones. His face, relaxed from sleep, was somehow

92

even more beautiful. Even his scar looked intentional—a near-perfect line down his cheek. He reminded her of the sirens she'd read about in books—beautiful enough to lure you in and kill you once you got too close.

And yet, he'd cared enough to drag her sleeping form to shelter and give her his blanket. Logically, she knew it was because he needed her to find the princess. That fact didn't stop the small flutter of butterflies in her stomach.

Raevyn shifted in his sleep, and Myla shut her eyes again. He let out a warm breath that wafted over her cheek. She felt his eyes dance along her face and tried not to flush. Not for the first time, she wanted to know what he was thinking and what he saw when he looked at her. A thick-headed, brash woman, no doubt. Or maybe—

"How long are you going to pretend to be asleep?" Raevyn asked, his voice low and raspy from sleep.

"Until you stop staring at me," she mumbled, a blush forming along her cheeks.

He huffed out a laugh, and she heard him get to his feet. She opened her eyes and watched him start to pack up his things.

"You didn't have to do that, you know," Myla said, handing him his blanket.

"As much as I enjoyed watching you stubbornly drown to prove your point," he replied, taking the blanket from her outstretched hands. "We've got an assignment to complete."

"Don't worry, I didn't think you were doing it out of the goodness of your heart," she spoke as she sat up.

"Because hunters don't have any?" The sarcasm in his voice was dry—nearly imperceptible—but it was getting easier for Myla to pick up on.

"Or brains," she retorted with a small smile. "It's a good thing you've got muscles, or I don't know where you'd be."

His lips pulled up in the corner. "You would know, recruit."

Her smile grew, though she tried to hide it. It felt easy to fall into this back-and-forth with him, even after being angry at him less than eight hours ago. He was nothing like she expected him to be. She'd expected him to be a stoic shadow who took everything seriously. Granted, he was serious most of the time, but he was witty and adept at sarcasm, which was good for her since it was practically her second language. It was oddly comforting, and after the week Myla had, she craved it.

"Let's just say we're anomalies with all three since you cared enough to keep me warm."

"Questionable since you almost killed yourself to make a point," Raevyn pointed out, grabbing some food out of his pack.

She rolled her eyes. "I would have been fine."

"Sure, who needs all their toes and fingers?"

Myla got to her feet and stretched out her back. "And here I thought I'd have to thank you. I'm not feeling very charitable anymore."

He snorted. "Never expected you to, sunshine. You're too damn stubborn."

Chapter 17

A day later, Myla and Raevyn made it to Roullon City—the first of many stops they'd make. Cassia City was the largest city in the kingdom, with more than forty percent of the entire population of Rosebourne living there. Roullon was one of the smaller cities on the outskirts of the capital. It was more of a place that people rode through on their way to Cassia City with a little over a hundred actual residents. The other hundreds or so milling around were travelers— precisely the sort of people she needed to talk to.

Myla tied her horse off next to the others outside the inn before grabbing all of her supplies and leading Raevyn inside. The inn was predictably crowded. The main area had a bar in the back with two sets of staircases on either side. Off to the left was a large fireplace with leather armchairs positioned in front of the hearth. In the center was a scattering of tables, most of which were occupied. Myla walked in between the tables, side-stepping a man who lurched into her path as he tried to keep his food down.

The woman behind the counter was wiping down a glass with a rag so dirty that Myla wondered what the point was. Her grey eyes met Myla's as she approached, and she plastered on an obviously rehearsed friendly smile.

"Welcome. How can I help you?"

"Do you have any rooms with two beds?" Raevyn asked, sidling up next to her.

Myla glared at him. "Seriously?"

"I'm sorry, sir, but this young lady was here first—"

"We're together," Raevyn cut the woman off.

"Not together, together," Myla added, not sure why she felt the need to clarify as her cheeks heated.

"She wishes," Raevyn put in, smirking.

Myla jabbed her elbow into his ribs, but he deflected—grabbing her elbow and pulling her into his side. Not expecting it, she fell against him, barely able to stay on her feet. Godsdamn asshole.

The woman glanced between them skeptically. "Right," she said slowly. "Well, you're in luck. We've got only one room left with two beds."

"Perfect," Raevyn smiled as Myla pushed away from him with a scowl.

Raevyn paid for the room and extra for their horses to be fed and given water. Myla was glad when Raevyn opted against getting hot meals. He probably thought the same way as her and didn't want to take the chance of getting sick like the man they'd passed. They dropped off all their supplies in the room and grabbed some dry meat before heading back downstairs.

Myla walked over to the fireplace and sat down in one of the armchairs closest to the fire. She finished her dry meat by the time Raevyn walked over with their drinks. Taking the mug from Raevyn's outstretched hand with a grateful smile, she settled farther into her seat. Her icy fingers gripped her mug of tea tightly as she suppressed a shudder. Fall was just around the corner, and there was a bite in the air to remind them all. She was honestly surprised that no one else had decided to sit by the fire, but a quick glance around the room told her that everyone else had dressed and packed for the upcoming cold weather with layers of fur and cloaks. Her own dark blue cloak was lined with fur, but it wasn't nearly as thick as others—making it clear that it got a lot colder here than it ever did in Cassia City.

The hot tea warmed her throat as she took a long sip, staring into the flames as she listened to the conversations around her. The two men behind her were talking about all the fish they'd surely catch once they made it to Naeron—the kingdom's main port city. Four women to her left were discussing their latest hunting trip and how much money their wares would go for when they got to Cassia City. She heard nothing that could possibly relate to the princess or a dragon. According to her father's journal, Roullon didn't have any sort of accounts that could lead to the princess. She'd hoped because of that it would be the perfect place for her to hide. As if it could be that simple.

"It's going to be hard to get any sort of lead if we don't talk to anyone." Raevyn pointed out.

Myla rolled her eyes. "I'm getting a lay of the land."

"So, in other words, you don't want to talk to anyone."

"What exactly am I supposed to ask?" She snapped. "It's not as if we can be forthright."

"So, you listen to people's tales from the road and see if anything stands out."

"And why would they tell me anything?" Myla asked, bringing her steaming mug to her lips.

97

He got to his feet. "Trust me, people love telling strangers stories that make them look good."

Raevyn walked off, but she stayed in her seat. She settled back, focusing on the conversation behind her. Did they say something about a flying beast, or was it lying geese—

"What's a pretty lass like you doing alone?"

Myla looked up to see a man twice her age leering down at her. From his long boots, excessive gold jewelry, and wide-brimmed hat tilted on his head, she knew he must be a pirate. Myla wasn't sure what he was doing so far inland, and she didn't care to find out.

Setting her nearly-empty mug of tea on the table, she got to her feet. "Just about to go to bed, actually."

He blocked her path as she tried to step around him. "Don't you want to hear what I have to offer? I've got a position on my ship that I know you'll be great at."

"You don't know anything about me or what skills I possess," Myla countered. "Regardless, I'm not interested. I don't need a job."

"I think you'll change your mind once I tell you what it is."

"Is *no* such a hard thing for you to hear?" She growled, pushing past him.

The man roughly grabbed her arm, short, yellow nails digging into her skin. He turned her to face him, barring rotten teeth. "Look, you ungrateful bitch—"

"Is there a problem here?"

They both looked up to see Raevyn standing over them. The glare Raevyn was giving him was so intense that the man's grip loosened on her arm. Myla snatched her arm back and glared at both of them. This was ridiculous. She hated that Raevyn could just waltz in, looking like he did, and everyone immediately saw him as a threat. Yet, at the

98

same time, people looked at Myla and thought she was an easy target. Fuck that. She didn't need anyone else to fight her battles.

"Nope, as a matter of fact." She reeled back and punched the man in the jaw.

The man stumbled back with a cry, nearly falling over one of the armchairs. His leg flared out, flipping the table with her tea on it. The mug shattered on the wood floor, causing the room to hush.

"I've got this handled," she told Raevyn before glaring at the man. "That's for laying a hand on me, asshole."

Not caring that all the eyes in the room were watching, Myla walked around the men and toward the stairs leading to their room. Unfortunately, Raevyn decided to follow her.

"What the hell was that?" He hissed, falling into step beside her.

"Just teaching the asshole a lesson," Myla replied. "You didn't need to step in."

"You also didn't *need* to punch him. You're lucky his mates didn't decide to step in. Are you always this short-tempered?"

She stopped in front of their door and fished out the key from her pocket. "Should he just get away with manhandling people? Maybe next time, he'll think twice before grabbing someone he perceives as helpless."

The door swung open, and she stepped inside with Raevyn close on her heels.

"I'm not condoning his actions, but you've got to pick your battles more carefully, or you'll get yourself killed. You can't hide behind your father's title out here because people don't know or care."

Myla tensed. "I don't hide behind anyone. That's the reason I punched the guy in the first place. I didn't want him to think—" She clamped her mouth shut, feeling her cheeks flame in embarrassment. She didn't want some random stranger to think she was weak. In all honesty, it was messed up and said a lot more about the kind of person she was than anything else. She'd always struggled with not caring what others thought—especially when it came to her strength. Even knowing this hadn't mattered because, she had let her indignation cloud her judgment. Raevyn was right. She needed to pick her battles more carefully.

"It doesn't matter," Myla finally said. "You're right. Besides, if I went around punching every person I came across that was an asshole, my knuckles would never heal."

"True." His lips twitched. "I'm honestly surprised you agreed with me so fast. I was expecting a fight."

She slumped down on the bed closest to the door. "Yeah, well, don't get used to it."

Chapter 18

Once Myla was sure Raevyn was asleep, she slipped out of their room. She didn't want to be put in the position where she'd have to fight Raevyn. Not only because she knew she would lose, but she was starting to fear she *wouldn't* kill him, and that made her vulnerable. Regardless, it was better for her to do this assignment on her own now that Raevyn had given her all the information he knew about the princess. Not to mention, she couldn't exactly use her 'special skills' with Raevyn around, and if she couldn't, she wouldn't stand a chance of getting close to the princess.

The dewy morning air drifted over her face as she stepped out onto the quiet street. Myla walked up to Cass and strapped her supplies on before swinging up onto the saddle. Heading off toward Blackwich, she pulled up a mental map of the kingdom. It was around a four-day journey from here, past a nearby mountain range. Thankfully, there was a path between two peaks, so she didn't have to brave the treacherous mountain paths.

Myla wasn't eager to sleep in the woods for that long but didn't have much choice. She'd been looking forward to sleeping on a mattress for a few nights before having to deal with the elements again. Not knowing what Raevyn's plans were, she didn't want to take the chance of staying the night only to have to wait until the next town to lose him. This way, he had no idea where she was going, so once she left this town in the dust, he wouldn't be able to find her.

Cass trotted along for only an hour before Myla felt her exhaustion settle into her muscles. She struggled to keep her eyes open as well as her head up. She thought about pulling off to the side of the road for a quick nap but wanted more distance between her and the town before she rested. She stifled a yawn as birds broke free from the trees behind her. She turned slightly and blinked in surprise to see four people dressed in all black riding toward her. One of them pulled out a dagger, the silver blade glinting in the faint sunlight. She cursed and spurred Cass forward. Fucking bandits. Bandits who were clearly more adept at riding than Myla was as she struggled to keep her saddle. They were easily eating up the distance between them, which meant running was out of the question. She was going to have to fight her way out of this.

She steered Cass over to the side of the road and pulled back the reins. Cass squealed as she skidded to a stop—hooves digging into the mud as she reared back. Myla lept off her horse and whirled around, pulling out her sword. The bandits had already dismounted, brandishing swords and daggers of their own. They charged toward her—slashing and stabbing with such ferocity and tenacity that Myla was forced to remain on the defense.

The bandits were sloppy—focusing more on brute strength than skill. None of them prioritized positioning their blades to defend their vulnerable points. Myla concentrated on their movements, waiting for one of them to make a mistake. A bandit slashed at her throat, and she ducked. She was level with his chest now—the perfect opportunity to drive her blade into his ribs. Before she could, the lifeless eyes of the hunter that had gotten her into this mess flashed in her mind. Her blade halted an inch from the man's chest. She couldn't do it. Even with death staring her down, she couldn't bring herself to take another life.

The man knocked her back with a knee to her chin. Myla bit down hard on her tongue—copper coating her mouth. She nearly fell on her ass but managed to land in a crouch. Another bandit lunged for her. Myla rolled out of the way before springing back to her feet. Her magic stirred in her stomach as frustration and panic raced through her. She pushed it down, willing herself to stay calm. If she used her magic, then she couldn't let any of them live. She wasn't even entirely sure if she *would* kill them all. The thought alone made her feel ill.

One slashed a deep cut into her right forearm before she could block it. She bit back a cry of pain and lashed out at him. He stumbled back, but she was able to cut a thin line across his chest. The move cost her. With her left side exposed, another bandit thrust their dagger into her side. White-hot pain shot through her, and she had a terrifying thought that this was how she was going to die. Not by trying to save a princess from a dragon but by a bunch of bandits only a few days from home. Fuck that. Maybe she wouldn't kill them, but she'd make sure they regretted perceiving her as an easy mark.

A new wave of adrenaline spiked through her, and, with a twist, Myla slammed the hilt of her sword into the side of a bandit's head. He crumbled to the ground in a boneless heap. She turned again to see one of the bandits had stepped away and was rifling through the packs on her horse. Myla cried out as she pulled the dagger out of her side and threw it at the bandit—striking his shoulder blade. He gave a shout of pain and fell to his knees. The scream startled Cass, and she took off through the trees.

Myla spun around to face the remaining two bandits, but to her surprise, Raevyn was there. At the sight of him, her magic flared. The feeling was oddly warm in her chest—different than how it felt when controlled by panic. It felt eerily close to relief. That couldn't be the case, though. She was clearly delusional from the blood loss.

Raevyn stood above the bodies of the remaining bandits, his sword glistening with blood. "Not the sort of display I expected from someone who supposedly murdered a dragon hunter," he remarked, wiping the blood off his blade on the dead bandit's tunic at his feet. "Rusty, after only three days without practice?"

Myla dropped her sword and clutched her side—the blood hot against her clammy skin. She knew she had other wounds, but they were dull aches compared to the crippling agony in her side. The adrenaline she had felt was wearing off, and her knees were weak. Her legs wobbled, and she took a stuttering step back. Her vision was fuzzy along the edges, and she tried to blink it away, but it only became hazier.

"Fuck you," she mumbled just as the darkness closed in, and she crumpled to the ground.

****

When Myla woke up, the first thing she noticed was that the sun was high in the sky, casting a welcome warmth over her face and neck. The second thing she noticed was that she wasn't alone.

In a flash, Myla was on her feet, pulling out the dagger from the sheath at her thigh before whirling to face the assailant. She winced as a sharp pain zipped through her side—nearly dropping her dagger from the force of it.

"For fuck's sake, sunshine, you're going to pull out your stitches," Raevyn said, rising to his feet from where he had been lounging under a tree. He tucked a small, golden pocketwatch he'd been toying with back into his pocket.

Myla scanned her surroundings as her memories came rushing back to her. They hadn't gone far from where she'd been attacked. The bodies were gone, but there were still streaks and pools of blood staining the road a few yards down. Cass was tied to a tree next to Raevyn's horse. From what she could tell, all her supplies were still there. She could feel the bandages on her hip and arm pulling gently on her skin as she moved. A quick glance down at herself revealed the shirt she had on wasn't her own. It was much larger, nearly falling off one shoulder. It smelled the same as his blanket had—like bergamot mixed with mahogany. It was frustratingly comforting, and all she wanted to do was bury her face in it and sleep for another few hours. Her want for answers won out in the end.

"What happened?"

"What? No, *'thank you for rescuing me—you're my hero'*?" His lips twitched as Myla's scowl deepened. "I'd settle for just a thank you too."

She pointed her dagger at him. "How did you find me?"

"You're not as quiet as you think you are. I heard you sneak out, and rather than chase you down, I was going to follow you until you made camp. Then I saw those bandits attack you and thought you might need some help."

"What'd you do with the bodies?"

"Threw them in a ditch nearby," he said, gesturing vaguely to the left of him. "I'd recommend we get moving as soon as possible before the smell reaches us."

Myla narrowed her eyes. "There is no *us*. It would be easier if I did this on my own."

"Easier to escape? Clearly, but I'm not going to deal with the consequences of letting that happen."

"I wasn't escaping. I'm going to bring the princess home, but I can't do that with you."

"And why's that?" Raevyn challenged.

"Because as soon as they see you, then they'll think we've come looking for a fight. The last thing I want is to fight a dragon and someone who can wield flames. Me alone is a lot less of a threat."

Raevyn barked out a humorless laugh. "You think they'll spare you and agree to *talk* just because you don't look like a threat? They've killed *hundreds* of knights just for getting too close. They won't give you a chance to go near them before they take you out. *I'm* your best bet at staying alive long enough for you to use whatever the fuck your special skill is to get to the princess. Their majesties didn't just pair us together so I can keep you from escaping. We're going to need our combined skills to complete this assignment, which means you're going to have to trust me."

"You're the one who said you don't trust criminals. Trust works both ways."

"And is that what you are? A criminal? A murderer? After your display with the bandits, I'm not so sure."

Frustration bubbled in her stomach, and she glared at him. "I had it handled."

"Really?" He took a step closer to her. "Because it *seemed* like you were trying very hard *not* to kill them."

"My first instinct in a fight isn't to kill. Unlike some."

Raevyn didn't rise to the bait. "So, you'd kill for a friend, but not yourself?"

She threw her hands up, immediately regretting the action. Pain lashed down her arm and hip, but she refused to let her pain show on her face. "Why would I lie about that?"

"Same reason why you might lie to their majesties. To protect a friend."

"Why is this so damn important to you?" She seethed.

"Trust, remember?"

Myla let her blade fall to her side and heaved out an annoyed sigh. "I may not have dealt the killing blow, but the hunter died because of me." That much, at least, was true. "I couldn't let Wrynn get punished and thought my father's title would protect me."

"Not that I believe in seers or prophecies, but if you took your friend's place, does that mean the prophecy was about him?"

She only shrugged. "Maybe? It wasn't completely clear, but since I was the only one disgraced, it would have to be me. Then again, I'm not a knight, either. I think the king was desperate enough to believe he'd finally found the person from the prophecy, and he didn't care if it didn't completely add up."

Raevyn hummed, looking thoughtful for a moment before he changed the subject. "Now that we have that cleared away, it's your turn."

"My turn to what? Trust you? I can't just trust you on a whim. You've done nothing to earn it."

"Does saving your life and stitching up your wounds count for nothing?"

"You could have ulterior motives I don't know about."

Raevyn rolled his eyes and let out a heavy sigh. "All I'm asking is that you try. And I will endeavor to do the same."

Myla clenched the dagger tighter in her fist—barely able to keep herself from flinging it at the tree next to his head just to see him jump. Ultimately, she loosened her grip and let out a sigh. She didn't have much choice in the matter, and as much as it pained her to admit, he had a point. Without his help, she might have died at the hands of those bandits. Her pride thought otherwise, but she ignored it. She wasn't helpless by any means, but her training was limited to a few months—professionally, at least. She'd been using a sword as long as she could remember, but it felt like child's play compared to what awaited her outside the training arena. If she was going to succeed on this mission, she needed to learn to be ruthless. The man standing in front of her may be her only option, but was quite possibly the best option, too.

"Fine. You can come along," Myla said finally after a lengthy pause.

Raevyn smirked. "How kind of you."

"On one condition." She sheathed her dagger.

"You're in no position to barter, sunshine—"

"You've got to train me."

He raised an eyebrow. "Train how?"

"Train me like a hunter." The thought of training like those who seek to destroy wielders like her made Myla's stomach twist. She reminded herself that knowing this could one day save her life. As they say, *to know thy enemy...* "If we're going to survive this, we both need to be merciless and cold-blooded."

He studied her, an amused gleam in his eyes. "You're asking for help?"

Her whole body stiffened, and she had to bite back her retort. His phrasing it like that made her want to take the request back. The flip side of knowing her enemy was he got a similar chance. She'd be exposing her weaknesses, and if he decided to turn it into a real fight—

"Never mind, I don't need—"

"Relax, sunshine, I'm only teasing. I'll train you. You're going to need to be at your best if we face a dragon."

Chapter 19

Myla wanted to scream. They had left the bloody scene behind and were back on track toward Blackwich. As if riding wasn't painful enough, she felt her wounds tug every trot and jostle in the saddle—sending fresh waves of pain through her body. Her wound from Wrynn had been like a paper cut in comparison. Raevyn had told her she'd needed over twenty stitches between the two wounds. Knowing that she was glad she'd been unconscious while he patched her up. He'd checked her stitches before they left and Myla had been surprised at the thorough job he'd done. It was even better patchwork than her sister's.

Cass jumped over a fallen tree, and Myla's body lurched. This time, she wasn't able to bite back her cry of pain.

Raevyn looked over at her. "First stab wound?"

"Of fucking course it is," Myla growled, clutching her side. "Getting stabbed shouldn't be a normal occurrence."

"Just wait until you've finished training, sunshine. You'll be so used to them that you won't even feel them."

"It's not likely I'm going to be seeing many battles. Ever since we signed a peace treaty with Adratus almost twenty years ago, it's been fairly quiet."

Raevyn shrugged. "There's increasing unrest along the southeast border near Auberteaux. If they rally enough of the neighboring cities and towns, I wouldn't be surprised if they decide to start a civil war."

Myla glanced over at him, furrowing her brow. "Really? Why is there so much unrest?"

"Auberteaux produces the majority of products that we trade with Adratus, and yet they barely have enough money to live. The citizens think the king and queen aren't charging enough for the products and that Adratus is taking advantage of us to their detriment."

"That's awful."

"Yeah, I was stationed near there for a while and heard all the stories. Nearly every night, there was some sort of riot in the streets. Production has slowed down considerably as a result, which is why there are so many knights stationed there. Their majesties thought it would motivate people to work. Luckily for you, I've become quite adept at sewing up wounds since their methods of motivation haven't been well received by the citizens."

A fresh wave of pain radiated from her side as if him saying that reminded her wound that it should be throbbing. Their discussion had been a welcome distraction, albeit short. She wondered if that had been his plan—to distract her from the pain—then she chided herself for the absurd thought. He was only keeping her alive so they could complete this assignment—no other reason.

"Were you stationed there because you were looking for the princess?" Myla asked.

"No. Let's just say my assignments play more to my strengths."

She understood what he meant, and the thought made her stomach churn. It had been easy to forget sometimes that his job involved killing dragons and possibly wielders. The first time she'd seen that side of him was with the bandits, and she'd missed the grotesque part. Riding side by side like this, Myla found herself letting go of that thought. She knew it was stupid, but she also didn't want to hold onto it. It only made her feel scared and upset, which could ultimately trigger her magic unconsciously.

"Not the rescuing type, then?" Myla asked, a slightly teasing tone to her voice.

"There's a reason I'm not a knight," he replied. His lips were pulled up into a half-smile, but she saw something pass along his face. It was subtle, but it made Myla wonder if there was more of a reason why he became a hunter.

"So, why did they send you with me?"

"Because I'm the best." He said it like it was a fact, which made him twice as arrogant.

She snorted. "It's a wonder, then, why you're not leading the entire unit of hunters."

"That's my father's—" He stopped himself as if realizing what he'd admitted. He took a deep breath and exhaled through his nose. "I suppose it doesn't matter at this point. He was the leader until he died last month."

Her eyes widened. "I had no idea. I'm so sorry for your loss," Myla said but knew it didn't mean much. Losing someone that close to you, even if you didn't have the best relationship, was a wound you always carried. And his was still fresh. She was lucky enough not to understand the pain, but she had seen it in her mother, who had lost her sister before Myla had been born. And she saw it in her father, who had buried more friends in her life than she could count.

He nodded stiffly, face stony. She'd expected him to look sad, but if anything, he looked angry. Somehow, she knew the anger wasn't directed at her. It made her wonder how his father had died and if Raevyn had been there when it happened. She didn't want to press him, though, so she changed the subject.

"My father never wanted me to be a recruit," she said, feeling the urge to share something in return. "I trained for two years with Wrynn before I completed the physical evaluation in disguise. There's no rule against it, so they let me. It wasn't until he said I passed that I removed the disguise."

Raevyn's gold-flecked eyes found hers, and the look he was giving her made her want to divulge all her secrets.

She looked back toward the road before continuing. "He couldn't take it back, so he was forced to let me enlist. And every day since, I've been working my ass off to prove to him I'd make a great knight. But after what happened with Wrynn and now the bandits...it makes me wonder if he was right."

Gods, she wasn't sure why she'd said all that. She felt naked in front of him—vulnerable in a way she'd only ever been with Wrynn and her family. It didn't feel right to trust him, of all people, with this part of herself. Yet, she couldn't help herself either. Maybe she was just lonely and missing home, but either way, she hated having to put up a front all the time. And with him, it was so easy to forget herself that it scared her.

Myla jumped when she felt Raevyn's hand on hers. He'd steered his horse closer without her noticing. He had to lean over to touch her, and his face was nearly level with hers.

"I'm going to help you prove him wrong. After you're done training with me, you'll be able to best the general himself."

His sincere expression and small smile made Myla believe him. They made her believe a lot of stupid, impossible things.

"I'm holding you to that, Telius."

He grinned, his dimple pulling lightly at the scar on his cheek. "I'm looking forward to it, sunshine."

****

Six hours later, they finally stopped to set up camp for the night. Myla slid off her horse, and as soon as her feet hit the ground, her knees gave out. She stumbled, grabbing Cass's saddle to keep from falling on her face. Raevyn snorted as he dismounted his horse with ease.

"I've never seen someone struggle so much," he remarked with a wry smile.

Myla flipped him off. "Piss off. I'm not used to riding—especially for that long."

Raevyn snorted again, barely able to suppress his laughter.

Her cheeks reddened. "Not like that, you deviant."

"I didn't say anything," he responded with a low chuckle.

"You didn't have to. Your thoughts are plain on your face."

Myla walked around, stretching her body. The tension in her muscles began to dissipate, and she barely kept herself from moaning at the relief of it. Once Cass was tied to a nearby tree, she grabbed her bedroll and laid it close to the fire Raevyn was beginning to build.

"You're pretty good at all this camping stuff," Myla commented as she wrapped her blanket around her shoulders. "How long have you been in service?"

Raevyn stepped away from the fire as it blazed to life. "Thirteen years."

114

Myla furrowed her brow as she studied his face. She thought he was only a few years older than her. Had she been that off about his age? He didn't have any wrinkles—not even around his eyes. That could just mean he never smiled. Given what little she knew about his history, she couldn't fault him for that.

"I can practically hear the wheels turning in your head," Raevyn said as he grabbed his bedroll and positioned it on the other side of the fire. "I was twelve when I was sent on my first assignment under my father's supervision. Though, I'd been training for years before that."

Myla's mouth dropped open. "Twelve? What the fuck, you were just a kid! How could they deploy someone so young? And how could your parents allow it?"

"Maybe things would have been different if my mother had been in the picture." Raevyn shrugged, laying on his back and crossing his ankles. "She died giving birth to me, so I never really knew her." He pulled out the pocket watch Myla had noticed earlier. He ran his thumb along the front, where something was engraved. It was too small to see from here, but it looked to be initials.

"Was that your mothers?" She asked softly.

He looked down at the watch and opened it. "Yeah. It's the only thing I have left of her. My father would be furious if he knew I had it. He never said as much, but I know a part of him blamed me for my mother's death. He always said he trained me to be a hunter because their team was dwindling, and they needed all the help they could get. But most days, it felt like a punishment for being born."

His tone was so matter-of-fact that it made her heart ache. He'd been just a child—forced and trained into being a killer. If his father hadn't been dead, she'd punch the man for doing that to his son. She thought of her sister at that age—so full of innocence and hope for the future. To have that ripped away was diabolical. Maybe Raevyn would have

115

gone down that path eventually, but he never got to choose. It made her wonder how he would have turned out if given the choice.

"Did you ever consider quitting?" Myla asked. "Or is that not something you can do?"

Knights had to serve for a minimum of ten years before they could be discharged. However, Myla had experienced that many who served were dedicated enough never to retire. She was certain her father would be one of them.

"In it for life, I'm afraid," Raevyn responded. "Though ours is usually fairly short."

She leaned forward, draping her arms over her knees. "Would you have chosen a different path for yourself?" She had to ask. He'd been so forthcoming recently that she wanted to capitalize on it.

"That's enough questions." Raevyn turned on his side and pulled his blanket up to his chin. "Get some sleep. And if you try to escape again, I will tie you to a godsdamn tree."

Myla snorted. "Kinky."

Her eyes widened slightly. Shit, she hadn't meant to say that out loud. She was blushing fiercely as Raevyn sat up on his elbow to raise an eyebrow at her. Myla flopped down on her bedroll and practically pulled the blanket over her head.

"Well, then, goodnight," she said way too loudly.

Raevyn chuckled low in his throat before she heard him settle back down. Myla buried her face in the thin cushion and barely kept herself from groaning in embarrassment. Rornja, give her strength.

Chapter 20

When Myla saw the lights of the small town of
Blackwich come into view three days later, she was more
than a little relieved. The last few nights had been hell with
her new wounds. The combination of sleeping on the ground
and riding a horse all day was excruciating. Raevyn assured
her the wounds were healing well, and she had no reason to
doubt him. He'd even been confident enough to promise
they'd begin training as soon as they left Blackwich. That
would only be in a few short days unless they got any leads.

Myla followed Raevyn inside the only inn in town,
which was a fourth the size of the last one they'd stayed at.
The lobby area consisted of a few tables and armchairs
scattered about the room without much reason. At the far
end of the room was a desk with an old man sitting behind it
with his head down. At first, Myla was afraid he was dead,
but then he let out a loud snore.

"Excuse me, sir," Raevyn stopped in front of the desk
and glanced down at the man.

He only snored louder in response. Raevyn sighed before slamming his hands down on the desk. The man shot his head up, looking around wildly.

"Wh-what, who goes there?" He mumbled, voice weak with age.

Raevyn flashed him a charming smile. "Ah, you're up. Good. We'd like one room with two beds, please."

The man blinked at him a few times as if he thought he was still dreaming. "Our rooms only have one bed."

"Then we'll need two," Myla said at the same time Raevyn responded, "That's fine."

She shot him a look. "I'm not sharing a bed with you. We can get two rooms."

"Maybe if you hadn't tried to run away, I might consider getting two rooms." Raevyn gave her a pointed look. "If you don't want to share the bed, you're more than welcome to sleep on the floor."

"You're the supposed gentleman. Shouldn't you be giving me the bed and offering to sleep on the floor?"

Raevyn snorted. "I'm no gentleman, sunshine. And I thought you, of all people, would resent those old rules, given you punched a man for perceiving you as weak."

Raevyn was right, and she hated it.

"You're the fucking worst," Myla told him.

Raevyn grinned. "Which is the closest I'll get to 'you're right.'" He turned back to the old man. "One room for two nights, please."

****

This wasn't going to work. Myla stared at the small bed, looking to be the size meant for a small child, *not* two full-grown adults. She looked at Raevyn, down at herself, and then back at the bed, mentally doing the calculations. They'd have to sleep on top of each other in order to fit.

118

"This is not going to work," Myla said, glancing over at Raevyn, who was busy pulling out a change of clothes.

"There's plenty of room on the floor," Raevyn replied, heading for the washroom.

Myla scowled as he closed himself in the washroom, and a minute later, she heard the sound of running water. Sighing, she walked over to her pack. Grabbing her silk shorts and top she wore to sleep in, she ducked behind the folding screen to change. She sat on the edge of the bed and pulled her hair out of her braid. Her fingers caught in the stands as she worked the braid out—sighing in relief as she massaged her sore scalp. It had been days since she'd taken it out—not wanting to deal with the messy waves that nearly reached the middle of her back.

Myla blew out the candle on the nightstand, letting the room fall into semi-darkness. She laid down on the stiff mattress and pulled the scratchy blanket up to her chin. It was freezing, and the room had no fireplace to help combat the chill wind creeping in from the busted window. Shivers raked through her body, and she curled in on herself. Myla tried to sleep, but it was nearly impossible when it was this cold. Minutes passed as she tried to distract herself with mindless thoughts to lull her to sleep.

The washroom door creaked open, casting a dim light over the bed. Myla peeked up to see Raevyn wearing nothing but a pair of shorts, his damp curls hanging loosely on his forehead. He hadn't even dried off completely. His broad chest glistened with a thin sheen of water, and Rojna, she'd never seen someone with so many muscles.

Myla quickly looked away before he could notice her staring. Burying her cold nose in the pillow, she attempted to steady her breathing. She heard him shuffling around the room for a few minutes before the mattress dipped. He slid under the covers, and the heat he was emitting was so inviting that she nearly turned around and curled into his warmth.

"You're shivering," Raevyn spoke, resting his hand on her hip.

Myla swallowed tightly, barely able to suppress a shudder at his touch. "Nothing gets past you." Her voice was a breathy whisper, not holding the same bite it usually did.

Raevyn chuckled and pulled her closer. Her back fitted against his chest as if they were two puzzle pieces. Her heart stuttered at the simple gesture and how good it felt to be held. It wasn't often that she felt small but in his arms, she did. It was far more comforting than she expected. Her entire life, she felt as though she needed to be big and strong in order to protect those she loved. She'd convinced herself she'd let people down if she was anything less. But, perhaps, she didn't always have to be. Maybe she could let someone else be that person for a change. Though, it couldn't be him—she knew that. So, why was it she kept forgetting?

"Is this okay?" He asked softly.

Warmth spread through her body, but it wasn't enough. Myla turned to face him and curled into his chest—resting her cold hands against his bare chest. Magic pulsed in her chest, but she ignored it, instead choosing not to overthink her actions for tonight.

"Only to stay warm." She allowed, tangling her legs with his.

"I wouldn't dare to assume otherwise," he said. Myla could practically hear the smile in his voice as he brushed his chin over the top of her head.

This was dangerous. So fucking dangerous, but her resolve was slowly crumbling, and she was finding it harder to fight her growing attraction.

****

120

Myla woke up alone. For a moment, she forgot where she was. When it came back to her, she blushed and buried her face in the pillow. It had only been a week, and Raevyn had found a way to worm under her skin. But, she reminded herself, it didn't have to mean anything she didn't want it to. It had just been a moment of weakness. After all, trying to keep your distance from someone always with you was like attempting to ignore a bug buzzing in your ear. She was only human—for the most part.

Myla got out of bed and went into the washroom. Splashing water on her face, she took in her sleep-disheveled appearance. It was all going to be fine. This feeling brewing inside her would pass because there was no other choice. She needed to focus on the princess and how to find her. Using her magic to lure the princess away from her dragon was out, but maybe she could sense magic in someone else. Was that a possibility? She wished that there was some kind of book to give her a better understanding of her magic. Supposedly, there had been thousands of such tomes, but they were destroyed after the old king triumphed in the War on Magic. All that history burned away with the ashes swept under the rug. Myla had accepted long ago that there would always be a big part of herself she'd never truly understand.

When the bedroom door opened, Myla peeked out of the washroom to see Raevyn walking in with a loaf of bread tucked under his arm and a steaming mug in each hand.

"Good morning, sleepy," Raevyn smiled, setting the goods on the desk across from the bed. "Or, I suppose good afternoon would be more appropriate."

Myla glanced out the window. It was hard to tell the time, given that a storm was approaching. That explained why she was able to sleep in so much. Or she was exhausted from nights sleeping on the forest floor.

"I'm surprised you left me alone after insisting that we had to share a room *and* a bed so you could keep me from running off," she replied, sitting on the edge of the bed.

"You didn't seem to mind when you wanted to cuddle with me," he quipped.

A blush crept from her cheeks down to her neck. "Only to keep warm—"

"Besides, I always had the inn in sight, and if you've forgotten, I'm a hunter. There aren't many places you could go that I wouldn't find you."

Gods, those words, even a few days ago, would have caused ice water to fill her veins. Now, it had the opposite effect. She swallowed tightly and tried not to focus on how his deep voice had curled around the words like a caress. The room that had been too freezing to sleep in suddenly felt like the inside of a fireplace.

Raevyn cut off a piece of bread and handed it to Myla, along with a mug. "And you wouldn't have breakfast, so you're welcome."

Taking the offered food, she took a bite of bread. Her eyes lit up. "Is this pumpkin bread?"

"Yeah, it's my favorite."

Myla smiled. "Mine too. They sold this downstairs?"

"Gods, no. The gruel they're selling downstairs is inedible. I got this at the bakery across the street."

"Did you talk to anyone while you were there?" Myla asked, finishing up her slice of bread.

"Yeah, I heard some promising legends," he said, handing her another slice of bread she graciously took. "But they were generations old, so it couldn't have had anything to do with the princess."

"Did you see anyone that could have matched her description?" She asked, taking a long sip of her tea. A shiver ran down her spine as the hot liquid warmed her chest.

"I did see someone with long white-blond hair, but it turned out to be an old woman with grey hair." He rubbed his arm sheepishly. "She didn't appreciate some random person grabbing her, so she beat my arm with her cane."

The laughter that bubbled from her was sudden and powerful. Her tea nearly spilled as she doubled over at the force of it. She couldn't help herself—the thought of an old woman beating around someone his size was too absurd not to laugh at.

"She had a cane," Myla managed to say between laughs. "And you still thought she might have been the princess?"

"Canes aren't just for old people," Raevyn replied, indignant.

"Grey and white-blond hair are fairly different, though," she countered, grinning.

"It was a very light grey."

Myla snorted. "I'm sure it was."

"Just for that, no more pumpkin bread for you," he said, hiding it behind his back as Myla reached for it.

"Oh, come on," she complained, reaching again only to have Raevyn spin away from her.

"Not happening, sunshine."

Myla lunged again, but he easily dodged, the back of his knees hitting the side of the bed. In hopes of getting him to fall back on the bed, she shoved him, but he barely budged. She tried again, but this time, he grabbed both of her wrists with one hand and twisted them so she fell back against the bed.

Myla glared up at him. "No fair."

He grinned and dropped the bread on her stomach. "Maybe after a few years of me training you, you'll last a few more seconds."

She kicked him, but he grabbed her foot before it could connect with his chest. "So violent."

She squirmed out of his grip and sat up, clutching the bread to her chest. "Arrogant ass," she countered.

His lips curved. "You wound me, sunshine." He put a hand to his chest as if she had actually hit him.

And looking up into his dark eyes, Myla thought, *I'm starting to think that's impossible.*

Chapter 21

The wind was biting, and a storm continued to tease the horizon. Myla tightened her cloak around herself as she walked beside Raevyn. The streets were fairly empty, with only a dozen or so loitering around the carts and stands lining the road. It was nothing like the markets they had in Cassia City, but with a small population, Myla wasn't surprised. They'd asked the innkeeper what most people did around here, and his response was mostly drink. It was too early to head to the tavern, but that was their next stop if their outing proved fruitless.

Myla lingered in front of a cart selling jewelry. The merchant smiled warmly at her and launched into her spiel about the history of her pieces. Interested, she listened, running her fingers over the silver bracelets embedded with small, pink gemstones. She was reminded of her sister. Rikia would have loved these bracelets. The thought made an odd mix of fondness and sorrow churn in her chest. She thought about buying it but decided against it. Who knew when she'd see her sister again?

Myla thanked the merchant and moved on. Her ears perked when she heard a man say something about a beast. She turned her head to see three men in their fifties gathered under a nearby awning as if it was already raining. Pretending to admire a cart of fresh fruit, she listened in—watching them from the corner of her eye.

"And then the beast attacked," the man with a short, grey bread was saying. His arms were flaring so spectacularly that he nearly hit the man next to him in the face. "The winged thing swooped and nearly had me in its grasp had I been a second slower. Its talons were as long as my body, and it would have swallowed me whole given the chance!"

Myla leaned closer, intrigued. That sounded an awful lot like a dragon. Was it possible—

"For fucks' sake, Garron." The man in the red hat next to him swore—shoving back the other man's flaring arms. "You need to stop telling that story. You were drunker than a pirate that night. That thing that attacked you was probably an owl. You know Orith's Forest is full of 'em."

"Owls don't attack people," the bearded man insisted. "'Sides, you weren't there, were yah? The creature was dark as midnight and had huge glowing eyes. I was lucky it only nicked me with a single claw." He pulled up his sleeve to reveal a long scar that extended the length of his forearm.

The man across from him with a blue scarf wrapped around his neck squinted down at the scar. "I thought yer ex-wife did that to you when she found you cheatin'?"

The bearded man pulled his arm away with a glare. "That was my other arm—this scar was from the flying beast. I'm telling you, never go into Orith's Forest if you fancy living."

126

A hand gripped her arm and she reached for her dagger. Before she could attack, Raevyn spoke low in her ear. "Follow my lead."

She relaxed, hand moving away from her dagger. "What's—"

He turned her around so fast she nearly fell against his chest. Her hands landed on his hard chest while his gripped her hips. Lips parting in surprise, she glanced up at him. Her voice caught in her throat when she realized how close their faces were. He leaned down and pressed his forehead softly against hers. Her heart stuttered in her chest and she was finding it hard to steady her breathing. His gold-flecked eyes were all she could see and she was engulfed by his scent. He overtook all her senses and she lost all rational thought.

Raevyn's nose brushed hers, and Myla found herself leaning closer—wanting to close the distance completely. His eyes widened just a fraction before they darkened with an emotion she could only guess at. Her hand reached up to cup his cheek a second before it dawned on her what he'd said before pulling her close.

"Raevyn!"

He let out a sigh that warmed Myla's cheeks, before pulling back. The sudden loss of him caused her to sway as if intoxicated. He didn't let go of her completely. Instead, he drew her to his side and turned to the man who'd spoken. Her senses came rushing back to her, along with a flush that traveled to her toes. She didn't have time to feel embarrassed before the man stopped before them. He was a well-dressed, middle-aged man. His grey hair was short, and his beard was well-groomed. Nearly as tall as Raevyn, the man cut an imposing figure in a burgundy suit. Even the wolf-capped cane, aiding a clearly injured leg, seemed part of the ensemble. The smile he flashed Raevyn was almost too perfect as he stopped in front of them.

"It's good to see you, my boy," the man said, clasping a hand on his shoulder.

Raevyn forced a smile and nodded. "Been too long, Mr. Rhaham."

"I told you to call me Leone," he chided gently, his smile never wavering.

"Of course. What brings you to Blackwich, Leone?"

Leone let his hand drop to grip his cane with both palms. "After the tragic departure of Mr. Kiao, their majesties bestowed on me the honor of governing this great city."

City was a bit of a misnomer, but Myla didn't say so. He most likely wouldn't acknowledge her anyway since Leone hadn't bothered glancing her way.

"Congratulations," Raevyn replied.

"Thank you." Leone nodded. "It's been a bit of an adjustment, especially for my daughter, Soleh. You remember her, don't you?"

"Of course—"

"Bit of a shame there aren't as many eligible suitors here for her. Doesn't stop me from trying." He pointed his cane at Raevyn. "I'm actually hosting a ball tonight. You should come. I know Soleh will be delighted to see you again. You had to leave in such a hurry last time you were in town."

Raevyn's grip on Myla's hip tightened. "That would be wonderful. My betrothed loves balls, don't you, sunshine?" He glanced down at her with a soft smile that definitely didn't make her insides melt.

Leone finally glanced her way. The smile he gave her was a lot less warm than the one he'd given Raevyn. His voice was dripping with sickly sweetness as he said, "I'm sorry, how rude of me. I'm Leone Rhaham."

"Myla Yules, sir," she replied with an incline of her head.

His dark brown eyes widened just a fraction. "No relation to General Yules?"

"The same. He's my father."

Leone studied her warily as if he didn't believe her. "His eldest daughter, I presume. Though, I'd heard she was a recruit."

Myla felt her eye twitch at his insinuation. It reminded her of what the queen had told her about looking nothing like her parents. Annoyed at the reminder, she had to fight to pull her lips into a convincing small smile. "I am. I took some leave to travel to Naeron so we can pick out rings."

"Best jeweler in the kingdom," Raevyn confirmed. "The engagement happened so fast that I wasn't able to get the ring she deserved."

Placing a hand on his stomach, she smiled up at Raevyn. "But I was happy to go with you. And not just to make sure you pick out the right one."

The grin he gave her in response made her forget, just for a moment, that they were playing a part.

"An arranged marriage, then?" Leone asked, voice full of mock pity.

Raevyn shook his head, not breaking his gaze from her. "From the moment I met her, I knew I wanted to spend the rest of my life with her. The first time I saw her, she'd barged in on a meeting between me and her father. She didn't even notice me at first. She just started ranting at her father about how she should skip a year of training given her obvious aptitude." He tucked a lock of hair behind her ear. "I didn't stand a chance."

"How precious," Leone retorted, barely able to hide his distaste. "My offer still stands for both of you, of course. I hope to see you tonight."

Raevyn finally tore his gaze away from Myla to nod at Leone. "Thank you. It was good to see you."

"You as well."

It wasn't until Leone was completely out of sight that Raevyn pulled away. A confusing torrent of emotions warred in Myla's stomach, but she ignored it. She didn't have enough time in the world to sort through that—nor did she particularly want to.

"Let me guess," she spoke, eyebrow arched knowingly. "Nobleman who has been trying to pawn his daughter off on you and won't take the hint that you aren't interested."

He nodded solemnly. "Essentially. It's been almost three years now. When I saw him, I sprung at the opportunity to get him off my back. Didn't anticipate the ball, though. That's not ideal."

"We're not going, right?"

"If we don't show up, he's going to think we were lying."

"This is ridiculous—"

"It's only one night, and everyone in town will be at this ball. We can gather intel while moonlighting as betrothed. Two birds, one stone."

"You know he'll find out eventually that we were never engaged. It'll be a temporary fix at best—"

"Since they're living here now, that news won't spread for a while. Hopefully, long enough for Leone's daughter to secure a match."

Myla wasn't to be deterred. "A whole night is a long time to pretend to like you," she retorted.

Her voice clearly didn't have the bite she'd intended because he grinned at her. "It's a plan then."

Chapter 22

"Absolutely not," Myla said, staring down at the dress Raevyn had laid out on the bed.

Granted, it was beautiful—a floor-length gown of shimmering blue fabric that resembled the surface of a freshly frozen lake. The bodice was low-cut and studded with gems that sparkled in the low light. Instead of sleeves, the gown had transparent tulle that would go over her shoulders and fall down her back like a cape. It was far more beautiful than any gown she'd ever owned—as few they were. It was also far too grand for a ball in Blackwich. Not to mention, Myla had sworn off dresses a long time ago—they weren't her style, and she hated how restricting they could be.

"It's one night," Raevyn called from the washroom.

"Where did you even find this on such short notice?"

"The dress shop here is surprisingly well stocked," he replied.

Myla ran her fingers over the gown, gnawing on her bottom lip in indecision. This whole plan was preposterous. It would be best if she just refused and they moved on to the next town. The princess wasn't here, and likely, there would be no information about her either. But what if?

It was that thought alone that got her into the dress. It definitely wasn't because the thought of being close to Raevyn all night wasn't entirely unpleasant. When she stepped out from behind the folding screen, Raevyn was waiting for her. Her throat dried as she took him in. He wore a white button-up under a shimming, silver waistcoat. The jacket he wore matched her gown and was adorned with an intricate silver design along the bottom that reminded Myla of a winter storm. His knee-length boots rested over white, form-fitted trousers. To finish off the ensemble, he wore a silver cape over one shoulder. He looked breathtaking—like a prince out of a storybook.

Myla swallowed tightly as she focused on Raevyn's face. A small smile played on his lips as he dragged his gaze over her. It was reminiscent of the first time they met, only this time, it felt more intimate. His gaze was like the sun, heating her pale skin until she was sure her chest was splotchy with the unease she felt at being seen so thoroughly. When his gold-flecked eyes finally met hers, Myla felt her heart thud against her ribs. She didn't dare assume the look in his eyes—didn't dare hope.

"You look stunning," Raevyn said, his voice delightfully raspy.

"You clean up nice yourself," Myla replied, looking away from his intense stare. "Well, let's get this over with."

Turning on her heel, she remembered a second too late that she wasn't wearing trousers. Her shoe caught the hem of her skirt, and she stumbled. Arms wrapped around her waist and steadied her before she could fall. Instinctually, she grabbed Raevyn's hands—holding them to her. They were warm against her cold fingers.

Myla let out a breathy laugh, leaning her back against him as she caught her breath. "I'm not used to dresses. Probably should have warned you. The last time I was forced into one, I almost ruined a wedding reception."

Raevyn chuckled against her ear, sending shivers down her spine. "Why am I not surprised?"

She allowed herself one more moment in his embrace before turning to face him. His fingers lingered a moment on her waist before falling away. They stood close together—dangerously close—but Myla didn't step back. Raevyn didn't either.

"Does your clumsiness extend to dancing?" He asked with an amused smirk.

"I would be great at dancing if I ever practiced," she replied with a barely contained smile.

He brushed back a lock of hair that had fallen over Myla's eyes. "I'd assumed it was because you didn't let your partner lead."

A trail of heat lingered in the wake of the soft caress of his fingertips against her skin. She had to swallow past the dryness in her throat before she could reply. "It's not in my nature to follow."

He grinned at her, exposing the dimples she was growing fond of seeing. "We'll just have to see about that."

This time, she couldn't suppress her smile. "Good luck, Telius. You're going to need it."

****

The Rhaham manor was only a short walk from the inn. Luckily, it was a paved path, so Myla didn't muddy her dress during the trek. The manor itself was larger than Myla's family home, but not by much. The outside was painted a light green with white accents. The surrounding land was what impressed her the most. Tall oak trees surrounded a lush, green yard that was dotted with bushes and flowers shaped like various animals. A wide stone walkway led up to a fountain with stone mermaids releasing water from their cupped palms. The walkway continued up to the manor onto a large porch decorated with potted bushes and stone statues of a few gods and goddesses. Myla wasn't surprised to see the queen goddess, Rornja, and the god of luck, Oros, among them. Those two were the most revived of all in the Old Faith.

A few dozen people mulled around the grounds, mostly men, dressed in evening garb. They formed a queue that led to the Rhaham family waiting just past the open doors. Myla and Raevyn got a few curious glances as well as blatant stares. It had been a while since she'd received this much attention, and it made her skin itch. When she'd gone to balls with her family, she never had to worry about receiving that much attention. Not only did her younger sister usually absorb the focus, but the court was full of beautiful women as well. It wasn't that she didn't think she was beautiful. She was just used to having more around her to absorb the focus so it wasn't overwhelming. With fewer women than men here, Myla was forced into the spotlight, and she hated it. She felt like a fraud dressed up like this. Even more so with Raevyn at her side as her supposed fiancé.

Raevyn must have noticed the stares as well, because he snaked an arm around her waist. He pulled her close to his side, so they had to walk in unison. Myla ignored the flutter in her stomach at the gesture, reminding herself it was all for show. This was all an act to get a nobleman off his back and hopefully find some helpful information about the princess.

134

When Raevyn's lips found her ear, Myla jumped, but he only whispered, "You need to relax. You look like you're going to be sick."

She pulled a face that she knew only proved his point. "Gee, thanks."

He squeezed her hip. "Just pretend I'm someone you'd want as your fiancé. I'm sure there's a man or woman back home you can think of."

Myla scoffed, though they both kept their voices low—cautious of others around that could overhear. "I can't even remember the last date I've been on, let alone think of someone I'd want to marry."

"What about Wrynn? You were willing to kill for him."

"He's like my brother. Absolutely no romantic feelings between us," Myla replied earnestly.

It wasn't the first time someone had assumed they were dating. They did spend a lot of time together, but she'd never seen him as a romantic partner. Nor did Wrynn ever give the indication that he wanted more than friendship.

"What about you?" She asked curiously as they slowly moved farther through the queue. "Anyone you're pretending I am?"

"Being a hunter doesn't really leave much time for a personal life," he responded dully.

"No other hunters caught your eye?"

"None that lasted. A physical release and nothing more."

An odd feeling churned in Myla's gut that she immediately squashed. It felt an awful lot like jealousy, and she couldn't allow that. It was ludicrous and, not to mention dangerous.

"Sounds like we're both fucked, so we should just turn around now—"

"Not happening, sunshine."

His grip on her tightened as he brushed a kiss against her temple. The touch was feather-light, but she felt the echo of it burn into her skin even as he pulled away. She hadn't expected it, so she stumbled a bit. Raevyn kept her from falling.

"You are the clumsiest almost-knight I've ever met," he told her with a small smile.

They were on the steps of the manor now. Anything they said from this point forward could be overheard by the Rhaham family. She needed to be careful of what she said. Glancing up at him, she was startled to find he was already looking at her. A blush crept up her neck at the fond look in his eyes. She reminded herself this was all for show, but it didn't stop the small bloom of hopeful optimism in her chest. Gods, what had she gotten herself into?

Chapter 23

Mr. Rhaham practically beamed at Myla and Raevyn as they approached. His eyes, of course, stayed on Raevyn, treating Myla as if she were some accessory of Raevyn's rather than a person. She didn't care. Instead, she focused her attention on the two women standing beside him. His wife was a petite woman with a heart-shaped face and olive skin. Mrs. Rhaham wore a modest, ruby gown that hugged her generous curves. Her silver-streaked, dark hair was pulled into an elaborate updo with faux flowers that matched her gown. Her brown eyes were kind as they locked with Myla's—a small smile tugging at her full lips.

Beside Mrs. Rhaham was Soleh, she assumed. To say she was beautiful would be an understatement. She had the same heart-shaped face as her mother but had her father's height. Her gown was an olive green that complimented her dark complexion. The bodice was decorated with gold leaves and showed a generous amount of cleavage. The skirt of her dress flowed off her in soft waves, thin enough to show the curve of her long legs. The dark strands of her hair were left to fall down her back in smooth, effortless curls that Myla envied. Her hair could never tame to waves like that, even with the help of a ladysmaid.

Myla had no idea why Raevyn wasn't interested in her. She was a vision. One that Myla herself was having a hard time ignoring. Perhaps she had a dull or cruel personality.

"So glad you could make it," Mr. Rhaham said with a broad smile. He'd changed from his earlier burgundy suit to a black and gold one. Even his cane had been switched out for one with a golden bird.

"Thank you for inviting us," Raevyn replied with a polite smile. He nodded to the women. "It's good to see you both again, Mrs. Rhaham and Soleh. This is my fiancée, Myla Yules."

Myla smiled at them and inclined her head. Both the Rhaham women looked surprised at the announcement.

"Fiancée?" Soleh asked, cutting a glance to her father. "My father failed to mention the happy news."

"Didn't I?" Mr. Rhaham didn't even look sorry as he shrugged. "My mistake. I thought I had."

Myla studied Soleh's reaction, bracing for jealousy, hurt, betrayal, or hate, but saw none. Soleh only looked annoyed at her father. That, at least, was a good sign. Myla didn't have to worry about a jilted lover.

"You're General Yules' eldest daughter," Mrs. Rhaham said as if just recognizing her. "I've seen you at some court events over the years. You're a recruit now, if I remember correctly."

Myla smiled and nodded. "Yes, I am. I've taken some time off so Raevyn and I could travel to Naeron to pick out our rings."

"Your father allowed you to join the knights?" Soleh asked, surprised.

Soleh's green eyes were wide as Myla turned her attention away from Mrs. Rhaham. She bristled at her words but relaxed as she interpreted the look on Soleh's face. She wasn't surprised that Myla was a recruit. She was surprised to hear of a father not trying to control every aspect of their child's life.

"After a lot of convincing and proving my skill," Myla replied. "He wasn't thrilled about the idea, but my determination rivals even his."

Soleh's lips twitched at that.

"That explains how you were able to wrangle Raevyn into a courtship," Mr. Rhaham said around a laugh.

Myla bristled, barely able to keep her face from morphing into a scowl. Raevyn stiffened as well, his finger digging into her hip. To hold himself or her back, Myla wasn't sure.

"Father," Soleh hissed in admonishment.

"I'm only jesting," he said with a wave of his hand. "Given the last time we spoke he was adamant about never marrying."

"Love tends to change minds," Raevyn said around clenched teeth.

"That or the privileges that come with marrying the general's eldest."

The tension in the room heightened, and Myla felt her magic tighten in her stomach as if readying to pounce. Usually, she only had to worry about her magic flaring when her emotions were out of control, but she was calm. Annoyed at the noble bastard, but not nearly enough to

139

warrant her magic perking up. It's almost as if it was responding to Raevyn's fury. Not that he could be that angry. This was all an act. He just happened to be a better actor than Myla imagined.

Thankfully, Mrs. Rhaham cut in before the conversation escalated any further. "Well, congratulations to you both. We hope you enjoy the party."

Raevyn relaxed slightly, turning his gaze to Mrs. Rhaham. "Thank you."

Then he ushered Myla away before anyone else could say anything. Myla caught Soleh's gaze, surprised to see the woman giving her an apologetic smile that felt like an olive branch. Before Myla could acknowledge it, Raevyn rounded them around the corner and into the grand ballroom. The floors were made of shining marble, with pillars erected along the outskirts. Large, floor-to-ceiling windows covered the far wall, giving a great view of the beautiful grounds beyond. A quartet was set up near the windows on a raised platform with tables of food along the opposite wall. The ample, open space was crowded with people mulling about, as well as staff carrying trays of drinks.

Raevyn's fury didn't wither away like she expected when they left the view of the Rhahams. He seemed genuinely angry, which wasn't something Myla was used to. He'd always been eerily calm. At worst, he'd gotten annoyed. This was something else entirely. It was a terrifying glimpse into what she'd have to face were Raevyn to find out about her magic. It made unease settle in her stomach as the reality she'd been trying to ignore for over a week loomed over her. Perhaps it was for the best. Myla had gotten far too comfortable around Raevyn as of late. This was just a reminder that he was a deadly hunter.

"Are you okay?" Myla asked hesitantly.

140

"Fine," he replied curtly. "That man just irks me, is all."

He seemed a lot more than irritated, but she wasn't about to say so.

"The audacity of that man," he seethed. "To assume and say to our faces that I'm only marrying you for status. As if that is the only reason I'd pick you over his daughter."

"Why did you turn her down?"

"I didn't. I told Leone I wasn't interested in a wife. I'm constantly on the road and am unlikely to reach middle age. I wouldn't subject any woman to that sort of marriage."

"A husband who's never home sounds ideal to me," Myla said, attempting to lighten the mood.

Raevyn glanced down at her, and she was relieved when a small smile tugged at his lips. "That I believe."

She returned the smile and tugged him toward the crowd of people. "Come on. Let's go mingle."

****

After an hour of mingling, Myla was ready to head back to the inn. She had expected the room to be full of denizens of Blackwich, but most were nobles from around the kingdom. Nobles that recognized both Raevyn and Myla. They were sucked into dozens of conversations that revolved around their fake relationship and were rarely able to change the subject to gain any information about the princess. The only useful information they got was another warning about Orith's Forest. If they didn't get any other leads, that's where they'd head tomorrow morning.

"I did not expect so many nobles to be here," Myla said as they broke away from yet another conversation about their wedding.

A staff member walked by, and she grabbed a glass from the tray. She took a long sip of champagne, nerves bubbling in her stomach. She'd never had much trouble lying—she'd been forced to keep an enormous secret her entire life. This felt different. Myla wasn't sure if it was because she was relying on another person to keep the lie going or if it was something else entirely.

"Me either," Raevyn replied, taking a glass of champagne for himself. "There's going to be a lot more untangling to do when we get back."

"When?" Myla asked, quirking an eyebrow. "That's very optimistic of you, Telius."

"What can I say?" Raevyn smirked, leaning down to brush a kiss on her cheek. "I have complete faith in my abilities."

Her smile nearly stretched across her entire face, and it took all her self-restraint not to turn her head slightly so their lips would brush. Pretending to be his fiancée wasn't nearly as hard as it should have been. They made a surprisingly good team when they trusted in one another. It felt good to fall into an easy, romantic rhythm with someone. It had been years since Myla had felt even a fraction of that. She would allow herself this one night. Then, come tomorrow, they'd go back to being unwilling companions. As for the thick, heavy tension between them, she was afraid to name—it would fade, too. It had to.

Out of the corner of her eye, Myla could make out Mr. Rhaham making his way toward them. She took hold of Raevyn's hand and pulled him toward the dance floor. To her surprise, he didn't fight her—just followed her willingly. She wasn't sure why that made her stomach somersault.

"I'll let you lead just this once," she told him, getting into position at the end of a row of couples. "Just to get out of talking to certain people."

Raevyn bowed along with the rest of his row. "How generous of you, sunshine."

With a roll of her eyes, she took his hand and allowed him to swing her into a dance.

Chapter 24

It had been years since Myla had been forced to a court function that required dancing. She'd always found a way to get out of it. As Raevyn spun her around the floor—surprisingly adept and at ease with the complex movements—she wished she'd gone to more. She had no idea what she was doing, and her muscles were tense, resisting the dance steps.

"How are you so good at this?" Myla hissed, nearly stepping on his toes.

"The question is, how are you so bad?" Raevyn teased, spinning her away only to bring her back against his chest. "You've surely gone to hundreds of balls like this."

"Sure, but I only danced if I was forced."

"It's similar to fighting. Just pretend I'm an opponent, and you need to interpret my next move."

Raevyn released her so he could step around her. When he faced her again, she quickly took stock of how he was standing, noting how he favored his left foot. He took her hands again, and this time, she was able to step with him. Raevyn grinned, and Myla felt a warm sense of pride swell in her chest.

"I knew you could do it, sunshine."

The magic in Myla's veins pulsed in her chest, causing her smile to falter. The random flare-ups were happening more often, and she knew it was because she was getting too close to Raevyn. Her magic was warning her that there was only one way their relationship could end. She couldn't allow herself to get invested.

The sound of the music cutting off and applauding brought Myla to reality. She forced a smile on her face, but Raevyn was giving her a concerned look. Stepping out of his hold, she stepped back toward the crowd. She needed space or fresh air. Preferably both. Raevyn stepped toward her, but Mr. Rhaham appeared at his side, halting his movements. Myla took the chance to slip into the crowd. She skirted the edges of the room, looking for doors that led out onto the grounds. When she could find none, she headed back the way she'd gotten in. She was near to the door when Soleh stepped in her path.

"Myla, do you mind if we talk?"

Myla looked up at her, an excuse on the tip of her tongue, but the look on Soleh's face made the words die in her throat. She looked pleading, almost, and Myla didn't have the gall to refuse her. So, plastering a smile on her face, she nodded.

Soleh smiled and looped her arm in hers. "Great, let's go outside."

144

She led her over to the corner of the room where Myla had failed to notice a door leading out onto the balcony. They stepped out into the cool autumn air, and she felt herself relax slightly. The music and sounds of the crowd died as soon as the door shut behind them. Even though she had no idea what Soleh would say to her, at least she was away from prying eyes out here. Soleh released her arm, and they both leaned against the railing, gazing out at the forest beyond.

"I just wanted to apologize for my father's behavior," Soleh said, breaking the silence. "He doesn't respond well to things not going his way. To put it mildly."

A small smile tugged at Myla's lips. "It's okay, really. He's not the first nor will be the last to wonder about Raevyn and me. No one expected Raevyn to settle down, or even me for that matter. The courtship was quick, but it felt right for both of us." Myla shrugged. "Not a lot of people understand it. Even my own father was skeptical."

"I'm surprised your father wasn't thrilled with the idea of a marriage to a high-ranking hunter like Raevyn."

"My father doesn't much care for the internal politics of court life. The only thing he cares about is whether I'm happy. Since our engagement was so sudden, he worried that I had been coerced into the whole thing. It took a lengthy conversation to convince him otherwise."

"That's surprising because just watching you two dance, I can tell you both care for each other deeply."

Myla flushed, scratching at the bandage on her forearm. "Yeah, more so than I ever expected."

The truth in those words made her heart clench, but she couldn't think about that now. She only needed to get through this night, and hopefully, these conflicting feelings would leave her by tomorrow.

Soleh smiled. "I'm happy for you both, truly."

"You aren't...upset at all? I know you never actually courted—"

"No, I never had any interest in Raevyn. It was my father who tried to push us together. He's been trying to find me a spouse for years now. No doubt pining for the day he can get rid of me."

Myla put a comforting hand on Soleh's arm. "I'm sorry. But on the bright side, once you find a spouse, *you* can be rid of *him*."

Her lips quirked at that. "Very true. Any interest in helping me pick out the best in the bunch here?"

A mischievous smile pulled at Myla's lips. "Only if we make a drinking game out of it. Any suitor we disagree on, we'll take a swig."

Soleh laughed. "I'm in."

****

Turned out, Myla and Soleh had very different tastes in people. One hour later, they were relatively drunk, and Soleh had only danced with two people. Raevyn hadn't found them either, which Myla was thankful for. She was having a lot more fun at this ball than she had anticipated.

"What about him?" Myla asked, gesturing to the tall, dark, and handsome man near the tables of food, deciding what to grab.

"Been there and would not recommend," Soleh slurred, taking a swig of champagne. "Let's just say only one of us left satisfied that night."

Myla snorted, the champagne bubbles burning her nose. "Just goes to show, don't trust a man who can't decide between two identical sandwiches."

Soleh laughed, leaning against Myla so much they both nearly toppled over. "Or feels the need to overcompensate his itty-bitty—"

"There you are."

The two women straightened and turned to find Raevyn. Unbidden, a broad smile broke across Myla's face, and she wrapped him in a hug. Raevyn's arms came around her as he returned the hug, his large hands warm against the small of her back.

"There's my fiancé," Myla said far too loudly. "Where have you been?"

Raevyn looked down at her, amusement lighting his eyes. "Got pulled into some boring conversations. Not having nearly as much fun as you two seem to be."

"We're looking for a good suitor for Soleh," she explained, leaning her head back to look up at him. "Turns out the only decent person here is you."

"Decent?" Raevyn asked, around a barely concealed smile. "That's high praise, sunshine."

"I know."

He shook his head and looked to Soleh. "I better get her to bed. Are you all right on your own?"

Soleh nodded. "Myla gave me a few pointers if anyone were to get too friendly."

"Eyes, balls, or boobs," Myla confirmed with a sage nod. "Best weak points."

Raevyn snorted. "Then you should be safe. It was good to see you again, Soleh."

"You too," Soleh smiled. "Take care of Myla. She's one of the good ones."

"I will."

Myla must be drunker than she thought because he sounded completely sincere in his declaration. Not to mention, she was having difficulty contemplating returning to how they usually were. It made her want to do stupid, reckless things while she still could. Before she could,

Raevyn began tugging her toward the door. Myla released him so she could hug Soleh goodbye.

"Good luck. I expect letters keeping me updated," Myla told her sternly.

"And I expect an invite to your wedding."

Myla pulled away, struggling to keep the smile on her face as reality set in. Even if her relationship with Raevyn was a farce, that didn't mean that her friendship with Soleh had to be. She'd figure out a lie when she returned home. *When* and not if, because Myla wouldn't entertain the alternative.

"Of course."

Myla waved before walking back to Raevyn. He wrapped an arm around her waist and led her toward the door. She allowed herself to lean into his warmth, knowing that they'd be nothing more than travel companions once they got out of view of the manor. *As it should be,* she reminded herself. What she was starting to feel toward him was only lust, which she could handle. It didn't matter that she was beginning to let down her defenses around him. Nor did it matter that sometime recently, she'd stopped expecting the worst from him. She had it handled.

The cold night air was a welcome reprieve on her flushed skin. It even sobered her up a bit, so she didn't have to rely so much on Raevyn to guide her. Though, she was hesitant to release him completely.

"How did you end up drinking with Soleh?" Raevyn asked curiously.

"She wanted to apologize for her father being an ass, and we ended up playing a drinking game to find a suitor for her. For every person we disagreed on, we had to take a drink."

Raevyn huffed out a laugh and shook his head. "That's surprising. Not about you, but Soleh always seemed

148

like the sophisticated type that wouldn't entertain a drinking game."

Myla laughed. "Honestly, I was surprised too. You really missed out on that one."

"All the more reason for her to find someone who deserves her," he replied, steering her away from a puddle.

Tilting her head back, Myla peered up at him. "That's a surprisingly gentlemanly thing to say, given what you claimed the other day."

Raevyn quirked an eyebrow. "Don't sound so surprised. I have my moments."

"Just not with me."

He smirked. "Now you're getting it."

Chapter 25

"Tell the sun to stop being so fucking bright," Myla pleaded, burying her face in Cass's mane.

Of course, Raevyn had to wake her up at the ass-crack of dawn after she'd spent the night drinking. And to make matters worse, the sun decided to come out after days of gloomy, cold weather. The one day, Myla had a head-splitting hangover.

"Yeah, I'll get right on that," Raevyn replied, sarcasm practically dripping from his tone.

They'd been riding for a few hours and were near Orith's Forest, where the thick trees would hopefully block out the harshest sunbeams.

"The sarcasm isn't appreciated," she muttered.

"But necessary for such a ridiculous question."

Myla mumbled some obscenities in his direction, but he ignored her. They rode in silence for the next few hours while she chugged water to fight her dehydration. By the time they entered Orith's Forest, the sun had nearly set, and Myla's headache dulled to a manageable light ache.

Ever since they'd left Blackwich behind, an odd tension had grown between them. It was almost as if Raevyn was forcing distance between them. The thought should have relieved her, but all it did was make conflicting feelings battle in her stomach. It frustrated her to no end, but as she did with all the things she didn't want to deal with, she buried it in the back of her mind.

"Shouldn't we set up camp outside the forest?" Myla asked as they continued on. "You know, in case there is some angry creature living here."

"There will be angry creatures living wherever we decide to make camp," Raevyn responded. "Besides, I'm fairly certain the man you heard was full of shit. If he did, in fact, face a dragon, he wouldn't have survived with only a minor scratch. He would have been scorched."

She nodded. "Probably."

"If I remember correctly, this river leads to a small lake, and we can set up camp near there."

"You've been here before?"

"I've passed through here a few times on various assignments. The only flying creatures I ever encountered were owls."

"What kind of assignments were they?"

"That's classified."

Myla sighed. Of course, it was. She wasn't sure why she bothered with all the questions. He had opened up a little about his past, but he never gave specifics of what he went through. Her curiosity was getting the better of her, she supposed. It certainly had nothing to do with her desire to be closer to him because that was just physical. Obviously, because anyone interested in men would find him attractive, even if they didn't find men attractive, anyone could appreciate his beauty. He looked like a godsdamn statue, carved perfectly in smooth marble. It would be annoying if it weren't so distracting.

Raevyn finally pulled to the side of the road at a small clearing hidden between a few rows of trees. Myla hopped off Cass—stretching out her sore muscles. Riding for so long was getting more manageable, and her stitches only mildly ached. She wanted to take off the bothersome bandages, but Raevyn insisted she keep them on for another day or two, especially since they would start training tonight.

After setting up camp and eating, Myla and Raevyn positioned themselves on the other side of the clearing—a safe distance from the fire but close enough to see their surroundings. Myla bounced on her toes and shook out her limbs, trying to loosen up her tense body. All their weapons had been stripped for this training lesson. Raevyn told her they'd work up to weapons.

"What do you know about taking down an opponent twice your size?" Raevyn asked, rolling out his shoulders.

"Use speed, and don't let them get a hold of you, or you're dead."

Raevyn nodded. "Good start. Let's see it in action."

He rushed toward her—faster than she thought possible. His fingertips brushed her biceps as Myla twisted away from him. She faced him again, but he was already in front of her, swinging his fist. She ducked and blocked his next punch aimed at her stomach. Her forearm throbbed at the impact, but she pushed through and rammed her elbow into his ribs. To her satisfaction, he took a step back, but it was short-lived as shockwaves reverberated through her arm. It was as if she'd elbowed a damn stone wall.

152

Myla stumbled back and raised her arms in a defensive position as he rushed her again. She thought he would punch her, so she lifted her arms higher. Instead, he gripped her wrist and pulled her toward him. She fell against his chest, and he wrapped his other arm around her waist—securing her in place. She struggled against him, but it was fruitless.

"Got you," he whispered, his hot breath brushing the stray hairs along her forehead.

"Not for long," she panted.

She wrapped her legs around his knees and pulled back with the entirety of her weight. He stumbled slightly, and his grip on her waist loosened just enough for her to twist her body so her side was flush against his chest. With her arm free, she aimed a punch to his throat. As expected, he released his hold around her waist to grab her wrist. Partially freed, Myla pushed away from his body. He tried to pull her toward him again, but she dropped down. She expected his grip to slip, but he stepped forward as she dropped, and she ended up on her back in between his legs. Before she could slide away, he dropped to his knees—trapping her waist in between his thighs.

"Not too bad," he admitted, releasing his hold to rest his palms on either side of her head and lean in close. "But this is one of the worst places you want to be pinned during a fight."

Heart beating wildly in her chest, she stared up into his dark eyes. Maybe a bad place during a fight, Myla thought, but perfect for other things—

Her thoughts drifted, and she felt heat flush through her veins and settle low in her stomach. She swallowed tightly as Raevyn's eyelids lowered as if he were thinking the same thing. He leaned closer—so close his breath brushed her lips like a caress. She was hyper-aware of every inch their skin touched and the firm grip of his powerful thighs

153

around her soft hips. Her arms stayed glued to her sides even though she wanted nothing more than to run her fingers through his coarse hair and trace the line of his scar—

Raevyn was suddenly on his feet, and the loss of his warmth was so unexpected that Myla nearly gasped. Whatever expression she thought she had seen on his face was gone—replaced with cool indifference as he held out his hand to help her up. Myla took it tentatively, and he pulled her to her feet.

"Nice first practice," he said. "We'll go again tomorrow."

She could only nod, feeling a pang of disappointment in her chest that was quickly replaced with annoyance for feeling that way. She should be glad that at least one of them had the good sense to keep things platonic between them. That or he was completely uninterested and pulled away before she could embarrass herself. Maybe she'd misinterpreted the looks he gave her in Blackwich. Or it had all been a ploy or act to get her to go along with his ridiculous plan. Her cheeks flushed at the thought as she watched him walk back to their camp, wishing she knew what he was thinking.

Chapter 26

Myla was still reeling as she collected another outfit, towel, and soap to bathe in the small lake nearby. She was going to take the chance to wash off the dirt and sweat from her skin before turning in for the night. Hopefully, the bath would also give her a chance to clear her head and any unwanted thoughts of Raevyn kneeling over her—

"Where are you going?" Raevyn called after her.

"To bathe," Myla called over her shoulder. "And there's no need to watch—I wouldn't try to escape without my supplies."

She headed into the trees and to the banks of the lake. A waterfall was nestled off to the right, and she walked over to it. She set her things down on the ground, and only once she was sure Raevyn was nowhere in sight did she strip down and ease her aching body into the freezing water. She wrapped her arms around herself and waded into the water until it was up to her neck. She rubbed the soap over her limbs and face as she tried to suppress her shivers. It felt nice to wash all the muck off her, but she didn't think she could handle the cold for much longer. Myla paused, the soap hovering over her sternum. There was one way to warm up the water, but it was risky.

Myla peered over her shoulder and squinted into the darkness surrounding the trees. She couldn't see Raevyn, nor could she hear anything. If she didn't practice soon, the tense knot in her stomach would only grow until she lost control of her magic. She'd learned that the hard way, and luckily, she was only in her family's company at the time. Since then, she hadn't let herself go longer than two weeks without using her magic.

Hovering her hands over the water, Myla reached for her magic. The water around her warmed enough to be comfortable but not hot enough to create steam. The knot in her stomach loosened, and she shivered as her cold skin acclimated to the heat. She scrubbed the rest of her body while keeping one hand hovering over the water to keep the temperature up. Once she was done, she waded under the steady stream of water. Closing her eyes, she felt her muscles relax under the soothing water pressure. It was so soothing that her body swayed. It wasn't until her back hit stone that she realized she'd drifted under the waterfall.

Blinking the droplets from her eyes, Myla looked back at what she'd bumped into. A small platform carved into the rocks led to what looked to be a cave. The moonlight shone through the water, casting eerily shadows across the stones. It was beautiful and peaceful. The rushing water created a barrier that blocked her from sight and drowned out the sounds of the world beyond. She could almost forget that she was on a dangerous journey.

Myla would have been content to stay here for hours but knew if she waited much longer, Raevyn would come looking for her. She started swimming back when something caught her eye. She turned to see a shimmering, black stone near the mouth of the cave. It was oddly shaped, though, and almost flat. Curious, she climbed out of the water and crouched next to it. Her eyes widened when she realized it wasn't a stone but a scale. One twice the size of her hand, which meant there was only one creature it could belong to.

****

"Raevyn!" Myla rushed into the clearing. Her hair was dripping on her face, and her clothes were askew, but she didn't care.

Raevyn jumped to his feet, hand resting on the hilt of his sword. "What's wrong?" He asked, glancing around as if a threat would appear at any moment.

"Look." She thrust the scale into his hands, practically bouncing with excitement. "Do you know what this is?"

He looked down at it, eyebrows pulling together. "Where did you find this?"

"There's a cave entrance under the waterfall. I found it there. It's a dragon scale, isn't it?"

Raevyn turned it over in his hands, inspecting every angle. "It sure looks like one."

"So the lead was real." Myla beamed. "We have to go check it out."

His gold-flecked eyes met hers as he frowned. "We should wait until the morning—"

"So they have time to get away? They could have heard me and already be attempting to escape. There's no time to waste." Myla rushed over to her supplies and grabbed her weapons—strapping them to her body.

"We need a plan," Raevyn insisted. "You've never faced a dragon, and frankly, you're not ready."

"I'm going," Myla said sternly, turning to face him. "This could be our only chance, and I won't waste it."

Without waiting for a reply, she marched back to the lake.

Raevyn let out a frustrated growl, muttering, "Stubborn pain in my ass," before following.

Myla walked to the lake and over to the cliff where the waterfall was cascading down. With her back against the stone, she shuffled behind the stream of water and onto the small platform she'd found earlier. Before she could walk into the cave, Raevyn grabbed her arm.

"Let me lead at least," Raevyn said, holding out a small, glowing stone.

"What is that?" Myla asked, squinting at the stone barely bigger than his palm.

"It's a glow stone," he explained. "Imported from Adratus. They're quite common along the shore of a local lake."

She hummed in interest before following him farther into the cave. The entrance was narrow, so she was forced to follow behind, unable to see their path. It wasn't long before the only light came from the stone in Raevyn's hand, which didn't help Myla. She was forced to follow Raevyn's silhouette and tripped on the uneven path more than once. Raevyn had no such issues.

"How far does the cavern go?" Myla whispered. "What do you see?"

"The cavern is widening. There appears to be an opening to a larger space several yards ahead."

"You can see that far ahead?" She asked dubiously. The glow stone barely illuminated a few feet in front of them.

"I have incredible night vision," Raevyn replied with a shrug. "I've explored thousands of caves such as this, so I am far more comfortable in the dark than most."

How one could find comfort in dark such as this, Myla didn't know, nor did she care to ask. She followed behind Raevyn until she saw the opening he'd spotted. They walked into a space with shadows clinging to the edges, making it impossible for her to know how large it was. She could, however, make out a bedroll next to a satchel positioned in front of the remnants of a campfire. Unsheathing her sword, Myla peered around the room, half-expecting someone to leap from the shadows.

"The place has been abandoned," Raevyn said, his deep voice echoing around the cavern. "If someone was here, they're long gone now. We just walked through the only entrance and exit."

Myla stepped up beside him and squinted around the room, trying to see what he saw. His night vision must be far superior to hers because she still couldn't tell how big the room was, let alone if there were any other exits. For some reason, she believed him without even a small doubt in the back of her mind. She didn't want to dwell on why or how she'd gotten to that point with him. Stepping forward, she headed toward the bedroll, hoping to find something useful in the satchel.

"Wait—"

But it was too late. Myla's foot caught on a thin rope, and she stumbled. A click followed by a loud crash echoed around them, and Raevyn cursed. She whirled around to face him, seeing a large boulder blocking their only exit.

"What the—" she cut off as a series of hisses bounced off the walls. Turning back around, she watched in horror as dozens of snakes slithered from the shadows toward them. Their red eyes were the only thing she could see, as their scales blended with their surroundings. Myla stepped back just as Raevyn came up behind her. One hand rested on the small of her back, and the other held a sword out in front of them.

"I should have known you finding that scale would be too easy," he said, jaw clenched.

"What do you mean?"

"Wielders have been putting up traps like this for hunters as long as they've been outlawed. I've encountered several, but none as elaborate as this. How does one even capture this many oxiacons?"

Heart thundering in her chest, she glanced up at him. "As in the most venomous snake in Rosebourne with impenetrable scales?"

He nodded gravely. "I can move the boulder out of the way, but I'll need time."

Taking the glow stone from his hand, she took a step forward and brandished her sword. "I'll give you as much as I can."

Raevyn flattened his lips in a thin line, looking like he wanted to argue, but gave a curt nod instead. He rushed over to the blocked exit while Myla faced the oncoming threat. Unlike her sister, she didn't have a crippling fear of snakes. Though, as several dozen pairs of eyes slithered toward her, she felt her breath catch in her chest. Facing all these oxiacons was a lot different than the occasional garden snake on the grounds of her family estate.

Steeling her nerves, Myla stepped forward and swung her sword. Her blade clinked against the scales of two snakes—sounding as though she'd hit a shield. The two flew back as if she'd swatted them with a bat. The hissing intensified as more snakes swarmed around her. She had to

160

get close to them in order to knock them back, and more than once, she barely avoided the fangs of another. The more she attacked, the angrier they seemed to get until all she could hear were their violent hisses. They were no longer closing in at a leisurely pace but actively attacking Myla. One managed to sink their fangs into her boot, centimeters from her toes. Digging her blade between the snake's jaw and her boot, she pried it off before flinging it back toward the neverending swarm.

"I don't know how much longer I can keep this up!" Myla called, lurching back to stop a snake from sneaking past her to Raevyn.

"Almost…got…it," he responded around strained breaths.

She thought about the river just beyond this cave. If she pulled it toward them, would it be enough pressure to move the door? Or, better yet, drown the sorry creatures. Though, knowing her luck, the snakes would be able to swim, and she'd kill both Raevyn and her. Not that using her magic was a possibility with Raevyn around. Only if she believed they'd die otherwise would she risk it. Even then, Myla wasn't entirely sure. She was starting to believe he wasn't the terrible person she'd painted in her mind—at least, not entirely. He had layers that Myla was only starting to uncover, and the optimistic part of her wanted to believe the best in him. Naive, she knew, but found she couldn't help herself when it came to him. Something about him made her want to believe impossible and stupid things.

"Got it!" Raevyn called.

Myla turned on her heel and didn't hesitate to run toward him. He stood with the boulder on his back, and his hands braced on the wall in front of him, creating a doorway under his arms. Sprinting forward, inches from Raevyn, she saw a flash of red spring toward her. She turned to knock the snake from the air but was too slow. The creature's fangs tore through her forearm, unable to latch on completely, but it was enough. A pain as though she'd been burned ripped through her arm, and she had to bite back a cry of pain. Raevyn called her name as he no doubt saw the blood leak down her wrist. She could feel the venom working immediately, burning acid through her veins. Her body felt instantly weak, and she used her remaining strength to throw herself through the doorway.

Falling on her side, Myla clutched her arm to her chest as if it could stop the burning pain. Sweat beaded on her brow and her mouth filled with cotton, causing words to clog in her throat. She'd been bitten before, even by a venomous snake, but it hadn't been an oxiacon. Those bites were child's play in comparison to what now tainted her blood. If she remembered correctly, she had only thirty minutes before the venom would reach her heart and kill her. The realization made panic flood through her and it took all her remaining strength not to flood the cavern with water.

A loud crash sounded before she felt hands on her shoulders. "Sunshine?" His beautiful face hovered over hers, but it was blurry along the edges—swimming in and out of focus. She had the absurd thought that she was going to die not having kissed him. She wondered if he'd be gentle or if he would claim her mouth with rough abandon. She expected the latter, and if she had been capable of speech, she would have asked him to kiss her before she left. One less regret to take to her grave.

Raevyn swept her up in his arms as if she weighed nothing before bolting through the cavern. He was swearing softly while simultaneously reassuring her that she was going to be okay. It was soothing, even with fear lacing his words. His voice always had that effect on her, even when he was driving her crazy. She could listen to his voice for days on end and not tire of him. Myla was glad now that it would be the last sound she heard as the darkness closed in on her.

Chapter 27

When Myla died, she always figured she'd end up in a comforting place where there was no pain and be surrounded by loved ones. So, when she opened her eyes to a thatched roof above her and a throbbing pain in her arm, she knew she was still alive. Alive and being treated by an old woman with dark, wrinkled skin, box braids, and dozens of bangles that clanked rhythmically in the otherwise quiet room. Her dark eyes were focused on Myla's wound as she rubbed thick cream into the scratch marks. The smell of it was enough to burn the hairs in her nose.

The woman wrapped the wound back up before casting her gaze on Myla. "Ah, finally awake I see. Good. I can tell the grumpy hunter he can see you now so he can stop hovering and worrying like a mother hen."

Myla blinked slowly, struggling to make sense of her surroundings and the woman's words. The pain, though present, wasn't nearly as bad as it had been. The fact that she was alive meant the venom had been taken care of, but it still had the effect of muddling her thoughts. Did the woman just say Raevyn was concerned for her?

"I'm sorry, what?"

The woman waved her off. "I'll let him explain, but tell him if you stay another night, it'll cost more than the pocket watch he gave me. Three nights is already generous."

Pocket watch? Certainly not his mother's because that would be absurd. He wouldn't give up the one thing he had left of his mother for Myla's life. Even if the king thought she was the only one who could bring his daughter home, it didn't mean Raevyn thought so, too. He'd scoffed at the idea of a prophecy, so why go to all the trouble of keeping her alive? It didn't make sense. Nothing made sense. And if she weren't in so much pain, she'd think she was dreaming.

"O-okay," she stammered, no doubt looking like an animal caught in a trap.

The woman only nodded before shuffling out of the room—much faster than Myla thought one her age capable of. She realized she'd forgotten to thank the woman as soon as she was alone. The door swung open again before she could call out, revealing Raevyn, who looked surprisingly disheveled. She'd never seen him in such a state before. His eyes were slightly bloodshot, with dark circles underneath. The curls on the top of his head were wild as though he'd spent a lot of time running his fingers through them. Not to mention he was wearing the same thing he had when she'd passed out, which, if the woman had been telling the truth, had been three days ago. What surprised her the most was the evident relief on his face as he strolled up to her bedside.

His lips twitched as he attempted to smile. "Hi, sunshine."

"You look like hell," Myla responded, surprised at her own words. She'd been thinking that but hadn't meant to voice it aloud. She was clearly still disorientated.

He let out a breathy laugh. "I could say the same about you."

"I almost died, what's your excuse?"

"You almost died."

Myla blinked, the admission and the sincerity in his expression causing her heart to flip. "I—I didn't think it would matter to you."

Raevyn scoffed, looking moderately offended. "I know you think I am some heartless hunter, but do you really believe so poorly of me to think I would not care if you died?"

"Honestly? I don't know what to believe. You've not the most expressive person I've met."

His fingers flexed where they laid on the bed, inches from her thigh. Almost as if he wanted to reach out and touch her. "I suppose that's a fair assessment."

In a move that surprised even herself, Myla took Raevyn's hand in hers—squeezing it gently. "Thank you for bringing me here and saving my life."

His expression softened and he squeezed her hand back. "You're the prophesied hero of this quest. I can hardly be expected to go on without you."

Thinking of the woman's words about the pocket watch he'd given up, she tightened her grip. "Did you truly give up the last thing you have of your mother to save me?"

Raevyn's voice was even as he responded, "it was just an object."

"But—"

He gripped her hand in both of his, looking intently into her eyes. "Yes, it had sentimental value, but I don't need it to remember who my mother was or how important she was to me. I needed—" He let out a breath as if taking the time to collect his thoughts. "I wouldn't let you die."

He looked as though he had more to say, but the silence stretched between them. Myla wanted to ask him why—why he wouldn't let her die. Why he sounded as though he might mourn her dead. If it was possible that he, too—

"I would have done the same for you," she admitted, feeling as though she owed it to him to be honest. "And not just because you're useful to have around."

He smiled at that, thumb running over her knuckles. It felt good—having his hands wrapped around her own—but she wanted more. She wanted to tuck herself into his warmth and feel the hard planes of his body against her own. More than anything, she wanted to kiss him. She'd be deluding herself for weeks, trying to convince herself that she hadn't wanted to do so almost since she'd met him. Perhaps it had started as lust, but now, staring up into his gold-flecked eyes, she knew it was far more than that. She'd inadvertently begun to care for him, and she suspected he felt the same way.

As if reading her thoughts, he gradually leaned closer. So slow, it was almost imperceptible. Before she knew it, his face was hovering over hers and she had to arch her neck back to hold his gaze. Her stomach filled with butterflies as he reached one had up to cup her cheek. His thumb lightly brushed her cheekbone before trailing down to draw across her bottom lip. Myla felt frozen under his soft touches—afraid that one wrong move would break the spell between them.

"Myla." His voice was rough along the edges, making heat pool in her stomach. "I—"

The door swung open behind them, and Raevyn jerked back. Myla's eyes swung over to the open door to see the old woman standing at the threshold.

"Time for you both to leave," she said sternly. "I have other patients that require this room."

Raevyn stiffened. "She only just woke up—"

"It's fine," Myla assured him, releasing his hand to swing her legs over the side of the bed. "I'm fine." Getting to her feet, she turned to the healer. "Thank you for everything, ma'am."

She waved her off. "Yes, yes. Off you go. Stay out of tall grass so I don't have to see you two again anytime soon."

Myla's lips twitched before she left the room with Raevyn close on her heels. He muttered something to the woman Myla didn't catch, but based on the tone, he wasn't pleased. Honestly, Myla wasn't either, but not because they were getting kicked out. She'd wanted Raevyn to kiss her and wasn't sure when another opportunity would present itself. Another part of her was relieved given getting any closer to Raevyn would surely end in disaster. The conflicting feelings weren't anything new. In fact, it had become so common that Myla had come to expect them. It was Raevyn that continued to surprise her. He seemed to be wrestling with the same feelings as she, if one moment he was pulling away from a kiss to nearly initiating one. It made her wonder what held him back.

The night air was crisp and Myla had to fight back a shudder as she left the healer's hut behind. Cass waited for her next to Raevyn's horse, both packed and ready. They chose not to travel far before setting up camp for the remainder of the night. With the fresh fire warming her and

167

Raevyn's bed roll far closer to hers than ever, Myla fell asleep almost instantly.

****

Myla dreamed of a dragon with eyes like hers—a bright, clear blue with a hint of green around the pupil. They stood on the banks of a river looking to be over twenty feet tall. They were covered in light blue and green scales and their underbelly was the color of pearls. The ridges along their back were a similar pearl color and their horns curled up and around their face—seeming to be made of seashells.

Myla, a soft, euphoric voice spoke in her mind. Myla wasn't sure how she knew, but she knew it was the dragon who spoke to her. The experience was surreal and almost familiar. The dragon was both new and felt as though seeing a long, lost friend. She'd never dreamt of her dragon, at least, that she could recall. But they'd always been with her—a hidden, steady presence in the recesses of her mind. But why would they reach out now?

"Did you gift me my magic? Where are you?" Myla asked, reaching a hand out as if she could touch them.

The dragon's ears perked, and they turned their head slightly, giving her a narrow view of what was behind them. She saw various houses with people mulling about and at least a dozen dragons. There couldn't be that many dragons living in harmony with humans—could there be? It didn't make any sense.

"I don't understand—"

The dragon focused back on her, leaning their head down slightly. *There is no time to explain. You must find the princess. She will keep you safe. Leave the scarred man—he will only bring pain as he's done to hundreds like us.*

Myla's heart clenched at the mention of Raevyn. She knew the dragon was right—had known all along, but it didn't match with the man she was starting to get to know.

Maybe it was denial, but she had always gone with her gut when it came to people. And her gut was telling her that Raevyn wouldn't hurt her. She prayed to the queen goddess, Rornja, that she wasn't wrong.

"I can't leave him."

The dragon snarled—*stubborn human. The magical blood he has spilled is far greater than any like him. You will be no different.*

Before Myla could argue, the dragon faded away replaced with a horrific scene. The trees around her burned as a group of six men and women in gleaming armor made from scales charged at three dragons, each bearing a rider. A Black woman with short cornrows sat astride the middle dragon—a giant brown dragon with gleaming yellow eyes. She lifted her arms, and the earth rumbled. Five of the assailants tumbled into a cavern the woman created, but one man jumped—landing on the other side of the trap in a crouch. He pulled out a dagger and flung it at the woman. It struck her neck, and she gasped at the same time her dragon roared in agony.

All three of the dragons blew fire toward the man, but he had already moved on—darting into the mass of burning trees. That's when Myla recognized him. It was Raevyn, looking to be a few years younger. He grabbed a jar of greenish liquid attached to his hip and threw it at the ground near the three dragons' feet before notching an arrow. The arrow soared through the air and lodged into the nearest dragon's eye—a smaller green dragon holding a curly, redheaded boy who looked no older than her sister, Rikia. The green dragon roared and spewed fire near Raevyn. The fire caught the liquid and exploded in a torrent of green flames. Both human and dragon screams filled the air with a force so strong that Myla fell to her knees. Tears streamed down her face as she watched in horror as the dragons tried to flee, but the fire had burned through their wings.

"Stop, please," Myla begged—who she wasn't sure, but she just wanted it all to stop. She didn't want to see this. She didn't want to think of Raevyn doing such awful things without even a hint of remorse. It hurt too much.

He did all of this just for who they were born as. The dragon spoke in her mind, urging her to understand. *He didn't—won't spare anyone. The old, the young, sick, or healthy, it does not matter.*

"Don't do this, please." Myla held her hand out to Raevyn, but he didn't acknowledge her. He let arrow after arrow fly, cutting off screams as he finished the job.

Heed my warning. This is his nature. He will not spare you.

Chapter 28

    With a start, Myla sat up, heart pounding in her chest and a scream lodged in her throat. Flames burned behind her eyelids as she blinked—not knowing if she was still stuck in that terrible place. The screams still echoed in her ears, and—

    "Myla? Myla, breathe. It's okay."

    Raevyn was crouched in front of her, hands outstretched and hovering over her shoulders. Myla flinched away from him and stumbled to her feet. She pulled the dagger out of the sheath on her thigh and held it between them. She was shaking, and tears were streaming down her cheeks. What she had seen—what *her dragon* had shown her—had been too much. Any trust she thought she had in Raevyn was crumbling away. She had let her attraction cloud her judgment. She wouldn't make that mistake again.

Raevyn was eyeing her warily as he slowly got to his feet. "It's okay. It's just me, sunshine—"

"Don't fucking call me that," Myla seethed, her voice as shaky as the rest of her.

He cautiously took a step toward her as if she were a spooked animal. "Whatever you saw, it was just a dream. You're safe."

A memory, she thought, *a horrific memory I won't forget.* But she couldn't fight him. She would lose—even if she dared to use her magic. He was used to fighting those with magic and had taken down many who had far more skill than Myla possessed. She would die before she ever found the princess. Terror coursed through her, merging with her magic. *No, no, no, not now,* Myla thought as her skin tingled. She needed to calm down, but she couldn't with the ghastly memory so fresh in her mind. She tried to think of something else—anything else—but she couldn't think with her heart thundering in her ears.

"Myla." Raevyn stepped toward her, leaving only a few feet between them.

He will not spare you.

Myla took a step back, casting her eyes down to the tops of his boots. Looking him in the eye was too risky. Her resolve would crumble if she saw any concern or care in them. It had already been weakened these past weeks, but she couldn't let her resolve fall completely. Any emotions she saw now would evaporate as soon as he knew. Maybe he did care, but he cared for the person he thought she was. Her magic roared inside her—wanting to protect her and get

172

rid of the threat looming over her. She was about to expose herself, and she'd be killed for sure. She needed to run—

Raevyn grabbed the wrist that held the dagger, and her magic burst through her. Myla gasped, dropping her dagger, and, at the last second, aimed her magic up into the sky. Storm clouds formed, thunder boomed, and lightning cut across the sky as rain poured down on them, soaking them in seconds. Raevyn looked up, brow furrowing, and Myla held her breath. Fuck, this was it. She was dead, and there was nowhere to run with his grip on her wrist—

Raevyn pulled her to his chest and wrapped his cloak around her to block the rain as he led them under a nearby tree.

"That came out of nowhere," he mumbled as he lowered them into a seated position.

He wrapped his arms around her waist and pulled her shaking body in between his legs. He rested his head on top of hers and rocked them gently.

"You're safe. You're safe," he whispered, brushing his lips over her forehead. "I've got you."

He didn't know. Myla's resolve shattered and tears streamed down her cheeks as relief flooded through her. Burying her face in his chest, she gripped his shirt tightly with both her fists.

"Promise me you won't ever hurt me," Myla whimpered, knowing it was ridiculous to ask such a thing— knowing it was impossible to promise but needing to hear it regardless.

"I promise. Of course, I promise." Raevyn hugged her tighter. "I'd sooner hurt myself than you."

Heed my warning.

****

Myla didn't sleep—too afraid of the memories her dragon might show her. Raevyn had dozed off some time ago

173

but hadn't released his hold on her. She hated that it was so comforting. She hated that still after watching that memory, she didn't want to believe Raevyn would hurt her. She knew it made her stupid and naïve—maybe she was. Her entire being was telling her she could trust him and that what he had done was what he had been trained to do before he had the self-awareness to make another choice. He had been brainwashed since he was a child that magic and dragons were the enemy, but maybe she could teach him otherwise.

Stubborn human.

I know, Myla thought. She wasn't sure if her own mind was replaying what her dragon had told her or if they were speaking in her mind. Nevertheless, she spoke to them, hoping her dragon could hear her. *I won't forget what you showed me and I promise to be cautious, but I have to go with my gut. And it's telling me I can't leave him. At least not yet. I need him.*

You will be no different.

Myla looked up at Raevyn, who was still sleeping deeply. His chest rose and fell softly against her side. His still-damp curls rested against his forehead, dripping lightly down the bridge of his nose. His head was back against the tree with his neck extended and exposed. He was completely at her mercy. She could pull out one of the many daggers she kept on her person and slice his throat—

You're wrong, Myla told her dragon. *I will be different.*

Chapter 29

When the sun started rising, Myla decided to take down their camp while Raevyn was sleeping. She was feeling restless after hours of arguing with herself about what she was going to do. In the end, her plan remained the same. She needed him if things were to go south with the princess and her dragon. It was clear from the vision her own dragon had shown her that he was a formidable opponent.

As for her feelings—there wasn't much she could do about that. There was a chance he felt the same, or it was equally possible that she was projecting her own feelings.

Yes, he'd worried for her safety and had been relieved she was alive, but that didn't mean he had romantic feelings for her. Had Wrynn been in a similar situation, Myla would have done just as Raevyn had. Perhaps he was starting to see her as a friend, but it wasn't more than that—it couldn't be— especially in the wake of the vision she'd seen.

"You're up early."

Myla turned from where she had been strapping her bedroll to Cass. Raevyn had gotten to his feet, but he didn't step any closer. He was giving her the same wary look he had last night as if he was afraid she would bolt.

Myla gave him what she hoped was a convincing smile. "Couldn't sleep, so I thought I'd be useful."

"How are you feeling?"

"Not like I want to stab you if that's what you're worried about," she replied, going for a joke, but it came out flat.

He took a tentative step forward. "I was never worried about that. I trust you."

Her heart fluttered at those three simple words. Fuck, he was making it really hard for her to ignore her feelings when he said things like that.

She shook her head. "How? You don't know me—not really."

He took another step forward. "I know enough to know you wouldn't hurt anyone without a good reason." Another step. "So, if you ever did stab me, I'd know you thought it was necessary."

"And that would make it okay?"

He shrugged. "I'd understand it better." Step.

She huffed out a breath. "You're crazy."

He smiled. "I know. I haven't been able to think rationally when it comes to you." Another step.

"What do you mean?"

"I've gone on hundreds of different assignments with hundreds of different people. The timeframe of which ranged from a few days to a few years. I used to try to befriend them, but after watching them die over and over—I stopped trying because I didn't think it was worth it. It hurts more to bury someone you've opened up to than a stranger, so I kept my distance." He was now standing in front of her, so close she could feel the warmth of his body like a tender caress. "I tried to do that with you, but you were so godsdamned persistent. And once I started to, it became so easy to just say things. Things I planned to never share with anyone."

"You must never share because you've given me almost nothing. You're still a mystery to me." She smiled softly, her heart beating irregularly in her chest.

"You don't need to know the gory details—not when you are fighting with nightmares of your own."

"You have nightmares? But nothing ever fazes you."

You didn't seem fazed when you murdered those magic wielders and dragons, Myla reminded herself as she fought the urge to hold on to him and never let go.

"I used to get them every night for years when I was younger. They've become more manageable, but they never truly go away." He brushed a curl away from her eye—his fingertips lingering on her cheek. "And things definitely faze me—especially when it comes to you, Myla."

Her name on his lips affected her in a way she hadn't been expecting. It was one of the few times he'd ever used her name and not that infuriating nickname. She leaned into his palm, stomach filling with butterflies. Gods, he wasn't playing fair. Her mind was telling her not to fall for it, but her heart was twirling in her chest.

"'Stubborn pain in my ass', right?" Myla asked, lips quirking.

"Among other things." He smiled. "I never stood a chance."

"Raevyn—"

There was a rustling somewhere behind her, and Raevyn shoved Myla behind him, pulling out two daggers from the sheaths on his chest. Stunned by the sudden shift, she was barely able to arm herself as someone emerged from the trees. She peeked around Raevyn's shoulder to see a woman with long black hair—the hairs framing her face dyed white-blond. She had a sword strapped to her hip, but she didn't pull it out even when she saw they were armed.

Raevyn shifted and Myla lost sight of the woman as he spoke, "What do you want?"

"I don't mean any harm," the woman replied. "I was only passing through."

Annoyed, Myla shoved past Raevyn to stand at his side. The woman glanced between the pair of them, but her eyes lingered on Myla. Her full lips pulled up into a flirtatious smile. The woman's eyes were the color of dying embers, an eye color Myla had never seen before. They were beautiful—*she* was beautiful with her tall, toned frame, sharp jawline, and tanned skin. Something inside her shifted, reacting to the woman's gaze in a way that was almost familiar, but she couldn't place why she thought so.

The woman tilted her head slightly as if she felt the same thing Myla had—her gaze turning from flirty to intrigued. She took a step forward, and Raevyn mirrored her, angling his body in front of Myla. Their eye contact broke as the woman narrowed her eyes on Raevyn.

"Why the hostility?" She asked, her voice calm. "I've given you no reason to think I'd harm either of you. I don't even have any weapons out."

"I thought you were just passing through," he snapped.

Myla had never heard that tone from him. He was livid, and she didn't understand why. The woman hadn't done anything, just walked into their camp by accident. There was no need to be this belligerent. Myla sheathed her daggers and walked around Raevyn to stand between them. Before she could walk far, Raevyn grabbed her arm—stopping her in place.

"What the fuck do you think you're doing?"

Myla glared at him. "Let go of me."

He glared right back. "Not unless you stop putting yourself in danger."

"You're being ridiculous."

"You heard the lady," the woman spoke up, hand resting on the hilt of her sword.

Raevyn pulled Myla to his chest—his arm like a vise around her waist. "Not going to happen, Aveis."

Chapter 30

"You know each other?" Myla asked incredulously.

"Unfortunately," Raevyn grumbled. "She's a liar and a thief. The last time we saw each other, I turned her in. How you're already out, I have no idea."

Aveis grinned. "You should know by now that there aren't many prisons that can hold me."

He huffed. "I don't care as long as you leave us alone. I'm not in the mood to chase you down to get back whatever you decide to steal from me."

"I would," she said, pulling out her sword and twirling it almost absentmindedly. "But I will not walk away when you're obviously holding this beautiful woman hostage."

"I am not. I'm keeping her safe from *you*."

Aveis glanced at Myla, and she felt the same flutter in her stomach at the look. It was then that she placed why it felt so familiar. It was the same feeling she'd felt every time she got closer to Raevyn. The thought immediately made her feel on edge. She'd been associating that feeling as a warning to keep her distance, but perhaps she'd been wrong. Her instincts were telling her one thing about both of them, but her magic was clearly trying to convey something else. Maybe it wasn't her magic at all, but her dragon warning her from them, but why? And who should she trust? Herself or a dragon who decided to make their presence known after over two decades?

"What say you, darling? Is this brute of a man holding you against your will?"

Glancing between the two of them, Myla decided to trust herself. "He just has a bad case of hero syndrome," she replied with a smirk. "Even though I've proven on many occasions that I can handle myself."

Raevyn glared down at her. "Yes, which is why I've saved you from nearly dying twice already."

"Once," she snapped. "I had the bandits handled."

He rolled her eyes. "Tell that to the twelve stitches in your side."

Myla huffed and tugged out of his grip before facing Aveis. "He's not a threat to me, other than his stubbornness."

"*My* stubbornness—"

"I've never seen you so possessive of one of your travel companions," Aveis said, cutting off his outrage. She

181

gazed between the two of them with newfound interest. "New lover? She can do so much better."

"Definitely not," Myla replied instinctively and instantly regretted the harsh words.

She cut a glance up to Raevyn, whose jaw was clenched. He wasn't looking at her, but she had felt him stiffen at her words. She hadn't meant it to sound so sharp. Sure, their relationship wasn't like that, but the *definitely* had been a tad strong, as if the thought was absurd. It was, but not because she didn't want him. It was absurd to want someone who could quite literally be the death of her.

"'Definitely not,'" she repeated with a grin. "Well, in that case. The name's Aveis, darling." She held out her hand and Myla took it. Aveis flipped their hands over so Myla's hand was on top and placed a lingering kiss on her knuckles. "Pleased to meet you. I hope to have the pleasure of getting to know you more...intimately."

"Fuck no," Raevyn snarled.

Aveis released her hold before rolling her eyes. "Pretty sure it's not up to you, Brute." Aveis looked back at Myla. "Why are you traveling with him of all people?"

"We're on an assignment together," she replied.

"Don't tell her that—"

"Don't tell me you're still looking for the last flame," Aveis admonished.

Last flame. Did she mean the princess and the dragon that took her? She supposed it made sense—the princess wielded flames, but no one was supposed to know that. Perhaps she was referring to the dragon since the story of the dragon kidnapping the princess was the first account of magic in decades. To the general populace, he would be seen as the last of his kind.

"None of your godsdamn business," he snapped.

"That's a shame because I might have a lead for you."

Myla perked up. "You do?"

"Oh yes," she smiled at her. "For a fee, of course."

"Not going to happen," Raevyn replied, grabbing Myla's wrist and tugging her away from Aveis. "Let's get out of here."

Raevyn's grip was firm, and even if Myla had wanted to, she wouldn't have been able to get out of it as he dragged them over to their horses. *Follow your gut,* her father had told her. And her gut was telling Myla to hear her out. Aveis knew something, and they needed all the leads they could get. Before she could argue, Aveis spoke up.

"If you change your mind, I'll be in Vallac for the next few weeks."

"Not going to happen."

****

They rode in silence for the next few hours. Raevyn was tense and still fuming. It made little sense to her that he would be this upset over meeting Aveis again if she had just stolen from him a few times. It was more personal than that, and Myla's curiosity was getting the best of her.

"So, Aveis—"

"Not in the mood to talk about her," Raevyn responded curtly.

"What if her insight will lead us to the princess—"

"It won't."

"You don't know—"

"I do. Just drop it, okay?"

Myla clenched her jaw. "I'm not going to just *drop it* because you don't want to talk about it. You're being childish."

183

He narrowed his eyes on her. "Childish is believing her in the first place. She'll say or do anything for a quick coin. Trust me, I know."

"Did something else happen between you two? Were you lovers—"

He snorted. "With Aveis? Gods no. Not only would I never because I have standards, but *she* would never because she's only interested in women. Clearly, since she wouldn't stop flirting with you."

"Oh," Myla replied, still slightly confused. "I figured she was only flirting with me to get under your skin because she thought we were..."

She trailed off, and his gaze hardened. "Yeah, well, you cleared that up real quick."

Myla cringed, looking down at the reins clutched in her hands. "I didn't mean to upset you. I just didn't want you to think that I thought—hells, I mean, I just didn't want to make things weird or awkward because I thought yesterday— and then you—" She sighed. "Doesn't matter. We're stuck together for the gods only know how long. No need to complicate things—not that I thought you wanted to."

The anger on his face vanished, replaced with the cool mask he put on to block her out. Her stomach soured at the sight, and she wanted so badly to take back her words and be brave, but her dragon's words were still echoing in her ears: *Heed my warning. This is his nature. He will not spare you.* If things were to go south, it was best not to get so close to the edge, even though it felt like she was already on the verge of falling completely.

"If that's what you want, then so be it."

Chapter 31

Myla jumped off her horse and stretched at one of many inns in Vallac. It had taken an entire day to convince Raevyn to come here and another four to travel. He hadn't wanted to run into Aveis, but Myla had insisted they needed to go to every town and city. What she didn't tell him was Myla hoped to run into Aveis so she could see what sort of insight she had. Raevyn clearly wasn't telling her everything, and she wouldn't let his petty rivalry get between her and her goal. Myla had no intention of becoming a nomad for the rest of her life.

After they dropped off their stuff in their room—one with two beds, thank the gods—they headed downtown. It was early afternoon, warmer than she had expected. Myla tied her hair up into a messy bun and pulled off her fur-lined cloak, draping it over her arm as they walked through the market. She felt like she was back in Cassia City with the enormous crowds and merchants yelling their wares. Though with the seagulls overhead and the smell of seawater in the air—she was reminded that she was near the western sea, far from her inland home.

Myla brushed her fingers over the silken clothes of various colors and designs—lingering on a light blue blouse with swirling white lines. Before she could ask how much, someone bumped into her, pushing between Myla and Raevyn. She stumbled, nearly falling on the table of wares, when she heard a yell. She turned. Raevyn was nowhere in sight, and smoke plumed from the welder's shop on the outskirts of the market, which was only a few yards from her. People were hurrying away from the shop, pushing through the crowded market and coughing up smoke.

"What—"

Someone grabbed Myla's arm and pulled her into a nearby alley. Myla grabbed her dagger and turned—brandishing it at the assailant who'd released their grip.

"Hello, darling," Aveis grinned, pulling back the hood of her cloak.

Myla let her dagger fall to her side. "For Rornja's sake—you couldn't have just tapped me on the shoulder or something?" She asked, sheathing her dagger.

"Had to get you away from that brute somehow," she winked. "Now that it's just the two of us—is he holding you hostage?"

Myla shook her head. "No, we are on assignment together—looking for the last flame. I'm actually glad you

186

found me. I was hoping we could talk more about the insight you had."

Her lips quirked. "You don't think I'm just a lying thief?"

Myla shrugged. "Possibly, but we're not exactly drowning in leads right now."

"Well, then you're in luck," Aveis replied, stepping toward her. "Because I can take you right to them."

Myla gave her a skeptical look. "Can you now?"

"Oh yes. We're actually pretty close. The princess saved my life once."

"How did you know she was the princess?"

"There aren't many people who are friends with dragons."

Her eyes widened just a fraction. "You met the dragon?"

"I only caught a glimpse of him flying overhead before she appeared and helped me dispatch a particularly handsy group of men who'd followed me from a tavern years ago. Normally, it would have been an easy fight, but I'd had a bit too much to drink, and they were able to sneak up on me. After she helped me, she disappeared without a word. I followed her—wanting to thank her but also not wanting to spook her. I found out where she was hiding but didn't approach her until she went into town again. We became fast friends, and I see her at least a few times a year."

"If that's true, then why would you take us to her when she clearly wants to stay hidden?"

Aveis shrugged. "Partly for the money—ten thousand gold coins, to be exact. And I know she's more than capable of taking care of herself if it turns out either of you have ill intent. I don't think *you* do, but the brute, most likely. And hey, maybe she'll kill him, and I'd be killing two birds with one stone—helping and impressing a beautiful woman *and* getting rid of a thorn in my side."

It's very unlikely that the princess could even hurt Raevyn. He'd taken down three wielders and dragons practically on his own, but Myla wasn't about to say as much.

"Won't she be upset that you're giving up her location for some coin? Do you do that often?"

"I've never," she replied, taking another step forward and backing Myla against the wall. "I don't know what is about you exactly, but you're different—I can feel it."

She put one hand on the wall next to Myla's head and reached up to stroke her thumb against Myla's cheekbone. Myla's breath caught in her throat at the simple touch and how it caused heat to flood into her system. Her magic tugged in her stomach like a hook on a line— tentatively reaching up and reacting to Aveis's touch. It wasn't painful but exhilarating, and for a moment, Myla forgot how to breathe. Aveis's face was so close that all Myla could see were her beautiful ember-colored eyes—somehow brighter than she remembered. Aveis brought her hand down to cup her neck, her fingers tangling in the stray hairs at the base of Myla's neck.

"Darling—"

"What the fuck is going on?"

Aveis's eyes narrowed, and she sighed in annoyance. "Way to ruin the moment, Brute."

Myla turned her head to see Raevyn standing in the mouth of the alley—his sword out and clasped tightly in his hand. His jaw was clenched, and he looked murderously at Aveis, not even sparing Myla a glance. She stepped out of Aveis's hold and stood between them.

"Raevyn—"

"Is this why you wanted to come here?" He seethed, cutting his glance to Myla.

"Yes—I mean, no. It's not like that—she can take us to the princess."

He scoffed. "As if."

Myla walked up to him and grabbed his arm. "Can I talk to you for a second?"

She didn't give him time to answer before pulling him away where Aveis couldn't hear them.

"Look, I know you don't like her—"

"Understatement," he grumbled.

"*But* you're going to have to trust me on this. Their majesties entrusted us with this assignment in part because of my special skill," Myla explained. "I know what I'm doing."

"Is your special skill making stupid decisions?" Raevyn snapped.

"I believe her. This is happening—whether you like it or not."

He ground his teeth together. "I thought you were smarter than this—"

"Don't," she warned, clenching her fists. "Do you trust me?"

"Sunshine—"

"Do. You. Trust. Me?"

"This isn't about you—"

"It is. You need to trust my judgment on this. It's the only way we're going to find the princess."

"With *her*—"

"Yes. Just, please. You told me before that you trusted me. Prove it."

He stared at her for a long moment, his nostrils flaring, before finally sighing. "Fuck. Fine. But when she inevitably betrays us, I *will* kill her."

"That won't be necessary," Myla said, relaxing. "Oh, I forgot to mention. She wants ten thousand gold coins as payment."

Chapter 32

It took Myla explaining that the money didn't matter since it wasn't even theirs for Raevyn to eventually calm down. He'd ranted and raved at both of them for several minutes about the outrageous fee Aveis required. They all agreed that they would pay Aveis half now and the other half when they found the princess. Aveis had a few loose ends to tie up but promised to meet them in front of their inn at dawn tomorrow.

For the first time since they started their journey, Myla allowed herself to hope. If Aveis turned out to be right, it wouldn't be long before Myla was reunited with her family again and knighted. Yes, there were still a few things she was skipping over—convincing the princess to come with them and getting past a dragon. But, with Raevyn by her side, that part would be easy enough.

However, it was hard to focus on her hope as they sat down for dinner a few hours later when Raevyn was still silently fuming across from her like a stubborn rain cloud that wouldn't go away. Myla was going to just let him stew, but as soon as their food was placed in front of them, Raevyn spoke.

"We can still back out of this."

Myla sighed in exasperation. "I know, but we're not."

"But—"

"We can argue until we're both blue in the face, but you aren't going to change my mind," she replied, cutting into her steaming chicken breast resting on top of rice and vegetables.

"I don't even have to entertain this idea. I can just throw you over my shoulder and get us out of here before she shows up tomorrow."

Myla took a bite of her chicken and shrugged. "You could, but you won't."

"I would if I thought I was protecting you."

"Why would she hurt me? Rob us, sure. But I don't think she's a murderer."

"Good murderers don't go around announcing that fact."

She rolled her eyes. "Why would she want to murder me?"

"She doesn't need a reason. She could just be insane."

"You're more than capable of defending us if necessary. Not that you will need to or not that I can't defend myself, either. You're being paranoid."

"You're not being paranoid enough," Raevyn snapped.

Myla just sighed and focused on her food. She wouldn't keep arguing with him. It was a waste of breath. Also, it was hard to explain why she was trusting Aveis in the first place. Raevyn knew her better and, obviously, didn't trust her for a reason. She told herself she was taking that into account, but in all honesty, she probably wasn't. She was following her gut and though it hadn't led her astray before, that could easily change. She couldn't exactly explain that to Raevyn. He would think she was being foolish. Maybe she was, but she knew she'd regret it if she didn't follow through with this.

After they finished eating, Myla got to her feet. "Are we still training tonight?"

"Of course," Raevyn replied, standing up. "You need it now more than ever since you decided to invite a constant threat on our journey."

****

After over an hour of Raevyn showing Myla how easy it was to beat her in a fight, she was fed up.

Myla shot to her feet and glared at him. "I get you're angry and want to show me how easy it is to get me on my back, but—"

"Phrasing, for fuck's sake, sunshine."

"You know what I mean!" She yelled, refusing to be embarrassed. "You're not teaching me anything. I will not let you use me to get your anger out."

She started to walk away when he grabbed her arm. "Wait, I'm sorry, you're right. Let's go again."

They stood across from one another. Myla was already extremely sore, but she was stubbornly determined to get in at least one good punch—preferably in his smug, unfazed face.

"You're not very fast, but you're strong—use that," Raevyn spoke, raising his hands in a defensive position.

Myla raised her hands in kind, but instead of punching him, she aimed a kick at his stomach. Before her foot could connect, he grabbed it and lifted her leg up. Her other foot slipped, and she fell hard on her back. The wind was knocked out of her, and she gasped. She rolled up into a crouch before Raevyn could kneel over her and swung her leg out. He jumped, and Myla threw herself at him—wrapping her arms around his waist and effectively knocking him to the ground. He gave a grunt of surprise, but her triumph was short-lived as he easily rolled them both over so he was on top. Resolved not to let him gain the upper hand, she kept their momentum going. They rolled a few more times before Myla was able to get out of his grip and stumble to her feet.

Raevyn stood up, a small smile forming on his lips. "Good, you're learning."

She rolled her eyes. "That sounds more insulting than anything else."

Raevyn shrugged. "I've learned that inflated egos turn people into stupid fighters. Just trying to keep you humble."

"Says the cockiest person I've ever met," Myla retorted, swinging her fist out.

Raevyn blocked her blow before it could connect with his jaw. "I'm very aware of the strength I have. You only think it's cockiness because it's too incredible to comprehend, so you think I'm exaggerating."

"Or," Myla replied, kneeing him in the gut. "You're delusional."

Raevyn wasn't even fazed as he grabbed her thigh and pulled her forward, trapping her knee between his hip and arm.

"That's more insulting to you since you haven't been able to beat me," he smirked.

"Are you sure about—" She started to pull out the dagger strapped to her thigh, but Raevyn's free hand shot out and gripped her hand, stopping the motion.

"Nice try."

She glared at him. "Cocky bastard."

He pulled her closer so they were only a breath apart. Her other hand fell against his chest, and she blinked up at him in surprise—her heart beating so loud in her ears that she was afraid he could hear it. He angled his face down, his gold-flecked eyes meeting her blue ones with such intensity that she froze, feeling her cheeks warm.

"I'm going easy on you, sunshine," he rumbled, causing a shiver to run down her spine.

Her mind tried to remind her of the agreement, not to complicate things—what they'd *both* agreed to. He hadn't fought her on it and had pulled away before. Whatever this was, whatever he was doing, it wasn't what she was thinking. His eyes only flickered down because she had run her tongue across her chapped lips. His eyes had darkened only because he was annoyed with her, per usual.

Myla cleared her throat and looked away—eyes focusing on the trees over his shoulder. "Yeah, well, maybe if you let me use weapons, it'll be more of a fair fight."

Raevyn blinked as if waking up from a deep sleep and then letting go of her. They both took a step back, and he crossed his arms.

"Sounds like an excuse, but fine. We'll start practicing armed and unarmed combat tomorrow."

Chapter 33

Myla was about ready to turn Cass around and go literally anywhere else. They had been on the road with Aveis for only two hours, and she and Raevyn had yet to stop arguing.

"For the last time, I didn't steal your precious compass!" Aveis argued, adjusting the pack strapped to her back.

"So, what, it just walked out of my pack the same day *you* decided to stop by my camp?"

"It was purely coincidental!"

"It was a family heirloom!"

"Enough!" Myla snapped, pushing Cass between their horses. "I get it, you hate each other, but for the love of Rornja, stop arguing. What did or did not happen doesn't matter. We're going to be stuck on the road with each other for—what did you say, Aveis? Two months?"

Aveis nodded.

"Two months," Myla continued. "I'm not going to deal with you two bickering for that long. So, just put it behind you for the time being. Once we find the princess, then you two can argue to your heart's content. Understood?"

"I give her a week before she steals our money and disappears into the night," Raevyn muttered.

Myla glared at him. "Not helpful."

"If it had been just you, then I would have already been on my way," Aveis admitted. "Not that I'd ever agree to help you in the first place. But I don't make a habit of robbing beautiful women."

"No, just have your way with them, then murder them."

"For gods' sake," Myla grumbled. "You know what? Never mind. I'm not even going to bother."

Myla stirred Cass forward, away from them.

"See what you did, Brute?"

"*Me?* You're the one—"

"I didn't come on this journey to chat with you."

Aveis's horse sidled up next to Cass, leaving Raevyn cursing behind them.

Aveis gave her a charming smile. "Sorry about that, darling. You're absolutely right, of course, but I just can't help myself sometimes because he's been so easy to rile up."

Myla only nodded but couldn't help but think it was so different from what she had experienced with Raevyn. He had always been the calm and collected one—often riling Myla up more than anything. She'd never seen someone get under his skin like Aveis did. Raevyn had said that nothing ever happened between them romantically, but she wondered if there was something more to their rivalry. Something that he didn't want to share.

"So, you two met when you tried to steal from him? How long ago was that?"

"Yeah, about seven years ago. I was only around thirteen and probably looked like I was eight from malnutrition, which I think is part of the reason he let me go with a warning."

"And you two have just been running into each other ever since?"

She shrugged. "We both travel a lot, and our paths cross, but not for very long."

"It doesn't take long to steal from someone," Raevyn retorted, coming up on Myla's other side.

"Why keep stealing from him when he didn't turn you in?" Myla asked Aveis.

"Because he's an easy target, and I needed the money."

"I caught you every single time!" Raevyn shot back, glaring at her. "That doesn't make me an easy target."

"Not every time. That compass was worth a small fortune."

197

"I knew it—"

"Forget I asked!" Myla tried to intervene, but a new argument had already broken out. This one, she knew, she wasn't going to settle.

She prayed to the god of war and quests, Dakdarr, for strength, knowing she needed all that help she could get to succeed with their unlikely band of travelers.

****

When they finally stopped to set up camp, Myla had a raging headache, and frustration was sitting heavily in her stomach.

"We need to talk," Myla announced, grabbing Raevyn's arm and tugging him away from where Aveis was starting a fire.

"I'm not leaving her unattended with all our stuff—"

"Not a request," Myla growled, pulling his arm with all the strength she had.

He didn't budge at first—not until she dug her fingernails into his bicep, and he looked over at her angry expression. He sighed but let her drag him into the trees far enough away that she felt confident that Aveis couldn't hear. She let go of his arm to hit him upside the head.

Raevyn blinked in confusion before narrowing his eyes. "What the fuck was that for?"

"Why the fuck are you acting like a child?"

"Me? She—"

"I swear to Rornja if you say, 'she started it,' I'm going to hit you again," she warned. "What are you not telling me? Why is she getting under your skin so bad?"

"Maybe because she's a liar but has somehow convinced you she's going to lead us straight to the princess as if it could possibly be that easy. Or maybe it's the fact that she waltzed in here and you—" He cut himself off, pressing his lips into a thin line.

"I what?"

"Doesn't matter."

"No, please, enlighten me."

He clenched his jaw, his body becoming rigid in barely suppressed frustration. "She came in, and you immediately trusted her even after everything I told you, and yet, I don't even think you trust *me*. Despite everything we've already gone through together. I told you I trusted you. Why does trust come so easily with her and not me?"

Myla blinked in surprise—taken off guard by the admission. She hadn't expected his issues with Aveis to revolve around Myla. Why would he care? But there was no mistaking the slightly hurt expression mixed with his own anger and frustration. Myla had the sudden urge to rub her thumb across his brow to smooth out the crease created by his scowl and assure him she did trust him. How could she not? But she didn't—couldn't let him know the sort of power he had over her. The silence stretched between them, his eyes becoming hard and his mask slipping back into place.

"Don't trust me enough to tell me." He nodded curtly and turned away from her. "Understood."

He walked away, and Myla's heart tightened at the sight. She wanted so badly to call out to him and tell him how she felt, but her dragon's words came back to her in sharp, agonizing clarity. *He will not spare you.*

Chapter 34

    Raevyn hadn't spoken to Myla in an entire week. He hadn't spoken to anyone, in fact, morphing into a silent, watchful shadow. Aveis had been elated by the turn of events, often pretending that Raevyn didn't exist and cozying up to Myla. Myla, on the other hand, was conflicted. She felt a knot of tension settle in her stomach, and it only grew the longer she didn't speak to Raevyn and the more distant he became. Then there was Aveis. She was clearly interested in Myla, and there was no denying that she was beautiful. Every time she was near or Myla felt her delicate suggestive touches on her skin, Myla's own body reacted with a flush of heat. If it had been any other time, any other place—Myla would have seized the opportunity to be with a beautiful woman.

But this wasn't any other time or place, and Myla's thoughts always seemed to drift to him. They drifted to his dark eyes, coarse curls, and cocky smirk. She wished she hadn't been a coward—that her dragon had never reached out to her—because all she did was doubt herself and doubt *him* when he had done nothing to her to deserve it. How could she even be sure if what her dragon showed her was true? Hells, she was going in circles. She wished her sister, Rikia, or best friend, Wrynn, were here. Either would help her sort through her complicated thoughts. Well, her sister definitely would, but Myla still wasn't sure how Wrynn felt about her having magic. The idea of him refusing to speak to her again sent a pang through her chest, but she pushed it away—one crisis at a time. Who knew, maybe she wouldn't ever see him again, and it wouldn't be a problem.

"What do you think, darling?"

Myla snapped out of her thoughts when she felt Aveis's fingers trail down her arm in question. They were walking their horses, partly to give them a break as well as to stretch out their own legs. Raevyn was a few paces behind them and, only quickly glancing over her shoulder occasionally, confirmed that. Aveis had been walking next to her, chatting, but Myla had gotten lost in her thoughts and missed the last few things she had said.

"I'm sorry, what did you say?" She asked sheepishly.

Aveis smiled and nudged her shoulder softly against hers. "I *said*: Roullon isn't far from here and only a few hours out of our way. We can stop there, go to a tavern, get a room at an inn—preferably one *together*."

Myla snuck a look back at Raevyn. The only indication he gave that he heard was his white-knuckled grip on his horse's reins. He didn't say a word, and Myla realized after a few seconds that she had been expecting him to. But he wasn't going to because he no longer cared since she had all but rejected him despite her true feelings.

Myla turned back to Aveis and gave her a small smile. "I wouldn't mind stopping in town for the night. As for our rooms, we'll see how the night goes."

Aveis's smile widened. "Deal."

****

They checked into the inn, and Myla ended up getting three separate rooms. She waited for Raevyn to say anything in objection, but he didn't. He just took a key from the desk as soon as the innkeeper set them down and headed up to his room. Myla took her own key and headed up the stairs with Aveis close behind. They agreed to meet up in about an hour after they had time to freshen up.

Myla set her bags next to the bed and flopped down on it—completely alone for the first time in weeks. Her relief was short-lived as the silence left room for her doubts and fears to creep in. Images of Wrynn lying unconscious on the palace floors, the hurt look on Raevyn's face after asking Myla to trust him, and the dragons and magic wielders dying at Raevyn's hand. She tried to push them away, but they were only replaced with her dragon's words, Wrynn's screams, and her own thoughts of doubt.

Fuck, she could really use that drink about now. She got to her feet and quickly got ready before heading back downstairs. Neither Raevyn nor Aveis was down there yet, so Myla settled by the fireplace and distracted herself with the chatter of the other lodgers. After years of practice, she had become good at repressing the thoughts she didn't want to deal with, but these were relentless. Specifically, her dragon's words. *There is no time, there is no time, there is no time.* Over and over, in a constant loop. Along with a consistent knocking as if there were a door in her mind, begging to be opened. She reached out for it, her fingers curling around the doorknob—

"Myla?"

She startled, looking up to see Aveis standing over her.

"Ready to go?" She asked with a small smile.

Myla smiled back and got to her feet. "Yeah, let's go."

She followed Aveis out the door and didn't need to look back to know that Raevyn had followed them. Aveis looped her arm with Myla's and led her down the street to the crowded tavern. They walked up to the bar where a tall, burly man covered in tattoos was serving drinks. A grin broke across his bearded face when he noticed the pair of them.

"Aveis! Long time no see. How've you been, kid?"

"Iandor, it's good to see you. I've been doing good—staying busy." Aveis smiled. "What about you? How's your husband and kids doing?"

"Good, good. The twins just turned nine—little hellions they are—but love 'em to pieces. How long are you in town for?"

"We're just here for the night." Aveis tugged Myla closer, and Iandor's eyes fell on her. "We're on a little adventure of our own."

He nodded. "I hope for your sake she's better company than the last one you brought around a few years ago that nearly impaled Thes with a butter knife."

Myla cut a look at Aveis, who chuckled. "She is. Myla here is squeaky clean. Training to be a knight, actually."

Aveis had asked her a few nights ago how she got mixed up with Raevyn, and Myla had panicked and couldn't come up with a plausible lie. Aveis knew Raevyn worked for their majesties, and Myla couldn't just say she tagged along for fun. Also, in case Aveis knew about dragon hunters, Myla didn't want to say she was a part of Raevyn's team. If it had bothered Aveis, knowing Myla was a recruit, she didn't give any indication. It didn't deter Aveis's advances either.

Iandor raised an eyebrow at Myla. "What are you doing with her thieving ass then?"

"She has good taste," Aveis cut in, giving Myla's arm a slight squeeze. "Clearly."

He snorted. "Clearly."

Aveis smiled and put a few silver pieces down on the counter. "If you're done insulting me, we'll take two ales, please, and keep 'em coming."

Chapter 35

The ale wasn't working. Myla was on her third drink in hopes that her thoughts would be lulled away for the night, but if anything, they got louder. Guilt clawed at her chest, and it didn't help that Myla kept catching Raevyn's eye, who hadn't moved from his booth in the corner of the tavern. Aveis and Myla were standing at a table near the band. Most of the people around them were dancing, and they had been too for a while. It hadn't been for long since the ale wasn't flowing through her system like it ought to have been. She often needed liquid courage to get herself to dance on a good day.

Myla took a long swig of her ale, refusing to look over at Raevyn again, even though his eyes were burning holes in the back of her head. *Leave the scarred man. Leave. The princess...she will keep you safe.* The door in her mind rattled—the door that must be her connection to her dragon. She knew if she were to open it, then her dragon's words would flood mercilessly through her mind, and she would never know peace again. She had enough doubt of her own. She didn't need theirs. She walled off the door as best as she could until the words were only faint whispers.

Aveis's fingers wrapped around Myla's hand, which had been resting on the table. "You okay, darling? You look like you've got something on your mind."

Myla looked up into her beautiful ember-colored eyes and felt that spark again. Her magic perked at the touch, rushing up her chest and to her fingertips. Her skin thrummed, but not in the way that indicated she was about to lose control—it was softer as if greeting Aveis. Aveis's touch was warm, as always. She never seemed to get cold, and her skin always radiated an alluring warmth.

Myla smiled softly. "I'm okay, just a lot on my mind."

Aveis pulled her closer, wrapping an arm around her waist. "I'd be happy to distract you if you wish."

She had to angle her face up slightly to look up at Aveis, who had a flirty grin and eyes focusing on her lips in a silent question. Perhaps the ale had been working because Myla didn't hesitate or think that perhaps it wasn't the best idea. She just wrapped her arms around her neck and leaned up. Aveis closed the final distance between them and kissed her. Heat coursed through her veins, but it wasn't the heat she expected to feel when kissing someone she was attracted to. It wasn't desire—the heat was surface level. She felt as though she had stood in front of an open flame for too long. It wasn't even near the level she had felt when Raevyn had almost kissed her. Aveis may be the safer choice, but she knew in her heart that it wasn't a choice—there was no competition.

Aveis reached a hand up to cup her cheek, her fingers catching Myla's curls as she deepened the kiss. Hells, she needed to stop this before it got too far. Myla moved her hands down to Aveis's shoulders and pushed her back slightly. She opened her eyes and smiled at Myla, brushing her thumb along her cheekbone.

Myla opened her mouth to say something—anything to explain things—but at the last second, she blurted out, "I'll be right back. I need to go to the washroom."

Fucking coward, Myla thought to herself as she walked away. Checking over her shoulder to make sure Aveis wasn't watching, Myla slipped out the front door and into the crisp air. She took in a deep breath, letting her skin cool from Aveis's touch. She ran her hands through her hair, cursing slightly. Why couldn't things be easy? Why did she have to be attracted to the person who would most likely kill her? When she had been told her mission, she never once dreamed that she'd end up here—agonizing over her love life, of all things. It was ridiculous. She needed to let it go and focus on what was most important—finding the princess.

Myla headed down the street, tucking her hands into her cloak pockets, not wanting to face Aveis just yet. The dark streets were mostly empty, and the noise of the tavern faded away the further she walked. She knew she should face Aveis, but what if she decided to back out of their deal because Myla rejected her? She didn't want to lead her on and wouldn't be able to do it convincingly with Raevyn always behind them. She didn't want him to think she had moved on with her—not that there had been anything to move on *from*.

Myla pushed the thoughts of Raevyn and Aveis out of her mind. She'd deal with it later. Right now, she wanted to let her mind wander away from them for once. Of course, that left her to deal with the aching homesickness she had been able to ignore the last few weeks with so much else going on. *Soon,* she promised herself. A month or so on the road then, however long it took to convince the princess to take her rightful place as heir. Shorter if it came down to a fight, which Myla hoped not. Then, she'd be on her way home to claim her reward and become a knight. Once home, she'd finally be able to explain everything to Wrynn, holding out hope that he'd accept her. He was one of the sweetest people she knew. The thought of him not accepting her was almost unfathomable.

Myla thought back on all the times Wrynn had helped her—her mind snagging on the first time she had tried throwing knives. It was a few weeks into training, and Myla stayed late one afternoon to practice throwing knives because she wasn't getting the hang of it and didn't want to fall behind. She had nearly impaled Wrynn, who was on his way out.

"Sorry!" Myla called, a blush spreading down her neck.

Wrynn laughed, pulling the knife out of the wall beside him. "No harm done. Do you want some help? I can give you a few pointers."

"You don't have to do that."

"I know," Wrynn said with a smile. "But I want to."

He came up beside her and got into position. "Put your right foot forward, a good foot away from your left." Myla mirrored his stance. "Make sure your body is relaxed, and hold the knife with your thumb on top." He readjusted her grip. "When you throw, pull your arm back so the knife is next to your face with the handle facing the sky. Then you throw it, but you don't need to put that much force into it." Wrynn demonstrated.

The knife soared through the air before sticking to the training dummy. Myla tried next. The first few bounced off the wall near the training dummy, Wrynn altering her stance until she got one in the target.

He grinned at her. "Good. Now, just do that a thousand more times, and you'll be an expert."

Myla smiled. "Sounds easy enough. Thank you for your help—for always helping me."

"Of course, Sea Storm. I was going to go grab some dinner. Do you wanna join?"

After that, they were practically inseparable. After training on the weekdays and Myla's extra training sessions, they'd find time to do something—whether it was walking around town or spending the night at either of their houses. They never tired of one another. Myla had come to see him as a confidant for all her problems and insecurities. Wrynn had too, telling her about the pressure he felt as the eldest after his father had died and how he had never dreamt of becoming a knight. Though the path he took wasn't what he had thought he wanted, it was a path he wanted to stay on.

Myla's vision started to blur with tears. She hadn't realized how much she had missed him—him and her family. And if things kept on as they were, she feared she might not ever see them again.

"Don't move," a deep voice hissed in her ear seconds before she felt a blade against the small of her back. "Give me all your money, and I won't have to hurt you."

Chapter 36

The stranger dug his blade farther into her back when Myla didn't move or speak.

"*Now,*" he barked.

Anger and frustration grew inside Myla—her magic humming in response, thrumming just under her skin. She was so fucking sick of people, men in particular, seeing a woman walking alone and assuming she'd be an easy target. It was ludicrous. All she wanted was to walk in peace and sort out her jumbled thoughts. She'd teach this asshole to think twice before assuming someone's strength from their looks.

Feeling confident from the daily sparring training with Raevyn, Myla spun on her heel—faster than the man could blink—and knocked the knife out of his hand. The blade went skittering across the cobblestones. He reached for another one in his belt, but she punched him before he could grip it. His nose cracked, blood splattering out, as he stumbled back with a cry. She didn't let him recover before shoving him against the stone wall of the building they stood next to. She pushed her forearm against his chest, pinning him in place as she pulled out her own dagger. She held the dagger against his skin. His Adam's apple bobbed against the blade, nearly cutting skin.

"I-I'm sorry," the man stammered, holding his hands up next to his face. "I-I don't want any trouble."

"You should have thought about that before you attacked me," Myla snarled, pushing the blade harder against the thin skin of his throat.

Lightning cut across the sky just before thunder boomed in response. Rain drizzled down—urged on by the insistent hum of her magic. She felt so angry and frustrated about how she ended up here, all she'd done and would need to do just to exist as she was. None of it was fucking fair. She should have never been put in this situation. She should be training with her best friend back home. The magic in her veins shouldn't exist, and she wasn't even sure if she wanted it anymore. Not when it might be the one thing that would keep her from the person she—

"Please, don't kill me," the man whimpered, blood blooming around the edges of her blade.

Myla blinked, realizing she'd been close to slicing the man's throat open—*too* close. She stepped back in horror, dropping the dagger to her side. The man edged across the wall hesitantly. When she didn't make a move to stop him, he sprinted away. Trembling, Myla pushed down her magic. The rain trickled to a stop, the clouds parting to reveal the full moon shining down. Gods, she'd been so close to killing that man, and for what? Wanting some money? Her anger had never been that out of control. It was almost as if it wasn't entirely her own.

Myla stiffened when she sensed someone else nearby. She lifted her dagger and looked around. Raevyn stood in the mouth of the alley, the moonlight outlining his body and casting a long shadow over her. Her entire body sagged as if sighing in relief, and her magic flared warmly in her stomach. He had come after her to ensure she was safe and watch her back even though he was angry with her. Even though she didn't deserve it after she practically told him she didn't trust him.

Tears collecting in her eyes, Myla dropped her dagger before launching herself at him. She wrapped her arms around his waist and buried her face in his chest, hugging him tightly.

"I'm sorry," she sniffled. "I'm so sorry. Of course, I trust you. I've always trusted you, but I was afraid. I was told that I shouldn't—but I shouldn't have listened. You've done nothing but show me I can trust you. And I don't trust Aveis more than you. I'm not even sure I *do* trust her, at least not entirely. But I know she'll lead us to the princess. I didn't want to tell you because I'm following my gut here, and I thought you'd be angry or think I was naïve. Maybe I am, but I still think we need her, at least for now." Myla fisted his cloak tightly. Fuck pride. For once, she allowed herself to be vulnerable. "Please don't be mad anymore. I need you." The truth of those last three words nearly cut her in half. Even if

212

she'd wanted to listen to her dragon, she knew now it was far too late. He'd buried himself under her skin so thoroughly that to try and detach herself would leave her in pieces.

Raevyn let out a shaky breath, wrapping his arms around her and hugging her back just as tightly. "Stubborn pain in my ass."

Myla chuckled wetly. "I know. Thank you for always having my back. I know I can always count on you."

"Always. Even though you drive me up the fucking wall sometimes, I'll always have your back." He ran his hand down her curls. "But I also know better than to step in to help when it's clear you've got things handled."

"He can be taught," she teased, earning a tight squeeze from Raevyn.

"Pain in my ass," he responded, but she could have sworn he sounded almost fond.

****

Myla headed back to the tavern with Raevyn at her side. Guilt settled in her stomach the closer they got to the door. She hadn't been gone for long. At least, she didn't think so. Either way, she needed to face Aveis and tell her the truth. Hopefully, she wouldn't be angry and refuse to help them. She hadn't realized that she had slowed down until Raevyn rounded in front of her. He had a pleased smile on his face.

Myla narrowed her eyes at him. "Why are you smiling like that?"

His smile widened. "Just thinking about you rejecting Aveis."

"Who said I'm rejecting her?"

"People who enjoy a kiss don't usually run away right after."

She flushed slightly. "Shut up. It's not any of your concern anyway."

"Sure it is," Raevyn replied, opening the tavern door for her. "Now I won't have to watch the painfully one-sided flirting on her part. It was getting embarrassing."

She walked past him, rolling her eyes. "You're taking too much pleasure from this."

Myla looked around the tavern and spotted Aveis standing beside the bar, talking to Iandor. As if she could sense her presence, Aveis turned around and caught her eye, smiling.

"Can I watch you break the news to her?" Raevyn asked from behind her.

Myla smacked his chest without looking back at him. "No, now give us a little privacy, will you?"

Raevyn chuckled before disappearing into the crowd. Myla met Aveis halfway, and Aveis's arm instantly wrapped around her waist—bringing her flush against her.

"There you are. I was worried you ran off. You okay?"

"Yeah, I just went outside to get some fresh air when someone tried to mug me. But, I'm okay," she rushed to assure as Aveis's eyes widened in alarm. "Not even a scratch."

Her smile returned, and she squeezed her hip lightly. "They're a novice if they thought you'd be an easy mark."

Myla smiled back. "Thanks."

"Now, come on." She tugged her toward the bar. "The night is young yet."

Chapter 37

After three weeks on the road together, Myla, Raevyn, and Aveis fell into a routine. Raevyn and Aveis were back to their bickering selves, but it wasn't as incessant or biting as it had been. Myla hadn't told Aveis in so many words that she wasn't interested in her romantically. She'd resolved to tell Aveis if she tried to kiss her again, which she hadn't. Aveis still flirted with her, but Myla didn't mind. Raevyn had become less sulky now that he knew Myla wasn't interested in her. Myla hadn't allowed herself to think too much about what that could mean for their relationship.

They arrived in Tanin early in the morning. Tanin was located on the eastern border of Rosebourne. Myla had been here countless times, visiting her uncle, his husband, and four kids. They'd since moved to Naeron, so she hadn't been in over three years. However, walking down the street felt like walking into her second home. The streets were bustling with life, and the entire city was cleaner and more colorful than Cassia City. The people who lived here were tan, friendly, and relaxed—often closing up shop to enjoy the salty sea and all its wonders. All restaurants and taverns had open walls, not needing to worry about unpredictable seasons as they only had mild temperatures.

It was cooler than Myla remembered, but it was because she and her family had always visited in the throes of summer. It was still warm enough that she had to tuck her cloak away and push up her sleeves. Aveis had left them as soon as they dropped off their stuff at the inn—proclaiming she had some business she needed to attend to. Raevyn was skeptical, but he had waved her off since he didn't want to follow her. Myla had an intrusive thought that Aveis was running away but didn't dwell on it. She was honestly slightly relieved to have some alone time with Raevyn. It wasn't as if they didn't have some sort of alone time when they were sparring, but it was different. As Myla looped her arm through his and tugged him along the streets, she couldn't help but think that this was more intimate—sharing a place she loved with someone she cared about.

As they walked down the streets, Myla recounted her fond memories of wandering the streets with her cousins. She pointed out the tavern she'd had her first drink in at only fourteen and told him she had sworn off drinking because alcohol tasted so awful.

"Obviously, that didn't stick," Myla smiled, tugging him away toward the bakery. "And here they have the best scones you'll ever taste."

They stepped into the shop, the smell of baked goods wafting over them, causing her mouth to water. In the display case were delicately decorated cakes and pastries. They were all so wildly different, from cakes decorated with suns and rainbows to pastries designed to look like fearsome creatures. Myla ordered two lemon-raspberry scones shaped like suns drizzled with light icing. They were still steaming when the baker placed them in a paper bag and handed them over.

They walked down to the beach and sat on the dock. Myla took off her boots and rolled up her trousers so she could dip her toes in the cold water. Raevyn did the same before they dug into their scones. Myla's eyes nearly rolled in the back of her head when she took her first bite. They were as good as she remembered. She was instantly transported to days on the beach, playing in the sea with her cousins. With Cassia being so far inland, Myla hadn't spent much time on the beach, so she soaked in all the time she could when visiting her uncles. They'd always joked that she had seawater in her veins. They didn't know about her magic, so they didn't realize how true that statement was. Staring out at the lapping waves now, Myla, for once, was happy to stay on shore if it meant being by Raevyn's side.

Myla glanced at Raevyn as he took his first bite. He chewed thoughtfully as she waited for his eyes to alight with pleasure, but his expression remained the same.

"Oh, come on!" Myla exclaimed. "You can't tell me that this isn't the best thing you've ever tasted."

Raevyn shrugged. "I'm not a big sweets fan."

"That is the most ridiculous thing I've ever heard. Who doesn't like sweets?"

"I like them just fine, but I don't usually crave them."

"Then you don't deserve to eat it," she replied, reaching to grab the scone, but he stuffed the rest in his mouth.

She gave him a disbelieving look, but the smile that broke across her face softened it. "Those are meant to be savored, not scarfed down, you deviant," she teased, the grin on her face spreading irrepressibly. She couldn't stop the rush of butterflies in her stomach either. Being with him like this, in a familiar place, felt like they were going on their first date. It all felt so normal and *right*. It made her forget all the reasons she needed to keep her distance.

He smiled in kind, exposing his dimples, which she found unbelievably attractive. Raevyn may be made of sharp edges, but when he smiled, and his dimples appeared, he was almost an entirely different person. The person Myla believed was the true self he had become accustomed to hiding. Every time she got a glimpse of his softer side, she found herself thinking of ways to keep that side around. It wasn't as if she didn't like all sides of him, even the side that loved to tease and antagonize her. It always thrilled her to be challenged, and Raevyn constantly was—whether it was in training or just a silly argument. It forced her to have perspective, and Myla liked to think she had the same effect on Raevyn. Then, maybe one day, he wouldn't see wielders as the enemy. Perhaps it was a tad optimistic, but in this moment with Raevyn, she allowed it.

"Desperate measures," he responded, his mouth still full.

Myla laughed, bringing her thumb up to his face to wipe off a bit of icing around the side of his lips. It had been almost instinctive, and she didn't realize what she was doing until her finger trailed along the slight stubble. His smile widened, and she blushed as she pulled her hand away.

"You're a mess," she admonished, the smile never leaving her lips. "I can't take you anywhere."

"I'll make it up to you," he promised, "by getting you a dozen of these for the road."

She grinned.

****

The sun was high in the sky as Myla and Raevyn walked between the booths set up along the harbor. Her new sea glass bracelet gleamed in the sunlight, casting blue and green reflections along Raevyn's arm, which was tucked in hers. Raevyn had seen it as they were wandering the booths and bought it for her.

"It matches your eyes," he had said, clasping it to her right wrist. Her insides melted at his thoughtfulness, and she felt lighter than she had in weeks.

Myla pulled him toward a booth selling fresh fruit, smiling widely as she bought them a small basket of berries.

"You have to try this." She held out a raspberry to Raevyn between two fingers. "Their fruit is amazing—all freshly grown not far outside the city."

Instead of grabbing the berry from her fingers as she had expected, he grabbed her wrist and brought her fingers up to his lips. Her magic swirled in her stomach, for once not incessant, but rather like butterflies. It felt almost like encouragement to keep close. It was so different than what she'd been feeling for weeks that she was stunned. She would have analyzed it more, but Raevyn's warm brown eyes were locked with hers—freezing her in place. His lips pulled up into a slight smile as he ate the berry, tongue swiping lightly against her fingertips. A blush crept up Myla's neck as heat flooded her system—thinking about what else he could do with his tongue.

Myla was transfixed on his dark gaze, her entire body tingling with desire. There was no denying the mirrored desire in his gaze. This time, she didn't have any ready excuse that would keep distance between them, and she didn't search for one. She was sick of fighting their chemistry and pretending they were just travel companions. It had been one thing when she'd thought only lust lay between them, but it felt bigger than that. Her magic, too, was trying to draw him in, against her dragon's insistence. Ever since she'd built a wall in front of the door to her dragon, she'd become better at deciphering between what was her own instincts and what were her dragon's thoughts. And her instincts pleaded for her to keep him close and trust him.

He pulled back slightly but kept hold of her wrist. "Delicious," he murmured, eyes darkening.

Myla swallowed tightly, unconsciously leaning into him as if she couldn't resist his pull of gravity. She followed the trail of his tongue along his lips—finding it increasingly difficult not to claim them as her own.

"I—"

There was a commotion off to their right, bringing them out of their daze. Raevyn pulled Myla closer to him, angling his body in front of her as knights ran down the street. Aveis led the charge, her black hair billowing behind her like a flag.

"For fuck's sake," Raevyn growled as Aveis changed course to dart toward them.

Aveis grabbed Myla's free hand without breaking stride—tugging her and Raevyn since he still had a grip on her other wrist.

"Time to go."

Chapter 38

"Are you fucking kidding me?" Raevyn growled as they rushed through the trees. "You stole from a *commanding officer?*"

"He was being a dick," Aveis replied, leaping over a fallen tree.

"You are infuriating! What the fuck were you thinking?"

"Would both of you shut up?" Myla hissed, barely avoiding a low-hanging branch. "We're trying to get away, which is hard when you're yelling at each other and giving away our location."

They stumbled into a clearing on the banks of a lake that spanned as far as the eye could see.

"Well, shit," Aveis said. "Any of you good swimmers?"

An arrow flew from the trees, narrowly missing Raevyn's shoulder. Shouts echoed along the branches, followed by more pounding footsteps. A dozen knights, if not more, were about to surround them, and even though they were all excellent fighters—Myla wasn't sure they'd be able to make it out of this. She and Raevyn might be fine, but Aveis could be hung for her crimes. Even if Raevyn didn't believe her, Myla did, and she knew that if she didn't get them out of this, she'd never find the princess.

I will be different.

Myla pulled the water toward them and wrapped it around them, creating an air pocket bubble. She heard the others gasp, but she didn't dare look at them—afraid of what their reactions might be. She pushed their bubble out into the lake, submerging them out of view of the tree line. They hit the bottom of the lake, sand pluming up around them and momentarily obstructing their view. Even when the sand settled, they couldn't see much. They were deep in the lake where light could not venture.

"Holy fucking shit," Aveis breathed somewhere to Myla's right. "This is insane. How can we even breathe right now?"

222

"Air pocket," Myla explained, sweat beating on her brow. "I won't be able to hold all of us for long. We need to get to the other side."

She shoved the bubble forward. Raevyn and Aveis stumbled, but Myla didn't allow their bodies to push through the air pocket. It took a few minutes, but they finally broke the surface, and Myla let the bubble pop as they tumbled onto the opposite shore. Myla landed on her hands and knees, head bent as she tried to catch her breath. Her magic was thrumming through her veins, heating her skin. She'd never used that much magic at one time before. She never had the need. She was glad to know that her limit was vaster than she imagined. She was physically tired, but magically, she could keep going. She wondered if one day she'd ever hit her limit.

There was a sound like a body thudding to the ground, and Myla looked up to see Aveis lying unconscious in front of her. Raevyn was standing over her with his sword out and pointed directly at Myla. She froze—heart hammering in her chest—as she stared up into the familiar brown eyes. Though all the warmth she had come to expect had vanished, replaced with icy anger.

"So this is your special skill," he spoke, his lips curling in disgust. His eyes flashed, looking golden in the setting sun for just a moment before returning to their usual dark roast coffee color. "I understand now why you kept it to yourself this whole time."

"Raevyn—" Myla tried, sitting back on her heels.

"Don't move," he warned, stepping forward with his blade extended in front of him. "Was anything you told me true? Why were you really arrested? Do their majesties know?"

The door in her mind that separated her from her dragon shuddered—their voice ringing out in muffled desperation.

"The hunter came looking for me that night, and Wrynn and I tried to fight him off. He got the best of both of us and brought us to the captain of the guard. The captain was the one that killed the hunter—"

"Lies," Raevyn snarled, grip tightening on his sword. "He wouldn't—"

"He *did*," she insisted. "Their majesties didn't want it getting out that they let a wielder free. They needed a water wielder for their prophecy—"

"Enough," he roared, his blade slicing inches from her skin.

Myla surged back, stumbling to her feet. The shock of him nearly cutting her made her question everything. She believed he wouldn't hurt her, but that had been the old her. She was exposed as the threat he'd been fighting since he was twelve. The affection she thought lay between them didn't stand a chance against his hate. Stubbornly, though, she didn't run. She wouldn't—couldn't. Not from him.

The door in her mind shattered, and her dragon's voice screamed at her. *Run, you stubborn human! He will kill you! The princess—*

"The king believes deeply in the prophecy. He'll do anything to bring his daughter home—"

"And kill the very people he employed for doing their jobs? That doesn't make sense! Why would they—after everything—" He ground his teeth together. His whole body tensed, and his eyes darkened in predatory focus. "I'm done listening."

He launched himself at her with deadly precision—moving so fast it felt as though he blended with the shadows around them. Myla dodged, his blade slicing through her shirt, a whisper from her flesh. Before she could unsheath her sword, he was in front of her again. His sword cut through the air, and Myla lifted her arms in defense. A large wave crashed into Raevyn, sending him toppling several feet away.

"Please, just listen to me," Myla begged.

Storm clouds rolled in, causing lightning to cut across the sky. Her magic swirled inside her—urged on by her desperation and apprehension in a nearly uncontrollable frenzy. She could feel her dragon's anger along the edges as well, pressing her magic to take over completely. Her dragon kept yelling at her—so loud that her head started pounding—but Myla refused to back down.

Raevyn got to his feet, sopping wet and sneering. "What you possess—it's not natural. It goes against the balance—"

Myla took a step toward him. "I was not made. I was *born* like this. There's nothing *unnatural* about it."

For fuck's sake, you ridiculous human! I showed you his nature, do not be fooled—

"Fuck the prophecy. You cannot be allowed to live."

In a burst of speed, he rushed toward her. This time, Myla was able to grab her sword. She lifted it up in time to catch Raevyn's. The steel squealed as he shoved his full weight into the blow. Myla's boots slipped in the wet sand, but she didn't fall. Raevyn's face was inches from hers, disgust written across every beautiful feature.

"You know me." She insisted, pushing back against him with all the strength she had. "We've been on the road together for months—can you really tell me you think I'm an abomination that needs to be dealt with?"

Raevyn's anger slipped just a fraction, but it was enough for Myla to see the anguish underneath. That one glimpse made hope bloom in her chest. It was short-lived as the look vanished a second before Raevyn shoved her. She stumbled and barely blocked his next blow. Despite his insistent strikes, Myla realized something. He was holding back. She'd been training with him for weeks and knew when he wasn't putting his all into a fight. Her eyes locked with his, and she hoped she wasn't making a terrible mistake.

Myla twisted around him, putting distance between them. He whirled to face her just as she let her sword thud to the ground. "I trust you," she said simply.

Her dragon roared, but Myla didn't move. Instead, she lifted her hands in surrender. It was possibly one of the most foolish things she'd ever done in her life. She'd never been fond of trust exercises, yet that's precisely what it was—a deadly trust exercise.

Raevyn let out a harsh laugh. "Surrendering already? And here I thought you'd put up more of a fight."

Anger bubbled to the surface, causing the lake behind her to react—pitching harder and faster against the shore. "I could say the same about you. I didn't take you for the type to toy with your prey."

"Is that what you are?" Raevyn asked, taking a step toward her. "Prey?"

"They don't call you hunter for nothing," she replied, taking an answering step forward.

They were standing so close now that the tip of his sword rested against her chest. Myla shuffled forward, the blade puckering her skin.

"What are you waiting for?" She taunted. "Kill me like the monster you think I am. Pierce my heart and prove that you're nothing more than a tool for their majesties to wield. Prove that you'd kill anyone—no matter who they are—just for being born different."

His eyes flashed in challenge, and the blade dug deeper into her skin, nearly drawing blood. She didn't even flinch, just stared up into his gold-flecked eyes—defiant to the end.

"Do it," Myla snarled. "Kill me."

His grip tightened, but it was trembling ever so slightly. "Stop it."

"Stop what?" She challenged, shuffling forward so the tip of the blade pierced her skin. A trickle of blood ran down her chest like a tear. Raevyn's eyes tracked the blood, Adam's apple bobbing as he swallowed. "Talking? Existing? You have that power, not me. So *end this*."

He bared his teeth. "You've manipulated me this entire journey. You knew there was a strong possibility we'd end up here, so you charmed me."

It was Myla's turn to laugh—the noise harsh and full of disbelief. "You think I planned this? You think I *wanted* this? I tried everything to stop my feelings from growing."

Pain flitted across Raevyn's face. "Please, Myla, don't—"

Her dragon pressed harder, and Myla's grip on her magic started to slacken. Her dragon was taking hold, and if they did, nothing would stop them from hurting Raevyn. She needed to tell him how she felt before it was too late.

"I'm in love with you, you arrogant ass." Myla spat the words at him like a curse, even though her heart was beating wildly in her chest. "Insanely and irrevocably. And, trust me, if I could stop my feelings, I would have. But it was completely out of my control. And despite your best efforts, might I add. I never thought of myself as a fool, but I must be to love you."

His anger slipped completely—exposing the torrent of emotions warring in his eyes. He shook his head, breath catching in his throat as if he was having a hard time breathing. "You really are a pain in my ass," he said around what sounded like a laugh. "Gods—I never stood a chance."

He let the sword thud to the ground before he captured Myla in his arms, kissing her fiercely. Then her magic burst from her.

Chapter 39

The magic inside her had built up to the point that there was nowhere for it to go but out. Rain poured down on them, lightning flashing behind her closed lids, and thunder rumbling the earth. The lake pitched toward them, splashing against their legs. Myla felt like she was in the eye of a hurricane, but she didn't care—not with Raevyn's lips on hers and his arms wrapped tightly around her, keeping her from slipping away.

His hands moved down her back, landing on her upper thighs as he lifted her off the ground with ease. Myla tightened her hold on his neck as he waded out of the water before pushing her against a tree, all without breaking their kiss. It was intoxicating: the touch, the taste, the feel of him. Myla could feel every inch of him, but it wasn't enough.

He moved his lips down her jawline, and Myla arched her head back to give him better access to her neck. He kissed and bit the sensitive skin, causing Myla to moan, her toes curling and liquid heat pooling in her stomach. She pushed her fingers through his hair, gripping the short strands in a desperate attempt to stay grounded. She'd never felt this out of control before. Her desire for him was melding with the magic inside of her, creating a tornado that she couldn't control. Her skin was humming from the heat of him and the static of her magic—so intense that she knew he could feel it. He groaned against her neck, the sound reverberating through her bones, and she wanted more—none of it was enough.

"Gods, I love you," he murmured against her skin, his teeth grazing her collarbone. "So fucking much."

Myla angled her face down and captured his lips with hers again, her heart filling with so much love that she thought it would burst.

"Raevyn—"

A crack sounded to their left, and Raevyn pulled them away just as a tree crashed mere feet from them—the trunk smoking and charred by lightning. That brought her back to her senses. The storm roared around them, filling the lake that had already been pulled up the shore to cover Aveis's waist, who was still lying unconscious. Myla swore as she jumped down from Raevyn's arms. She thrust out her arms, pushing the lake back and slowing the storm. The rain trickled to a stop, and the clouds lightened before parting, revealing the midday sun.

Myla was soaked to the bone, but her skin thrummed with heat—making a shiver run down her spine. Panting slightly, she turned to look at Raevyn, a sheepish smile on her face.

"I promise every time we kiss, I won't create a hurricane."

Raevyn's lips twitched as he pulled her toward him, capturing her lips in a gentle kiss. "I'll take it as a compliment. There wasn't even a drop of rain when Aveis kissed you for the first time."

She rolled her eyes. "Cocky bastard," she smiled, resting her head against his chest.

****

It wasn't long before Aveis woke up. Myla and Raevyn had curled up near her—partly for warmth and partly because they couldn't keep their hands off each other. Aveis sat up with a wince, gripping the back of her head with a groan.

"What the fuck happened?" She narrowed her eyes at Raevyn. "Did you fucking knock me out?"

"I'm honestly surprised it was the first time I did," Raevyn retorted.

Aveis glanced between the pair of them, obviously confused by their closeness. "Right."

Myla got to her feet, and Raevyn followed suit, intertwining their fingers. "We should get moving. One of us will have to grab our supplies before we leave."

Aveis got to her feet as well, a wary expression on her face. "So, we're just not going to talk about it?"

"About what?" Myla asked, even though she knew exactly what she was talking about.

Aveis raised an eyebrow. "Oh, I don't know. The fact you have magic and now this—" she gestured between Raevyn and Myla. "Is a thing. Did you knock me out so you both could have some alone time? Who the fuck does that?"

"I don't have to explain myself to you," Raevyn snapped.

"It's complicated," Myla said sheepishly, flushing slightly.

"Right," Aveis said again, dubiously. "If you don't want to tell me, fine. I'm assuming you're going to be collecting our supplies, Brute?"

"Me? You should be the one to do it since you put us in this situation to begin with."

"I'm the one with the target on my back," she responded. "And you're the biggest and therefore can carry the most stuff. Besides, I'm sure you don't want to send Myla in alone."

"Myla and I can both go together."

"One person will be less conspicuous—"

"The fuck it is—"

"It's okay," Myla cut in, squeezing Raevyn's hand. "I'll stay with Aveis—make sure she stays out of trouble."

Raevyn looked down at her with a troubled expression. "I don't know—"

"For gods' sake," Aveis said, exasperated. "I know you both just hooked up and everything, but you don't have to be attached at the hip. I think you'll both last ten minutes away from each other."

He glared at her, lip curling up in a snarl. "Just because she's not interested in *you*—"

"It's okay," Myla cut in, stopping the argument from going any further. "We'll be fine here."

Raevyn's eyes softened as he gazed down at her. "I'll hurry back."

Myla smiled, raising up on her tiptoes to kiss his cheek. "I know you will."

Raevyn squeezed her hand before pulling away. He glared at Aveis once more before disappearing into the trees. Myla settled back on the ground, resting her back against a tree trunk.

"So damn possessive," Aveis muttered before sitting down next to Myla. "I'm sorry about this, darling."

Myla turned to look at her, confused. "For what—"

She felt a sharp pain along the back of her head before the world fell into darkness.

Chapter 40

Myla woke up with a throbbing headache. She blinked—disoriented because it appeared night had fallen and she wasn't where she had been. She sat up, looking around wildly. She was in a forest somewhere, but she couldn't hear lapping water, which meant they were far from the lake. She reached for the dagger strapped to her thigh, but it wasn't there—none of her weapons were.

"Welcome back, darling," she grinned, the campfire between them casting ominous shadows across the sharp lines of her face.

"Where are we?" She asked. "What's going on?"

"I apologize for knocking you out," she responded, getting to her feet. "I had to get us out of there, and I didn't have time to explain everything properly to you."

Aveis walked around the fire to crouch in front of her. Myla scooted back as far as she could but didn't make it far, her back slamming into the trunk of a tree a foot behind her.

"I always knew you were special," Aveis said, her voice soft, almost wistful, as she reached up to tuck a loose curl behind Myla's ear. Her fingers lingered a moment longer than necessary.

Myla pulled back, a chill creeping up her spine. She forced herself to meet Aveis's gaze, the unease in her chest growing. "Explain what to me?" she asked, though her voice trembled despite her best efforts to sound sure.

Aveis's eyes flickered with something unreadable, and she leaned closer, her smile more knowing than comforting. "Raevyn is a dragon hunter. One of the best, they say. I don't know why he didn't kill you when he had the chance. Maybe he saw something in you, too. But he would have eventually. You know that." She paused, her expression hardening. "Which is why I never planned to take you to the princess."

Myla's stomach twisted, the words sinking in like stones. She opened her mouth to speak but couldn't find her voice.

Aveis tilted her head, watching Myla closely as if studying her reaction. Her lips parted slightly, but she didn't immediately speak. The silence stretched between them, thick and heavy.

"Then why—" Myla finally managed to ask, her throat tight.

Aveis smiled again, but this time, it was different. There was no warmth in it, only a quiet certainty. Slowly, she extended her hand between them, palm up, and for a moment, nothing happened. Then, with a faint shimmer in the air, a small flame bloomed above her hand, flickering like a star caught in the palm of her fingers.

Myla's breath caught, her heart pounding. She stared at the flame, disbelieving. "You... you're..."

Aveis nodded, her eyes never leaving Myla's face. "I am the princess."

Myla's lips parted in surprise. "But, what? Why would you go with us and tell us you would bring us to the princess? Just for the money?"

"For you," she responded, letting the flame die. "I felt it as soon as I met you. There was something special about you, but I couldn't figure it out until earlier today."

I could have told you that weeks ago.

Myla was startled at her dragon's voice speaking in her mind—clearer than it had ever been.

How did you know? Myla asked her dragon.

Because I'm not completely oblivious. How many times did I tell you to go with the princess? But, no, you had to make things more complicated.

Myla tried not to scowl at her dragon's words as she asked Aveis, "Why tell me now?"

"You saved me, and I plan to return the favor. You can come with me and stay with me and Drathal—"

"Who's Drathal?"

"My dragon. We've found a place where we can live without being bothered. You'll be safe there with us. I don't know what you did or said to convince Raevyn not to kill you, but it won't last. That's why I had to get us out of there." Aveis reached up to cup Myla's cheek. "We can be together."

Myla's mind was reeling—trying to make sense of everything she'd been told and Aveis's offer. Aveis thought Myla had manipulated Raevyn and used his attraction to her to stay alive. Aveis didn't know that Myla and Raevyn loved each other—wouldn't believe that Raevyn would let her live with magic because of that love. She would never trust Raevyn, and Myla couldn't defend him without alienating herself from her. This might be her only chance to get close to the princess and convince her to come home. Even if that meant leaving Raevyn behind, she had to do this. They'd never get a chance like this again. She needed to play her part convincingly, even if it broke her heart.

Myla smiled softly, leaning into her touch. "I'd like that, but I have so many questions."

Aveis settled down across from Myla. "Ask anything, darling. There doesn't have to be any more secrets between us."

"How have you been able to hide in plain sight? And your hair—I thought it was supposed to be white."

"Yes, Drathal and I have been going from place to place for years," Aveis said, her voice steady but her eyes distant, as if she were pulling the memories from deep within. "Until about two years ago, when we found a place to settle. A place no one would think to look for us." Aveis shifted, brushing a few strands of white hair from her face. Her gaze lingered on the strands for a moment, her expression almost absent. "I became a thief to survive," she continued, her words softer now, almost like a confession.

"To be able to feed myself—and Drathal. He's the only true family I've ever had. The only one who didn't betray me."

Myla tilted her head slightly, watching the princess. Gone of the suave, confident thief she'd met weeks ago, replaced by a woman who wanted nothing more than to belong somewhere—a safe haven. That was something she could understand. Myla was lucky enough to have a family that supported her, but she could never truly be herself if the kingdom continued to hunt dragons and magic wielders like animals. Aveis, on the other hand, had the luxury of being a princess and could change the kingdom for the better of those like them. The fact that she ran away at all spoke to something larger. Myla found herself listening intently, her heart heavy with curiosity—and something more.

Aveis met Myla's gaze, and there was a flicker of vulnerability in her eyes. "As for my hair," she continued, her fingers absently tugging at the white strands that framed her face, "the reason it's like this—why it looks so... unnatural—is because I was sick for most of my childhood."

A pause hung in the air, thick with unspoken words. Myla's heart began to race, her stomach churning with a deep sense of dread. All of what Myla knew of the princess's past came from Raevyn and the king. She was eager to learn her side of things, though the way her voice faltered now made Myla's pulse quicken.

The silence stretched on, and Myla found herself leaning forward without realizing it, her sympathy growing in the pit of her stomach.

"They poisoned me," Aveis whispered, her voice so quiet it was almost lost in the stillness. Myla felt the words before she fully understood them, the weight of them pressing into her chest like a sudden, suffocating cloud. Aveis's hands trembled, and she tugged at the white strands again, her fingers moving absently as if to distance herself from the memory. "My parents. They poisoned me every day...tried to trap my magic inside me, keep it locked away. They thought they could control me. Force me to be something I wasn't."

Myla's breath caught. She had always known that Aveis was different—stronger and more capable than most gave her credit for. But this... this was something else entirely.

"My hair," Aveis continued, voice thick with bitterness, "this was the price they made me pay. It's not just the color. The sickness—it left its mark on my body. I've never been the same." Her eyes flickered toward Myla, and for the first time, there was something raw, something fragile in her gaze. "And it's why I can't escape it. Why I can never run far enough."

Myla's heart twisted. There was so much pain in Aveis's voice, so much sorrow. The image of Aveis—charming, fierce, and always in control—seemed to fracture in that moment, replaced by something more vulnerable. She wasn't just the mysterious, untouchable woman who'd captured her. She was a victim, too.

Myla's voice barely rose above a whisper. "I'm sorry."

Aveis looked at her then, her gaze softening just slightly as if Myla's words reached her in a way she hadn't expected. She didn't reply at first; she just swallowed hard, a bitter smile tugging at her lips. "There's nothing to be sorry for. It's just the way of things." But the way she said it sounded more like a question than a statement.

Myla's heart clenched at the quiet desperation in her voice. She thought of her own interaction with the potion and how detached she had felt—like a part of her had been cut away. She couldn't even imagine what it would have been like to constantly have the potion in her system, slowly eating away an essential part of herself until there was nothing left but a hollow space. Sorrow clawed at her chest at the thought of a child going through that day in and day out.

"So, you ran away from home?" Myla asked softly, as if afraid to ask. She remembered Raevyn saying that the princess's life was hard, but to run away from home at *eight* years old was inconceivable to her.

"Not exactly. When I was eight years old, my parents sent me away," she answered. "They didn't tell me where I was going or why or even when I'd come back. All they said was when I came home that, I would be cured. They had always thought of my magic as a sickness and had done all they could to cure me of it. They had created potions that held my magic in, but couldn't take it away completely. At the time, I was happy to go. All I had ever wanted was to make my parents happy. I thought that if my magic was taken from me, then my parents would finally love me." Aveis sighed. "I think my father did love me—in his own sort of way—even if he was trying to change me. My mother, I know, hates me and has since the moment I was born. I left the castle with a caravan of people—determined to come back changed and be the princess my parents wanted and the kingdom needed.

"We weren't far into the woods when our caravan was attacked by bandits. I'm not sure if anyone but I survived. They only took me so they could use me for ransom. I would have used my magic to get away, but my parents had given me a potion earlier to suppress my magic. I could feel it at the tips of my fingers, but I couldn't reach it. It was in that moment that I wished for my magic in a way I had never done before. I had always seen my magic as a fault because that was all I had been taught. I cried and begged—terrified out of my mind. Then I felt something tug at my magic. Something was reaching for me, and I heard Drathal in my mind for the first time. He told me to hold on and that he was coming for me.

"It didn't take long for Drathal to show up. He blotted out the entire sun before he landed in front of us. The bandit and I were thrown from the horse. I hit my head, and my vision was blurry as I watched Drathal swallow the man whole. There was a moment when I thought I was going to die, but Drathal looked at me, and his eyes were the same color my mother had told me mine had been when I was born. The color that told her I was a demon of some kind, and it was only with the potion that my eyes became a more *human* color. But, looking into Drathal's eyes, the last thing I thought about him was that he was a demon or a monster. It felt like a part of me was finally whole. I wasn't afraid after that. Even when he scooped me up in his claws and flew away. I passed out along the way, and when I woke up, Drathal was curled up beside me, and food and water lay by my head. He told me that I could stay with him. That if I wanted to stay, then he would keep me safe, and I wouldn't ever have to be afraid. He said that if I wanted to go back to Cassia, then he would take me but warned that I would never be safe there so long as magic was in my veins. I looked up at him, and the connection between us felt like home—home in a way that being with my parents would never be. So, I decided to stay, and he kept his promise."

"Do you ever regret staying?" Myla asked softly.

Aveis shook her head with a scoff. "No. Of course, I have thought of 'what ifs,' but the more I thought about it, the more I knew I had made the right decision. Rosebourne will never be safe for people with magic—you know that as well as I do. With him, I am allowed to be as I am and not feel faulted for having magic because magic is a gift. A gift that will keep me safe."

Myla knew she was treading on dangerous water but decided to push just a bit farther. "You are the princess and heir to the throne." She spoke slowly. "Would it not be within your power to change the law and make magic legal again?"

240

Aveis huffed, straightening her legs—the tip of her right boot brushing against Myla's thigh. "That law is centuries old. There is no human alive that remembers how it was. All the people know is what they've been taught, which is that dragons and magic wielders are evil. If I were to take the throne and try to change the laws to bring back magic—there would be riots, and I have no doubt that the people would stage a coup to get me off the throne. There wouldn't be many who would see the change as good."

"But—"

"But nothing," she replied, her tone brooking no argument. "I wouldn't—couldn't ever go back there while my parents are still alive. I'd be powerless, and even if I were to go back after they die, no one would see me as a leader. Everyone thinks I'm dead—best to keep it that way."

Myla nodded. "I'm sorry. I didn't mean to upset you."

Aveis took a deep breath, and her expression softened. "You didn't," she said, reaching out to take Myla's hand. "It's just a sensitive subject, is all."

"Understood."

Myla would have added that she wouldn't bring it up again but decided against it since it would be a lie. This was her chance to convince the princess to take her throne. She was adamant now, but with time, Myla thought she could persuade her. If she could convince Aveis that she could make Rosebourne a safe place for her, Drathal, and all others with magic, then Aveis would come with her. A fight was out of the question now. Aveis may not see herself as a princess, but she was, and maybe this was the gods' way to bring change to Rosebourne and to fix a centuries' old mistake.

Chapter 41

"I have some questions of my own," Aveis told Myla, leaning forward so her elbows rested on her thighs. "How did you end up on assignment with a dragon hunter when you have magic?"

"Unfortunate coincidence," Myla lied. "As you know, I'm still a recruit, and usually recruits aren't sent on assignments until they're knighted, but I think because my father's the general and I've been one of the top recruits—they made an exception. From what little Raevyn told me, I think they're running low on dragon hunters."

"They tried to recruit you to become a dragon hunter?" Aveis laughed. "How ironic."

"Kind of—this was sort of a trial run, I think. But, obviously, I wasn't going to hurt the princess—you or your dragon." Myla added quickly. "I honestly didn't think we were going to find you. But, I also held out a little hope, wanting to meet someone that's like me and maybe find a place where I can be safe."

She can be that place if you stop fucking lying, her dragon snarled.

You don't know that, Myla snapped back. *Besides, having her assume the throne would have positive, long-lasting outcomes. She can bring magic back to this kingdom.*

You're naïve if you think one person will change things.

It starts with one person—I would help her, and I know there are more of us out there. We owe it to them to try. Maybe it'll even get you and whoever else out of hiding.

Her dragon hummed but didn't add anything else.

"And what of your family? I'm assuming they know about your magic. It's surprising that the general of all people decided to let you live."

Myla wanted to say that it wasn't surprising since he was her father, but hesitated, thinking about Aveis's own experience. Her parents hadn't killed her but had poisoned her daily, slowly sucking the life from her.

243

"I was lucky," she admitted, feeling a pang of guilt in her chest. "I know they have no problems with me, but the rest of the kingdom...I have to do what's best for me. They'd understand."

She nodded solemnly. "It can be lonely sometimes, but we have each other now."

Myla smiled, feeling grateful for the sentiment, but the guilt remained. She really hoped she was making the right decision.

****

Aveis didn't tell Myla where they were going, and Myla didn't ask—knowing that she'd find out in due time. It had been about two weeks, and Myla couldn't stop thinking about Raevyn. She could imagine his face when he went back to the lake to find them missing—imagine the thoughts that must have run through his head. He probably thought that Aveis had kidnapped her or worse. Myla wished she could have explained everything to him and hoped one day she'd get the chance to.

She was surprised when they rode into Naeron around midday. Given that Naeron was the largest port city in the kingdom, it didn't seem like the best place to hide. There was always a large number of knights stationed here at any given time. Her surprise only grew when they headed toward the dock, where Aveis told Myla they'd be taking a ship to get to their final destination.

The sun was high in the sky with no clouds to block its heat. They bypassed people unloading cargo, causing the unsteady wood under Myla's feet to rock precariously. She stumbled a little as she tried to keep up with Aveis, who was gliding between people with ease as if she'd done it thousands of times before.

Aveis walked up to a tall, stocky man and tapped him on the shoulder. He turned to face them, a scowl appearing on his face when he locked eyes with Aveis. His

244

red hair was unruly—the long curls barely contained under his wide-brimmed hat. He wore a thick brown overcoat over a white, billowy shirt that was tucked into black leather trousers.

"Hello, Captain Enjorren," Aveis grinned.

"Not a chance, wench," the captain snarled. "Yer debts need settling before stepping foot on me ship."

"As if I ever would," she replied sweetly. "I've got enough gold to pay my debts and pay for another trip."

He glanced at Myla before turning his green eyes back on Aveis. "Another landlubber costs extra."

"Of course," Aveis replied amicably. "I believe this should suffice."

She handed him a small velvet sack laden with gold coins. He took it and immediately handed it to the man next to him. He was slightly shorter than the captain, with thick dreadlocks held back in a maroon bandana. He wore a similar outfit, but his overcoat was dark blue, complimenting his rich umber complexion. The man scanned the contents before nodding.

"This'll cover it," the man confirmed.

The captain huffed. "Any hornswoggle, and I'll toss ye overboard me self."

Aveis saluted to him before looping her arm in Myla's and tugging her onto the boat. "Aye, aye, Captain," she called back.

"Keep 'em in yer sights, Keenstone," the captain ordered the man next to him as he snatched the sack of gold from his hands.

"Aye, Captain."

"Are you going to tell me where we're going?" Myla whispered. "I didn't realize we'd be leaving the kingdom."

Aveis squeezed her arm in reassurance. "You'll see in a few days. We're not technically leaving the kingdom."

An island, then. A brilliant place to hide, especially when they could fly away to escape if necessary. Myla followed Aveis below deck, where they set their supplies down next to two hammocks. They had restocked on supplies the day after they left Raevyn behind, going into a nearby town outside Tanin. Myla had been surprised and a little disappointed when Raevyn didn't show up. For the past few weeks, she'd expected him to, but now that they were sailing away to some remote island—she gave up on that hope. If he hadn't found them yet, he wouldn't now. She was on her own.

Chapter 42

Do you have a name? Myla asked her dragon that night as she struggled to fall asleep. She was feeling nauseous from the rocking ship. She'd never been on a ship in her life and had never imagined how unsteady it would be. The hammocks around her never stopped swaying, and there were many on the crew who snored quite loudly.

Of course, I have a name. Her dragon huffed in annoyance.

Myla waited for a beat, but when they didn't elaborate, she added, *and it is...?*

Vavna.

And why did you decide to reach out now? If I didn't know any better, I'd think you wanted to keep me alive.

Vavna huffed again. *Our fates have been intertwined since the moment of your birth. I've tried to ignore it as much as I could, knowing where you were, but whether I liked it or not, our bond only grew the more you used your magic and the more you grew. It was only a matter of time before you would become too hard to ignore. That day came when you lost control of your magic after watching your friend get attacked.*

Thinking back on the night that started all this made Myla grimace. She knew in her heart that the law was wrong, but regardless, she'd started a chain event that killed a hunter and nearly her best friend. There wasn't enough hope in her to think that they'd be the only ones negatively affected before she succeeded in her quest.

I admit, I was curious, Vavna continued. *And I peeked through the door between our bond, and I've been able to tune into your thoughts. We would have been able to communicate earlier had you not stubbornly shut me out after I tried to save you. I will be able to live without our bond—I've seen it firsthand—but it's a long and taxing recovery. It is inevitable since mortals live short lives, but it is easier to recover from a broken bond caused by natural death.*

So, it only matters to you because it affects you in the long run? Myla asked, slightly perturbed.

Yes, so if you'd stop making stupid decisions—I'd appreciate it.

I'll try my best, she responded dryly. *Any other words of wisdom?*

Yes, don't betray the princess or let her find out that you want her to take the throne. It'll end in your death.

****

The next few days, the captain put Myla and Aveis to work. Since Myla knew nothing about sailing, she was forced to do the grunt work. On the first day, she had to swab the deck. Even though it didn't seem to make much of a difference despite her scrubbing until her skin cracked and the sun faded from the sky. Today, she'd been assigned to the kitchens. She didn't know the first thing when it came to cooking but didn't argue—wanting to do anything but clean. Pirates were disgusting, to say the least, and there were more than a few incriminating stains she was forced to scrub yesterday.

Myla stepped into the kitchen to see an older man around her father's age. He was tall and muscular, with colorful tattoos running up his arms and neck. His bald head was already gleaming with sweat as he leaned over a pot on the stove.

"Hi," Myla said when the cook didn't acknowledge her entrance. "The captain asked me to help you today."

The man grunted as he added some seasoning to the pot. "Great, it was a long time coming. You can start by cutting this onion."

He tossed one to her without looking at her, and Myla barely caught it. She turned the onion over in her hand,

248

not entirely knowing what to do with it. She had very distant memories of watching her mother cook as she sat on the counter—chubby legs swinging back and forth as she asked her mother if she could taste. But that had been before her father was promoted to General, and they were able to afford a bigger house with a full staff of cooks and cleaners.

The cook didn't seem to be in a talkative mood, and she didn't want to ask what to do and be given the same look the captain had given her when she said that she didn't know anything about sailing. Besides, cutting an onion couldn't be too difficult. She placed the onion on the counter and grabbed a knife. She started cutting into it—the skin of it flaking off as she did so. The onion slipped precariously under her grip as if it were a living thing trying to get free. She was so focused on the task and not cutting herself that she didn't notice the cook walk up to her. The knife was suddenly plucked out of her hands, causing her to jolt. She looked up to see the cook glaring down at her.

"What the hell are you doing?"

"Cutting the onion," Myla replied, but it sounded more like a question.

He squinted at her. "Have you ever worked in a kitchen before?" When Myla shook her head, he sighed. "I asked for an assistant, and he gave me a novice. Fantastic."

"I'm only helping for the day."

He raised an eyebrow. "Why's that?"

"Because I'm being dropped off tomorrow."

"Tomorrow? But the only land nearby is..." he trailed off before squinting at her. "Why are you being sent to the cursed island?"

"I'm going with Aveis. Why is it cursed?"

"You'd have to ask her that," He replied before gesturing with the onion. "You need to peel this first." He started pulling the purple layers off the onion to reveal the white underneath. "Then you cut it into small bites." He demonstrated how small by cutting up half the onion. He placed a few more onions beside her and gestured to them. "Think you can handle it?"

Myla nodded. "Yes, sir."

He harrumphed and went to the other side of the counter, where he started cutting up meat. For the next few hours, they worked. The cook—Marione, Myla had learned—showed her various tasks, and Myla found that she didn't hate cooking. It definitely beat cleaning. She was starting to get into a rhythm, and she couldn't help but think about training with the other recruits back home. Marione reminded her a lot of her father in how he taught—which was show once and then throw them into the fire. Lucky for Myla, she was used to picking up on things fast and cooking didn't seem to be much different.

"How long have you been a cook?" Myla asked.

"Ever since I was a wee lad," the cook replied. "I grew up in Naeron, and as soon as I was old enough to work, I got a job on a ship. Their cook took me under his wing and taught me everything I know. It wasn't long until I was skilled enough to work on my own."

"Why work on a ship? Now that you've got the skills, can't you work for a tavern or somewhere in the city?"

Marione shrugged. "I supposed I could've, but I never thought about it. Regardless, I enjoy being at sea."

"And what do you know about the cursed island?" Myla couldn't help but ask. She wanted to know as much as she could. Maybe he'd tell her something Aveis wouldn't.

The cook stiffened, pausing his stirring for just a moment before continuing. "Not much. I've heard rumors and have seen things that I can't quite explain, but I know nothing for sure."

"Like what?"

For a moment, Marione didn't speak, and Myla thought he wasn't going to answer. Finally, he looked over at her. "The only thing I know for sure is that Aveis has been hitching a ride on this boat for the last few years, and those she brings with her are never heard from again."

A chill ran down Myla's spine. "Do you know who they were?"

He turned away and continued stirring the stew of meat and vegetables. "Most were knights."

Myla thought of the king's words when he sent her on this mission: *We don't know where the dragon is keeping her, and we have scoured the kingdom, but those we have sent have never been heard from again.* Aveis had told her she'd never offered to take anyone to the princess, but what if she was lying? What if, when she caught wind of someone trying to find her, she killed them to keep her secret? What if that's what Aveis was doing to her?

"Thank you for telling me."

He took the spoon out of the pot and covered it with a lid. "That ought to do it." He turned to look at her again. "I could help you. This ship is heading to Adratus. You could make a new life there."

Myla was taken aback by his offer to help a near stranger as if it were that simple. Maybe it was.

She gave him an appreciative smile. "Thank you for the offer, but this is something I've got to do."

Marione nodded.

The rest of the time, they cleaned. It was nearly noon when Marione gave her a bowl of stew and told her she could head out before the rest of the crew showed up. She was grateful for that, wanting some time to herself before she saw Aveis again. She took her bowl and headed to her hammock.

I thought you said staying with the princess would keep me safe, Myla snapped at her dragon. *Did you know she's been luring people to their deaths?*

This may come as a surprise to you, but I don't know everything. And besides, she's been luring people she perceived as threats. She thinks you're a victim like she is.

Myla felt herself relax, but only slightly. *I suppose that makes a bit of sense. But what if Raevyn was right about her?*

Vavna snarled. *Nothing that man told you is true. He's been manipulating you from the beginning. He is the one who would have been the death of you—not the princess.*

You don't know him like I do—

No, I know him better. He has killed dozens of my friends and family. He would have done the same to you once he had the chance.

But he didn't—

One hesitation doesn't excuse all the terrible acts he committed.

Myla sighed but didn't argue further, knowing it was fruitless. She finally had someone to work out her thoughts with, but they turned out to be even more stubborn than she was.

Hardly.

Myla shut the door between their connection. Even if she didn't believe Vavna when it came to Aveis and Raevyn, she knew that she didn't have a choice. She needed to take this opportunity. Whatever happened, and for whatever reason, it was out of her control. She couldn't focus on any of that. She needed to stay alert and be ready for anything. Tomorrow could just be the beginning or be her end.

Myla pretended she was asleep when Aveis came below deck hours later. She was surprised when Aveis brushed a kiss on Myla's forehead before climbing into her

252

own hammock. She really hoped it wouldn't turn into a fight in the end.

Chapter 43

The following day, Myla was awoken by Aveis at dawn, telling her they were near the island. Myla quickly braided her hair and changed into a pair of leather trousers and a white blouse—not bothering with a corset. She tied up her knee-high boots and slipped a dagger in each boot along with another sheathed to her thigh. She strapped her sword to her waist. She was glad she had it on her when they left Raevyn. She had gotten the blade from her father when she became a recruit. It had been crafted and explicitly balanced for Myla, and her initials were even engraved on the hilt. It was a gift she cherished more than anything.

Having packed the night before, Myla grabbed her supplies and followed Aveis up to where the captain and first mate were. The captain was looking off in the distance with a spyglass. The sky was still dark, the sun behind them barely penetrating the thick fog around them. Myla squinted, but she couldn't see the island. Before she could ask, the captain set the spyglass down on the map in front of him.

"Ye know what to do, wrench," Captain Enjorren said, pointing. "Keep her steady onward southeast. Or don't and drift out to sea for all I care."

Myla turned to the captain, eyes wide. "You're not getting us closer than this?"

The captain scoffed. "That ain't part of the bargain."

"It's okay," Aveis smiled, taking Myla's free hand. "We'll get there quick enough with your help." She winked.

Myla nodded, catching her drift. "Okay," she replied, heading toward one of the rowboats with Keenstone close on their heels.

"If ye ruin another dinghy, I'm raising me fee!" Captain Enjorren called to their backs.

Aveis only rolled her eyes—not bothering to respond. Keenstone helped them into the rowboat and handed them the supplies.

"Good luck," Keenstone said, giving Myla a look she couldn't quite discern, but it made dread fill her stomach.

Myla gave him a nod before he lowered the rowboat into the water. Once the boat landed, Aveis untied the ropes on either side before using the oar to push their boat away from the ship. They each took an oar and started rowing away, heading in the direction the captain had told them. Only when they were hidden in the fog did she use her magic to propel the boat toward the island. It wasn't long before she saw the island in the distance. Jutting out in the middle of the island was a mountain, and on top was a stone castle overgrown with ivy. On the left side of the castle, a large portion of the stone wall had been caved in, and various cracks and holes littered the remainder of the castle. Other than that, the castle seemed to be in good shape.

"What exactly is this place?" Myla asked curiously.

"An old royal vacation spot, if you can believe it," Aveis responded, stretching out her legs. "It hasn't been used for decades and has become forgotten. But, since it is still officially owned by the crown, there are no occupants."

"Aren't you afraid that Captain Enjorren will tell any of the knights stationed in Naeron that you're living here?"

Aveis shook her head. "Enjorren and I have an understanding. He doesn't like to interact with the knights any more than I do. He's done plenty of illegal things in his time, and so long as it's profitable to him—he won't jeopardize it."

When they got close to the shore, Aveis jumped out of the boat and pushed it onto the sand. Myla helped her push it until it was a few meters away from the water. The shore made way to a jungle that surrounded the mountain. The trees in front of her were a lot smaller than those toward the back of the island—as if the trees were newly grown. Myla could imagine that Aveis and her dragon had burnt the original trees, and they were only starting to grow

255

back. There was a path in front of her that led through the jungle and up to the mountain. Along the side of the mountain, Myla could see stairs that had been built into the rock. She also saw rope hanging down from the mountain that led up to the castle. She looked up to see if she could see anyone or anything within the castle, but it was too dark and foggy to make out much. She thought she saw a shadow move through the cavern on the left side of the castle, but she couldn't be sure. From what she could tell, they were alone. The only sounds were the lapping waves and insects in the jungle.

"Home sweet home," Aveis smiled, holding out her arms. "Come on, I'll show you to your new room."

Myla followed Aveis toward the path leading up to the castle. They stopped in front of the cliffside, where a plank of wood tethered with ropes led up to the castle.

Myla eyed it skeptically. "What is this?"

Aveis smirked, placing the bags on the plank. "A faster way to get us up the mountain."

"How exactly does this work?" Myla asked, her grip on her bag tightening in anticipation.

Aveis pointed up the cliff, and Myla's eyes followed the rope to see it disappear inside the castle. "Drathal knocks over some boulders in a net that are connected to this plank. As it falls, the momentum brings us up."

"Are you telling me this thing launches up into the air?"

"Essentially."

"I think I'd rather take the stairs than be launched into the air, thanks," Myla responded, taking a step back.

"I get it. You're scared. No shame in that. You can take the stairs, and I'll meet you up there in about an hour."

Myla tensed and narrowed her eyes slightly—the competitive side of her rearing up. "I'm not scared."

"Oh?" Aveis asked as she tied her bags down to the plank with a spare piece of rope. "Then prove it."

Myla knew Aveis was goading her, but her need to prove Aveis wrong was too strong to ignore. "Fine."

Myla walked up to her and dropped her bags down on the plank. Aveis grinned and tied them down with the rest of the stuff.

Aveis straightened and held out her hand. "Hold on tight, darling."

Myla stepped onto the plank and took hold of Aveis's hand, and one of the ropes tethered to the plank. Aveis's grip was firm, and the touch alone caused warmth to spread throughout her body. Aveis radiated heat—more so than anyone she knew. Myla just hoped so wouldn't get scorched.

"Ready?"

Before Myla could answer, Aveis whistled, and she heard a crash before they were shot upward. Myla screamed as her stomach dropped—nearly losing her footing, but Aveis kept her in place.

"Get ready to jump!" Aveis called over the wind.

Myla turned her head to gape at her, silently cursing the stubborn side of herself that got her into this situation. "What?"

"Now!" Aveis called.

Aveis jumped into the window and—with Myla's hand in hers—she could only follow. Myla swore and dove into the window. She had expected to land on stone but was pleasantly surprised when she landed on a mass of pillows. Her weapons dug into her, but Myla couldn't help but laugh as the adrenaline rushed through her. She sat up and turned to Aveis, who was on her knees and grinning at her.

"That was fucking insane," Myla replied, causing Aveis to laugh.

257

She got to her feet and started pulling their supplies in from the window. "That's nothing. Just wait until you ride on the back of a dragon for the first time. There's nothing like it."

Myla got up and helped Aveis grab the bags. She didn't add that she might never experience it since her dragon didn't like her much.

Maybe you'll grow on me, Vavna responded. *Like a fungus.*

Would you stop reading my thoughts? Myla snapped back.

Then stop making them so loud.

You're insufferable.

Right back at you.

Myla rolled her eyes as she was led out of the room and down the hall. The hall looked similar to those in the palace in Cassia, except these halls were worn with age. They looked as if they had been cleaned, but there were cracks in the walls, and the rugs along the ground were torn. The chandeliers above her were broken in places but were all lit, casting rippling shadows along the ceiling.

They walked nearly to the end of the corridor before Aveis stopped in front of a doorway. Myla peered inside to see a room about the size as the one she had at home. There was a large canopy bed in the middle of the room with two large bookcases on either side. In front of the bed was a wardrobe, and next to it was another door that led to a washroom. On the same wall as the bedroom door was a desk, and across the room was a large window seat. The entire room was beautifully decorated in shades of blue and gold. It was also covered in a thick layer of dust that nearly made Myla sneeze.

"Sorry about the state of the room," Aveis said sheepishly. "I didn't find the need to clean all the rooms in the castle—just the ones I use often. I can help you clean up."

Myla shook her head. "No, it's fine. This room is more than generous, and I won't have a hard time cleaning up."

Myla ruffled through her supplies, pulled out her bar of soap, and shaved off a few pieces before throwing them into the room. She set her supplies down by the door and walked over to the window, pushing it open. She stepped back until she stood next to Aveis and held her hands out in front of her. She took a deep breath and reached for her magic. She felt the ocean far below her and pulled. A current of water rushed through the window, and Aveis took a step back as the water filled the room, but Myla didn't allow the water to pass the doorway. She swirled the water until the shavings of soap dissolved. She pressed the water in the nooks and crannies of the room—bringing the dirt out until the water was opaque. Then Myla pushed the water out of the room, making sure that every drop was leaked out.

"That's amazing," Aveis breathed, coming up to stand beside her again. "That would have been extremely helpful when I was scrubbing this place down."

Myla smiled at her. "It can be quite useful," she agreed.

"I never thought I'd see another wield magic. I never thought..."

"You'd meet someone else who understands," Myla supplied, and Aveis smiled at her.

"Yeah. My ancestors destroyed that hope. I thought Drathal and I were the last of our kind. I thought the gods must have a fucked-up sense of humor to give magic to the princess of the kingdom that wiped out dragons. But maybe there are more people like us out there," Aveis said, eyes searching hers. "Do you know of anyone else? Or anything about your dragon?"

Myla almost told her she'd been hearing her dragon for weeks now but hesitated. If she told her about Vavna, then Aveis would try anything within her power to get there with Drathal. Then, there would be no chance she could convince Aveis to go back home. It started to click in her head why Aveis had taken Myla to their hiding place despite not knowing her very well. She hadn't done it out of the goodness of her heart—she was out to get something, just as Raevyn had warned her. Aveis wanted this information from Myla ever since she saw her do magic. She'd been trying to get closer to her just as Myla had been doing. They'd both been out for something this entire time. But how could she use this information to help her?

Myla shook her head. "No. I didn't even know about you until the king and queen told me before they sent me away with Raevyn."

Aveis nodded, looking slightly disappointed, but the look was quickly replaced with her easy smile. "Come on, there's something I want to show you."

Chapter 44

Myla followed Aveis down the hall and down a set of stairs. They walked to the end of the hall and to a set of double doors. She pushed them open, and Myla's jaw dropped as she took in the grand library. She had never seen a library this big. The ceiling was several meters high, and all the walls were covered in floor-to-ceiling bookcases. There was a second-floor landing that looked over the rows of bookshelves encasing a small open area in the middle with tables and desks. Spiral staircases were placed on either side of the room, leading up to the landing and holding even more books. Myla had only ever gone to the library at the university in Cassia. She had thought that was impressive, but this library was at least twice the size.

"This is amazing," Myla breathed, eyes roaming the room in an attempt to take it all in.

Aveis smiled. "Yeah. It's my favorite place in the entire castle. It took me weeks to clean and dust it all."

Myla followed Aveis inside and to a table that had a pile of books stacked on top. "These are all the books I found about magic," Aveis said, gesturing to the pile. "I thought you'd like to look at them."

Her eyes widened as she looked over book covers depicting dragons and magic wielders. "But I thought they were all destroyed."

"Most were," Aveis agreed. "But the queen at that time was an avid scholar. She thought burning books should never be an option, no matter the circumstance. She had been overruled in that regard, but she had kept as many as she could and hid them in this castle. I found them in a hidden compartment behind a bookcase."

Myla brushed her fingers over one of the covers. "Are you sure it's okay for me to look at these?"

"Of course. You have every right to this knowledge. Hopefully, it'll give you a better understanding of yourself and your magic."

****

Myla spent the rest of the day reading. Aveis had left her to it, for which Myla was grateful. Myla wasn't sure if she'd ever get a chance to read about magic or dragons and wanted to learn as much as she could. She spent the first few hours in the library before hunger insisted she take her studies to her room so she could get some of her rations.

Myla learned dragons lived for centuries. That humans were born with magic, and only in rare cases did magic manifest later in life. A dragon's magic was vast, and their human only got a small fraction. Humans could use more of their dragon's magic than what was given, but only if the dragon was alive and allowed it. When a magic wielder's dragon died, then the human's magic was significantly weakened. The stronger the bond between a dragon and their human, the stronger their magic was. Myla hadn't seen the depth of Aveis's magic firsthand, but she knew her connection with Drathal must be extremely strong. The magical bond between a magic wielder and their dragon varied, and as it strengthened, they could communicate in what they called 'mind speak.' This would only work if both parties were open to the connection.

Myla set the book on the bed next to her. She closed her eyes and reached for her magic, as she had done countless times. She felt the water in the air, in the clouds above her, and the ocean below her—humming in her mind and through her blood. She reached down, trying to find the bottom in her well of magic. She kept reaching until it felt like her skin was on fire. She gasped, opening her eyes just in time to watch the tornado of water she'd unknowingly created fall.

A knock sounded at her door, and Myla jumped. She quickly pulled the water out of her bed and the floor and shoved it out the window before calling for her to come in.

Aveis stepped inside with a smile. "Hey, how do you like the books?"

Myla returned the smile. "They're extraordinary. Thank you again for letting me read them."

"Of course. I'm glad you're enjoying them."

"I was just reading about mind speak. Do you hear Drathal? How exactly does it work?"

"I'm not entirely sure," Aveis admitted. "He is this sort of presence in my mind, and if I want to speak with him, then all I must do is tap into it."

"Have you always felt his presence in your mind?"

She shook her head. "I only felt it the first day we met. When Drathal decided to let me in."

Myla nodded. "Does it work on other dragons? Is that how other dragons speak to one another—through mind speak?"

"Partially, yes. They also speak to one another as humans do."

"You mentioned you thought a place existed where other dragons were living—how come Drathal never tried to reach out through mind speak to find it?"

Aveis's face fell as if a terrible thought crossed her mind. "Mind speak between dragons only works if they have a bond. It doesn't have to be strong, but at least one sort of interaction has to take place for the bond to manifest. Drathal didn't have many such connections since he was so young when the war started, and he lost them all when they were slaughtered."

Myla's stomach dropped. "That's awful."

"Yeah, he's been cut off from his kind ever since. He's yet to cross paths with any other dragon and is convinced he is the last of his kind. That is until I told him about you. He'll never say so, but your existence gives him hope as it does me."

Myla smiled, trying not to wince as a sharp pang of guilt pierced her chest. "I'm glad."

"Going through the books, are you wondering about your own dragon and how to reach out?" Aveis asked.

"Yeah. I tried reaching out to them but didn't feel anything." Myla lied.

"Give it time. I'm sure they are just waiting to show themselves. Dragons don't trust humans—for good reason. Drathal had planned never to make himself known to me but ultimately chose to save me, and I will always be grateful for it."

"How are you so sure my dragon's alive?"

"Your magic," she said simply. "You're strong. Moreso than I think even you know. I've seen it, and I can feel it."

"Feel it?"

"Yeah. I felt it when I first saw you, but I wasn't sure what it was. Can you not feel mine?"

Myla thought about how she'd felt when she first met Aveis. She'd instantly been drawn to her, and her magic had reacted to her presence in a way that Myla now recognized as familiarity. She'd thought that attraction had caused her magic to reach out, but it had really been her magic's way of telling her that Aveis was like her. She hadn't consciously known that Aveis was a wielder, but her magic did, and apparently, Vavna had too. Myla couldn't help but think maybe that was why Aveis had come onto her as well—not recognizing the connection for what it was. Just another way Myla was deceiving her, she thought with a stab of guilt, even though that hadn't been her intention.

"I guess I can."

Aveis smiled knowingly before gesturing out the door. "I was just about to make supper if you wanted to join me."

265

Myla got to her feet. "Sounds great."

Chapter 45

Myla couldn't help but stare as Aveis moved about the kitchen as if she'd done it countless times before. She was usually a person who moved through life seemingly at ease despite her circumstances, but here in the kitchen, it was different. The ease with which she moved was more believable and not full of the usual bravado that had always felt like a mask to Myla.

Aveis grabbed some pork and started cooking it over the stove as Myla prepared a salad. Aveis had another pot cooking with rice to go along with their meal. Myla definitely wasn't as adept in the kitchen, so when Aveis handed her a thorough receipt, Myla took it gratefully. It was definitely a lot easier to follow than a middle-aged man grunting at her.

They were silent as they worked, and Myla's mind wandered to Raevyn yet again, but she wouldn't let herself dwell on him. She needed to focus on the task at hand, which started with getting to know Aveis better.

"How did you learn to cook like this? Are you just gifted, or was there a lot of trial and error involved?"

"Most of it was trial and error, but I knew the basics before I came here."

"I didn't know they taught princesses how to cook," Myla said, surprised. "That seems like a task reserved for those below your class."

"It is. I wasn't supposed to learn how to cook, and I hadn't meant to. When I was younger, I always felt like an outsider, and I hated even going down the hallways and seeing anyone because they always gave me looks that ranged from fear to disgust. Which, of course, made me feel like absolute shit. So, you can imagine my relief when I found a secret passageway in the library to get around and avoid people entirely."

Aveis flipped the pieces of pork over, pressing the flat end of the spatula against each piece. They sizzled, and the savory smell wafted over Myla, making her stomach growl. "The passage led to a grate in the kitchen, but before I could grab a little snack, I saw the Royal Cook making biscuits. I was so fascinated with what he was doing and how all those seemingly random ingredients could make something so delicious. It just seemed so magical to me at the time. I got a little too close to the grate, trying to get a better look, and ended up knocking it over." Aveis smiled softly. "The cook looked at me, and it was clear that he recognized me. I waited for him to give me a look like everyone else did, but his expression softened, and he held out a spatula for me and asked if I wanted to help him.

"After that, I came back every day for months, and he showed me how to make a plethora of things. I remember he said that if being a princess didn't work out, I was always welcome to work in his kitchen. If anyone else had heard that, they would have been scandalized, but I was so happy because being in the kitchen had become a safe place for me, and the thought of just *being* without having to worry about anything other than the food I was making—it felt like a dream."

Myla smiled. "He sounds like a great man. And he obviously taught you well."

Aveis nodded. "He was, and he did." Her smile faltered a little. "But then my parents found out, and they were furious with me and the cook for 'putting me to work like a peasant.'" Aveis transferred the cooked pork onto two plates, along with a generous helping of rice for each of them. "They fired him and told him that he was lucky they didn't hang him for his so-called crimes. I cried and begged my parents not to do it and that it wasn't his fault. Of course, they didn't listen to me, so all I could do was apologize to the cook. He smiled at me and knelt down in front of me— telling me not to worry about him and that he was glad to have gotten the time to get to know me." A tear trickled down her cheek, and she quickly wiped it away. "I never saw him again, but I never forgot what he taught me."

Myla placed a comforting hand on Aveis's shoulder. "I'm so sorry."

Aveis looked up at her—eyes sparkling with unshed tears—and smiled. "It's okay. I just hope that he was able to find a job. A better one where he's appreciated for his talent and treated with the respect he deserves."

Myla squeezed her shoulder. "I hope so, too. Who knows, maybe you'll see him again one day."

Aveis raised an eyebrow. "If he stayed in Cassia, then I doubt it."

Myla just shrugged, pulling back to load their plates with the finished salad. They walked over to the table with their plates and sat beside each other.

The more she learned about Aveis, the more she started to believe her dragon. It was clear that Aveis wasn't planning to kill her. If she had wanted to, she would have had plenty of opportunities. Aveis trusted Myla, at least to the extent that she didn't think Myla would betray her. She needed to capitalize on that trust to get Aveis to listen to her. She needed to figure out what would convince Aveis to leave this all behind.

She was thinking about what she could say to bring up Cassia when Aveis broke the silence.

"What's it like?" Aveis asked, almost shyly.

Myla looked at her. "What's what like?"

"Living in the city. I can barely remember it, and what I remember is behind stone walls. The only time I went out into the city was when I was leaving it."

Myla thought about it for a moment. She knew she should be explaining how great the city was and convincing Aveis to go back. But, in all honesty, she didn't enjoy living in the city. She enjoyed being close to her family and having everything she needed close by, but the city was noisy, dirty, and full of people. Myla had never been much of a people person and enjoyed her solitude.

Pushing past all that, she thought about the times she enjoyed being in the city: going out to dinner with Wrynn, shopping with her sister, visiting the library with her mother, and shadowing her father while he was on patrol when she was little. There was so much to do around the city, and when she was with the ones she loved—the city became a little brighter.

"With every place, it has its perks and downsides. I think any place can be wonderful if you're surrounded by the right people. Most of the time, I can barely stand the city since it's loud and messy, but when I'm with my family or friends—that doesn't matter. All I care about is who I'm with and not where I am." Myla blushed slightly. "I know that's not the answer you were looking for—"

"It's not, but I think that's an even better answer." Aveis smiled at her, ember eyes bright. "Drathal and I have been comfortable here for many years. But I would give it all up if I could find a place to live with people like us."

Aveis scanned Myla's face—obviously looking for something or some kind of reaction on her face to indicate if she had any sort of information on such a place. The guilt rose up again, but Myla kept her face carefully neutral, pushing back the relentless guilt.

"Is there such a place? Do you think there are more people like us?"

"I'm not sure. They would need to be expert hiders to stay under my parents' radar for so long, especially with their secret force of highly trained dragon hunters always on the prowl. I wasn't supposed to have powers, but the fact that I did meant that there was at least one dragon out there. Now, with you, there's another one. It's possible there is an entire colony living under our noses."

"That can't be possible, right? How would they remain hidden?"

Aveis shrugged. "Dragons wield all sorts of magic. Perhaps there is a power that keeps them hidden. There are many books about magic here, but thousands more were destroyed after the War on Magic. Who knows what is possible."

"How would you find them?"

"I'm hopeful you'll be able to help in that regard."

"How?" Myla asked, feigning innocence.

"With your connection to your dragon. You can use it to communicate with them and find out where they're hiding."

"Even if I were to connect with them—how are you so sure they'd tell me where they're hiding?"

Aveis smiled. "You can be quite convincing when you want to be."

I hope that's true, Myla thought to herself. *Or this will not end well.*

"I'll try."

Chapter 46

Myla stayed up late reading, trying to absorb as
much information from the books Aveis gave her as possible.

The chapter she was currently reading was talking about how emotions affect the wielder's magic—but not just their own emotions. Their dragon's emotions affected the wielder even more so than the wielder's emotions. When their dragon's emotions were strong, they could overpower the wielder, and they'd become vessels for the emotions and be forced to respond in kind. It had a physical trait as well. The most common trait was the wielder's eyes changing to the color of the dragon's scales or underbelly.

Myla thought about what happened when Raevyn found out she had magic. She had felt Vavna's emotions over her own, and her control of her magic slipped the harder Vavna pushed. She wondered if her eyes had changed colors or if it only happened when Vavna took over completely.

Can you control me? Myla asked Vavna. *Like a puppet if you wanted to?*

Vavna chuffed. *If I could, I would have the half a dozen times you made stupid decisions.*

Myla's lips twitched. *But I felt your emotions that day. You were desperate for me to run from Raevyn, and I almost lost control of my magic.*

I can only tap into your magic if you allow it. I imagine it feels a bit like losing control, but I cannot control what was given to you.

If I allow it, will I know what's going on?

That, I do not know. I've heard that it feels a bit like an out-of-body experience.

Can I control you if you allow it?

No. Vavna huffed. *As if I'd allow such a thing in the first place anyway. The magic is mine, first and foremost. Without us, humans would not have it.*

Myla set the book aside and looked at the candle flickering on her nightstand. She wondered if Aveis ever let Drathal take over her magic. Perhaps it was the only way she could go through with killing those knights trying to find her. Or maybe killing came as easy as breathing to her. She had learned a lot about Aveis, but she didn't know who Aveis truly was. Perhaps she wasn't the ruling type. Perhaps she wouldn't bring Rosebourne into a more tolerant future, but who else had the means to do it if not her?

Sighing, Myla blew out the candle and lay in bed— hoping a good night's rest would provide some clarity.

****

The next day, Myla decided to make breakfast for Aveis. She needed to get Aveis to open up to her more and thought a kind gesture might help.

Myla headed into the kitchen and grabbed the cookbook. She flipped through it until she found a recipe for pancakes. She scanned through the instructions. It seemed simple enough. First, she needed to beat the eggs. She grabbed a few eggs and dropped them into the bowl before proceeding to whack them with a wooden spoon. The eggs cracked—pieces of the shells flying out. She looked down at it and frowned. She didn't remember pancakes being crunchy, but maybe the shells dissolved when cooked. She grabbed a bag of flour and poured some into the egg mixture. A cloud of flour burst in her face. Startled, she dropped the bag, and it landed on the edge of the bowl, causing it to tip—the mixture leaking out onto her shirt and shoes. Cursing, Myla righted the bag of flour and pushed it away from the bowl.

"What is going on here?" A familiar voice asked, sounding extremely amused.

Myla tried to wipe the flour from her face but only succeeded in smearing it everywhere. She rubbed her eyes and blinked until her eyes cleared, and she saw Aveis leaning in the doorway.

"Making breakfast. Obviously." Myla chuckled awkwardly.

Aveis nodded, barely able to hide her smile as she strode toward her. "I see. I don't remember any recipe that calls for putting flour on your face and..." she looked down at the remaining mixture in the bowl. "Are those eggshells?"

"The recipe said to beat the eggs. So, I did," she replied, holding up her wooden spoon.

Aveis laughed as Myla blushed in embarrassment at struggling so much at a common task.

"That's not what they mean by beating, darling," Aveis said. "But I can see where the confusion came from. I'll show you."

Aveis pushed the dirty bowl out of the way and grabbed a clean one before showing Myla how to crack an egg. "You don't want any of the shells in the batter. And beat is just another way of saying stir but with more vigor. As for flour, it's easier to spoon it in, so it doesn't make as much of a mess."

Myla watched her work, passing her the ingredients as instructed. She figured now was as good a time as any to ask some questions, and she seemed to be in an amicable mood.

"Has anyone ever recognized you before? I know you look a lot different, but when you were a kid, it's hard to believe no one asked any questions."

"Most people think I'm dead, and I didn't use to go out into the open when I was younger," Aveis replied as she stirred in the remaining ingredients. "I took what I needed or foraged for it. I knew that a child buying a bunch of supplies would raise suspicion, and I didn't want to risk it since I didn't know how to protect myself back then. I'm not afraid like I used to be."

"It must have been hard—and lonely."

"It was at times," she admitted. "But I had Drathal, and it was enough."

"Was?"

Aveis smiled softly at her. "Until you. I didn't realize how good it would feel to have someone around who understands it all. I wouldn't wish what we've gone through on anyone, but it's nice to have the company all the same. And I don't plan on letting you go any time soon, darling. Hope you're up for that."

Myla swallowed tightly—a mixture of guilt, unease, and sadness filling her chest. This was becoming increasingly difficult. Aveis had gone through so much, and all she wanted was to live in peace. Perhaps she could make the kingdom a safer place for people like them—but who was Myla to ask that of her? Myla was leading Aveis on for her own gain. Aveis might be doing the same thing, but that didn't alleviate Myla's guilt.

Even if it was starting to feel like Myla was more of a captive than anything, given that Aveis would never let her go knowing her secret. Aveis didn't deserve to be manipulated, especially after everything she's gone through. Not only that, but she couldn't help but think she was betraying Raevyn, too. She wished she could just leave, but it was out of the question now. She was stuck.

Vavna, I don't know what to do. I think I made a mistake coming here.

The only mistake you've made is letting yourself fall for the scarred man. He's clouding your judgment. You could be happy with her if you choose to let go of your past.

It's not that simple. Haven't you ever been in love?

Long ago. It's a vulnerability I'm glad I no longer have.

Aveis grabbed the bowl of batter and brought it over to the stovetop, where Myla had set out a greased pan. Aveis poured the batter onto the pan in small circles.

276

"You know, this was supposed to be my thank you," Myla said, leaning on the counter across from Aveis. "But I'm a wreck in the kitchen."

"That's okay. You can do the dishes," she said with a smile.

Myla smiled back. "Fair enough."

Aveis gestured to the pan and held out a spatula. "Do you want to do the honors?"

Myla took the spatula and peered down at the little cakes. She tried to slip the spatula underneath one of them, but it started folding in on itself. Aveis came up behind her, placing one hand on her hip and the other over Myla's hand, holding the spatula.

"Like this," Aveis whispered in her ear.

Myla stiffened slightly as Aveis's hand guided hers and helped her flip the pancakes.

"You need to be quick," Aveis said, holding onto her hand for a few seconds longer than was necessary before stepping back.

Myla swallowed thickly before turning to face her. "Right, thanks."

Aveis grinned. "I'll make a cook of you yet."

Chapter 47

After breakfast, Aveis offered to teach Myla some
tips and tricks to controlling her magic. Despite the

despondent feelings she'd been carrying, Myla couldn't help the spark of excitement she had about the prospect. She'd never worked on her magic with anyone else, and not only would this be an excellent opportunity to learn new things, but it would also give her a chance to see Aveis's power firsthand. She wanted to know as much as she could about Aveis's power and strength if this all went south and she was forced to fight. The more Myla learned about Aveis, the more she hoped that wouldn't happen.

They decided to go to the beach to practice so Myla could use the ocean. They stood on the shore, and Myla breathed in the salty air—instantly feeling relaxed by the sound of the crashing waves. That was until her brain helpfully reminded her of the day she had with Raevyn in Tanin, and she felt her heart break all over again.

"Magic is attuned with your emotions." Aveis began, coming up to stand next to Myla. "Negative emotions such as anger or fear are the strongest motivators for your magic. They can bring out the most in your magic, but it is highly unpredictable. That's why it's important to focus on positive emotions when trying to use your magic and stay in control. Two possible positive emotions you can focus on are joy or love."

"What do you think of?" Myla asked curiously, glancing up at Aveis.

Aveis closed her eyes and held out her hands in front of her, palms up. "I think of the time when I felt my magic intertwine with Drathal's, and our bond solidified. It had been months since I decided to stay with him, and by then, I knew Drathal would always keep his promise. He took me on a ride across the ocean, and it was at that moment that I felt completely safe and whole." Twin flames bloomed above Aveis's palms, reshaping until they resembled a dragon and a woman. She pushed them away, and they flew across the ocean before disappearing. Aveis opened her eyes and turned to Myla. "Now you try."

Myla closed her eyes, and flashes of Raevyn's dark gold-flecked eyes immediately filled her mind. She thought of all their almost moments and how they had ultimately led to their first kiss amidst a hurricane. A torrent of emotions warred in her chest, and she felt her magic zip through her veins. She tried to grab onto it, but it slipped through her grasp.

Myla opened her eyes and gasped as the ocean in front of her rose—creating a wall in front of them that blocked out the horizon line. Before she could stop it, it crashed down on top of them, drenching them and nearly pulling them out to sea.

Myla wiped her face, spitting out seawater as she turned to look sheepishly at Aveis.

Aveis pushed herself to her feet, flicking her damp hair out of her eyes. "I told you to think of a *happy* memory."

"Sorry, it just popped into my mind—I couldn't stop it. Let me try again."

Myla closed her eyes and thought about her birthday the year before. It wasn't a grand affair—just dinner with her family and Wrynn—but it had been perfect. Their discussions were lively, drinks hadn't stopped flowing, and laughter filled the halls. Myla's heart had been full of so much love and gratitude for all those around her. She couldn't have asked for a better day.

She smiled at the memory and held onto it as she reached out to the ocean in front of her. She willed it to part—revealing the sand underneath. She pushed the waves back together and urged them to spiral. Soon, a whirlpool formed, and she expanded it as much as she could until it was several yards across. She lifted the whirlpool up so it swirled above the surface and pushed it out. It danced along the water for a while before collapsing.

Myla was panting softly as she turned to look at Aveis, who had a wondrous expression on her face.

"Can you control water in all forms?" Aveis asked, intrigued.

Myla nodded, creating a ball of water in her hands that she solidified. Then, she turned to mist and allowed to brush against Aveis's cheek, leaving a wet smear.

Aveis chuckled softly as she wiped her face. "That's impressive."

"What else can you do?" Myla asked, trying to come off as nonchalant and missing by a mile.

Her lips twitched. "A lot, darling, I assure you."

Aveis turned away from her and reached her hands out, creating a life-size horse made entirely of flames. It trotted in place, the sand beneath its hooves crystalizing. Aveis walked over to it and brushed her fingers lightly down the horse's mane. "They act like a normal horse would, but I cannot ride them for very long. It takes longer for me to burn than others, but I burn nonetheless."

"What if you didn't ride it but used it to pull something?" Myla suggested.

Aveis gave her a small smile. "That's not a bad idea."

Myla pushed the water toward Aveis, creating an ice board beneath her feet, making sure to encase her boots for added stability. "Now you can create reins and get pulled along the water."

Aveis looked down at her feet and then up at Myla. "I'll try only if you accompany me."

Myla thought about refusing, but Aveis reached out her hand with a soft smile on her face, and Myla couldn't resist it.

Myla nodded and walked over to her. She made the ice board longer and froze her boots to the board as well.

The horse trotted in front of them, and Aveis pulled out a sword, the blade of which was made entirely of coal. She held it out in front of her, and two thin cords of flame shot out of the sword, creating a bridle around the horse's face. As soon as it was attached, the horse lunged forward. They lurched backward as the board slid awkwardly against the sand before crashing into the water. Myla grabbed Aveis around the waist—holding on for dear life—as they sailed across the water. Aveis laughed, placing her free hand on top of Myla's.

Myla peered around Aveis to see the horse wasn't running on top of the water but a few inches above it. Aveis jerked the sword to the right, and the horse complied, turning sharply around. Their board was nearly top-sided, but a quick burst of Myla's magic steadied it. The horse was charging toward the shore, and Myla braced herself for a rough landing. When they got close enough, Aveis lifted her sword up, causing the reins to fall away. The horse disintegrated just as it touched the shore.

Thinking fast, Myla tightened her grip around Aveis's waist and liquified their ice board before they made it to shore. They fell back—the water breaking their fall. Myla's feet touched the sand, and she righted herself and Aveis before pushing the water away from them, creating a small pocket. They both spluttered, and only when Myla was sure that Aveis had her footing did she release her hold.

Aveis turned to Myla, grinning widely. Myla was surprised when Aveis brought her into a tight hug.

Aveis pulled back but kept her hands on Myla's hips as she said, "That was fucking insane."

Myla laughed. "Yeah. Who knew fire and water could work so well together."

Aveis brushed a lock of dark hair out of Myla's eye. "You know what they say—opposites attract."

Chapter 48

Myla wasn't sure if this was a good idea. After they had practiced for a few hours, Aveis suggested she meet Drathal. Myla assumed she would meet Drathal eventually but wasn't sure what to expect. What if Drathal could read her thoughts and figure out that she was sent by Aveis's parents? What if Drathal had the ability to manipulate her mind and coerce her into doing things?

That is ridiculous—Drathal has no connection to you. His magic is flames, not mind manipulation.

Are you telling me that some dragons have *that gift?*

Perhaps.

"It will be fine," Aveis assured Myla as they walked down the hall. "I won't let him hurt you if that's what you are worried about."

Myla glanced up at her. "You won't?"

Aveis's lips twitched. "Of course, darling. I've grown rather fond of having you around."

Myla looked away, guilt appearing like a slash across her chest. "T-that's good."

Aveis smiled as she pushed open the grand doors at the end of the hall. Myla followed behind tentatively. The room was a giant ballroom with white marble floors, high ceilings, and tall windows on either side. There was an enormous hole in the left corner of the room that Myla assumed Drathal used as an entrance. Off to her right, Myla saw a bed, nightstand, and wardrobe set up. And lying in front of her—taking up the majority of the room—was Drathal. He was the most terrifying creature she'd ever seen. His entire body was thick with muscle and covered in maroon scales except for his underbelly and inside of his wings, which were a smoky yellow. He had thick spikes running from the base of his neck to the end of his tail. Two large horns curled up from the base of his skull, and his eyes were the same color as Aveis's.

Drathal lifted his head where it had been resting on his sharp claws. He growled softly, the noise deep and reverberating in her chest. Myla tensed but resisted the urge to run from the room. Barely.

"Drathal, this is Myla. She is our guest," Aveis said.

Drathal looked at Aveis and growled again, causing Aveis to roll her eyes. They stared at each other, and Myla assumed they were mind-speaking. Eventually, Aveis sighed, and Drathal turned his attention back to Myla. He brought his face closer to hers until it was only a few feet away.

Don't move, Vavna warned her. *Show that you mean no harm.*

He bared his teeth, and Myla remained utterly still. His eyes bored into hers, and Myla tried to come off as unthreateningly as possible. Not that she stood a chance against him, but she wanted him to know that she didn't want to hurt him. He widened his jaw, and Myla saw flames blooming in the back of his throat. She flexed her fingers—reaching out to the ocean below her to help her if necessary—but still didn't move.

Drathal closed his mouth and placed his head back on his claws, growling softly. Myla didn't realize how tense she was until she felt Aveis put a hand on her shoulder.

"You've passed Drathal's test. A ridiculous test but one that he thinks is necessary." Aveis said, squeezing her shoulder comfortingly.

Drathal growled again, and Aveis turned to him. Something passed between them, and Aveis scowled, removing her hand from Myla's shoulder.

Aveis looked at her. "I'll come get you in a few hours for supper."

Tamping down her curiosity, Myla nodded and left the room. She desperately wanted to know what they were talking about but knew it wasn't her place. She just hoped that if it was about her, it would be good things. She needed Aveis on her side.

Thinking a nice bath would soothe her, she headed to her room. The interaction with Drathal hadn't been what she'd expected. She didn't think he'd be so calm. He was wary of her, of course, but when she pictured seeing a dragon, she always thought their first instinct would be to attack.

I take offense to that notion, Vavna snarled. *This is why I didn't even want to bother with you—your kingdom has brainwashed you.*

I'm sorry, I don't know anything when it comes to dragons or magic. Maybe you can enlighten me?

Are you asking me to relay millions of years of history?

Of course not, but maybe the highlights? Like, what really happened during the War on Magic?

Myla stripped off her clothes and eased into the warm water, all the tension in her body dissipating. She sighed and closed her eyes.

Vavna huffed. *The war started when a large group of magic wielders attacked us. Hundreds of us were killed—not expecting such a betrayal from someone we've bonded with. Chaos erupted, and many dragons fled while others stayed to fight alongside their magic wielder. Turns out, an order had been given to all magic wielders to take the hearts of their dragons to spare their own lives. The promise of their lives had been a lie, but many magic wielders fell for it, and when they showed their dragon's heart—they were killed on the spot. Magic in a wielder is greatly diminished when their dragon dies, but it's not entirely gone, which was enough for those without magic to warrant killing them.*

286

Do you know what started it? Myla asked. *We are told that magic wielders and dragons became too powerful.*

Vavna snorted. *Of course, they'd tell you that. Fear was a motivator, but not in the way you're thinking. We didn't learn until later what truly caused the change. It was sudden—none of us did anything or knew what was happening until it was too late. I was one of the ones who fled. Since I had not bonded, it was easier for me.*

Fled to where you are now?

Not exactly.

But, you're with other humans—you showed me.

I am, but I am still of the mind that you are more trouble than you're worth.

But you're stuck with us?

Until you all eventually die out—yes. Unfortunately, we are.

Chapter 49

Myla was having a hard time falling asleep. Her mind wouldn't let up, thinking over everything she had done and learned thus far. Everything seemed so simple when she started this journey, but it only grew more complicated the more she learned about Aveis and the more she talked with her dragon. Dread and worry had set up camp in her chest, and she could do nothing to deter their stay. She was so fucking paranoid that when she heard a scream, she thought it was all in her head—an illusion of her frustrations.

The second time she heard it, she knew it wasn't her imagination. She was instantly out of bed and putting on her robe over her nightgown. Grabbing her sword, she ran out of her bedroom toward the noise. For a moment, she thought that someone had broken in, but that didn't make sense. If someone had gotten in, then she would have heard Drathal. Unless...

Myla pushed open the grand double doors, brandishing her sword as she took stock of the situation. There didn't seem to be any threat. Drathal was curled up in the middle of the room—his eyes narrowed on her as he growled in warning. Myla dropped her sword and raised her hands in a placating gesture.

"I'm sorry. I thought I heard—"

Another scream tore through the air, and Myla followed Drathal's gaze to see Aveis lying on the marble floor with Drathal's arms circled protectively around her. Myla hadn't noticed her at first because she was covered, but now, she was burning like a fallen star.

Aveis screamed again, and Myla thought she was being burned alive. She started running toward her, and Drathal snarled, tail swinging out to block her path.

"Please," Myla said, lifting her hands again. "I just want to help. I promise."

Drathal stared at her, his teeth gleaming as he growled. Aveis screamed again, and Drathal looked down at her, his eyes filling with pain.

"Please," she said again. "I can help."

Drathal looked at her again before reluctantly moving his tail. Myla went up to Aveis and knelt next to her—careful not to touch the flames leaking off her. Myla lifted her hands and pulled the water from the ocean toward her. She settled the water over Aveis's body, cocooning her like a blanket. A large plume of steam wafted up, blinding her for a moment. Using one hand to keep the water over Aveis, she used her other to push the steam away. When it cleared, she looked down at Aveis. Her tan skin was splotchy, but Myla didn't see any burns, and miraculously, her hair wasn't singed. Myla wasn't sure what had caused her to scream. She seemed to still be in a deep sleep.

Aveis started tossing and turning, her eyes squeezing shut as a pained expression took over her face. She mumbled under her breath something that sounded like "*no*" and "*please.*" Myla reached her free hand out and brushed her fingers along Aveis's cheek and hair.

"It's okay," Myla said softly. "You're safe. I won't let anyone hurt you. I promise."

Aveis's hand shot out and gripped Myla's forearm. Her touch was searing, and Myla flinched. She leaned down so her forearm rested in the water, cooling Aveis's touch. She stayed like that for Myla wasn't sure how long, whispering soothing words until Aveis's grip fell away and the flames dissipated. Once Myla was sure Aveis was calm, she pulled the water off her and directed it out the window. She looked around for a blanket but couldn't see one—most likely having been reduced to ash by Aveis's flames. Shrugging off her robe, she settled it over Aveis before getting to her feet. She looked up at Drathal, who was looking at her with something akin to gratitude. Myla nodded to him and smiled softly before grabbing her sword and heading back to her room.

****

Myla didn't sleep well that night. Aveis's screams kept echoing in her ears, and she couldn't stop thinking about what might have caused them. Did she have nightmares about things she had done—the things that Marione had alluded to on the ship? Or perhaps they were nightmares from her time in the palace?

As the sun started rising, Myla gave up trying to sleep and got out of bed. On her way out, she grabbed one of the books on magic Aveis had let her borrow, which was full of different magic techniques. She had to wander around for a bit before she finally found the stairs that led down to the beach.

She sat down on the sand and placed the book on her lap. Flipping through the pages, she settled on the one she had left off on. It demonstrated the ability to do two different moves at once—one with each hand. She had tried a few times but had been unsuccessful. Setting the book down beside her, Myla took off her boots and got to her feet before wading into the water. Using one hand, she pulled a small amount of water toward her and formed a small ball hovering over her hand. With the other, she tried to create a whirlpool in the lapping waves. The water ball started to lose its shape as the water in front of her tried to swirl. She tried to focus on both, but the ball burst right as the whirlpool formed.

Myla groaned and dropped her hands. The ground shook, and she nearly tumbled face-first into the waves. She turned around and saw Drathal had landed on the shore, nearly crushing her book. Myla froze—eyes wide and unsure. Drathal gazed at her before lying down on his stomach. He nudged the book with one claw before drawing something in the sand. Myla cautiously walked up to him and looked down at the drawing. She had to turn her back to Drathal to understand what she was looking at. It was a swirl, and above it was a circle. Myla blinked and looked up at Drathal. He nodded toward the water. Myla did as instructed and, just as the image showed, created a sphere of water above the whirlpool. With both in her sight, she was able to concentrate on both tasks, and neither faltered.

Myla grinned and turned back to Drathal. "Got any more tips?"

Drathal blew smoke out his nose and opened his mouth. Myla thought she had offended him somehow, and he was going to light her on fire. She braced for his attack, but he lifted his head up and blew fire into the sky. He turned back to her and gazed at her expectantly.

"You want me to blow...water?" She asked, confused. "Like a faucet?"

He chuffed and drew what looked to be a spike in the sand.

"You want me to spit icicles?" She asked, raising an eyebrow.

He nodded.

Myla looked down at the seawater lapping around her knees and frowned before turning her gaze on Drathal. "Don't suppose you have a glass of water with you? Something a little less salty?"

Drathal only stared. Myla sighed and reached down, pulling water up and into her mouth. She grimaced as the salty water hit her tongue—sucking all the moisture out of her mouth and throat. She then spat it out, forming icicles before the droplets hit the surface.

"That's a neat trick and all, but I don't understand why I needed to spit the water first."

Drathal bared his teeth—no, he *grinned* at her. It was terribly unnerving.

"You just wanted me to put seawater in my mouth." Myla realized. "Did you just play a trick on me?"

Drathal's grin widened as someone spoke from behind him. "He may look like an ancient scary beast, but he can be a trickster, too, when he's not grumbling and growling."

Drathal huffed as Aveis walked out from behind him. Myla was shocked and more than a little embarrassed. How long had she been standing there? Had she watched her put seawater in her mouth and spit it out like an idiot?

Her cheeks flushed, and she quickly changed the topic. "Aveis, how are you? Did you sleep okay?"

Aveis blushed slightly. "Yeah, I did. Drathal told me what you did, and...thank you. It was really kind of you."

"It was nothing. Do they happen often? Your nightmares?"

Aveis looked away. "I usually manage them with a draught, but I ran out a few nights ago."

Drathal got up and flew into the sky, back toward the castle. Aveis watched Drathal go for a moment before turning back to Myla.

"I suppose you have a right to know what they're about, given how you helped," Aveis replied, sitting down on the sand.

Myla walked out of the water and sat down next to her—careful not to get too close. "You don't have to tell me if you don't want to. I won't push you."

"It's okay. I want to." Aveis took a deep breath before continuing. "I usually have nightmares about the things I had to do and the people I hurt to survive, but last night..." she reached a hand up and brushed her fingertips along the scar she had running down the side of her neck that was usually hidden by her long black hair. "Was about the night I got this scar—before I had even met Drathal. I was around seven years old when someone tried to assassinate me."

Myla's eyes widened, and her heart dropped at the thought of a young Aveis being targeted and hurt in such a way.

"Almost everyone in the palace knew of my powers. It was nearly impossible to keep it a secret. Even when I was young, I knew no one liked me. They never bothered to hide their disdain—not even my mother. So, it could have been anyone in the palace who hired the assassin to kill me."

Aveis brought her knees up to her chest and wrapped her arms around them.

"He must have made a noise or something because when I woke up, his blade was at my throat. I brought my hands up and turned my head just as he sliced. My hands were covered in flames, and I touched his face before he could move away. He screamed as my flames tore away his skin. I gripped my neck with my other hand, not realizing it too, was burning. It was the first and last time I was able to burn myself with my magic. I think it somehow knew I needed it to."

Aveis fell silent, gazing off into the horizon.

"And the assassin?" Myla asked softly. "What happened to him?"

"By then, the guards had come in, and they took him away. He was hung for his crimes the next day, and a few weeks after that, I was sent away. My parents said it was for my safety, and maybe it was, but they never told me where I was going. Maybe it was their way of getting rid of me for good."

"That can't be true. If it were, then they wouldn't be trying so hard to bring you back."

"They're trying to kill me, not bring me back," Aveis snapped. "Whatever Raevyn told you—it was a lie."

"He said that the king and queen think a dragon kidnapped you. That the dragon hunters were only meant for Drathal."

"They should know by now that I don't want to leave."

"And you don't? Want to leave, I mean?"

Aveis glared at her. "Of course, I don't. If I did, I would have left."

"Right, of course. I just meant—don't you ever wish things were different and you could go home?"

"It's useless to think of such things."

They were quiet for a while, the only sounds being the waves crashing along the shore and birds flying overhead.

"I'm sorry that happened to you," Myla spoke quietly. "And I understand why you don't want to go back. Drathal makes you feel safe. You aren't a defenseless child anymore, and you're more than capable of taking care of yourself, but you're safer with Drathal. He's your home, and you never think about going to Cassia because you don't think he can go with you."

"I know he can't," Aveis said, looking down at Myla. "And I won't leave him. Not unless he asks."

Myla nodded. "I don't think he'll ask. I saw last night how much he cares for you."

"He wants what's best for me. He tried to warn me against you, but I shut that down pretty quickly. You've more than proven yourself in my eyes."

Guilt settled in her chest—her constant companion these few weeks. "Thank you."

Aveis smiled slightly. "Thank *you*, darling, for helping me last night."

Myla returned the smile. "Glad I could help."

Chapter 50

Myla and Aveis stayed on the beach the rest of the day. Drathal joined them as they practiced their magic. Myla was in the water—manipulating the waves around her, while Drathal and Aveis remained on the beach. Not for the first time, Myla wanted to be able to understand what they were discussing. Whatever it was, Aveis was amused, grinning like she didn't have a care in the world. At one point, she even laughed and turned to look at Myla and wink.

Myla waded out of the water toward them. "What are you two giggling about?"

Aveis wrapped an arm around her waist and brought her to her side, kissing her temple. Myla was surprised by the touch but allowed it—not wanting to spoil her good mood.

"You," she teased. "Drathal's just critiquing your form, and I told him I'd love to see him use magic in the water."

Drathal huffed and lifted his nose up at them.

"Obviously, he's too scared," Aveis grinned.

Drathal's nostrils flared, and he snarled at her. Aveis's grin widened, and Drathal rolled his eyes at her before stalking toward the water.

"This should be good," Aveis whispered to Myla.

Drathal shuffled into the water until he was up to his chest. He then turned to give Aveis a smug look. Myla never thought of dragons having such distinct facial expressions, but today alone had proven how wrong she was. She couldn't hear Drathal's thoughts but could guess as much just from the look on his face. She figured now Drathal was telling Aveis that she was wrong and that he wasn't afraid of anything.

After spending the day with them, Myla was feeling far more at ease around the dragon, especially given the fact that he'd been good-humored enough to joke with her. So, with a small smile on her lips, Myla decided to have a little fun of her own. With a flick of her wrist, she created a wave that barreled into Drathal. He stumbled—nearly falling in. He huffed out a puff of fire and shook the water off his face, and Aveis laughed.

"That's for my form!" Myla called to him, grinning.

Drathal narrowed his eyes and splashed them with his wing. They both shrieked as they were doused. Drathal gave them a victorious look as Myla pulled away from Aveis.

"You don't want to get in a water fight with me," Myla spoke, stalking toward the water.

Aveis laughed and watched as Myla and Drathal got into an epic water war that only ended when Drathal picked Myla up with his claws and held her upside down until she admitted defeat. Myla waded back onto the shore—panting and soaked—to Aveis's side.

"A little backup would have been nice," Myla pouted.

Aveis smiled and pulled her into a hug. "I know better than to get between a rock and a hard place."

Myla huffed. "Yes, well, I would have won if he hadn't cheated."

"Most definitely," Aveis said, nuzzling her face in Myla's neck. "But it's for the best. Drathal is an awful loser."

"So am I."

"But I can make it up to you in a way I couldn't with Drathal," she murmured, her breath hot against her neck. "If you're interested."

Drathal snarled and shook the water off his scales and onto them as if to point out they weren't alone.

Aveis laughed and pulled away. "Later then."

****

A few hours later, they were all starving. Rather than going back up to the castle to cook, Myla suggested fishing. Though, with her trick, it should be a quick and easy feat. She'd done it a few times in the past, but that had been with fish she could see. She wasn't entirely sure she could manage it in such a large body of water.

Myla walked into the water and held her palms over the rippling waves. She closed her eyes and concentrated on the depths of the water far in front of her. She searched for disturbances in the depths—something to indicate another creature within. Finally, she felt something and focused her magic on that spot, encasing the thing in a ball of ice before pulling it toward her. It collided with her, and she stumbled back, barely able to keep hold of the slippery ball. She looked down at it to see three fish swirling around in the water, unable to escape the thin layer of ice.

Myla grinned and tossed it to Aveis on shore before turning back and repeating her process to catch about a dozen more. Aveis had created a bonfire, cooking the fish on a stick while Drathal released them from their icy containers. Once Myla was done, she walked up to them and sat by the fire—shivering as the frigid water settled over her skin. She could pull the water off of her, but she was tired and content with settling closer to the fire and to Aveis, who sat next to her.

"Nice job, darling," Aveis said with a smile, wrapping an arm around her shoulders.

"You too," Myla smiled. "Those fish smell amazing."

"He's too impatient to wait for cooked ones," she nodded toward Drathal, who tossed one ice ball into his

298

mouth. "It's a good thing I got these three because I don't think Drathal's going to give us any of the others."

Drathal turned to them with a grin before popping another ball in his mouth. Aveis smiled and shook her head at him. Myla smiled, too. When Aveis had said that he was a jokester, Myla hadn't believed her until this moment. It was a refreshing change of pace to see them so playful, and Myla was terrified of doing anything to disrupt it. The thought of bringing up going back to Cassia now that she was getting closer to them was daunting. The smile on her face slowly fell as unsettling thoughts rushed through her head. She had gained their trust just as she had hoped, but in doing so, she had learned how precious and rare their trust was. She wanted to hold on to it and protect it as no one had before. She didn't know if she could jeopardize it, which scared her even more.

"You okay, darling?" Aveis asked, nudging her side. "You look like you've seen a ghost."

Myla shook her head—pushing the thoughts out of her head and forcing a smile on her face. "It's nothing, just got lost in thought for a second."

Myla took the offered fish from Aveis and started pulling the scales back for something to do.

"If you're sure," Aveis said, not sounding convinced but letting it go.

Aveis lowered her arm to rest around her waist as she held another fish over the fire. Myla watched the flames as she ate her fish—letting her thoughts drift away. She was determined not to let her thoughts ruin this moment. She knew at some point she would need to face all of it, but today wasn't that day.

After they ate, Aveis and Myla rested next to the dying embers and watched the stars above them. Drathal curled up like a cat next to them—his tail reaching out to wrap around them for extra warmth and protection. It didn't take long for Myla to fall into a deep sleep.

Chapter 51

The next few days, Myla allowed herself to ignore her conflicting feelings and to take things as they came. She didn't let herself think about her assignment and her looming indecision. It wasn't until she dreamt of Raevyn for the third night in a row that it became impossible to ignore any longer. This would be so much easier if Aveis was a villain, but the more Myla learned of her, the more she believed Aveis wasn't. She's just a woman trying to survive in this world. But, regardless, Myla owed it to herself and her family to at least try to convince Aveis to come home. Aveis didn't believe she had the capability to change Rosebourne, but Myla knew she could. She'd need to give it time, but Myla believed she had it in her.

"Would you consider taking the throne if your parents weren't in the picture?" Myla asked as they sat down to eat dinner.

Aveis looked up from her steak and furrowed her brow. "Why do you ask?"

Myla shrugged. "You told me you didn't think Rosebourne could change, and I wondered if you really meant your parents. And perhaps, if they were gone, you'd have more faith in yourself and the kingdom."

"Perhaps, but I am no leader. I would love to bring Rosebourne out of the hateful and jealous past, but I don't think I'll be the one to do it."

"If not you, then who? You are the only heir to the throne. I think the gods gave you your magic for a reason.

You can help people like us—however many of us are out there."

"It doesn't matter now. I won't be able to do anything while they're alive," Aveis replied, taking a bite of her food. "If I were to return now, I would be nothing but a pawn that they'd try to wield to their advantage."

"But as you've said, if you return after they're dead, no one will have trust in you as a leader. They might not even believe you're the true princess. You need the king and queen's endorsement if you ever hope to help Rosebourne."

Aveis squinted at her. "Why is this so important to you?"

"Because I don't want anyone else to die for possessing magic. We were both lucky, but if there are others out there—they won't be spared."

Aveis looked away. "I know you're right, but I don't ever want to go back there. I can't."

Myla reached across the table and took hold of Aveis's hand. "I understand. What you went through was traumatic, and the thought of going back to them scares you, but you wouldn't be alone this time around. Drathal and I would be with you."

Aveis shook her head. "I wouldn't put Drathal in that position. I couldn't risk it."

Myla nodded. "I get it. But would you think about it, at least?"

Aveis looked up at Myla and squeezed her hand. "I'll think about it, but I'm not making any promises."

Myla smiled. "Thank you."

****

Myla woke up that night with a disturbing feeling that she wasn't alone. She sat up quickly and grabbed the dagger she kept on her nightstand before getting to her feet.

She squinted in the darkness, her eyes falling on a figure looming next to her open door—too tall and broad to be Aveis.

"I see you're not a prisoner," a familiar voice drawled. "I don't know whether to be relieved or angry."

The dagger in Myla's hand clattered to the ground as she launched herself at Raevyn—wrapping her arms tightly around his neck as tears collected in her eyes. He gave a grunt of surprise, large hands landing on her hips.

"Raevyn, I'm so happy to see you," she said, burying her face in his chest. "I've missed you."

Raevyn pulled her away slightly so he could look down at her face. "Not so fast, sunshine. What the fuck is going on? Why did you run away?"

Myla's heart clenched at the hurt expression on his face. "I didn't want to, Aveis knocked me out and—"

His hold on her hips tightened. "She fucking kidnapped you? I knew it—"

"At first, she did," Myla cut him off. "But I decided to go willingly with her because she's the princess."

"Sunshine—"

"It's true! I've seen her do magic firsthand, not to mention I've met her dragon—"

"You did *what?*"

"It's okay, I'm fine. He didn't hurt me, and he won't because he knows I'm not a threat—"

"They're mindless beasts—"

"They're not," Myla said sternly, pulling out of his grip to glare at him. She could feel Vavna's anger as well, bubbling just under the surface of her own. "What we've been taught about dragons, magic—it's all wrong. Our history is built on lies—"

"And this dragon told you that?" Raevyn cut in scornfully. "Or was it the lying thief?"

"No, my own dragon did."

For fuck's sake, Vavna growled. *You tell* him *that, but not the princess?*

Myla ignored them. "I know this is hard to wrap your head around, but I need you to trust me. I can convince Aveis to come and assume her place—"

"There was never an option where this didn't end in a fight. Aveis will never come back willingly, and her dragon won't allow it either. You've done well leading us here, but it's time for me to do my job."

He headed toward the door, but Myla grabbed his arm. "No, please don't do this. Drathal doesn't deserve this. He's done nothing wrong—"

Raevyn curled his lip in disgust. "That beast has a name?"

"Yes," Myla insisted. "And complex feelings, emotions, and thoughts. All dragons have ever done is protect themselves from us. *We* betrayed them—not the other way around. And for what?"

"For balance—"

"That's bullshit!" Myla's magic surged at her anger, humming just along the edges of her control. "The crown felt threatened by their power and tried to put an end to it."

"That's not—"

"Isn't it? That's exactly what the king and queen are trying to do with the princess. They're trying to take away her power and hold her under their thumbs just to prove they can. But guess what? They couldn't do it without magic themselves." Myla held out her hands, pulling the water from the air, and swirled it around their bodies like a small tornado. "They've been searching for her for a decade, and I found her within a few weeks. They may pretend to hold all the power, but they hide behind those who truly have it. And I don't think I want to help them anymore."

"So, what do you plan on doing?" Raevyn snarled, taking a step toward her, unafraid of her display of magic. "Stay here? Stay with *them*? Leave your friends and family behind as if they mean nothing?"

"Of course not," she snapped, taking an answering step forward until they were only a heartbeat apart. "But I won't be the reason she's trapped again."

A roar cut through the silent night, and Myla flinched. She ran over to the window that overlooked the beach, and her heart caught in her throat when she saw dozens of armed men and women storming the shore.

Myla shot a look at Raevyn, heart pounding in her chest. "What the fuck did you do?"

"What was necessary."

Myla tried to rush past him, but Raevyn wrapped an arm around her waist, pinning her back against his chest.

"Let go of me," she growled, squirming.

"I won't let you put yourself in danger again."

"Fuck. You." Myla snarled.

"I don't care if you hate me for it—I will always do what is best for you."

"Then you leave me no choice."

Myla pushed down water particles from her tornado and froze them against the stone floor under their feet. She then lifted her legs up and pushed as hard as she could against the wall. He stumbled, feet slipping against the ice, and fell on his back. Her back slammed into his chest, and he gasped as the air was knocked out of him, causing his grip to loosen. Myla rolled off of him and stumbled to her feet.

"Myla!"

She ran toward the door, grabbing her sword that was leaning against the wall. She turned at the last second to see Raevyn getting to his feet.

"Please, don't do this."

"I'm sorry," Myla said, her throat tight with emotion.

Before he could stop her, Myla slammed the door shut and froze the hinges. The door shuddered as he slammed against it, calling out her name with such desperation that her heart cracked—a sliver of it lodging in her throat.

Run, you stupid human, Vavna growled. *You've wasted enough time.*

Myla nodded before turning on her heel and sprinting down the hallway toward the stairs—hoping she could stop all of this before it turned into a fight that she wouldn't be able to win.

Chapter 52

Myla took the stairs two at a time, nearly tripping several times but being able to keep upright. By the time she made it to the bottom, she could see several people gathered on the shore. Myla ran to them and was relieved to see her father and Wrynn among the group. Her father looked up, and a smile spread across his face as Myla barrelled into him.

Myla hugged him tightly, face buried in his chest. Even though he shouldn't be here, she was glad to see him all the same. This was the longest she'd ever been away from her family, and she had missed them all terribly. Dad returned the hug, squeezing her just as tightly.

"Thank the gods, you're safe," her father murmured in her hair.

Myla pulled back. "Of course, I'm okay. But what are you doing here?"

He furrowed his brow. "The dragon hunter—Raevyn—told us you were taken by the princess and her dragon. Once I got the message, I asked their majesties if I could send a rescue team, but they refused. All who are here," he gestured to the surrounding knights, "came of their own accord—to bring the princess and you home."

Myla was surprised to hear that Raevyn already knew about Aveis. He couldn't have known the entire time. He would have told her or, at the very least, not been trying to get rid of her the whole time. Had he just suspected when Aveis took her? Had he been following them that close and saw her do magic? Or had he followed them all the way here and saw Drathal? But, if that had been the case, they would have noticed him. She supposed it didn't matter now. The damage was done, and she had to stop things before they got any worse.

"I appreciate it," Myla replied, looking over everyone and smiling when she caught Wrynn's eye. "But I've got it under control. I'm so close to getting Aveis—the princess—to come back on her own. I just need more time, and if she sees you, then all my work will be for nothing."

"I'm not leaving you again," her father said firmly.

Before Myla could argue further, she heard a roar. She turned to see Drathal descending from the castle with Aveis astride his back. Her father pushed Myla behind him and drew his sword.

"No! You've got to go. If you retreat now, they won't attack you. I promise," Myla said frantically, trying to get her father to look at her.

Dad pushed her back again just as Drathal landed—causing the ground to shake. Myla stumbled back and fell into Wrynn's arms. Myla straightened and turned to Wrynn, putting her hands on his shoulders.

"You've got to go now, please," Myla said, panic flooding into her voice.

Wrynn looked from her to her father. "We won't leave unless General tells us to."

Myla groaned in frustration, letting go of him. She stood in front of her father and faced Drathal and Aveis. She had dismounted, brandishing her coal sword dancing with flames. Her eyes found Myla instantly, and Myla sucked in a breath when she saw they were completely red.

"You," Aveis snarled, stalking toward Myla.

Myla put her hands up in a placating gesture. "Please, Aveis, this is just a big misunderstanding."

Aveis bared her teeth, her eyes flashing from red to her normal color as she struggled to suppress her own anger as well as Drathal's. "I trusted you." Aveis was trembling with rage, and Myla could feel the heat emanating off her as if she was standing in front of a forest fire.

"You can still trust me. Aveis, please—"

Her father pushed Myla behind him when Aveis was a few feet away. "I won't let you hurt her."

Aveis's eyes cut to Dad's, and she sneered. "I'm afraid you've got things backward, General. It is your daughter who has done the hurting, and I plan to return the favor."

Myla tackled her father to the ground as Aveis slashed out with her sword—the flames missing them by inches. Myla grabbed her sword and got to her feet. She held it out in a defensive position.

"Aveis—" Myla was cut short when Aveis lunged.

Myla was barely able to keep her footing as their swords collided. Her blade hissed in protest as their swords scraped together. Aveis's eyes were like pools of blood, and Myla knew she wouldn't be able to get through to her in this state—not when she was allowing Drathal's emotions to take over. She had to get her Aveis back. Myla pushed Aveis back, and she heard Drathal roar again. She was only dimly aware of the other knights charging toward Drathal as she kept her focus on Aveis.

Aveis yelled and charged again, striking over and over again, and Myla was forced to fall back. She stumbled against a rock and fell on her back. Aveis brought her sword down, and Myla rolled out of the way before jumping to her feet. Aveis discarded her flame sword and launched herself at Myla. Myla only had time to drop her own weapon and reach her arms out before Aveis knocked her to the ground. The breath was knocked out of her, and Myla gasped, reaching her hands up to grip Aveis's shoulders as she straddled her. Her hands were glowing bright orange as she took hold of Myla's wrists.

Myla screamed as the flames burned her skin. She planted her feet on the outside of Aveis's ankles and flipped them over using her hips so Myla was on top. Aveis released her grip, and Myla stumbled to her feet. Aveis wasn't far behind, and Myla pulled the sea toward her just as Aveis lunged again. She ran into an ice wall but quickly melted her way through. Fast enough that Myla wasn't expecting it, she landed on her back again. Aveis brought her hand up—the palm engulfed in flames—and brought it down toward her neck in a sharp arc. The flame died as Myla shot a blast of water toward it just before it hit her skin—Aveis's nails cutting long scratches along her neck.

"Aveis, please, don't do this."

Aveis's eyes flashed, and for a split second, Myla saw her fiery eyes before they were gone. Aveis wrapped her fingers around Myla's throat and squeezed. Myla gripped Aveis's hands, trying to wrench them away from her throat. Before Myla could use her magic, Aveis's grip loosened, and her eyes rolled in the back of her head, and then she slumped forward onto Myla. Myla instinctively wrapped her arms protectively around Aveis. She looked up to see Raevyn standing over them, an empty syringe in his hand.

"We've got to go. *Now*," Raevyn said, reaching down to pull Aveis off her.

"Just leave them be," Myla snapped, jumping to her feet as he slung Aveis over his shoulder. "We don't have to do this."

"This will be our only chance to bring her home. The only chance *you* have of going back to your normal life. It's either your freedom or hers, and I'm not allowing you to be the martyr."

"Raevyn—"

Drathal roared again, and Myla looked up to see he'd spotted them and was heading their way. Myla swore, looking between Drathal and Raevyn. She felt like her heart was being pulled in two different directions, and she was frozen in indecision.

"I—"

"Myla!"

She turned to see Wrynn running toward them. He stopped only long enough to grab her arm and tug her toward the retreating rowboats. She was relieved to see her father among those escaping.

"We've got to go."

Raevyn shoved Aveis into Wrynn's arms as if she weighed no more than a sack of potatoes. Wrynn stumbled under her weight, releasing his hold on Myla to balance Aveis across his shoulder.

"Take the princess to the ship. Myla and I will take care of the dragon," Raevyn commanded.

"But—"

"It's okay," Myla said, giving Wrynn what she hoped was a reassuring smile. "We'll be right behind you."

There was no going back now. Drathal would kill them all for touching Aveis. She had to protect her family no matter the cost.

Chapter 53

"What's the plan, sunshine?" Raevyn asked.

Drathal had turned his attention to Wrynn and Aveis—his roar, this time sounding almost panicked.

"We can't kill him," Myla said, picking up her sword and sheathing it at her hip.

"But—"

"No," she replied sternly, pulling the water and creating a whip that slashed against Drathal's face so he would turn his attention to her.

Drathal snarled at her—massive jaw widening as flames built in the back of his throat. Drathal unleashed a barrage of flames, and Myla could barely create an ice wall that blocked them and the rest of the knights from the attack.

The rowboats were finally on the water, and once Drathal's flames had ceased, she pushed the water back toward the sea, propelling them forward. Drathal spread his wings and started upward but almost immediately came crashing down with a shriek of pain. One of his wings was bent at an odd angle, dark red blood coating the inside. He got up and headed toward the sea, but Myla intercepted him with Raevyn by her side.

"Grab hold of my waist," Myla commanded, and Raevyn didn't hesitate.

Myla pushed the water back from the shore, pulling it up with them floating on top of it. It was only when they were taller than Drathal did she stop. Raevyn's grip tightened, and he swore softly.

Drathal's fiery eyes locked with hers, and Myla's heart tugged because all she could think was that it was *her* eyes.

"I'm sorry," Myla said, eyes filling with tears.

Drathal roared again and shot a blast of fire toward them. Myla pushed them out of the wave, and as they fell back, she turned the wave into ice and shoved it toward Drathal. The ice slammed into Drathal just as they hit the water—Raevyn's grip never faltered. Raevyn propelled them up by kicking off the ocean floor. They surfaced, gasping. Myla wiped the water off her face and looked to see Drathal lying motionless under the mountain. Myla was terrified that she had killed him, but his chest was rising and falling softly. Myla let out a breath of relief and waited to see if Drathal would get up again, but he didn't.

"Are you okay?" Raevyn asked, turning Myla around in his arms so they were face to face.

Myla nodded, but that wasn't entirely true. She was exhausted both physically and mentally. She had done what she needed to save everyone, but that didn't mean it was easy. Aveis had trusted her, and she'd broken it in the cruelest way possible.

"Hey." Raevyn reached up to cup her cheek. "You saved us all. You're going home a hero, Myla."

Her mouth soured at the thought—thinking she was anything but a hero.

Vavna?

The silence that greeted her was deafening.

****

Myla created an ice board for Raevyn and her, then propelled them forward toward the ship. The board nearly crashed into the ship as they neared it, Myla too tired to slow their propulsion. She grabbed onto the ladder embedded in the ship and started climbing with Raevyn close behind. She pulled herself up onto the deck, where she was met with half a dozen swords pointed directly at her.

Myla lifted her hands in a placating gesture, scanning the knights' faces in hopes of seeing a familiar face. They were all sneering at her with various expressions of fear, disgust, and anger.

"Not another step, dractactus," the knight to her right growled. He looked to be only a few years older than her, and he had light brown hair and brown eyes.

Raevyn stepped in front of Myla, blocking her from the glowering people.

"Look—"

A familiar face burst through the crowd, and Myla stepped around Raevyn just in time to be nearly tackled by Wrynn as he hugged her. Myla laughed and returned his hug with equal enthusiasm. She saw her father push through the crowd and told everyone to stand down. They begrudgingly lowered their weapons.

Wrynn pulled back and grabbed her face to assess her. "Are you hurt? What the fuck were you thinking, taking on a dragon?"

Myla pulled his hands away from her face but held onto them with her own. "I'm fine. Mostly tired, is all." Myla looked over Wrynn's shoulder at her father. "I need to talk to you both."

Her father nodded.

"We can't just let her go!" One of the other knights shouted—a short woman with grey streaks in her black hair. "She's a dractactus. Our law states that she is to be put down on sight."

Her father turned to the woman and glared. "She saved our lives. She defended us against a dragon and has brought our princess home when thousands have failed." He turned to the rest of the knights. "Her magic is to remain a secret. That's an order. If I find out that any of you have revealed her secret, you will be dismissed and executed for violating a direct order. Is that understood?"

The knights around her exchanged looks before nodding solemnly.

"Dismissed," he barked, and the knights broke away to head below deck.

"Where is Aveis—I mean Zaya, the princess?" Myla asked. "I need to talk to her."

"The princess," her father said in a tone that told her he didn't approve of Myla using her familiar name. "Is in the captain's quarters for now."

Myla started walking toward the room under the helm when her father blocked her path. "But you can't talk to her."

"Why not? I've got to explain things—"

"She tried to kill you, Myla," He looked down at her throat, where Myla was sure bruises were starting to form. "I'm not letting you anywhere near her."

"She wouldn't hurt me. She thinks I betrayed her, but once I explain—"

"Not going to happen. The chains we put on her haven't been properly tested, and I will not take the risk of them failing and you getting burnt to a crisp."

"What chains?"

"They're meant to suppress her magic like the potion. As long as they're on her, she can't access her magic," Wrynn chimed in.

Myla stiffened and felt her heart constrict. She remembered Aveis telling her about her childhood and how the potion had felt like a poison, slowly sucking the life out of her. The thought of her having to endure that kind of pain again made her stomach twist, and anger bubble up inside her.

"You can't keep those on her," Myla said through clenched teeth. "You don't understand what it's like—"

"She's too dangerous and unpredictable." Her father cut in. "I won't risk those on this ship."

"But—"

"I'm not negotiating with you." Her father put his hands on her shoulders. "Your mission is done. When we get home, you'll be knighted just like you've always wanted. You don't have to worry about the princess anymore. You can go back to your normal life."

"It's not that simple," Myla said, her voice cracking as she tried to tamp down her emotions.

Her father scanned her face, the corners of his mouth turning down slightly. Finally, he sighed. "I'll think about it, okay? But tomorrow. You need to rest now."

Myla nodded. "Okay. Thank you."

He nodded and released her before looking at Wrynn. "I need you to stay by her side until we get to Naeron. I don't want to take any chances."

Wrynn nodded. "Yes, sir."

Her father looked at Raevyn, his eyes narrowing slightly. "I appreciate you sending word about my daughter, but I don't want you anywhere near her. Without her magic, you would have died along with the rest of us, so I don't care about whatever oath you took—"

"It's okay, Dad," Myla said, reaching out and taking hold of Raevyn's hand. "He already knew."

No matter how angry she was at him for bringing them all here and turning things into a fight—she still missed him. She understood where he was coming from and might have made the same decision if their roles were reversed, but it was going to take some time to work through that. At least he listened to her and didn't kill Drathal. That, at least, was progress from what Vavna had shown her. Also, she needed her father to understand that Raevyn wasn't a threat—to Myla, at least.

"What do you mean he already knew?" Her father asked.

"It's a long story, but he won't hurt me or tell anyone. I trust him."

"Myla—"

"Tomorrow," Myla promised her father. "I'm too exhausted right now."

Her father sighed but nodded. "All right."

Myla smiled at her father before following Wrynn and Raevyn below deck. She kept her head down as she passed the knights with the rest of the ship's crew. Wrynn led them to the only cabin below deck. It was a spacious cabin complete with a four-poster bed and wardrobe. There was another door off to the left that led to a washroom.

Myla flopped down on the bed—exhaustion weighing heavily over her. It didn't take long for the exhaustion to pull her down into darkness.

Chapter 54

Myla startled awake, gasping, a scream forming in her chest. She looked around wildly, forgetting for a moment where she was. Her dreams flashed through her head, no longer making any sense: hundreds of dragons flying through the sky and blotting out the sun; Aveis with a crown on her head getting pulled to the bottom of the ocean by glowing green chains around her ankles; Drathal sitting on top of a castle while the world around him burned; and Raevyn calling out to her as she tried and failed to make her way toward him.

The bed dipped as Raevyn sat on the edge, reaching up to cup Myla's cheek. "It's okay. You're okay, sunshine."

Myla blinked and looked out the port hole to see the sun rising in the distance. "How long have I been asleep?"

"A day and a half, give or take. We'll be at port in about a day."

That would explain her dry mouth and the hunger clawing in her stomach. As if reading her thoughts, Raevyn pulled back and grabbed the tray from her bedside table before setting it on her lap.

"Eat. You must be starving."

Myla didn't need to be told twice. She ate the vegetable stew greedily until it was entirely gone. Myla wiped her mouth with the sleeve of her shirt and took a long sip of water.

"Don't think you're off the hook," Myla said as soon as she came up for air. "I'm still unbelievably upset with you."

"That seems to be your common response when I save your life."

Myla pointed her spoon at him. "Don't even start with me. I had the situation well in hand. It didn't have to end like this."

"Maybe not, but it would have taken you years to convince Av—the princess, to assume her place as heir. This was quicker and more effective."

"It should be her decision! We took away her choice!"

"It was never a choice," Raevyn argued, plucking her spoon out of her hand and setting it down on the tray. "It's her birthright. She's just been hiding from her responsibilities for a decade."

"She was hiding from her abusive parents!"

His face softened slightly, but his voice remained firm. "I understand, and even though I don't like her, I would never wish that on anyone. But I was given a choice between helping you and helping her, and I chose you. I will *always* choose you. Guilt doesn't need to fall on you. The only part you played was saving your family."

"I'm not trying to relieve myself of guilt. I want to make things right before it's too late."

Raevyn's expression hardened, and he reached out to grip both her hands in his. "You can't. Myla, I need you to think about this. Perhaps you could have convinced her, but she doesn't trust you anymore. She thinks you betrayed her—"

"I can explain things—"

His grip tightened. "She won't listen to reason. You were the only person alive that she brought to her home. Any explanation you throw at her, she will dispute. If you let her go, she'll run off with Drathal and will never be heard from again. You'll never find her, and you'll never go home and be with your family. You'll be forced into exile—if the

320

king and queen don't decide to kill you first. Aveis will have a rough few years, but she'll never have to worry about food or a place to sleep. And once her parents die, she will be queen. She'll have the power to change the kingdom for good and bring Drathal back into her life. Who knows, maybe she can even convince the king sooner—if he loves her as I expect he does."

Myla looked down at their hands, tears filling her eyes. "It's selfish—"

"You're allowed to be. It doesn't make you a bad person." Raevyn lifted her chin. "You're not alone in this. I'll be by your side—if that's what you want."

Myla pulled away from him. "You didn't trust me—haven't trusted me to make the right decision when it concerns my future."

"Myla—"

"No. You've told me you trusted me but haven't shown me. Even when you allowed Aveis to come with us on our journey, you were trying everything in your power to make me change my mind or undermine my decision. I was right to trust Aveis to take us to the princess. Maybe I wouldn't have ever been able to convince her to come home on her own had you not intervened, but you didn't trust me to try. I never asked you to come in and 'rescue' me. I am more than capable of making hard calls when I feel the time is right. I never asked for your help—"

"You never *would* ask for help—" Raevyn cut in.

"I would have." Myla snapped. "If I thought I needed it. Which I didn't."

Raevyn clenched his jaw, looking as if he wanted to argue, but just sighed. "Okay, I understand—I do, but I couldn't just leave you. I didn't know if you were okay, and it was killing me. I'm sorry. I should have found a way to talk to you before I contacted your father."

321

Myla softened, but only slightly. "It's going to take a lot more than sorry."

Raevyn nodded. "I'll do whatever it takes."

****

Myla fell asleep for a few more hours, curling up under Raevyn's watchful eyes. She was still half asleep when she heard Raevyn speak.

"Anything to report?"

"Everything's been fairly quiet as far as I can tell. But it's not as if they'd tell me otherwise." Myla recognized Wrynn's voice reply.

"You know them fairly well—anyone you can think of that we should be worried about?"

There was a long pause before Wrynn said warily. "What would you do to those I mention?"

"Whatever was necessary."

Myla fell back asleep.

****

When Myla woke up again, Raevyn was gone. She sat up with a yawn, rubbing the sleep from her eyes. Squinting, she saw Wrynn leaning against the wall next to the door. He smiled at her.

"Welcome back to the land of the living, Sea Storm."

Myla snorted and swung her legs over the side of the bed, stretching out her limbs.

"What have I missed?" Myla asked.

"Just the entire voyage. We'll be sailing into port within the hour."

Myla nodded, her eyes scanning her best friend's face. If he hadn't known about her magic before, he did now. He didn't seem angry or disgusted, but Myla needed to be sure.

322

"I'm sorry about everything that happened that day in the throne room. I begged them to let me speak to you before I left, and I would have tried harder if Raevyn hadn't been with me. He's not a problem anymore, but that's a story for another time." Myla launched into what happened that night with Desmond, leading to the hunter finding her and the mission the king and queen had given her. By the end, tears had filled her eyes. "It was stupid of me to think I hadn't been caught. I should have done more. I should have told my father sooner—"

Wrynn walked over and sat next to her. "It's okay. I understand. I'm not angry." He wrapped an arm around her shoulders and brought her into a side hug. "I'm just glad you're okay."

Myla blinked at him. "What? Just like that? I'm the reason they attacked you, and I've been lying to you for years! How can you forgive me?"

"Magic is a capital offense. I understand why you never told me about it. I would have done the same thing if our roles were reversed. Besides, I always thought our history of destroying magic was insane. I never understood why they made that decision, but I never questioned it because I thought it was ancient history. Obviously, there's a lot the crown is keeping from us. As for what happened with their majesties, you didn't know what would happen."

"Yeah, but I could have stopped it if I had told them the truth when they gave me the chance."

"It's okay," Wrynn squeezed her shoulders. "As you can see, I healed up quite nicely, and we're finally on our way home. Everything turned out all right."

Not everything, Myla thought, guilt settling in her stomach at the thought of Aveis.

She rested her head against his shoulder. "I've missed you. I have so much to tell you, and I want to hear everything I missed."

Wrynn chuckled. "Yeah, you do. And it better start with what happened between you and the dragon hunter."

Chapter 55

Myla filled Wrynn in on all that had transpired in the last few months. She started with her father's warning to keep her distance from Raevyn to meeting Aveis, then ended with her plan to convince Aveis to take her throne after spending time with her on the island.

Wrynn shook his head in disbelief. "I can't believe you got both a dragon hunter *and* a princess to fall in love with you."

"Aveis isn't in love with me," Myla argued. "She might have been attracted to me, but it didn't go any further than that."

Wrynn snorted. "Right. She's been eluding knights and hunters for over a decade but lets you stay in her hiding spot after only a few weeks with you because she was attracted to you. That makes sense."

"You're forgetting the part where I have magic, and I'm the only other person she's ever met with it. She thought I was a victim of Raevyn's and brought me to her hiding spot to save me."

"Yes, but I don't think she'd risk it if she weren't a little bit in love with you."

"It doesn't matter either way. She'll hate me forever now," she responded glumly. "Rightfully so."

"Maybe not. I think if she truly cares for you and wants you in her life, then she'll forgive you. You just need to give it time, Sea Storm."

Myla smiled slightly, feeling a warm rush of affection at the nickname Wrynn had given her when they had met. At the time, Myla thought it was so random, but Wrynn had explained how her eyes were the color of the sea and that she had the ferocity and determination of a storm. Some might have taken that as an insult, but Myla had felt oddly touched because the quality that got her into trouble more often than not was something that he liked about her, and it made her feel seen. Usually, she hated that because it meant being vulnerable, but Wrynn had seen through her and still decided to stick by her, and she loved him for that.

"Thanks, Wrynn, but I'm not going to get my hopes up. What I did was unforgivable. I don't think I deserve forgiveness."

"None of what happened is your fault. If she can't see that, then I don't think *she* deserves you."

Myla squeezed his hand. "You're too kind."

It was much too kind because Myla knew in her heart that much of what happened was, in fact, her fault, and Aveis deserved at least some kind of explanation. Myla got to her feet and almost immediately fell over as a wave of dizziness overtook her. Wrynn shot to his feet and took hold of her arms to steady her.

"Careful. You used a lot of magic—I'm assuming that equates to training too much. You should take it easy."

"I need to see Aveis. It's already been too long."

"Okay, I'll take you up there."

She pulled away from Wrynn and started toward the door. Her knees buckled slightly, but she was able to keep from falling to the ground. Wrynn followed her out—hovering behind her in case she stumbled. They went above deck, where the crew was bustling around, and the birds chirped loudly as they flew by. Myla walked up to the helm, where her father was talking to someone she assumed was the captain. She stood out from the crew with her more formal attire, a long red overcoat with gleaming golden buttons and a black wide-brimmed hat resting low on her forehead.

"I need to see her," Myla said by way of greeting.

Her father sighed and muttered something to the captain before turning to her.

"Myla—"

"Please, Father."

Myla felt Raevyn's presence behind her before he spoke. "Absolutely not."

Myla sighed in annoyance. She hated that she felt comforted by his presence and his warm hand against the small of her back even when she was still furious with him.

"I wasn't asking you," she snapped at Raevyn, eyes trained on her father. "This is important."

Her father flattened his lips in a hard line. "I don't think it's a good idea."

"She can't hurt me—"

"That's not strictly true—"

"I can defend myself regardless," Myla cut in. "Please. I need to explain things to her."

Her father took a deep breath, letting it out through his nose. "Fine, but you only get a few minutes."

Myla smiled and gave him a tight hug. "Thank you."

"Now, wait a damn minute—" Raevyn started, but her father cut him off.

"We will stand outside the door the whole time, and if I hear anything to warrant concern, I'll pull you out immediately, understood?"

"Yes, Father. But you have nothing to worry about."

"We'll see about that."

They started toward the captain's cabin, but Myla didn't make it far. Raevyn blocked her path and glared down at her.

"This is a stupid idea."

Myla poked his chest. "You don't have to like everything I do. Now get out of my way."

"Why are you so fucking stubborn?" He seethed.

"Just to drive you crazy," she responded sweetly.

She stepped around him, but he grabbed her arm. "She won't be in a talkative mood."

"Then it's a good thing I'll be doing most of the talking."

When he didn't release his grip, she glared up at him. "Is this how you show you trust me?"

He released his grip but kept his hand hovering over her arm as if it was taking all his strength not to pull her into his arms and protect her from danger. "Fine, but if I hear even a *scuffle*—"

"I know." She gave him a small smile. "You'll barge in like the knight in shining armor you think I need when we both know *I'm* the knight in this relationship, and I'll end up saving you."

His lips twitched as he tried to hide a smile. "Yes, that."

She grinned before following Wrynn and her father to the captain's cabin. The men stood outside the door while she walked in. She made sure to bolt the door behind her. The room was similar to the one below deck but was twice the size. There was a four-poster bed and a nightstand on the right side, sidled next to a porthole. In the middle of the room was a long table set for two, and on the left was a grand desk. There was also a wardrobe and a folding screen in one corner. The entire room was decorated in dark reds and gold, from the rugs to the blankets on the bed. Aveis was sitting in the middle of the bed, slumped forward, and staring at the chains fastened around her wrists.

"Aveis—"

Aveis's head snapped up, and she snarled before lunging at her.

Chapter 56

Myla didn't have time to react. Aveis barrelled into her, and she crashed to the floor—knocking the breath from her lungs. She reached up and took hold of Aveis's hands before she could scratch her eyes out.

"How could you!" Aveis snarled, struggling to break out of Myla's hold.

Myla flipped them around so she was on top. "Please, let me explain!"

"Myla?" The doorknob rattled, and before they all started banging on the door. "Open this door!"

"I'm fine!" Myla called as she pinned Aveis's chained hands above her head.

Aveis struggled and bared her teeth. "For now."

The door shuddered in its frames, but Myla ignored it and focused on Aveis. "Please, let me help you."

"Unless you're planning on taking these fucking chains off me and taking me back to Drathal, then *not* interested."

"Please, I didn't want this to happen like it did."

"I don't want to hear your excuses," Aveis struggled under her grip but couldn't break out of Myla's hold.

"I wanted you to come back on your own. I was never going to force you."

Aveis laughed, but there was no humor in it. "You drugged me and dragged me here, then proceeded to chain me up. That's the definition of forcing me."

Myla released her hold and got to her feet, putting her hands up—trying to show she meant no harm. "I never wanted this—"

Aveis got to her feet and snarled. "Bullshit! I trusted you! How could you—" Her voice broke, and tears collected in her eyes. "Just leave me alone. I never want to see you again."

"Aveis, please," Myla reached for her, tears collecting in her own eyes, but Aveis stepped back and glared.

"Don't fucking touch me."

The door slammed open, and her father, Raevyn, and Wrynn stumbled in. Raevyn stepped between them as her father pulled her back by her arm.

He glanced down at Myla, eyes narrowed. "Times up."

"But—"

"*Now.*"

Myla looked at Aveis, but she had turned away—shaking from anger or tears, she wasn't sure.

"I'm sorry," Myla told her, voice thick with emotion.

Aveis stiffened but didn't reply as her father pulled Myla out the door.

****

Myla didn't see Aveis for the rest of the voyage. Her father wouldn't allow it, and Myla knew Aveis wouldn't see her, anyway. Myla debated writing her a letter or something, but Aveis would just rip it up. Myla needed to explain everything to her. She needed her to understand. Her heart was aching thinking about Aveis hurting and believing that she had betrayed her. She had to make it right—but how? She couldn't exactly break her out and the selfish part of her didn't want to. As Raevyn had said, this would be her only chance to bring Aveis home and be able to stay home herself. If she let her go, Aveis would never go back to Cassia, and Myla could never go home and be with her family again. Myla would find a way to make it up to her, or hopefully, Aveis would understand one day.

From Naeron, they took multiple carriages to Cassia. Myla wanted to ride with Aveis, but it was out of the question. Her father rode with Aveis alone, and Wrynn, Raevyn, and Myla rode in their own carriage—for protection, her father had said. Aveis had fought them every step of the way, but without her magic, she was outmatched. Myla hated that they were treating her like a prisoner and not like the princess she was.

She hoped that when they got to Cassia, things would change, and they'd take the chains off her. She knew it was wishful thinking, but perhaps after all these years, her parents had seen the error of their ways and would let Aveis use her magic freely. Perhaps even Drathal would be welcome in the kingdom's capital. Stupid and naïve, she knew, but it was the only thing she could think about without breaking down with sadness and guilt. She hoped she hadn't made a grave mistake.

They traveled nonstop to get to Cassia as quickly as possible. The King and Queen didn't know of their arrival and would be upset at her father for going behind their backs. But all would hopefully be forgiven when they saw their daughter for the first time in over ten years.

During the voyage, Raevyn explained everything that happened after they were separated. It had only taken him a few days to find them, but before he could confront them, he had seen Aveis do magic. He knew then that she was the princess and decided it would be best to follow for the time being in hopes that Aveis was taking Myla to Drathal and they could finish their assignment. When he saw them go on a ship, he asked around the docks to figure out what route the ship took. He knew Aveis wouldn't have gone to the neighboring kingdom of Adratus, and there was only one island near the ship's trade route that could possibly be their destination. Then he wrote a letter to Myla's father asking for help.

"Why would you ask my father for help?" Myla asked.

"Because I knew that if, for whatever reason, you decided to side with Aveis, I would be outmatched because I would never have hurt you. And we needed the princess alive in order to fulfill your end of the bargain."

Once they made it to Cassia, Myla's father dismissed the soldiers that had come with them—thanking them for their service and reminding them of their order to keep their mission a secret. In case things turned out for the worse, her father didn't want anyone getting dragged down with them. Wrynn, however, refused to leave their side, not caring about the possible repercussions.

Her father had alerted the Royal Guard of their arrival, and they were now following Captain Oyvim through the palace halls toward the throne room. Myla felt tense being around him again, after what he'd done to the hunter, but kept her face neutral. Wrynn looked slightly uncomfortable as well, but Captain Oycim acted as though they'd never met before. She was fine with that and hoped after this, they'd never have to interact again.

Myla and her father flanked Aveis on either side while Wrynn and Raevyn brought up the rear. Myla had tried to catch Aveis's eye, but she refused to look at her. There were bags under her eyes, and Aveis's usually vibrant skin paled slightly as if she was getting sick. Despite this, she held her head high and shoulders back—ready to face whatever came her way. She didn't try to run this time. Maybe because she knew it was pointless, or perhaps a part of her wanted to see her parents again (no doubt a small part if that part even existed).

Her gaze traveled to the chains around Aveis's wrists. They looked to be regular chains, but Myla could see needles embedded along the inside—injecting the potion into her veins. On the ride there, Myla had asked Wrynn about them, and he told her there was potion inside the bands around her wrists that slowly dripped through the needles and into puncture wounds. The potion lasted a week and needed to be refilled using a locked section embedded on the side of the wristbands.

Myla thought of her own encounter with the potion. It had terrified her to be cut off from her magic so absolutely—as if losing a limb. It drained her, and she felt exhausted until the potion wore off. If they never took the chains off, would Aveis always feel tired and weak? Could her parents do that to her for the rest of her life?

The guards beside the doors to the throne room saluted to the captain before opening them. Myla's heart lurched—thinking about the last time she had been in this room and how it had changed everything. She turned to Wrynn, who gave her an encouraging smile and a nod. If Wrynn could face going back here, so could she. Myla swallowed hard and turned to face the doorway where the captain had returned. He nodded to Myla's father and gestured for them to head inside.

Chapter 57

Myla walked into the throne room and up to the dais. She knelt and bowed her head, following her father's lead. Aveis didn't follow suit. Her eyes stayed fixated on her parents, with her lips curled into a sneer. King Otois immediately got to his feet and walked up to Aveis—his eyes wide and full of tears. Queen Deona followed after as if realizing that was the next right step. Her eyes were dry as she forced a sickly-sweet smile on her face.

The king pulled Aveis into a hug. It was clear that Aveis wasn't expecting it. Her body went rigid at the touch, and even if she wanted to hug him back, she couldn't with the chains binding her wrists in front of her. He pulled back and put his hands on her shoulders, eyes scanning her face. The queen nodded to them, kneeling, and Myla got to her feet along with Raevyn, Wrynn, and her father.

"You've grown up so much," the king murmured, tears falling freely down his cheeks. "I'm so happy you're finally home."

Aveis seemed taken aback by her father's reaction, but she steeled herself and stepped away from her father and out of his grip. "This isn't my home. Drathal is my home."

Striking the king would have hurt less if the expression on his face meant anything.

Queen Deona just rolled her eyes. "Over ten years, and yet you have not changed from the tantrum-throwing child you were when you left."

Aveis turned to glare at her mother. "Over ten years, and yet you have not changed from the heartless bitch you were when I escaped this hellhole."

"How *dare* you—"

"It would be best to table this discussion for another time," the king interjected. He wiped the tears away and squared his shoulders—turning back to the powerful and intimidating king Myla remembered.

The queen let out a breath and forced a smile back on her lips. "Yes. We owe you a debt of gratitude for bringing the princess home," she spoke, dark brown eyes turning to Myla. "I'll admit, I did not think you would succeed even with one of our best at your side, but am gladdened you have."

Myla let the jab roll off her and inclined her head. "I am happy to have assisted, Your Majesty."

"And as promised," the king drew his sword—the sword stained with the blood of countless slaughtered dragons and magic wielders—and pointed it at Myla. "Do you swear your devotion and loyalty to the crown?"

Heart hammering in her chest, Myla only hesitated for a moment before replying, "I do."

"Do you swear to safeguard the helpless and do no wrong even if it leads to your death?"

"I do."

"Do you swear to be an agent for the rest of your life and to never betray the crown or their causes to the full extent of your abilities?"

"I do."

The king nodded. "Then kneel, Myla Yules."

Myla did—bowing her head as she dropped to one knee. For the first time, Myla felt Aveis's eyes on her like twin flames burning a hole in the side of her face. Shame rose up inside of Myla. This wasn't how she was supposed to feel the day she got knighted. This had been her dream since she was a child, but this wasn't how it was supposed to go. She wasn't meant to become a knight by standing on the back of someone she had grown to care for.

"I dub thee Dame Myla Yules," King Otois touched the flat edge of the blade on each of Myla's shoulders. "Knight of Rosebourne and personal guard to Princess Zaya Griffin. Now rise."

Myla got to her feet and turned to look at Aveis. She looked as shocked as Myla felt, but that shock quickly turned to anger.

"No fucking way," Aveis snarled. "I don't want her anywhere near me."

"She was the only one that was able to bring you home safely," The king replied. "I trust she will continue to keep you safe. There is no other in this castle I can say the same for."

"And," the queen added. "It is not up for discussion. You may be a princess, but we're the king and queen. Therefore, you have no power over us."

"And we're your parents," the king said, glaring at his wife. "First and foremost. We only want to keep you safe."

"I will never be safe here! Don't you understand? If anyone finds out what I can do, I'll be killed even with your protection. The only place I'll truly be safe is by Drathal's side." She held out her wrists. "And with these chains, I can do nothing to protect myself."

"Which is why you have a personal guard."

"Yes, with abilities—"

"That makes her a suitable knight," the king interrupted, no doubt to keep Myla's magic a secret from Raevyn. She shuddered to think what would happen if their majesties knew Raevyn was aware of her magic. Would they kill him like the other hunter? It was more plausible they'd kill her since she'd served her purpose in bringing their daughter back. She'd prefer that over having another suffer for what she was.

"No, I mean—"

"Enough!" The queen threw up her hands. "Myla, the captain, will show you your new living quarters, which will be adjacent to Zaya's. General, though you went against our wishes to aid Myla, we will let it slide only because you have helped bring the princess home. We will not be so generous the next time you disobey us."

Myla's father bowed. "Thank you, your majesties."

The queen waved her hand at Wrynn and her father. "You both are dismissed. Tell Captain Oyvim to come in as you leave."

Wrynn and Dad bowed again. They each gave her one last look, the worry evident on their faces. Myla gave them what she hoped was a convincing smile, but when their worry deepened, she knew she had failed. They hesitated only a moment—to do or say what, Myla wasn't sure—before leaving the room. Raevyn stood off to the side and slightly behind her, silent and steady like a shadow. Aveis was silently fuming next to her. Her hands were balled into fists, and if she had her magic back, Myla was sure that her hands would have been consumed with fire.

The captain walked into the room and bowed deeply. "Your majesties."

"Have the rooms been made up for them?" The queen asked. At the captain's nod, she continued. "Show them to their rooms. Zaya, once you've cleaned up, we'll be expecting you for dinner. Raevyn, we require a status report before you're dismissed."

Aveis curled her lip. "I will not take orders from you—"

"Please, Zaya," King Otois said. "It'll give us a chance to talk properly."

Aveis looked at her father, and her gaze softened ever so slightly. She sighed. "Fine."

Myla bowed to their majesties one last time, eyes flickering back to Raevyn. He gave a subtle nod and a look she deciphered as he would find her later. She straightened before following Aveis and the captain out of the throne room. They walked down the winding halls until they reached two sets of doors in the palace's west wing.

"I will await here until you are ready, Your Highness." The captain bowed to Aveis and turned to Myla. "While the princess is at dinner, you will have time to go home and pack your things. You must be back by eight. That should give you plenty of time to collect what you need. I will escort the princess to and from dinner tonight, but after, you will not leave the princess's side. Their majesties do not trust anyone other than the two of us to guard the princess. If there is an emergency, you must find me to reprieve you."

So much for never seeing him again, Myla thought before nodding. "Understood, sir."

"How do you expect me to bathe and change with these," Aveis interrupted, thrusting her wrists out, causing the chains to rattle.

The captain turned his gaze to Aveis and fished out a key from his pocket. "Apologies, Your Highness."

Myla sucked in a breath, thinking that he would remove the bonds completely. From the hungry desperation in Aveis's eyes—she felt the same. The captain, however, only removed the chain that connected the two bands on her wrists.

Aveis sighed. "That's not what I had in mind."

"I'm under direct orders to keep the bands on you for the time being, Your Highness."

Aveis just rolled her eyes and disappeared into her room.

"Palace armor will be provided within a fortnight that you will be expected to wear daily." Captain Oyvim continued, turning his gaze back to Myla. "There is a door that leads from her room to yours in case there are any incidents. That door can't be locked from either side. Princess Aveis's room will remain locked at all times while she's in there, so no one—not even the guards who will be posted outside her door—will be able to enter from there. If someone were to somehow infiltrate the princess's room, you would be her first line of defense." The captain fished out two keys from his pocket and handed them to her. "One key is for your room, and the other is the only key to her room. If, for some reason, the door adjoining your two rooms has been obstructed in any way, you'll be able to go around and get into her room from the front. You are not to give this key to anyone else. Understood?"

"Yes, sir."

"Good. You're dismissed."

Myla saluted before turning on her heel and heading down the hall, hoping she'd be able to find her way out.

Chapter 58

Myla was able to find her way back to the throne room, where she waited near the doors for Raevyn to come out. After nearly a half hour of waiting, Myla turned to leave. She was trying to think of where he would go after this. Would they send him on another assignment so soon? Did he have a place he called home? She didn't have to wonder for long as Raevyn pulled open the grand double doors and strolled out. He spotted her immediately and walked over to her. Without breaking stride, he looped his arm with hers and dragged her away from the guards stationed outside the throne room.

"What did you tell them?" Myla asked as soon as they were out of earshot of the guards.

"I told them the highlights of our journey, excluding the more personal details that weren't relevant."

"So they don't know that you know about me?"

Raevyn gave her a sideways glance. "Of course not."

Myla nodded, feeling slightly relieved. "What did they have to say?"

"They were mostly curious about your relationship with the princess and what became of the dragon."

"What did you tell them?"

"I told them she was drawn to you from the beginning, and I didn't know why. And I told them that the dragon was still alive."

Myla stiffened. "And they asked you to finish the job, didn't they?"

Raevyn nodded solemnly.

"You can't, Raevyn, please," Myla replied urgently. "Drathal has done nothing to deserve this. They don't have to be the enemy—magic, dragons, all of it. We were told that they got power hungry, but you know that's not true. People in power felt inadequate, and they took it out on innocent people. You don't have to be their assassin. Please—"

"I don't have a choice," he said softly. "This will be for the best. The princess will lose most of her magic, and their majesties won't be forced to inject that concoction into her system, which makes her sick."

They stepped outside the palace doors and into the circular courtyard surrounded by tall stone walls. The sun was just setting, casting the ground in shadows. The courtyard was full of people bustling to and from the bridge that led into the heart of the city, their chatter echoing off the walls around them. She pulled out of Raevyn's grip and took his hand—dragging him over to a quiet alcove and out of the light snowfall.

"Taking away her magic would be like taking away the part that makes her who she is," Myla insisted. "The only people it would help is their majesties."

"Myla—"

"Please." She took hold of his bicep as if her grip would knock some sense into him. "I'm asking you to help me."

Pain filled his expression, knowing just how much it meant to Myla if she was asking for help. "That's not fair, sunshine—"

"I know, but I know you don't want to do this. Magic doesn't have to be the enemy."

Raevyn lifted his arm but let it fall back to his side—fighting the urge to pull her close. "If I don't kill the dragon, they'd know. It—he isn't going to just leave Aveis here. He'll come for her eventually, and it won't end well for anyone. They won't go quietly. People—*innocent* people—will get hurt or worse."

Myla's heart dropped, knowing there was truth in his words, but still couldn't condone killing Drathal. "There has to be another way. We could let her go—"

"No," said Raevyn firmly. "Their majesties would blame you and hang you for the crime. Since you are the only one with the means to help her escape now that you're her personal guard."

"Not if we do it now that she's not under my watch—"

"It's too risky. I won't let you put yourself at unnecessary risk—"

"And I wasn't asking for your permission," Myla snapped. "Whatever decision *I* decide to make will be my own, and *I* will deal with the consequences. You don't have to agree with my decisions, but you have no right to try and stop me."

"I'm just trying to protect you—"

"Don't give me that bullshit." She pointed an accusing finger at him. "That's just your excuse not to trust me. I'm not asking you to agree with me all the time or to not fight me on decisions you think are wrong. I'm asking you to let me make them and not make them for me. And if that's so hard for you to do—then I'm not sure where that leaves us."

Raevyn tilted his head back to look at the sky and ran his hands through his hair. He let out a frustrated breath before looking back at her. "Okay, fine. I don't think it's a great idea to break her out now, especially since you have no idea where she'll be or how to get her out of the castle. Plus, she'll be with their majesties most of the time, which doesn't leave you much of a window to enact any sort of plan."

"Okay—that's reasonable, but do you have any better suggestions?"

"There isn't a choice here, Myla. I have to kill him."

Myla took a step back from him as if his words were a physical blow. "If you go through with this—if you kill Drathal—I won't ever forgive you."

Raevyn flinched, reaching out toward Myla. "Sunshine—"

"Don't." She took another step back. "There will be no coming back from this. If you hurt him, then the next time you see me, it'll be as your enemy."

Raevyn clenched his hand into a fist and lowered his hand. He stared at her for a long moment. She wasn't sure if he was waiting for her to change her mind, but she didn't speak. She didn't even let her expression soften from the stony resolve. She wouldn't allow her feelings to cloud her judgment. Not for something as important as this. She loved him more than she had ever loved anyone, but they wouldn't be able to come back from this. If he continued to fight against the very thing that made her who she was—there could be no future for them.

Finally, Raevyn said. "So be it."

Chapter 59

Myla parted with Raevyn, still unsure of what he planned to do. She had a sinking feeling in her gut that he would do as he always did—as Vavna warned her he would. But there wasn't anything she could do. If she went after him, she'd be abandoning her post, and all she had done and everyone she'd hurt to get to this point would be for nothing. She had to leave it up to Raevyn to decide. She really hoped that he made the right choice—for Aveis's sake and her own because she wasn't sure if she could handle the heartbreak.

Fuck, Aveis—Zaya, the princess, whatever she had to call her now. That was its own issue. She was her personal guard. She never expected the king and queen to trust her with such a task. It didn't make sense. They didn't know her. Myla did possess magic, but magic wielders had been known to turn on one another, just as Vavna's history indicated. For all they knew, Myla hated the magic in her veins and wanted to destroy all magic. She had been taught that, after all. Whatever the reason, Myla would protect Aveis at all costs. Myla cared for her even if Aveis didn't believe it herself. And perhaps this would give her the opportunity to make it up to Aveis.

Myla walked down the cobblestone street until she reached her house. She knocked on the door, and almost immediately, it opened. Her mother embraced her, and tears collected in Myla's eyes as she hugged her back just as fiercely.

"I'm so happy you're home, honey," her mother mumbled into her hair.

Her mom pulled back only so she could usher her inside, where she was greeted by Rikia, Wrynn, and her father. Rikia hugged her tightly.

"Good to see you too," Myla grinned—glad to let the dread and guilt settle in the back of her mind for now.

"So, tell us everything!" Rikia said, pulling Myla over to the couch. "We're all dying to hear."

Myla sat down between Rikia and Wrynn, feeling the guilt start to rise back up in her chest. She didn't know how much of what happened, and she wanted to tell them. Her unlikely relationship with Raevyn—definitely not. Also, all the intimate details of Aveis's past trauma weren't hers to share. So, she started from the beginning, telling them of the various cities and towns she visited, meeting Aveis, and her days on the island with her and Drathal. They were just as confused as she was about Aveis letting Myla stay in her hiding spot, but Myla explained that Aveis had been trying to gain something from Myla as she had. She didn't go into much detail about the days that followed. Only described how she had slowly gained Aveis's trust as well as Drathal's to the point that she was able to learn from them about her magic, how they were able to survive on the island, and what they did to keep each other safe.

Her father rubbed his chin. "Very interesting. She never tried to attack you?"

Myla shook her head. "She didn't see me as a threat until after she thought I betrayed her."

Her father scowled. "And the knights that went after her? Did she tell you what became of them?"

"No, but when we hitched a ride on a ship, one of the crew members told me she'd taken knights to her island before, and they were never heard from again."

"Killed them, most likely," he responded, his voice somber.

"Do you think Drathal will come for her?" Her mother asked. "If their bond is as strong as you say..."

"I think he will. It will quite possibly be a suicide mission, but Drathal loves her. He'll protect her at all costs."

"Shouldn't we alert the king and queen? We should prepare for an attack." Wrynn replied.

"They already know. Raevyn..." Myla trailed off, looking down at her hands. "I tried to convince him, but I don't think I got through to him."

"Of course, you wouldn't have," her father said, not unkindly. "That's who he was trained to be."

"He let me go, didn't he?" Myla argued. "People change."

"Killing a human being and a monster are two very different things."

"He's not a monster," Myla snapped. "We know nothing about dragons because our history with them was erased. I was with him for weeks—he's intelligent and cares for Aveis as if she was his own flesh and blood. He's never attacked anyone that didn't initiate it."

Her family exchanged looks, but no one spoke up to counter her. Myla sighed and slumped back into the cushions, running her hands down her face.

"This has become so fucking complicated. Even if Raevyn decides to let Drathal live or if he's able to heal enough to get here before Raevyn finds him—Drathal will come here. He'll do whatever is required to save Aveis."

"If the dragon only wants the princess, and the princess wants to leave, then I don't think we should stand in their way. The princess has been brought home, so that means that Myla has fulfilled her end of the bargain. If she leaves afterward, they cannot fault Myla. That's what's most important." Her father responded, leaning forward and resting his elbows on his knees.

"I'm her personal guard—tasked with keeping her safe. If I let her go, they *will* fault me."

"The princess said it herself: being with Drathal is the safest option. Besides, put up a convincing fight, and they won't be able to hold it against you. You won't be able to use your magic in front of anyone else, and it was your magic that got us off that island in the first place. It's risky, but I think it's our safest option." Dad reasoned.

"I think you're right. If Drathal comes and they leave without hurting anyone, then we should let her. I just can't help but think, what if she could change things?" Myla asked. "There's a possibility that she could change everything once she becomes queen. If she leaves now and waits for her parents to pass before coming back and claiming the throne—it'll be madness. No one will accept her as a ruler. But, if she stays and proves herself to the people before her parents' demise, then it'll be a smoother transition, and she'll have a better chance to create a better, safer Rosebourne for people like us. That's what I was trying to convince Aveis to do, and I think I was getting through to her. Obviously, this isn't my choice to make, but shouldn't I at least try in the meantime?"

Her family all exchanged uncertain looks. Finally, Wrynn spoke up.

"You can try, but what's the likelihood you'll succeed?"

"Slim to none," Myla admitted.

"There's no harm," Rikia replied.

Myla nodded and got to her feet. "Well, I've got to go pack. I'm due at the palace shortly, but we need to meet up again soon. I'm not to leave Aveis's side, but you can visit me in my rooms, and we can catch up."

They all nodded in agreement before she headed upstairs. She packed up all her remaining clothes and a few knickknacks that she didn't want to leave behind. On their way to Cassia City, Raevyn had given her the supplies she had left to follow Aveis, which she had been grateful for. Once packed, she headed back downstairs to say goodbye to everyone—promising to see them again soon. She hated leaving. There seemed to be so much more to say, but she had run out of time. Soon, she reminded herself. She wouldn't be too far from home any longer.

Chapter 60

Wrynn offered to walk with Myla back to the palace. She was grateful for the company and the distraction from her troubling thoughts. She kept thinking about what Aveis had implied about why she, too, wasn't in chains. Myla knew Aveis was a flight risk, which was why she needed them, but why would they allow Myla to access her magic?

"Why do you think the king and queen didn't put me in chains like Aveis?" Myla asked.

Wrynn looked up at her—seemingly coming out of his own thoughts. "Probably because they don't want anyone to know you have magic, at least not any more people. The guards can rationalize keeping their daughter alive even with magic, but someone with no ties to royalty? It would make them look soft and sympathetic toward magic wielders."

Myla nodded. "I suppose that makes sense. They have no reason to believe I would rise against them—not after bringing their daughter home and securing their line of succession. Plus, they'll never believe that Aveis and I are plotting against them since she hates me so much."

"Would you plot against them if given the opportunity?" Wrynn asked carefully.

"Of course not," Myla responded immediately—instinctively—but she thought about it for a moment.

She'd taken an oath promising to protect the crown no matter the threat. She'd sworn her loyalty to those that have done their best to wipe out the magic humming under her skin. She'd always seen her father as a just leader and aspired to be just like him because that's what she wanted. After going on this mission and learning more about who she was, she wasn't entirely sure she wanted to follow their orders. Not if it went against her morals.

"Maybe," she said softly after a few moments.

She waited for him to be affronted—to step away from her and to call her a traitor. Instead, he grabbed onto her hand and squeezed it in reassurance.

"You'll figure it out, and I'll support you. I can't imagine what it must be like for you, but I know you're a good person, and whatever you decide will be what's right for you."

Myla smiled at her friend, grateful to know that he would stand by her. "Thank you, Wrynn."

****

Once they made it to the palace gates, Myla parted ways with Wrynn with a promise to see him tomorrow. It was a few minutes to eight by the time she got there. The captain was waiting for her in front of Aveis's door. Myla saluted to him, expecting him to nod and be on his way, given that being a personal guard was way below his pay grade and no doubt he had many other duties to deal with. When he didn't, Myla slowed to a stop.

Captain Oyvim looked over her shoulder before turning his gaze back to her and gesturing to her room. Myla walked up to the door and opened it with her key. The captain followed her inside, shutting the door behind him. The room was the same size as her own back home. A large four-poster bed with twin bookcases on each side occupied the far wall, nestled up in the center under the window. A desk was set up next to the door, and a dresser with a mirror was against the right wall next to the washroom door. In the left corner was a large armchair and footrest near the door that led into Aveis's room. The entire room was decorated in shades of light grey and pale gold.

"What do you know about the dragon from the island?" He asked as Myla set her bag down on the bed.

Myla blinked, surprised by the question. "What do you mean?"

He flattened his mouth in a thin line. "The princess threatened the king and queen with the beast's presence—claiming it'll come for her. Based on what you've observed during your time there, do you think that is a possibility?"

Myla felt her heart drop, but she was careful not to let her emotions show on her face. "Difficult to say. It is a beast after all—hard to anticipate whether it has the capacity for the complex emotions it'll need to make such a decision."

Captain Oyvim's lips twitched into a smirk. "Quite right. I figured the princess was only grasping at straws, but I will have the guards keep an eye out, regardless."

Myla nodded and saluted as he left the room. Once the door shut behind him, Myla strode into Aveis's room using the adjoining door. Her room was twice as large and was decorated in shades of bright pink and gold. In front of her was a small couch and armchairs surrounding a wooden coffee table. At the far end of the room was a four-poster bed with hanging sheer drapes. Along the right wall was a vanity table and a full-length mirror. On the left wall across from the sitting area was a door that led into the washroom, and a large desk settled far to the right of the door.

Aveis was standing next to the desk wearing a ridiculously frilly dress that tightened around her waist and cascaded down her legs in thick layers of pink silk and lace. Her hair had been left down to fall in waves along her spine. Myla felt the urge to laugh, given that the outfit was so far from something Aveis would have chosen herself, but her worry killed the laughter from her chest.

Aveis whirled around, brandishing what looked to be a letter opener. She relaxed her stance slightly when she saw it was Myla, but she didn't lower her weapon.

Myla marched up to her—not as worried about the letter opener as she ought to have been given their last two meetings. "Are you out of your mind?"

Aveis blinked in confusion before narrowing her eyes. "What are you talking about?"

"Why would you tell them about Drathal?" Myla hissed, lowering her voice ever so slightly in case the guards were already posted outside Aveis's door.

"I don't—"

"The Royal Guard will be looking for him now. We both know that Drathal will come for you, but any chance of a sneaky entrance has now been blown because you couldn't keep your mouth shut." *That is, if Drathal gets away before Raevyn shows up,* Myla thought but didn't want to say as much to Aveis.

Aveis's lips parted slightly, and her eyes widened as she realized what Myla was saying. The shock quickly faded, and she glared at Myla. "What's it to you anyway? You're the reason I'm here in the first place. You obviously don't care about either of us."

Myla clenched her jaw—anger boiling up inside her. "I understand you're upset. Rightfully so, but if you think for one second, I didn't care about—don't care about you still—then you're a fool."

Aveis bared her teeth and thrust out the letter opener so it rested against Myla's chest. "The only foolish thing I did was trust you in the first place. I should have listened to Drathal, to begin with, and I wouldn't be in this mess."

"I never lied to you. The only thing I didn't tell you is that your parents wanted me to bring you home."

"Yes, and as a reward, you were to be knighted just as you've always wanted and would be able to come home. So, of course, you sold me out."

"I never sold you out! I wouldn't—"

"Stop it! You got what you want from me—what more could you want? Do you want the fucking crown too? Because you can have it. I never wanted it."

"I don't want anything from you! I just want you to understand—"

"I understand perfectly. You chose yourself over me. Plain and simple." Aveis pushed the letter opener against Myla's skin, causing her to step back. "Now, get the fuck out of my room. Next time you barge in—I won't be so amiable."

To make her point, she pushed the letter opener harder against Myla—nearly drawing blood—before stepping back and turning away from her. Myla wanted to say more—wanted to plead with her to understand—but she couldn't bring herself to do it because she knew Aveis was right. She was in the wrong, and there was nothing more she could say now to make things better. Especially if she wasn't willing to listen, she'd have to prove it to her with actions. What those actions would be, Myla wasn't sure, but she'd be damned before she gave up on her without a fight.

Chapter 61

Myla woke up to Aveis screaming. Myla bolted out of bed and ran into Aveis's room, grabbing her sword as she did. She brandished the blade, squinting as her eyes adjusted to the darkness. She turned in a circle, looking for a threat, but found none. Aveis screamed again, and Myla ran over to her. She was thrashing in bed with her eyes screwed shut and her covers thrown off her. Her skin was gleaming with sweat, and she kept mumbling something that Myla couldn't understand. She was clawing at the bands around her wrists to the point that her fingernails were broken and bleeding.

Myla dropped her sword to pull Aveis's hands away from the metal bands. Aveis fought against her as she held her hands against Aveis's chest—shaking her softly and telling her to wake up. Aveis gasped, eyes flying open. She sat up, and Myla let go of her hands. Aveis was looking around wildly as if trying to figure out where she was.

"It's okay. You're okay. You're safe," Myla whispered softly, brushing a lock of hair from her eye.

Aveis's eyes focused on Myla, and tears started streaming down her cheeks. Myla sat on the edge of the bed and pulled Aveis into her arms. She couldn't help it—she had never seen Aveis break down like this. Myla was surprised when Aveis didn't pull away and instead hugged her back, burying her face in her chest.

"I've got you," Myla lulled, rubbing soothing circles along Aveis's back. "It was just a dream."

Aveis suddenly pulled back and out of her arms, scooting away until her back was against the headboard. "They're never just dreams," she snarled. "They're memories. And here I thought that no memory could top almost being assassinated, but congratulations—your betrayal hurts much more."

Tears welled in Myla's eyes, and her heart squeezed painfully in her chest, making it hard for her to breathe. "Aveis—"

"Leave!" Aveis pulled her knees to her chest and buried her face in them. "Please, for the love of the gods, haven't you hurt me enough?"

Myla had to swallow the sob rising up in her throat as she got to her feet. She grabbed the sword and walked back into her room. Only when the door shut behind her did she allow her tears to fall.

****

Myla barely slept that night. When the sun started rising, Myla gave up on trying and got ready for the day. She slipped on a pair of red cloth trousers, a white blouse, and a black corset. She was slipping on her knee-length black boots when there was a knock on the door. Myla walked over and opened it to reveal a young man pushing a cart of food.

"Dame Yules," the man dipped his head, blonde curls falling into his eyes.

Myla opened the door wider to let him in.

"This is for you and the princess," he said, lifting the lids off the trays and storing them in the lower compartment of the cart. "She told me to give it all to you since she wasn't hungry."

"Okay, thank you."

He nodded and left, shutting the door behind him. She knocked on the adjoining door before poking her head in. Aveis was sitting at her vanity with an older woman, fussing with her hair. Aveis's makeup had already been done—black outlined her eyes, red powder was dusted along her cheeks in an attempt to make her look less pale, and her lips were painted a dark red. Aveis didn't look at Myla, but the older woman nodded to Myla in greeting before returning to her task. Another woman shuffled through the exquisite gowns of various colors in Aveis's wardrobe.

Myla returned to her room, pushed the cart into Aveis's room, and set it up in the sitting area. Myla wasn't too hungry herself, but the food smelled delicious, and she ended up eating her whole plate to give herself something to do. It left a weird aftertaste in her mouth, but she pushed past it and settled back in the armchair to watch the older woman place a tiara of woven gold, diamonds, and sapphires on Aveis's newly styled updo. Aveis stared at the tiara in the mirror and scowled. The other woman had grabbed a terracotta-colored gown with a lace design around the bodice the color of cream. It was beautiful and would pair really well with Aveis's eyes, but Myla couldn't help but think that all the dresses and frills didn't pair with the woman she had gotten to know. Trousers were definitely better for travel, but Myla was sure if Aveis had been interested in dresses, then she would have worn them at some point.

"Is it completely necessary for her to get all dressed up?" Myla asked. "Couldn't she just wear trousers?"

The two women looked at her in shock—as if she had asked if Aveis could walk around naked.

"Princess Aveis is to be reintroduced into court and the kingdom today. She cannot wear *trousers*," the older woman responded, appalled.

357

Myla looked to Aveis for confirmation, but her scowl only deepened.

"Oh, I wasn't aware. When are they making the announcement?"

"This morning, the princess will meet with their majesties and their court. Then, this afternoon, she will be announced to the rest of the kingdom."

Aveis didn't look happy about the prospect but allowed the two women to pull her behind the folding screen to help her into the gown. When she walked out, one of the women placed a thick necklace of diamonds around Aveis's throat. She looked like what Myla always thought a princess would look like, but it wasn't Aveis. She kept stepping on the thick layers of fabric around her feet, and her head dipped from the weight of the tiara. The women were fussing around her—trying to tell her how to walk and how to stand.

"Could you give us a minute?" Myla interrupted.

"She's due in the antechamber soon."

"It'll only take a moment," Myla promised.

They nodded and bowed to Aveis before scurrying out of the room. Once they were gone, Aveis slumped down on the couch—causing her skirts to fly up. Aveis cursed as she pushed the fabric down, and Myla let out a small chuckle.

Aveis glared at her. "I'm glad you find this all so amusing."

Myla's smile disappeared. "I'm sorry."

Aveis just rolled her eyes, grabbed a roll from the cart in front of her, and took a large bite—causing the paint on her lips to smear. When she finished the roll, Myla got to her feet and held out her hand. Aveis squinted at the offering before getting up herself.

"Can I..."

358

Myla reached out her hand toward Aveis's lips but didn't move closer until Aveis gave a subtle nod. She brushed her thumb along her lips to fix the paint and wiped off the excess that had smeared around her lips.

"Now, chin up and shoulders back," Myla instructed. "Act like you're going into battle. Show no weakness or discomfort. You're a princess, and everyone else is below you. If you don't act like that, then they'll eat you alive—trust me. I wasn't always a part of the royal court, and I learned quickly that if you don't act like you belong, then no one will treat you like it."

"None of this matters anyway. Drathal will come for me soon, and I can leave this dreaded hellhole behind and everyone in it."

"Is that what you really want? What if he gets hurt trying to come here or, worse, killed?"

"Of course, I don't want him to get hurt," Aveis snapped. "But I can't stay here, and I also can't communicate with Drathal with these damned bands on my wrists."

"Why can't you stay? I know, given some time, your father will see how much they're hurting you, and because he loves you, he'll remove the bands. He just doesn't trust that you won't leave him again."

Aveis laughed, but there was no humor in it. "Leave? I didn't *leave*. I was sent away to be *fixed*—whatever the fuck that means. He never would have tried to change me if he truly loved me."

"You're right. What they did was wrong—I'm not trying to make excuses for them. More than anything, I want you to stay, but I know my wants don't matter in this case—only yours do. Things will get better—"

"You're only fooling yourself into thinking things will get better to relieve your guilt," Aveis snarled. "I won't make it that easy."

"Av—"

The door opened, and the older woman stuck her head in. "Apologies, Your Highness and Dame Yules, but it is time."

Chapter 62

Myla followed Aveis into the antechamber, and they were met with an uproar of people in fancy garb yelling at one another. Myla wasn't sure what she was expecting—but it definitely wasn't that. Myla scanned the crowd for her own family but was surprised when she didn't see them. They were members of the royal court, so they should have been invited. Unless, since they already knew of the princess's arrival, they decided not to come.

The king and queen sat on two golden thrones on the dais, overlooking the entire affair. King Otois was scowling—hands balled into fists on the armrests. Queen Deona looked almost amused as she lounged on her throne.

The room didn't quiet down as they made their way over to the dais. If anything, it got louder. Aveis stood next to her father, and Myla stood behind the thrones next to Captain Oyvim. The king got to his feet, and all the voices spluttered to a stop as if he had blown out a candle.

"I have heard all your concerns and considered them as you are all valued members of my court." The king proclaimed, deep voice echoing across the vast room. "However, your concerns are unfounded. You have heard rumors that the princess possesses magic, but that is no longer true. This long decade, the princess has been through rigorous procedures to remove the vile disease from her body. I am pleased to tell you all that she is cured."

The crowd started murmuring amongst themselves as Myla tried to hide the surprise from her face. That was the story they were going with? It was absurd—no one was going to believe them. Especially if they had family among the knights and royal guards, they had been sending soldiers to find Aveis for over a decade. She knew they had kept it on the down-low as much as possible, but no matter what they tried to do, people talked, and Aveis hadn't necessarily been discreet by killing anyone who got too close. Besides, most knew that magic couldn't just be taken away without taking away their life.

"And to prove it," King Otois continued. "A demonstration is in order."

Aveis tensed at that, and looked at her father before turning her gaze to Myla with fear evident in her eyes. Similar to when—

"Dame Myla Yules, please step forward," the king turned to Myla and motioned her forward.

Myla swallowed tightly and stepped up to stand by the king's side.

"A few months ago, Myla was sent to check on Zaya's progress and bring her back once she was cured. During that time, they became close friends and confidants. There is no one else in this world besides her own parents, to whom Zaya is closest. And as you are likely aware, magic is similar to a ferocious beast—it cannot be tamed. Especially when it feels threatened, or those it cares for are threatened."

Myla took a step back, but Captain Oyvim was there. He wrapped his arms around her and held her arms down before she could escape. Aveis rushed toward them but was stopped by her father's arm around her waist. She snarled something to him—something Myla couldn't hear against the hammering of her own heart. He hissed something back, and she stopped struggling, but only slightly.

Another guard came up to the dais and pulled out a small dagger. Once he got close enough, Myla kicked the dagger out of his hand, causing it to skid down the steps. She brought both her legs up and kicked the guard away—the momentum pushed her back against the captain. He stumbled, his grip on her loosening. Myla twisted and wrapped her ankle around his knee and pulled. He fell to one knee, and Myla broke out of his hold. She stumbled to her feet and away from him, drawing her sword. A small group of guards were advancing toward her—backing her into a corner.

"You've made your point!" Aveis yelled, pulling from her father's grip. "I'm magicless! Now, stop this!"

The guards stopped advancing and turned to look at the king. The king looked out to the crowd. They were murmuring and shuffling—doubt still clear on their faces.

King Otois's blue eyes fixed on Myla, and her heart dropped at the resigned look he gave her. "Kill her."

Aveis screamed as the guards closed in on her. Myla felt her magic stir in her stomach, but it was stuck as if it were being held down by something. Fuck—the potion. They had slipped the potion into Myla's food! That's why it had a weird aftertaste! How had she not noticed the feeling before? Had she been that absorbed in her guilt, or was it some sort of late-effect potion? It was pointless to think of such things now. It wouldn't change the fact that she was completely surrounded. She wouldn't be able to beat them all, but she would be damned if she didn't try.

Myla lifted her sword higher and charged. Her sword clashed with the guard closest to her, and she parried—twisting around him to meet the guard behind him. Myla swung her sword, the blade cutting into the gap in her armor. Another guard came up behind her and slashed a long cut along her back. Myla gritted back a yell and turned to return a blow. Their blades locked, and she pushed him back, causing him to stumble down the dais.

Someone grabbed her arm from behind, and she twisted around to slam the hilt of her sword into their face. They released her, and she slashed out at the next guard. Sweat dripped down her face, curls clinging to her forehead and the back of her neck. Myla heard Aveis yell again, and she turned to look—afraid that she might be hurt—and was met with a dagger to her gut.

Captain Oyvim grabbed Myla's arm and pulled her close so he could whisper in her ear. "Stay down."

He pulled back and released the dagger. Myla stumbled back, dropping her sword to grab the dagger with both hands. Blood bloomed along the sides of the dagger— darkening her black corset. She knew she should have felt some sort of pain, but all she felt was shock and dizziness. She blinked as her vision blurred. She looked at Aveis, who had fallen to her knees, her makeup smeared from the tears streaming down her face. Aveis reached out a hand to her as Myla's knees gave out, and she fell back. Ridiculously, Raevyn's words popped to mind, telling her that after completing training, she'd be so used to stab wounds she wouldn't feel them. Unfortunately, she wasn't used to them yet as the pain appeared—sharp and sudden as the dagger shifted in her stomach at her collapse. She gasped and choked on the blood rising in the back of her throat—the darkness closing in around her vision. The last thing she saw was a circle of armor surrounding her before darkness overtook her.

Chapter 63

Myla woke up in a dark room. She tried to sit up but immediately slumped back down as a searing pain pierced her abdomen. She hissed and gasped as another wave of pain shot across her back when she laid back against the pillows. To her surprise, Wrynn appeared above her—looking like he had just come from training in his brown cloth trousers and loose-fit white shirt. His hair was mussed up, no doubt from running his hands through the strands like he always did when he was nervous or upset.

"Try not to move," Wrynn soothed, running the back of his hand along her cheek. "You need to rest."

"What happened?" Myla asked, voice raspy. "How did I get here?"

Wrynn sat down on the edge of her bed, pain evident in his expression. "They took you here after what happened in the antechamber, and a medic tended to your wounds. I came here after training, hoping we could talk, and found you here with the princess. She filled me in on what happened."

"Aveis, is she okay?"

"She's fine. She was shaken up a bit but wasn't harmed. She's resting in her room now with the captain stationed outside her door."

"I don't understand why they did it," Myla replied, flinching as she tried to get into a more comfortable position. "They wanted to prove she didn't have magic, but trying to kill me after they appointed me her personal guard doesn't make sense."

"The princess said that they weren't going to kill you. They wanted to get a rise out of her to play the audience." Wrynn's face fell. "They supposedly weren't going to hurt you much either, but when you fought them—they didn't have a choice." He said the last bit mockingly as if he didn't believe that for a second.

"I suppose this is my punishment for what happened to you."

Wrynn intertwined their fingers and squeezed her hand. "You got mixed up in the king and queen's power manipulation bullshit, but none of what happened is your fault."

Myla chuckled softly. "I am not without fault, you know. I think a lot of what happened could be considered my fault."

"Not for this," Wrynn insisted. "You got hurt because you cared for someone. That's majorly fucked up."

"I'm surprised she even cared enough to show a reaction. I would have thought she'd be glad to get rid of me."

"I can't speak for her, but speaking from my own experience, I know that strong feelings like that don't just go away even when it's clear that it's never going to happen. It doesn't stop your heart from wanting what it wants."

Myla looked up at him curiously. "Thinking about someone in particular?"

He rolled his eyes. "No, I just happen to be more knowledgeable than you in matters of the heart."

Myla snorted. "How can I forget? You're such a sap."

Wrynn smiled, rolling his eyes again. "You should go back to sleep. I'll find some food for you to eat when you wake."

He started to pull back, but Myla held onto his hand. "Wait. I just want to say thank you for always being there for me. I don't know what I would do without you."

"Probably spiral into a hole of self-blaming and doubt. You also probably never would have grown out of your angsty teenage phase—walking around in dark colors and makeup and writing poetry about how no one understands you."

Myla laughed, wincing slightly as her abdomen flexed. "Don't make me laugh. I got stabbed, remember? And how did you know about that?"

Wrynn grinned. "I didn't—I just assumed."

"Asshole," Myla grinned back.

"Now, go back to bed. I'll be here with a plate of food when you wake."

Myla settled back into her pillows. "So bossy."

Wrynn kissed her forehead. "Love you, Sea Storm."

Myla smiled and closed her eyes. "Love you too."

****

Myla was put on bed rest for two days before she convinced the medic she was fine. During the entire time, Wrynn visited when he could, as did her sister, who was working with the royal physician, Erlan (a position she'd earned while Myla was away). They had both been sworn to secrecy about Myla's injury. Their majesties didn't want their general to be upset at them. Myla hadn't seen Aveis at all since what happened, either. Myla could hear her pacing her room often—the only indication Myla had that she was all right.

Myla couldn't help but feel hurt. Aveis hadn't shown her face these last few days. Especially since they were only one room away, she supposed it showed how little she felt toward Myla. She must be a great actor because Myla believed Aveis would mourn her death. Wishful thinking on her part. There was a part of her that didn't want to face Aveis—to see the utter disregard on her face—but it was her job. A job that she was starting to really regret being given.

Myla steeled herself and walked into Aveis's room. Aveis was standing next to her bed, dressed in trousers and a loose-fitted red blouse. She whirled around, and her eyes widened when she saw Myla.

"What are you doing up? You should be resting."

Myla blinked, taken aback by the concern in her voice. "I'm fine."

Aveis shook her head, tears welling up in her eyes. "It's not fucking fair," Aveis growled.

Myla startled. "What?"

"After everything you did to me, I shouldn't give a damn about what happens to you. You shouldn't have any power over me."

"I'm sorry—"

"You should be! You broke my fucking trust, and yet seeing you get stabbed and collapsing—not knowing if you were alive—" Her voice broke as tears started falling freely down her cheeks. "It somehow hurt worse."

"I didn't think you'd care, given that you tried to kill me back on the island."

"I lost control of myself." Aveis wrapped her arms around herself and looked down. "I let mine and Drathal's anger and hurt take over my magic like I haven't done since I

368

was a child. If I would have succeeded…I don't know if I ever would have recovered from that."

Myla reached out to her. "Aveis—"

She took a step back. "But that doesn't mean I forgive you. I don't think I ever can."

Myla felt her heart clench, but she nodded. "I understand. I don't expect you to forgive me, but I want you to know that I'm going to fix this. I never knew how bad it was, and if I had, I would never have helped bring you here. I'll make it right. I promise."

Myla couldn't continue to try to convince her to stay. It wasn't right. This kingdom had a rotten core and poisoned those in charge. Whether or not Drathal came for her—Myla would get her out of there before it too poisoned her. Even if it meant she could no longer have the future she had dreamt for herself.

Aveis turned away from her and wiped her eyes—not bothering to reply.

I don't know if you're listening, Vavna, but if you are—I'll make things right. No matter what happens to me, I won't turn my back on magic. I promise.

Chapter 64

The next day, Erlan and Rikia came to the princess's chamber to refill the potion into Aveis's bands. It supposedly needed to be refilled every week. As soon as Aveis saw the potion, she charged the physician. Myla got between them—not wanting her sister to get hurt in the crossfire. It took her and the two guards stationed outside her room to hold Aveis down so they could administer the potion. Every scream and yell Aveis let out felt like a physical blow to Myla. She had to squeeze her eyes shut to stop tears from streaming down her cheeks.

As soon as they were done, they tentatively let go of Aveis. Aveis had slumped in the chair, exhausted. The bags under her eyes were darkening by the day, and her normally tan skin was obtaining a green sheen. She snarled at them but made no effort to attack any of them, so the guards left with the physician.

"Hey, Rikia," Myla called before her sister could leave.

She turned to her. "Yes?"

"Do you mind taking a look at my stitches? Just to make sure everything looks normal?"

Rikia looked the way Erlan had left. "Are you sure you want me to do it? Erlan—"

"I'd rather it be you," she insisted.

She nodded and looked at Aveis once—who hadn't moved from her slumped position—before following Myla into her room. Myla waited until the door shut behind them before she spoke.

"Is it possible for you to get a hold of the potion they give Aveis?" Myla asked, her voice barely more than a whisper.

"No, he keeps it locked up somewhere that no one but him, the king and queen, and the captain of the guard knows. I only ever see it when we're on our way here. He won't even let me hold it. Why?"

"What about the key? Does Erlan keep a key to the bands?"

Rikia shook her head. "No, only the king has a key."

"Could you get something that looks just like the potion but is harmless?"

Rikia narrowed her eyes. "What are you planning?"

"The potion is clearly making her sick—it may even be killing her. I can't stand by and let that happen."

"But she's dangerous. She tried to kill you for Rornja's sake."

"Yes, but Dad's right—we've got to let her go. Drathal might be on his way soon. I'm not sure how long it'll take for his wing to heal, but she needs to be ready if she has any chance of escaping."

"If anyone finds out—"

"They won't. And even if they do, they'll blame me. You have no reason to help Aveis."

"Exactly, Myla. In the last few months, you've been sent on a suicide mission, nearly died multiple times, and got stabbed because of the princess. If you help her escape, then you'll be killed. Dad may not think so, but I think he underestimates what their majesties are capable of."

"Please, Ri, I know it's risky, but I owe her this much."

"You don't—"

"I do," Myla insisted. "I just need you to get me a similar-looking potion, and I'll take care of the rest."

Her sister looked at her and, seeing the apparent desperation on Myla's face, resigned with a sigh. "All right. I'll see what I can do."

Myla hugged her tightly. "Thank you. You're the best."

She hugged her back just as tightly. "I know," Rikia replied, causing Myla to snort.

****

For the rest of the day, Aveis ignored Myla and the food offered to her. She spent the entire time in her room reading and sleeping. Myla checked on her every now and then, but Aveis gave no indication that she noticed. Dinner rolled around, and when there was a knock on her door, she expected a servant with food for her, but to her surprise, it was Wrynn holding a tray of steaming grilled chicken, mashed potatoes, and vegetables.

"Hey, Wrynn. Did you get dismissed and are now working in the kitchens?" She teased with a smile.

"Your father wouldn't dismiss me even if he wanted to. Our numbers are dwindling as it is."

"Wait, what?"

Wrynn cringed. "I wasn't supposed to tell you that. Forget I said anything."

Myla let him in and shut the door behind him. "Too late for that."

Wrynn sighed and set the tray down on the desk. "A few people from our little rescue team resigned after discovering about you and how the king and queen promoted you. They think the king and queen have become sympathetic toward those with magic, and they didn't want to be a part of protecting that." He handed a plate to Myla before sitting at her desk with the other plate. "Once they left, rumors started going around. Nothing incriminating you from what we can tell. It was more incriminating the princess. Now that she's back, people are asking questions about where she went and why. During their announcement of her return to the entire kingdom, all they said is that she's been returned and that they're happy about it."

Myla poked at her food from her perch on her bed—no longer very hungry. "Shit, I had no idea."

"Yeah. People are even starting to question Desmond's assignment since he left the day after you did."

"Desmond left on an assignment? Where? When will he be back?"

Wrynn shrugged and took a bite of his potatoes. "No idea. It was all confidential. I don't even think your dad knows. The order came from Captain Oyvim."

"But members of the royal guard don't send recruits on assignment. That doesn't make any sense."

Myla thought about the last time she had seen Desmond. She'd figured he hadn't pieced together that she was a wielder, but what if he had? What if he found out about Myla's assignment, thinking it was some sort of reward, and decided to report her to Captain Oyvim? Though, she doubted he'd wait that long to make his suspicions known if he'd had any. Maybe it had something to do with the hunter Captain Oyvim had killed. Was it possible he'd recruited Desmond to take the hunter's place? Desmond's family were respected members of the court, so if Captain Oyvim had been actively recruiting for a replacement, they'd know about it. Myla had no doubt that Desmond would seize it to become a hunter if given the opportunity. He'd never been shy about telling anyone in earshot that he'd preferred it over being a knight. But, since hunters were hand-selected by their majesties and their captain, Desmond had been forced into the recruits.

"It didn't make sense to me either."

"You don't think he became a hunter after what happened to the one that turned us in?"

Wrynn scoffed. "If he did, then good riddance, but it seems unlikely. He's not even the best recruit in your year. Why would they choose him?"

It was a good point, but it didn't make the unease in Myla's stomach dissipate. "What other scenario is likely? Unless he said something stupid enough to get himself banished." Or he saw something like Myla using her magic to try and stop a hunter. The timing of it all was too convenient for the two things not to be related. Had Captain Oyvim killed him, too, to cover their tracks? The thought made her nauseous, so she set her plate on her nightstand.

Wrynn gave her a reassuring smile. "Regardless, it doesn't matter. I, for one, will be glad not to have to deal with his bullshit every day."

She nodded, but her thoughts were miles away. Desmond may have been a pain in her side, but he'd also brought her to Raevyn, Aveis, and Vavna. Despite everything that happened afterward, Myla would always be grateful for the time she had with them—time that gave her clarity to figure out who she wanted to be rather than who she always thought she was meant to be.

Chapter 65

Two weeks later, Myla had what she needed. Rikia had formulated a harmless potion with the same green shade as the other potion. Myla slipped the harmless potion into her sleeve and walked into Aveis's room. Aveis was standing by her desk with the letter opener in her hand, knowing full well who was on their way here.

"I need you to kick Erlan in the face," Myla said by way of greeting.

Aveis turned her steely gaze to Myla and glared. "I'm planning to do a lot more than kick, darling."

Myla nearly gasped at the familiar nickname and felt a spark of hope for the first time since she had left the island. "I have a plan, but I need you to kick the potion out of Erlan's hand."

"Why—"

A knock sounded, and Myla walked over to let Erlan, Rikia, and two guards in. Aveis raised her letter opener like a dagger, but Myla quickly disarmed her before she could attack. Aveis glared at her and was about to say something when the two guards took her by each arm. She struggled as they forced her into the desk chair. Myla knelt down and took hold of her thrashing legs. Erlan and Rikia came over, and Erlan pulled a syringe from his jacket pocket. He leaned down, and Myla loosened her grip enough to free one of Aveis's legs. Aveis's foot connected with the physician's face.

He fell back with a yell, the syringe dropping from his grip and by Myla's knee. She leaned down to grab it— making sure her back covered the guards' lines of sight of the syringe—and quickly switched it with the one in her sleeve. She held the syringe out to Erlan, who was getting to his feet, holding his bleeding nose. He cursed and gestured to Rikia, who stepped forward and took it from Myla's outstretched hand. She administered the fake potion into Aveis's bands before slipping the empty syringe into her jacket pocket.

Once they left, Myla took the syringe from her sleeve and walked to Aveis's washroom. She cleaned the potion out of it, took the needle off the end, and threw it away in Aveis's garbage. She slipped the remaining part of the syringe into her pocket to give to Wrynn when he came by later to dispose of it. Aveis had stood up from her chair and squinted suspiciously at Myla when she walked out.

"What did you do?"

Myla smiled. "I replaced the potion with something harmless. Give it a few hours; it should be out of your system for good."

Aveis didn't seem convinced. "We'll see."

****

When Captain Oyvim showed up at Myla's door, she was afraid she had been discovered. She braced herself for the accusation and told herself to fight if she needed to, but he was alone. He beckoned her outside her room, and Myla followed him out into the hallway. To her surprise, the two guards who were normally posted outside Aveis's door were gone as well.

"We've just been sent word that the beast has left its island and is coming here. We're expecting it at any time. Anyone we could spare is on their way to intercept it before it reaches the palace. You are to keep the princess in her room until I come back. Do not tell her the beast is nearby. We will dispose of the beast as quickly and quietly as possible, but until then, you and the princess are not to leave her room. Is that understood?"

Myla saluted, her heart pounding in her chest in anticipation as she tried to keep her face from giving anything away. "Yes, sir."

Captain Oyvim nodded before turning on his heel and heading down the hall. She waited until he was completely out of sight before Myla hurried into Aveis's room. Myla quickly did the math in her head—it would have taken Raevyn about as long as he'd been gone to get to the island. Myla wasn't sure how fast dragons could fly, but if Drathal could have gotten to Cassia in less than a day, then that meant that Raevyn let him go. Or it's possible that Raevyn didn't make it to the island before Drathal left. Which meant she still wasn't sure if Raevyn would have gone through with killing Drathal. She really hoped for the former, but that did nothing to diminish the knot of tension she'd been carrying since he left. One crisis at a time, she thought. Perhaps when she's an official fugitive, she'd meet Raevyn again on the road and know for sure.

Aveis was standing in the middle of the room, looking down at her bleeding wrists with melted metal at her feet.

"Thank the gods, the potion wore off," Myla said, rushing to her washroom to grab some gauze. She came back and started to wrap up Aveis's wrists. "Drathal is here. This is your chance to leave. I'll help you sneak out of the palace and meet up with him. You'll need to find a new place to live—"

"No."

Myla blinked and looked up at Aveis, dropping her newly bandaged wrists. "What?"

"I'm done hiding and running. It's time I end this. Once and for all."

"What are you planning?"

Aveis looked up from her wrists into Myla's eyes—the same dying ember color was tinged with red along the edges. "I'm going to become queen."

"You can't—"

Aveis gripped Myla's chin, angling her face up to hers. "This is what you wanted, isn't it? Why you dragged me here in the first place."

"Not like this, and you know it."

Aveis brought her other hand up to run a finger down her cheek. "You think you can stop me?" She smirked. "You've been repressed your entire life—just scraping the surface of your magic." Her fingers heated, nearly burning Myla's skin. She tried to pull back, but Aveis's grip was firm. "Not so fast, darling. You're not getting away."

"Please, don't do this," Myla begged, fingers closing around the hilt of the dagger strapped to her thigh.

"You've hurt me—more than I thought possible—and I plan to return the favor."

A knock sounded at the door, and they both turned in time to see Erlan and Rikia walk through the open adjoining door from Myla's room. Erlan's eyes widened as he noticed Aveis's bare wrists.

"Run!" Myla yelled, but it was too late.

The door behind them burst into flames.

Chapter 66

Erlan and Rikia fell forward from the force of the flames behind them. Erlan's medical bag went flying along with the contents—one of which was a familiar green potion. Myla rammed her elbow into Aveis's arm, causing her grip to falter. Myla dove for the potion, but Aveis had the same thought. With a quick whip of fire, she snatched the potion—pulling it toward her outstretched hand.

She twirled it around her fingers, grinning madly. "Too slow. The fact you decided to grab for the potion just proves my point that you've barely scratched the surface of your magic."

Myla got to her feet, placing herself between Aveis and Rikia. "Please, don't hurt them—they've done nothing—"

"Except inject poison in my body for weeks," Aveis snarled.

"Please, she's my sister."

Aveis looked between Rikia and Myla before letting out an annoyed sigh. "Fine."

She sagged in relief. "Thank—"

A rope of fire shot out faster than Myla could react. It wrapped around Rikia's waist, and she was flung across the room. Myla screamed as her sister slammed into Aveis's bed—the wood cracking and breaking under the impact. Myla ran to her sister's side. She heard a whoosh of flames, and Erlan's scream of agony was cut off as fast as it had come.

Myla crouched next to her sister, pushing the broken boards off her. She was unconscious—the back of her head wet with blood—but she was breathing. Her relief mixed with her anger. Her magic thrummed under her skin, causing the sink in Aveis's washroom to explode—water gushing out and flooding the floor.

She turned on her heel, lifting her arms, but Aveis was already there. She thrust a syringe into Myla's chest, and Myla gasped as she felt the tether binding her to her magic snap. The water around her fell uselessly to the floor.

Aveis grinned, pulling Myla to her chest. "Can't have you getting in my way, darling," she purred. "Besides, this is only a fraction of what you deserve."

Aveis shoved her away and wrapped a thin rope of flames around her wrists before using that to tug her toward the door. "Now, it's time to take my place as queen."

****

Myla couldn't do anything but follow Aveis as she dragged her down the hallway. Anyone they passed that tried to stop them, she took care of them by either vaporizing them or flinging them across the hall. Of course, this caused a panic, but Aveis strolled through the halls toward the throne room as if she had all the time in the world. Myla kept desperately reaching out to her magic—to Vavna—in an attempt to escape, but it was useless. The last time she was injected with the potion, it had taken nearly half a day for it to return.

The four guards stationed in front of the throne room didn't even have a chance to scream as Aveis reduced them to ash. Aveis blasted the doors off their hinges and sauntered in. Their majesties were on their thrones, Captain Oyvim in front of them. His sword was already out, and pointed at her.

"Not another step," he ordered.

Aveis laughed. "As if you can stop me."

He charged toward her, and she allowed it, creating a sword of flames for herself. He brought his sword down in a sharp arc. Aveis brought hers up to meet the blade, and as soon as they collided, Oyvim's sword split in two. He stumbled in surprise, but it was enough for Aveis to twirl around him. Myla could only watch in horror as her sword burst from his chest—the flames eating through flesh and armor as if it were dry grass. His lips opened in a silent scream, and the light left his eyes seconds before his body clattered to the floor.

Aveis grinned at Myla, her ember eyes dancing with satisfaction. "It's the least he deserved after stabbing you, darling."

Myla shook her head, fear clawing at her chest. "Aveis—"

Aveis tugged her forward. Myla stumbled, falling to her knees in front of Aveis and next to Captain Oyvim's corpse. "You were right all along, darling. I can change this kingdom for the better, and it starts here and now." She reached down and ran the back of her hand against Myla's cheek. "And you can be by my side if you stop fighting me."

"I—"

Aveis suddenly whirled around and encased her parents in a cage of flames—the pair of which were trying to sneak away to the door behind the thrones to escape.

"So rude," Aveis tsked. "We're trying to have a conversation here. You'll have to wait your turn." Aveis turned back to Myla with a smile. "Sorry about that, darling. What were you going to say?"

Myla stood on a precipice. Either she could defend a king and queen who didn't believe she was worth protecting, or she could back up someone who could bring magic back to the kingdom. It should be clear—she had believed that Aveis was the key to a better kingdom. But, looking into her reddening eyes and having watched all she had killed just for standing in her way—Myla couldn't stand behind her. If she went through with this, killing their majesties to assume the throne early, people would believe that magic was to blame. She'd be setting them even farther back. She had promised Vavna she wouldn't turn her back on magic and planned to keep that promise, which meant she couldn't let Aveis go through with this.

But she was powerless now. Refusing would only get her killed. No, she had created this villain, and it was her responsibility to stop her.

"You're right—this is the only way," Myla smiled at Aveis, reaching up to grab her hand. "I'm on your side."

Aveis grinned. "I knew you'd see reason." She snuffed out the rope of flame around Myla's wrists before pulling her to her feet. "Now, let's finish this the way we started it. Together."

Chapter 67

Myla followed Aveis up to the dais, still reaching for her magic—hoping for some spark—but a vast emptiness greeted her. They stopped in front of their majesties just as the roof caved in. Myla ducked and stumbled back as Drathal crashed in from the ceiling. Stone and debris littered down around them, but Aveis didn't even flinch. Drathal landed on the dais, claws nearly crushing the thrones mere feet from where their majesties were imprisoned in flames. Snow fell heavily through the hole in the roof, coating Myla's face. She tried desperately to reach out to it and manipulate it, but her magic wouldn't respond.

"Are you happy now?" Aveis asked her parents, twirling her flame sword before pointing it at them. "You made me into the monster you always feared I'd become." She strode forward and leveled the flaming sword at her mother's throat. "Drathal and I would have been content to live on that island forever, but you wouldn't let me be—too afraid of what I'd become. You just had to intervene." She pressed the sword against her flesh and smirked when she flinched. "Well, no more."

An arrow shot through the air, and Drathal gave a warning roar, allowing Aveis enough time to twist her body. The arrow whizzed inches from her ear and bounced harmlessly off Drathal's scales. Myla and Aveis whirled around to see Raevyn and Wrynn standing next to the ruined doors. Raevyn was already notching another arrow while Wrynn rushed forward with his sword drawn. Myla's heart soared at the sight. Raevyn was here, which meant he didn't go after Drathal. She had gotten through to him. But her hope was quickly dashed as she thought she had more than just herself to get out of this mess now. She wasn't sure she'd be able to get them all out of this without someone getting hurt.

"I was really hoping you'd show up," Aveis smirked, lifting her arms.

"No!" Myla tackled Aveis just as she let loose a barrage of flames.

The flames veered off course, shooting up and catching onto the wooden boards above them. Aveis kicked Myla off her just as Myla grabbed her dagger. She toppled back and twisted into a crouch, brandishing her dagger. Aveis got to her feet and sneered at Myla.

"You always did have a soft spot for that brute."

Aveis lashed out a whip of flame that Myla barely avoided. She stumbled back and into Wrynn, who pulled her out of the way as she blasted streams of fire at them. Smoke was filling the room despite the gaping hole in the ceiling, and Myla struggled to see as she and Wrynn stumbled through the wreckage toward Raevyn and the door.

"Some of your magic would be nice right about now," Wrynn said, coughing as he inhaled a gulp of smoke.

"I would if I could." Myla caught Wrynn before he could go careening to the floor after stumbling over a piece of stone. "But she injected me with that potion that suppresses magic."

"Well, fu—"

A line of fire burst in front of them. They skidded to a stop, barely able to stop from running straight into it. Myla whirled around, still gripping her dagger, as Aveis walked through the flames. The edges of her clothes were singed and burning in some places, but she didn't seem to mind as a crazed smile tugged at her lips.

"Stop, Aveis, please."

Aveis laughed, but there was no humor in it as she lifted her flame sword. "I don't think so. You're seeing me through to the end of this, darling. You will get front-row seats to me burning down this kingdom to make way for a new and better one—all with the knowledge that it's *all your fault*."

Vavna, if you can hear me, please help. I know I don't deserve it, but I need you. Please.

Myla stepped in front of Wrynn. "I won't let you hurt them. Do whatever you want to me, but let them go."

"They both helped bring me here. That alone is enough for me to warrant killing them. Especially the brute. He's been a thorn in my side for long enough. Besides, with them out of the picture, I'm confident you'll see the error of your ways and beg to be by my side—as you should."

Drathal roared in pain, and Aveis spun on her heel. Through the smoke and haze, Myla could make out Raevyn dodging Drathal as their majesties snuck away. Aveis had used too much magic, which caused the prison holding their majesties to falter, and they didn't hesitate to flee. Drathal tried to bite Raevyn, but he twisted away, lifting his sword up in a defensive position. As Drathal turned his head,

Raevyn's sword tore across Drathal's jaw, and Aveis cried out as blood bloomed from the wound. The flames around them rose in her fury—making the throne room almost unbearably hot. She thrust her arms forward—pushing all the flames toward Raevyn and Drathal.

"Raevyn!" Myla screamed.

Fear and desperation shot through her, and Myla felt Vavna for the first time in weeks—pushing magic through her.

Make it count.

Time seemed to slow as she felt a rush of magic race through her, breaking through the barrier that kept it at bay. The pipes around them burst, water pouring out of every available space, extinguishing all the flames. Myla created a wall of ice between Raevyn and Drathal, giving him enough time to dive out of the way as Drathal spewed fire. Aveis rushed toward them—Myla close on her heels. Aveis lifted her arms to hurtle fire, but Myla turned the floor under her into solid ice. She slipped and crashed to the floor. Myla encased her in ice just long enough for her to pass her. She collided with Raevyn, who spun her away, so he was in front of her as Aveis burst through her cage.

"Enough!" Aveis roared, flames dancing along her arms. "I'm done playing games."

Aveis rushed toward Raevyn, flame sword up and poised to attack. Myla pushed herself in front of Raevyn and created a blade of ice. Their blades clashed, and Myla kept a steady stream of magic pushing into the blade to keep it from evaporating. Aveis swung over and over, and Myla met every blow—letting Aveis stay on the offense until she eventually tired herself out. She heard Drathal roar and rush toward them, but she focused on Aveis.

"We could have been an unstoppable team!" Aveis snarled as their blades locked together. She pushed forward, trying to knock Myla off balance, but Myla stayed grounded.

"Why you chose to align yourself with those that seek to destroy our kind, I will never understand."

"I didn't—I wouldn't—" Myla spun out of the way as Aveis pushed away from her and swung another attack. "I believe you are the queen Rosebourne deserves. But if you take the kingdom by force, then no one will follow you. If you just wait—" A flame whip shot out of Aveis's sword and coiled around Myla's wrist, pulling her to the ground.

"I'm done waiting!" Aveis roared, stepping toward her. "I won't be a prisoner any longer, and I won't stand idly by as I've done for the last decade. It's time for Rosebourne to start a new era with me on the throne."

Myla looked into her eyes, which held so much hate, and felt her stomach twist. She tried to get to her feet, but at the movement, the whip heated up, causing her to flinch. "I don't want to fight you."

"I'm not buying the innocent act. You won't fool me twice, darling."

Myla grabbed her wrist and extinguished the flames coiled there with a burst of her magic. "You were right about everything. I'm sorry I hurt you. I'm sorry I brought you back here. You deserve to make this choice, and I won't stand in your way this time."

Myla slowly got to her feet, and Aveis allowed it, watching her with eyes as bright as the surrounding flames.

"Just let us go—you've got what you wanted. The throne is yours."

Aveis's eyes narrowed. "And you expect me to believe you'll just let this go? That you won't stab me in the back the first chance you get, as you've done numerous times?"

"So long as my family isn't in danger—it does not matter to me who sits on the throne."

"I suppose—"

Myla tackled her to the ground as Raevyn rose behind her—whether he planned to stab her in the back, Myla didn't want to find out. She gave a grunt of surprise, and Myla quickly rolled off her to stand between Raevyn and Aveis. Aveis got to her feet. The surprise on her face was quickly replaced with anger as she glared at Raevyn.

"That was the last time, Brute."

Myla encased them in a bubble as Aveis's magic crashed into them. Sweat beaded on her brow at the exertion of flowing so much magic into the shield. She felt the bottom of her well of magic for the first time. She crumbled to one knee as the bubble around them slowly shrank.

Raevyn crouched next to her. "Sunshine—"

"We don't have much time," Myla panted. "I'm going to distract her, and I need you to get out of here. Get my sister—she's injured and in Aveis's room. Take her, the rest of my family, and Wrynn. Get them out of here. Protect them like you would me. Aveis won't hurt me—"

"Myla, don't do this. She'll kill you—"

"Please." The bubble was nearly touching their backs—Aveis's flames barely faltering. "I need you to do this for me. There's no one else I'd trust to keep them safe."

"Myla—"

It was now or never.

"Go!"

Myla got to her feet and pushed her water out—driving it into Aveis. Aveis was thrown back across the room. Drathal roared as she fell on her side with a groan. Myla stumbled, and Raevyn caught her before she fell.

"Raevyn—"

"I'm not leaving you." He insisted and tugged her toward the exit.

Wrynn appeared panting and covered in soot at her other side and helped Raevyn pull her toward the exit. Drathal tried to stop them with a burst of flames, but Myla used the last of her magic to shield them as they hurried through the throne doors.

"My sister—"

Raevyn scooped her up in his arms and nodded to Wrynn. "Her sister's in Aveis's chambers. Meet us at Myla's house as soon as you've got her. She's been hurt."

Wrynn gave a firm nod and dashed down the hall. Raevyn ran in the other direction as Aveis stumbled out of the throne room in a fury of flames.

"You're mine, darling. And I'm not good at sharing."

Chapter 68

Myla was having difficulty keeping her eyes open as Raevyn ran through the corridors. Aveis's laugh echoed off the stone walls, and she could feel the heat of her flames dancing across the rug and tapestries on the walls. She was going to burn the whole fucking palace down. She hoped everyone had evacuated and Wrynn and her sister got out safe.

Raevyn shoved the courtyard door open—his stride never slowing even as he slipped on the icy stone.

I'm sorry, Vavna. Myla wanted them to know in case this was it. *Thank you for my magic. I know I haven't always treated it like a gift, but it is—a gift that brought me to you.*

Stupid, sentimental human. You will not die on me. Do what you must and make your way to me.

A rush of magic zipped through Myla like a shock of electricity. She gasped—eyes flying open as lightning cut across the sky, followed immediately by the boom of thunder.

"Raevyn, I'm okay," Myla said, struggling in his grip. "Let me down."

Raevyn obliged just as Aveis sauntered out into the courtyard.

"I'll admit," she said, lips pulling up into a crazed smile. "You're stronger than even I gave you credit for. But a little storm isn't going to stop me."

Fire built up around them, encasing them in a ring of fire. Myla took Raevyn's hand and tugged him toward the archway that led to the training yard. She encased them in a bubble of water so they could charge through the flames before letting it evaporate. Aveis yelled after them, but Myla didn't stop. The training yard was filled with soldiers—half charging toward them and the other half fighting Drathal, who had flown down from the throne room. Leading the charge toward them were her parents and a man she'd never seen before. He was a tall, muscular Black man with a bald head and sharp features. He looked a lot like—

Myla was jerked back as Raevyn froze. When she looked back at him, his eyes were glued to the other man with her parents.

"Raevyn—"

"Myla!"

They all skidded to a stop in front of her. Her father's large hands landed on Myla's shoulders, and he scanned her—looking for any injuries. "Are you okay? What about your sister—"

"Hello, son."

Myla looked over at the man, but he only had eyes for Raevyn. Raevyn had paled as if he'd seen a ghost.

He swallowed thickly. "Father." He nearly choked on the word.

Myla's jaw nearly dropped. "What—"

An explosion sounded behind them, and Myla turned to see Aveis. Her arms were down, her palms out and facing toward them, creating a trail of fire behind her that caught on the grass. Myla turned back to her parents.

"We've got to go. We can't stop her—"

"Raevyn will," his father spoke, his voice deep with an icy edge that nearly made Myla shiver.

Raevyn shook his head, utter panic and terror warping his features—an expression Myla had never seen on his beautiful face. "Please, don't—"

Raevyn's father spoke a phrase—the words in no language she'd ever heard before—full of hard consonants that seemed to be pulled from the back of his throat. Raevyn's grip on her hand fell away, and Myla turned to him. A chill ran down her spine as shadows built around him— oozing off him in inky tendrils. The shadows wrapped around his body, extending from his fingers in the form of claws before closing around his face, giving him the form of a monstrous beast with glowing gold eyes.

Myla choked, reaching out a hand to him. "Raevyn—"

Raevyn—the *creature*—turned his gaze toward her and bared shadowy teeth that she knew could do as much damage as any blade.

"Kill the princess," Raevyn's father ordered.

"Wait—" Her father tried, but it was too late.

Raevyn bounded toward Aveis without a second glance. Aveis didn't even have time to react. Raevyn pounced on her, and she screamed as his claws dug into her shoulders. Drathal roared before breaking away from the other soldiers to get to Aveis. His claws closed around Raevyn's body before Drathal flung him across the training yard. Myla whirled on Raevyn's father.

"What did you do to him?" She growled, the storm around them intensifying at her torrent of emotions.

He gave her a cool expression as if he couldn't be bothered with her. "I only reminded him who he really is. A monster. Just like the princess."

"He has magic?" Myla's heart clenched in her chest as realization dawned on her. Her magic had been trying to tell her the entire journey. All the flares and instances where her magic reacted to Raeavyn's presence hadn't been a warning to stay away—it was like calling to like. It had been the same with Aveis. She felt stupid for not having put it together sooner. She supposed she never could have imagined a hunter having magic—it didn't make sense. "But how did you command him to change like that?"

"Extensive training."

Myla shook her head—too horrified to imagine what he meant by that and turned away from him.

"Wrynn is on his way to our house with Rikia." She told her parents. "She got hurt—I don't know how bad. I'll meet you there soon, and we'll get out of here—"

"There's no need to run," Raevyn's father interrupted. "Raevyn has this handled."

Myla turned to see Raevyn locked in a fight with Drathal. Drathal was on his back with Raevyn above him. His shadow claws dug into Drathal's arms as Drathal tried to hold him back from ripping open the soft skin of his underbelly. He sputtered fire at him, but the shadows cocooning his body seemed just to absorb the flames. Blood pooled on the grass from the various wounds across Drathal's stomach and chest. Aveis was lying on the grass a mere few feet away—unmoving. Myla turned back to her parents, who were both shaking their heads, knowing precisely what she was thinking.

"Meet me at the house," Myla said before she sprinted toward Raevyn.

Chapter 69

Myla lifted her arms and pushed a wave of water between Drathal and Raevyn. They were forced apart—Raevyn turning end over end before landing on his feet, his claws digging into the grass to stop his propulsion. Drathal tried to flee with Aveis's unconscious form wrapped gently in his talons, but Raevyn got a good swipe in one of his wings, which grounded him. Raevyn snarled, his gold eyes flickering from Myla to Drathal.

Myla lifted her hands up in a placating gesture. "Raevyn, come back to me. Please—"

He lunged at her with inhuman speed. She created an ice dome around her, but he burst through it. His claws gripped her shirt before he threw her behind him. Myla crashed into the ground with a yell—grass, snow, and dirt flying around her. Before she could stand, Raevyn was there, hovering over her with his teeth bared and poised to close around her throat. Through the shadows, she could just make out the outline of his face. She tried to reach through the shadows, but it was as solid as flesh. At her touch, he froze, his gold eyes dimming slightly.

"Raevyn, I need you to snap out of it. We're safe. *You're* safe. Whatever your father did to you—we'll figure it out. I won't give up on you."

"Myla!"

She turned her head, heart climbing in her throat at the desperate fear in her mother's voice. Raevyn's father was running toward them, his lips forming around words she knew would mean her death. Her parents were behind him— her mother kneeling over her father's still form. An immense crowd of soldiers rushed past the general after Raevyn's father. To fight Drathal or him, Myla wasn't sure. She looked back at Raevyn.

"I'm sorry for this."

She pushed Raevyn off her with a wave of magic before jumping to her feet. She turned to Raevyn's father and encased him in a dome of ice before he could finish whatever phrase he wanted to utter. The soldiers behind him didn't slow—charging toward Raevyn and Drathal. Drathal snarled and released a torrent of flames that wiped out the first line of soldiers. He was stopped from killing the rest when Raevyn jumped on Drathal's back. He roared, shaking in an attempt to buck Raevyn off. Aveis sat up, rubbing the back of her head, but was immediately on her feet when she saw Drathal. Aveis launched herself at Raevyn like a giant fireball—knocking them both off Drathal's back.

Myla swore before dashing toward her parents. She knelt next to her mother. "What happened?"

"The hunter knocked him out when he tried to order the soldiers to stand down."

Myla was relieved that it wasn't something worse. She looked down at her father and back at the fight raging on behind her. She had to stop this before it got too far. She didn't want anyone else to die today.

"If I tell you to run as soon as Dad wakes up, would you?"

"Not without you."

Myla sighed. "Of course not. Fine, I'll be back."

She got to her feet, and her mother followed suit, grabbing her arm. "I know better than to tell you not to go out there, but please be safe."

Myla smiled and nodded. "I will. I love you."

Myla ran into the fray. Once she reached the end of the crowd of soldiers, she launched herself up with a burst of magic. While in the air, she created an ice barrier from the courtyard wall to the castle, separating Drathal, Aveis, and Raevyn from everyone else. She landed in a crouch that she rolled out of before jumping to her feet. Aveis and Raevyn were locked in a fight—Aveis burning so bright that Myla could barely look at her. Raevyn's shadows were straining against the burning light. To her relief, the creature's form was slowly shrinking. Drathal bared his teeth before clasping them around Raevyn. He threw Raevyn, who slammed into Myla's ice wall. The wall cracked but held as he crashed to the ground.

Raevyn was instantly on his feet and rushed back toward Drathal and Aveis. Myla didn't let him get far. She pulled the rainwater toward Raevyn and wrapped him in a bubble—cutting off his air supply. Aveis took a surprising step back, eyes darting over to Myla.

"Go!" Myla shouted. "He won't stop until you're dead!"

Aveis looked from Raevyn—the shadowy creature struggling to break free—to Myla before nodding. She rushed toward Drathal. Myla was so focused on ensuring they'd escape that she didn't notice Raevyn's attack. She let out a choked gasp as an arrow made from pure shadow tore through her stomach. She fell to her knees, the grip on her magic slipping as pain shot through her. Blood splattered from her lips as she let out a guttural cough. Someone screamed inside and outside of her mind.

Myla!

She blinked up to see Aveis rushing toward her with flames pouring off of her, looking like a shooting star. Raevyn was running toward her as well, but Aveis intercepted him. She placed herself between Myla and Raevyn and then screamed. Myla had to close her eyes from the sheer intensity of the light. She heard a crash before she fell to her side—unable to hold up her weight anymore. The light dimmed, and she saw Aveis kneeling over her, panic filling her ember eyes. She reached down and pulled the shadow arrow from her stomach. Myla lurched, a scream tearing its way through her throat.

"Just hold on, darling," Aveis soothed, reaching down to press her fingers against her wound.

Flames licked her skin, and she cried out—the pain causing her vision to darken around the edges. Aveis's hands pulled away a second before she was flung away from her. A large blue and green form appeared in front of her, shielding her from Aveis.

You're not dying on me.

Vavna?

A large, scaly head, nearly three times the size of Myla's entire body, turned to look at her. They craned their head down and rested their snout against her wound. Myla flinched as they blew a small puff of air so cold it burned. But, as soon as the pain ebbed away, relief filled her. Her wound felt as if it had happened weeks ago rather than minutes.

Thank you.

Vavna pulled their head back. *Climb on, stubborn human. I'm getting you out of here before you get yourself killed.*

Myla got to her feet to see Aveis and Drathal staring at Vavna—shocked and awed. Aveis slowly got to her feet, her mouth opening and closing as if she wanted to say something, but no words came out. Off to their right was Raevyn, lying unconscious. The shadows had disappeared, revealing his torn clothes and various cuts along his dark skin. But he was breathing, thank the gods.

The ice wall behind them shuddered, cracks splintering across the surface. Myla clambered onto Vavna's back. It wouldn't be long before the army broke through. Aveis seemed to think the same thing because she let flames build up around her. She locked eyes with Myla and Myla gave her a small smile. Despite everything, Aveis had tried to save her, and she was grateful for it.

"Thank you," Myla said.

She reached toward her, taking a few steps forward. "Wait—"

Vavna snarled at her, and Aveis slowed to a stop. Drathal stepped up beside her and snarled in kind. Before Myla could intervene, the wall behind her crumbled.

Time to go.

Myla had just barely settled between two spikes along Vavna's back when they flew up. Myla gripped the spike in front of her for dear life, thighs quivering from the effort to stay seated.

We have to get Raevyn and my parents—

Vavna huffed. *Yes, yes, fine.*

The soldiers charged toward Drathal and Aveis, but they didn't have a chance against her barrage of flames. Vavna swooped down and captured Raevyn in their claws before sailing over the soldiers' heads. Myla caught a glimpse of Raevyn's father, who had broken out of his icy prison to glare at them. Her parents were where she had left them—her father struggling into a sitting position. Their eyes widened at the sight of Vavna, and her mother let out a surprised scream as Vavna scooped them up before shooting into the sky. She glanced down at the training yard to watch the remaining soldiers flee from Drathal and Aveis.

Aveis had gotten what she wanted—the throne was hers.

Chapter 70

They made a quick stop at Myla's home to grab Wrynn and Rikia. Myla was relieved to find that her sister was okay—the injury to her head was minor. Not wanting to waste time packing, they all piled onto Vavna's back. Raevyn was draped across Myla's lap, secured with a rope around her own waist. With no other idea of where else to go, they headed to Naeron, where her mother's brother and his family lived.

Thank you for coming after me. After everything...I didn't think I would ever hear from you again.

I told you before, stubborn human. Our fates are intertwined, and I will not stand idly by and allow you to die before you're ready. Vavna paused before adding. *Also, I saw the effort you put into learning from your mistakes to become better. I see now that you've only been trying your best, which is all I can ask of you. Even though I think you're wrong about most things, it appears you were right to be wary of the princess.*

Myla smiled. *I think that's the nicest thing you've ever said to me.*

Don't get used to it. The one thing you should remember about me is that I never sugarcoat things. And I won't lie to you. I ask that you do the same.

Of course. It wouldn't be very convincing anyway— since you can read all my thoughts.

Which is annoying, so I'm going to teach you to block out your thoughts the first chance we get.

So, what's next for us? Myla looked down at Raevyn and ran her fingers through his hair. *I can't just leave him like this. There has to be some way we can help him. Do you know what happened to him? Does he have magic? His father turned him into this creature with just a command—have you ever heard of such a thing?*

No, but I have long given up being surprised by the cruelty of humans. He clearly has magic, but he doesn't have any control over it. Whatever brainwashing his father did, it was thorough.

Myla's heart tore at the thought of young Raevyn going through such trauma and how he must have thought about himself for being gifted with magic. Though he never would have thought of it as a gift. Her stomach soured at the thought of how much he hated magic and all he had done to try to destroy it with magic in his own veins. Had his father been controlling him all the times he'd spilled magical blood? What could he have gone through to make it so that he killed for something that he himself had? Is it possible that he doesn't know about his magic? Wouldn't he have told her if he knew? Myla felt a slash of hurt at the possibility that he hadn't trusted her enough to tell her. Of all the things she would understand, it would be magic and the conflicting feelings one had for it when everyone told you it corrupted you.

Do you know of a way I can help him?

Vavna hesitated a moment before admitting *I might know of someone.*

Myla brightened. *Who?*

Do not get your hopes up. She lives in our hidden city, and if I were to bring you there, you could never leave. The human king would not allow such a thing, and neither would my queen. Our secret must remain, and they would not jeopardize it unless you prove your loyalty, which might take years—decades—if at all. It is even possible that they would kill you and the hunter at first glance without even hearing you out. The scarred man is known and feared by the entire city.

Could you not convince them to hear us out?

Luckily for you, the human king knows and trusts me. I can get you an audience with him far from the city. It will be your job to convince him to allow you access.

Myla's eyes trailed over Raevyn's face. She thought of their adventure, of all he had done to help her, even if it wasn't entirely what she wanted. They still had a lot to work through, but she wouldn't let that stand in the way of his safety. She wasn't lying when she said she would become his enemy if he rose against magic, but this was different. There were too many unknowns. She needed to know the truth before she could sort things out with Raevyn.

I'll do whatever it takes to save him.

****

Once they landed in the woods near Naeron, Myla's heart tightened. She had barely been home a month and had to say goodbye to her family again. Despite wanting them by her side, she knew it was selfish. This had all started when she was discovered with magic, and every decision she'd made since had only put those she loved in danger. They would be better off without her.

Myla's family slid off Vavna's back. Her father helped her down with Raevyn in her arms. She undid the rope and laid Raevyn down softly on the snowy grass. She looked up at her family and couldn't help the tears that filled her eyes.

"I'm not going with you," she said, voice cracking.

"Myla—" her father started, but she cut him off.

"Vavna is going to bring me to someone who can help Raevyn. But I don't know how it'll play out, and I won't put any of you in danger anymore. If they agree to help, I might never come back, but I've got to do this for Raevyn."

"Will you be safe there?" Myla's mother asked, tears spilling from her eyes.

Safer than you'll ever be in this kingdom, Vavna replied.

Myla nodded. "If I'm convincing enough."

Her mother captured her in a bone-crushing hug. "I trust in you. Go and do what you think you must. We'll be waiting for you to return because I know you will."

Myla buried her face in her mother's curls. "I love you."

"I love you too, sweetie."

She pulled back only to be nearly tackled in a hug by her sister. "Don't do anything stupid. I won't be around to stitch you up."

Myla choked out a laugh through her sob as she squeezed her sister's small frame. "No promises."

"You're the worst."

Myla smiled and pulled back. "I love you too."

Her father was next, powerful arms encasing her in a tight hug. "I'm proud of you. You've grown into a strong and capable woman—exceeding all my ridiculously high expectations of you."

403

"Thank you." She pulled back to smile wetly at him. "I love you."

"I love you too."

Myla turned to Wrynn, who had crossed his arms in stubborn resolve. "If you think I'm going to let you go off on some stupid adventure without me again, you're out of your godsdamn mind."

"Wrynn—"

"My family is already on their way to Naeron, where I know they'll be okay. My extended family will care for my siblings and mother. They don't need me, but you do."

"I can't ask you to come with me."

"Then it's a good thing you aren't asking."

Myla stared into his narrow, dark eyes. "There's no way I'm going to convince you otherwise, is there?"

His lips quirked. "Not a chance."

Myla smiled. "Then I won't waste my breath."

She turned back to her family and tried not to think of the fact that this might be it. She reminded herself that this was for the best—that she could rest easy knowing that her family was safe and wouldn't have to fear for their lives so long as she stayed away. Aveis was on the throne, and maybe things would get better. Perhaps the hidden city would come into the light within her lifetime. Despite its absurdity, she let herself hold on to that hope. It was the only thing that allowed her to turn her back and go on without her family.

Chapter 71

A day later, they made it to the meeting spot. Vavna told her they hadn't filled the king in on Raevyn since they didn't think he would come if he knew it had to do with the hunter. And Raevyn still hadn't woken up. She'd been able to bandage all his wounds, but she only knew what was wrong on the surface. She didn't know if the reason he hadn't woken up was because he had used too much magic and was recuperating or if it was something much worse. She was helpless to do much else and prayed to the queen goddess, Rornja, that it was the former.

They met near the eastern border between steep mountain ridges, far from any cities or towns. A place that only something with wings would ever venture. Waiting for them on the plateau was the king and his dragon.

The king did not look as she'd expected. She expected someone far older than her, but the young Black man before her couldn't have been older than her early twenties. His hair was plaited down to the base of his neck. A crown of shimmering scales plated to a golden band was resting on top of his head. He was a few inches taller than her, muscular, and his eyes shone the color of freshly grown grass. The dragon behind him was broad and taller than Vavna, with horns jutting up from their skull—reminding Myla of the snowcapped mountains around them. Their underbelly was the color of soil, and their scales were a shade darker than their green eyes.

His eyes darted between the trio, gaze snagging on Raevyn lying unconscious next to them. The king threw out his hands—palms to the ground. Myla stumbled as the ground trembled before a crack broke across the floor mere feet from Myla's feet. Wrynn wrapped his arms around her waist and pulled her away from the chasm the king had created between them. The dragon behind him growled, and Vavna stepped forward to stand next to Myla—baring their teeth.

"What is this?" The king snarled, glaring up at Vavna. "You didn't say anything about a hunter."

Vavna snarled something, but Myla couldn't make it out this time. The dragon stared down at Vavna, lips pulled back into a snarl.

"We come in peace," Myla interjected, stepping out of Wrynn's grasp.

The king turned his steely gaze on her. "Who are you, and what do you want?"

"I'm Myla Yules, and this is Wrynn Einar." She gestured to Wrynn and then Raevyn. "And you already know who this is. We've come seeking refuge from Cassia City and help for Raevyn."

Myla then explained everything that had led up to this point—how she had been discovered with magic and sent on a dangerous mission to save the princess and bring her home. She admitted she had to force Aveis home, even if it hadn't been her intent, and how that had inevitably led to

Aveis taking the throne for herself and Raevyn's display of magic.

"His father brainwashed him or cursed him—I don't know. He becomes a mindless beast at his father's command. I know—"

"How?" The king demanded.

"I don't know. He hasn't woken up since. That's why I need your help. Vavna said there was someone in your hidden city who could help wake him up, and if you do, I promise we'll tell you anything you want to know."

"Has this been done to anyone else?"

Myla shrugged. "I don't know—"

"Would the hunter know?"

"Possibly. I can promise you he'll tell you anything he knows."

"How could you promise such a thing on his behalf? He has killed dozens of our kind, and bringing him into the heart of my city is a tremendous risk. A risk I'm not sure I can take. Why should I squander this opportunity to end his life?"

Myla stepped forward until she was standing in front of Raevyn. "Because you and your people need the information only Raevyn could give you."

Before the king could reply, his dragon snarled something, and he looked up at them. A silent conversation passed between them before the king looked back at their group. His eyes trailed over each of them, lingering on one in particular.

"And if he has no information? Or if he becomes a threat?"

"Then you kill us, and I won't stop you. I trust Raevyn and know he won't hurt any of you. He's already proven that to me."

The king seemed surprised. "You'd stake your life on that trust? The life of your friend here as well?"

Myla looked over at Wrynn, who gave her an encouraging smile. He would stand by her. "Yes."

"Let's say, hypothetically, the hunter has valuable information, and I decide to let you all live. Why should I let you stay? How can I be sure that you all have good intentions?"

Myla wasn't sure how to respond. He should let them stay because she had magic? Because they had nowhere else to go? Because she needed their help? Those things didn't matter to him. Raevyn could have valuable information, but if he didn't—

"We can tell you we will keep your secret and do our part in helping out however we can around the city, but you have no reason to believe us," Wrynn replied, stepping forward on Myla's other side. "We can tell you that Raevyn has become a changed man and been forced to do the awful things you claimed. The same goes for us, saying we have good intentions, but there's no way to prove those things to you. So, it's up to you to decide how much Raevyn's insight is worth, and trust your gut. Do you think we're going to break your trust and expose this place so we'd have to find another place to seek refuge? Do you think we'd even succeed if we attacked your city with just the three of us?"

The king stared at Wrynn for a long moment—green eyes intent. Wrynn held his gaze and didn't falter. Myla felt an odd twist in her stomach, as though she was intruding on an intimate moment, but she couldn't look away.

"Based on your heartbeat, you aren't lying or, at the very least, believe you're telling the truth. But that doesn't mean you won't change your mind later."

Wrynn shrugged—as if the king casually mentioning he could somehow hear or feel heartbeats from a relatively far distance away was completely normal. "Then I guess you'll just have to keep a close eye on us."

The king's lips twitched ever so slightly. "You'd like that, wouldn't you?"

"Oh my gods," Myla muttered.

She hadn't meant to say that out loud, but it did the trick of pulling the king out of his intense staring contest with Wrynn. He looked them all over again before his gaze settled on Myla.

"Vavna trusts you for some unknown reason, and I owe Vavna a life debt, which is the only reason I'm considering this. I trust their judgment and can't let this opportunity pass on to gain insider knowledge about the hunters and their tactics. If they have found a way to curse magic wielders or whatever on a larger scale—it could be detrimental to our kind. I owe it to my people to figure out how it is done and if there is a way to stop it. I make no promises that we can even help your hunter, but we will do what we can. But this is your only warning: if you step even a toe out of line, it'll be the last thing you do."

Myla let out a relieved breath. "Thank you, Your Majesty." Myla bowed deeply.

Myla straightened as the king climbed back onto his dragon's back. "I will take you to our city. But make no mistake, this isn't an invitation to stay. I will decide what will be done once the hunter is awake."

"Of course, Your Majesty," Myla responded.

"Do you have a name?" Wrynn asked. "Or do we just call you sir?"

The king's lips pulled up into an almost smile. "You can call me that if you'd like. But for more casual interactions, you can call me Kerei."

The dragon shot up in the sky—a plume of snow kicking up in their wake. Myla rubbed the dirty snow from her face and turned to face Vavna.

"That went well, I think."

Vavna squinted down at her. *I can't tell if you're being sarcastic or not.*

"I mean, it could have gone a lot worse. Why does the king owe you a life debt anyway?"

That's a story for another time. Now, let's go before the king changes his mind.

Vavna lowered themselves to the ground. Myla and Wrynn climbed onto their back, and Raevyn hung awkwardly between them. Vavna flew into the sky in the direction the king went. Myla wasn't even entirely sure where they were going. They were flying high above the clouds, the ground below them hidden. For all she knew, they were flying out of the kingdom.

Half a day passed like that, so when Vavna told her they were almost there, Myla sagged in relief. Her thighs and ass were aching from being saddled for so long. She longed to bathe and sleep for days but couldn't relax until she knew Raevyn was being taken care of. She blinked the exhaustion from her eyes and took in their surroundings—not recognizing anything. They were somewhere in the mountains, but that could have been in any direction since Cassia was in a valley surrounded by mountains on all sides.

Vavna tucked in their wings and nosedived toward the mountains. Myla gasped and feared they would crash, but as they got closer, a gap appeared between the ridges, just big enough for them to get through. As soon as they cleared it, Vavna threw out their wings to stop their fall. They glided over a bustling city amongst grand trees hidden between the ridges of the mountains. It should have been visible from the air, but it was as if the entire city was covered in a mirage that only cleared when they got close.

Wrynn slid off Vavna's back before turning to help Myla with Raevyn. They looked around in awe, and Myla realized this was the same place Vavna had been when they first reached out to her months ago. A city of dragons and humans living in harmony as a backdrop, only this time, everything was covered in a thick layer of snow.

Welcome to Magesanctum.

About the Author

Brooke Anderson is a fantasy writer based in the mountainous Salt Lake City, Utah. When she's not conjuring up magical worlds and witty dialogue, you can find her painting and spending time with her trusty sidekick, Izzy the dog. Her debut novel, which is as funny as it is enchanting, is a testament to her love for LGBTQ+ representation and size-inclusive characters.

Inspired by authors like Kimberley Lemming and TJ Klune, Brooke's writing is a perfect blend of humor and heart. Her stories transport readers to whimsical realms where anything is possible, and where love knows no boundaries. She brings a fresh perspective to the world of fantasy fiction, breaking free from the traditional norms and stereotypes.

Brooke is a proud advocate for diversity and inclusion in literature, and her commitment to representing marginalized voices shines through in her writing. Her unique blend of magic and humor has earned her a loyal following of readers who can't get enough of her imaginative storytelling. Get ready to embark on an unforgettable adventure with Brooke Anderson – a newcomer writer of heartfelt, LGBTQ+ inclusive, funny, and size-inclusive fantasy fiction!

Be sure to follow her on TikTok for updates and information on new releases!

@authorbrookeanderson

Made in United States
Troutdale, OR
01/19/2025

27800192R10256